A DAGGER for CATHERINE DOUGLAS

EUAN MACPHERSON

authorHOUSE

AuthorHouse™ UK
1663 Liberty Drive
Bloomington, IN 47403 USA
www.authorhouse.co.uk
Phone: UK TFN: 0800 0148641 (Toll Free inside the UK)
UK Local: (02) 0369 56322 (+44 20 3695 6322 from outside the UK)

© 2021 Euan Macpherson. All rights reserved.

No part of this book may be reproduced, stored in a retrieval system, or transmitted by any means without the written permission of the author.

Published by AuthorHouse 12/01/2021

ISBN: 978-1-6655-9457-8 (sc)
ISBN: 978-1-6655-9458-5 (hc)
ISBN: 978-1-6655-9456-1 (e)

Print information available on the last page.

Any people depicted in stock imagery provided by Getty Images are models, and such images are being used for illustrative purposes only. Certain stock imagery © Getty Images.

This book is printed on acid-free paper.

Because of the dynamic nature of the Internet, any web addresses or links contained in this book may have changed since publication and may no longer be valid. The views expressed in this work are solely those of the author and do not necessarily reflect the views of the publisher, and the publisher hereby disclaims any responsibility for them.

CONTENTS

Prologue vii

Chapter 1 1
Chapter 2 6
Chapter 3 17
Chapter 4 28
Chapter 5 36
Chapter 6 47
Chapter 7 54
Chapter 8 63
Chapter 9 70
Chapter 10 81
Chapter 11 87
Chapter 12 97
Chapter 13 108
Chapter 14 117
Chapter 15 128
Chapter 16 132
Chapter 17 137
Chapter 18 144
Chapter 19 152
Chapter 20 159

Chapter 21 167
Chapter 22 174
Chapter 23 181
Chapter 24 190
Chapter 25 201
Chapter 26 211
Chapter 27 217
Chapter 28 222
Chapter 29 229
Chapter 30 234
Chapter 31 243
Chapter 32 250
Chapter 33 257
Chapter 34 266
Chapter 35 273
Chapter 36 282
Chapter 37 292
Chapter 38 302
Chapter 39 309
Chapter 40 318

Epilogue. 329
About The Author 331

PROLOGUE

The horse sailed through the air with nodding head and flapping forelegs, the rest of its body heavy and stiff.

Elisabeth stood on her own in the centre of the courtyard with bare toes peeking out from under the folds of her long gown. Holding up a hand to shield her eyes from the sun, she watched with a strange sense of disbelief as the horse gradually grew bigger.

A loose thread on her sleeve caught her attention. She stared hard at it, murmuring to herself, "Must remember to fix it."

A cacophony of wailing voices and running feet filled her head. The priest came running down the winding staircase inside the tower and out into the courtyard. People were scattering this way and that.

Here came the horse, big and brown and dropping over the wall to splatter on the flat stone floor of the courtyard. Then it was lying motionless on its side with its head resting on the stones. It might have been sleeping but for the fact that its belly had broken open and a red mess of entrails was spilling out.

No more talk, now, of chivalry and the rules of war. Now it was only about desperation and the pressing need to win at any cost. Nothing lay ahead but slow starvation, surrender and death.

It would be a slow death stuck inside a castle like prisoners—unable to move, unable to do anything but wait and watch and brace yourself for the next missile, hoping it might miss its target. They were like criminals locked in the stocks to be jeered at by the mob and pelted all day long with stones and rotten fruit.

They were unable to fight back, unable to do anything but suffer this torture. Sometimes, she would stand in the courtyard shaking her fist at the skies above, cursing the God who had forgotten her. "I'm going to win this one, with your help or without it!" she would shout at the clouds and at the seagulls.

She repeated, *I will not surrender, I will not surrender,* over and over in her head. They could starve her to death, but they couldn't make her lift a white flag or raise the portcullis.

Endurance. That was her father's way. Taking a defeat and keeping on going—fighting and fighting till there was no difference between victory and defeat; fighting and fighting and keeping on fighting till the enemy grew as tired of it all as you were. If you could endure the defeats and keep on fighting, eventually the enemy would just give up and walk away. Battles might be lost, but wars were won by determination, and you could always win, whatever your circumstances, if you had the will to keep going.

Starvation or surrender—that was the choice. And she would hold out another day and then another day, praying every night for Zizka to come.

In the corner of her eye, a tall, broad-shouldered man was walking across the courtyard. He made her feel tiny, like a small child.

His calmness came not from courage but from relief and fatigue, from the exhaustion of worn-out emotions. He was simply too tired to be afraid, too tired to care. "You are all right?" he asked.

A puff of wind caught the stink of rotting guts. She hesitated. There were words she could not say. Two hundred pairs of eyes watched her— men who all thought they could make a better defence of the castle and women who thought it, too.

"Yes, Paul," she said. "I'm all right."

"They did the same at Nekmir," Paul Horvat said, looking at the horse. "The best thing to do it is to cut it up and throw it back over the battlements at night. They will be hoping we drop it out the sluice gates, but you can't do that—can't open the gates."

Every sentence Horvat spoke began with the words, "When I was at Nekmir." He thought he should be in command, and maybe he would have been but for his low birth. But when her husband failed to return, when the rays of sunshine glinting off rusted metal exposed the Holy Roman Emperor's army coming through the forest, Elisabeth had known she had no choice but to close the gates and take command.

Another man had come over to stand beside them. Not as tall as Horvat or as broad, he still dwarfed Elisabeth. He wore a coat of mail[1] with a sword hanging from his belt as if he expected the enemy to come over the walls at any moment. This was Franz Bauer.

"Do you think, if we boiled it long enough, we could eat it?" Bauer asked. "They ate worse than this on the Crusades."

"And you would know, would you?"

"I've heard stories."

Elisabeth thought of her father, poisoned in a tavern in Lubeck as he was recruiting an army to fight Sigismund. "They'll have poisoned it," she said.

"Perhaps."

If the enemy couldn't take the castle by force, they would take it by disease, catapulting corpses over its walls till the defenders dropped down one by one, their stomachs retching and their faces ravaged by boils. And when there was no one left alive, when there was no one strong enough even to stand up and wave a white flag, when the corpses lay all around and the stench of the dead smelled stronger than the sewers of Lubeck in midsummer, then they would send couriers rushing south with the news that God had granted them another glorious victory.

"Could we cut the horse and catapult the pieces back at them?" Elisabeth wondered aloud. Let Sigismund learn what it was like to walk about with rotting entrails on his tunic. All of a sudden she laughed to herself, thinking, *If we all have empty bellies, then the smell can't make us sick.*

Paul Horvat cast her a sideways glance. This was the way people cracked up; after five or six months of bombardment, you would see them standing in the courtyard by themselves, laughing like idiots.

Elisabeth saw him looking at her and somehow stifled her laughter.

"This is a good sign," Bauer said.

Horvat looked at him as if he, too, had gone insane. "What is?"

"The horse."

"It is a good sign that they are still bombarding us?"

---

[1] Often called chain mail, it was a shirt made of metal ringlets to stop a blow from a sword.

"Do you think they would be tossing dead meat over the wall for their own men to climb over? They're not ready to come over the walls yet."

"When I was at Nekmir—"

"You weren't at Nekmir," Franz Bauer said.

"Yes, I was."

"You turned up late, after it was all over."

"I was there," Horvat growled.

"Be quiet, both of you," Elisabeth said.

"I was there—you ask Albert Sobieski."

"How are we going to ask him?"

"Be quiet!" Elisabeth screeched. "We should clean this mess up."

"I've been saying that all week," Paul Horvat added.

Bauer shot him a sideways glance. "And nobody else has been saying it?"

"Get them scrubbing on their knees; it takes their minds off the army sitting outside the gates. This is what I learned at Nekmir."

"On you go, then," Bauer said.

Horvat looked around. "Where are the scrubbers?"

"Lead by example."

"He's right," Elisabeth said. Cleaning the courtyard would keep people busy. "Get buckets and shovels," she added.

Horvat turned to Bauer. "You'll find some in the kitchen."

"Me?" Bauer knitted his brows. "Are you asking me to go?"

"I'm a knight. I can't do it."

"You don't give me orders"

"I'll go!" Elisabeth shrieked, her hands over her ears. Then she turned, running across the flat stones to the tower and up the winding staircase to the chapel.

She pushed open the scratched wooden door and found herself looking at a stone statue of Mary. The stone eyes had no pupils, which gave the statue an omniscient quality, as if it could see everything, everywhere. She sat down on a wooden bench, keeping a respectful distance from the statue.

Horvat was judging her with every word he spoke. Every word he uttered implied that he had been in these situations before—and she had not.

And he always seemed to be right. Maybe they were lucky that the emperor was sending dead horses over the walls, because that meant he was planning for a long siege. And that might give Zizka time to arrive.

But where was Zizka? There was never any news.

And no, she thought to herself. *I disagree. We were not lucky this time.* Because if they'd sent over a fresh horse, we could cut up the meat and roast it. But it was always old horses that came over, horses that had died from the glanders and then been left to rot for a month or two till they were stinking and bloated with gas.

But this time, maybe she had been lucky—the last horse had dropped down onto the battlements and stuck there, impaled on the stone, its open eyes staring into the courtyard. They knew if they pushed it over the wall Sigismund would just catapult it back at them, so they'd hacked it to pieces where it was and taken the flesh and bones in buckets down to the sluice gate, where they'd threw it out for the crows. For the rest of the week, she had spent her time cleaning the blood off her hands, face, and hair. But no matter how many times she washed her gown, it still stank of rotting innards.

Every time she plunged her gown into a barrel of water, Horvat stared at her disapprovingly. And he shook his head and rolled his eyes every time the bucket dropped down into the well and was raised back up again.

"One day, you will lower the bucket, but there will be no water in the well," he said.

"There is plenty water," she said.

"Today, there is. But what of tomorrow?"

"Tomorrow, Zizka will be here."

She was on her knees, clasping her hands in prayer. "Please, Lord, help me hold this castle till Zizka arrives," she pleaded.

"You talk like it is this transitory world that is important, not the afterlife. One day, this castle will crumble to the ground."

Elisabeth turned around. The priest was standing in the doorway. But she was too tired, just too tired, for his pompous pronouncements. Her eyes flared with anger. "It's easy for you to talk love and peace. If I open the gates, that army outside will slaughter my people. They won't touch you, but they'll slaughter everyone else—if they don't rape the women first."

The priest stepped forwards, his black robes trailing across the wooden floorboards. Once he had been fat and filling out his robes. Now the folds of loose material were conspicuous. "You want to save the lives of your people?"

"Yes!" Elisabeth shouted.

"How can you give them what they already have? They have life."

"They won't if Sigismund's soldiers enter the castle."

"They have eternal life, which neither you nor Sigismund can take away."

Why am I explaining my actions to him? Elisabeth wondered. "You want me to surrender so you can fill your belly again?"

"How would surrender give meaning to your life?"

"I don't know what you want from me!" Elisabeth shouted.

"I don't want anything from you."

Except to confuse me with endless riddles.

"Do the right thing for the right reasons; that is all I ask. Fight only if this is the best way to serve the Lord."

The heavy footsteps of Paul Horvat came clanking up the stairs. For once, she was glad to see him. She stood up, brushing past the priest, and walked to the door. But she was stopped by Paul Horvat's bulky frame that filled out the doorway.

"I thought you were going to the kitchen?"

"I'm going there now," Elisabeth said. And immediately, she was angry with herself. Why was she always explaining herself to him?

"They're moving the sow," he said.

"They're moving it *this way*?" Elisabeth ejaculated involuntarily. Immediately, she regretted it.

"Where else would they be moving it?" the priest asked.

For several days, the carpenters had been building a sow. Now they had finished, and Sigismund was ready to use it.

The sow—a battering ram with a protective cover. Called a sow because the battering ram protruded out from under the roof like the long nose of a fat-bellied pig, the men would push it forwards under the wooden roof. You couldn't shoot arrows at them. You couldn't pour boiling oil on top of them. You couldn't do anything except watch as they battered down your front gate.

So now everyone knew the enemy's plans. Once they moved the sow into position, the soldiers would climb inside and slowly roll it forwards towards the castle. Nothing Elisabeth could do would stop them. And if help did not come within a day or two—

"How do you attack a sow?" Elisabeth said. She was thinking aloud, not meaning to ask a question.

But Horvat couldn't resist giving the answer. "We could soak arrows in bitumen and set fire to them," he suggested. "That's what we did at Nekmir. A sow makes an easy target from twenty yards."

"Zizka saved you that day—not your arrows of fire."

"We held out long enough for Zizka to arrive. We did our job."

"And Zizka will come again," the priest said. "Let us pray for that."

Elisabeth walked out of the chapel and down the stone stairway.

CHAPTER 1

An orange arc blazed across the night sky as a fireball fizzed over the wall of the castle. The long arm of the trebuchet shuddered, lurching back and forth. Creaking and groaning, it came shakily to a standstill like an overweight drunk man.

"Have you ever wondered if you joined the wrong side?" Sean Campbell asked. He was looking up at Melnik Castle, its white towers reaching above the trees where they glinted in the starlight like the prongs of Lucifer's trident.

It was a witch's castle, standing on a rock jutting out above the junction of two rivers. And inside it was the witch, standing over her cauldron cackling and casting spells.

Or so they had been told. But this witch was a beautiful twenty-five-year-old woman with long black hair. Abandoned by her cowardly husband, she was holding the castle against the Holy Roman Emperor.

"Aren't knights supposed to rescue the damsel in the tower?" Campbell asked.

"As soon as I saw it"—Alan FitzRoland shook his head—"I knew it would cause us trouble." He was craning his neck, trying to look up at the castle. "I can't see anything for the trees."

They were standing by the bank of the River Elbe; its black waters were silent and deep. "I don't know what I'm doing here," Campbell muttered.

FitzRoland shot him a sideways glance. "It's a bit late for that."

"I always wanted to make my name. Now I just want to go home."

"It'll be worth it. People will talk about you differently when you get home."

"When will that be?"

"You can't talk like that." FitzRoland gave him a sharp look. "We're fighting for God, for the Pope, for the Holy Roman Emperor."

FitzRoland made a disappointing audience. Campbell looked away, looking up at the trees and picturing the steep castle walls beyond. "Don't you admire that woman in there?"

"I've already told you; you can't talk like that."

"You make a bad decision, and then you're stuck with it."

"Don't talk so loudly." FitzRoland had one eye on the man who was approaching along the riverbank.

"I never said I wanted to come here. This was what my father wanted."

"What else were you going to do?"

"My father can preen himself, boasting to the king that he sent his son to help the Holy Roman Emperor. He'll tell the story as if he's the one who's making the sacrifices."

The man who was approaching stepped on a tuft of grass; the wet mud underneath gave way. His right leg slid into the river while he grasped the overhanging branch of a tree. FitzRoland laughed.

"Did I ever tell you about Janet MacRory?"

FitzRoland rolled his eyes. "All the time."

"I left her at home to come out here."

"What would her father say? You're the second son of a second son. You don't have land to inherit or a title."

"I might be married to her by now, if I'd stayed in Scotland."

"You didn't want to get married. You wanted to make your name, fighting on the continent."

"It wasn't supposed to be like this."

"What was it supposed to be like?"

"I don't know what I'm fighting for."

"Yes, you do."

Hanging onto an overhanging branch of the tree, the man pulled himself out of the river.

"I used to think about Janet, her belly swollen with my child, skinning the deer I brought home from hunting. I used to picture her standing over an open fire with flecks of soot in her hair."

"She'll have lost her shape by now," FitzRoland said cruelly. "Children make a woman big in the hips and small in the chest."

"She said she would wait for me."

"You don't believe that, do you?"

Campbell winced visibly. "Janet—"

"Make your name; get a title and some land. The women will be queuing up."

"Sir Alan! Sir Alan!" The approaching man was waving an arm to attract their attention.

"My daughter will be nearly two years old." FitzRoland smiled briefly.

"Sir Alan!"

Campbell's eyes were on the approaching man and the water dripping from the rim of his tunic.

"Sir Alan!"

"What is it, Calvin?"

"Orders from Sigismund!" Calvin called out. "You are to take the castle."

FitzRoland frowned. "What does he think we're trying to do?"

"You are to enter the castle."

"What?"

"You are to raise the portcullis for the rest of the army to enter."

FitzRoland's frown deepened. "How am I going to do that?"

"Climb in through the sewer."

"The sewer is blocked."

"One of the bars is loose."

"How do you know that?"

"These are your orders from Sigismund."

"Who loosened the bar?" FitzRoland persisted.

"You must do it tonight."

"What?" FitzRoland was aghast.

"He asked who loosened the bar," Campbell intervened.

"And I told you that these are orders from Sigismund."

"We'll use the darkness to make an approach tonight and test the bars," Campbell suggested. "If one is loose, we attack tomorrow."

"No." Calvin shook his head. "We cannot wait."

A knot tightened in the bottom of Campbell's stomach. "Where is Zizka?"

"We attack tonight," Calvin said.

"I asked about Zizka. Where is he?"

"We attack tonight," Calvin said. "You will get into the castle and raise the portcullis for the rest of the army to follow."

"We can't climb the sewer in full body armour," FitzRoland said.

"Then take your armour off."

"Is this a suicide mission?"

"Your job is to raise the portcullis; the others will do the fighting."

"The sentries will have full body armour; we will not," Campbell said.

Calvin smiled a cruel smile. "You are always telling us that the archers are cowards who stand a safe distance from the battlefield. Here's your chance to do some real fighting."

"You want two men to take a castle?"

"Sigismund will create a distraction. The sow will draw the sentries to the other side."

FitzRoland turned to Campbell. "We need to discuss this."

"There is no time for discussion," Calvin said. "You have your orders."

FitzRoland's eyes were still on Sean Campbell. "It was your opinion that I wanted."

"Sigismund doesn't have anyone else stupid enough to do it. Therefore, the burden falls on us."

"You have your orders." Calvin turned and walked away.

"You came here to make your name," Alan FitzRoland said to Sean Campbell. "Now's your chance."

Sean Campbell watched Calvin's retreating back grow smaller. He had come here to do God's work, rescuing damsels from towers guarded by dragons. Instead, he was going to raise the portcullis.

And he knew what would happen next. In would rush an army of men who wanted a woman, any woman at all, because they had gone so long without one. In would rush an army of men grown bored by their idleness and frustrated by their impotence—an army of men who knew that legends were not made and honours were not won by sitting on grassy slopes while the defenders mocked them from the parapets.

If Elisabeth surrendered now, they would punish her for her defiance. Out would pour the pent-up frustrations of ten thousand men; they would have her on the table in the great hall, one after another, her legs held open while her clothes were tossed onto the fire amid much hooting and revelry. Then they would make their way through every room in the castle to satisfy their lust on the washerwomen, cooks, milkmaids, and any pretty-looking drummer boys.

The siege had gone on too long now; it could not end except in death for Elisabeth or, perhaps, if she was lucky, an unwanted pregnancy to a man she did not know. For Sigismund, it could not be allowed to end in dishonour and having to live the rest of his life with men sniggering about him behind his back—*to be beaten in battle by a woman.*

Sigismund. The man you fought for. A disgrace to chivalry. A man who stood a safe distance from the battle zone, in no danger himself, and who catapulted boulders and rotting tree trunks smeared with flaming pitch over the walls. Sigismund—the unholy Roman Emperor.

"If there's a horrible job to do, you give it to the Scots." FitzRoland's angry voice shook Campbell from his dreaming.

Campbell shrugged his shoulders wearily. "Didn't they show you how to climb up a sewer when you were training to be a knight?"

"I must have slept in that day."

CHAPTER 2

"I wanted Janet MacRory to be proud of me; that was all."

"Oh, get on with it."

"I didn't realise how young I was. The stupid ideas I had in my head."

"Hurry up!"

A streak of orange shot over Campbell's head. On the far side of the castle, burning arrows fizzed through the air. The sounds of men shouting, thuds, and clanks floated across the night sky.

"I'm going home to tell Janet MacRory I climbed up a sewer to kill a young woman."

"Hurry up!"

They were making their way up the hill, through the trees. The flat soles of their leather shoes stepped silently across the carpet of pine needles. They wore coats of mail, and they had daggers thrust into their belts.

They came out of the trees and the tall, stone wall of the castle rose above them. Far below them, the River Labe flowed into the Vltava. FitzRoland followed the curve of the moat and the wall eastwards. The water in the moat was black like the night sky.

The faint smell of mutton was in the air. "Who's roasting a sheep?"

Psychological torture—something for the defenders of the castle to smell. "I haven't eaten mutton in such a long time," Campbell grumbled. He closed his eyes, imagining his teeth sinking into a piece of soft, greasy mutton that was dropping off the bone.

FitzRoland jumped.

Campbell grimaced and then jumped. He let out a gasp of shock as the cold water hit him. Then FitzRoland came splashing towards him, and a wave of water hit him in the face. He gasped again.

He was up to his chest in water. His hands were cold; his feet were cold. He walked unsteadily and slowly across the moat. The stench of excrement was in his nostrils.

"I'm feeling sick," Campbell said.

There was an arch and a dark tunnel below the waterline. Ducking his head and pulling his shoulders in, FitzRoland crawled into the small space. He waded along the muddy floor and then climbed up onto a cold stone ledge. The only light in the passageway was starlight, but Campbell's body had blocked most of that when he'd entered the tunnel.

FitzRoland looked up. He seemed to be at the bottom of a well. He was barely able to make out some iron bars. He reached up and tugged at the first bar. It did not move. He tugged at the second, which did not move either.

Behind him, Sean Campbell's hands began to shake. He was cold and wet. Already, he was feeling claustrophobic. He was silently wishing that the bars had not been loosened, and they could go back and tell Sigismund that they could not get into the castle. The fault would be someone else's, not theirs.

There was a scraping sound. Some crumbling mortar came down on FitzRoland's head. "I think this one's loose," he said.

Damn.

FitzRoland had two hands on the bar now. He was shaking the bar in its setting, loosening more mortar. Then he was pulling downwards as hard as he could.

There was a scraping sound and then a dull thud and a groan. FitzRoland fell backwards as the bar came loose and dropped into the water with a splash.

"If Sigismund has a man on the inside," Campbell said, "he doesn't need us to raise the portcullis."

"Nobody loosened the bar," FitzRoland said. "The mortar is old."

"You mean 100,000 buckets of urine loosened it?"

"Something like that."

FitzRoland pushed his head into the gap between the bars. Pulling his shoulders in, he slowly squeezed his arms through. Then he was lifting himself up and pulling his legs in until he was standing on the remaining bars.

"Can't see a thing," FitzRoland complained. He was feeling the wall with his fingers, feeling for fingerholds and toeholds in the stonework.

Campbell waited.

Pressing his back against one side of the sewer and his feet against the other, FitzRoland slowly pushed himself up. Then he let himself drop back down.

"What is it?" Campbell asked. But he knew what the problem was—the stonework was too slippery to climb.

"Can't get a grip with these shoes," FitzRoland said. He bent over in the small space and began pulling his boots off.

Campbell felt his heart sinking. He pulled off his leather shoes, with their smooth leather soles, and took a length of string from his pocket. Not thinking about what the shoes might be smeared with, he tied them around his neck.

Then he went forwards slowly, his bare feet on the slimy floor of the sewer. "Too late to get cold feet," he joked, but FitzRoland was already grunting his way up the sewer and did not seem to hear.

The bars were above Campbell's head. He grasped them and pushed his head through. He pulled his shoulders in and, then, his stomach. He was through the bars now; he pulled himself to his feet, and it felt good to be out of the water and standing on what was left of the iron grille.

Standing erect, enjoying a momentary relief, Campbell was completely enveloped by darkness. At least, outside they'd had the starlight. Now there was nothing—unless, upstairs, somebody took a candle into the water closet.

Feeling the wall with his fingertips, he got a grip on something. The wall was damp and slimy, but the stone was rough. He pressed his back against the wall of the sewer and lifted his right leg till he found a toehold. He pulled himself up, feeling for a toehold with his left foot. Flecks of crumbling mortar and dried faeces rained down on him as, above, FitzRoland slowly dragged himself upwards.

Up he went. One fingerhold at a time. Toe-hold by toe-hold. Pushing his back against the wall, his arms splayed out.

All his muscles were straining. Every time he kicked or scratched his toes, he winced. He was hanging on with his left foot and right hand, feeling for a hold with his right foot. He looked down; it was an instinctive reaction, but it was a waste of time in the blackness. As he looked back up, he arched his back. He could feel his shoes swinging against his chest. Then he got a good foothold with his right foot and pushed himself upwards as the string began to slide around the back of his neck.

One shoe was caressing his cheek now, and the other was hanging down. He raised his left to feel for another fingerhold and nudged the shoe that was now sitting on his shoulder. Suddenly both shoes, and the string, were hurtling back downwards to ricochet off the walls of the sewer and land on the iron bars at the bottom.

If you ever get out of this sewer, you'll be fighting in your bare feet, Campbell was thinking. Better not to think about it. Better just to keep on climbing.

Better not to think about someone going to the toilet above and dropping shit and pee on top of you. Better just to keep on climbing.

Better not to think about what you're digging your fingers into every time you take a fingerhold in the wall. Better just to keep on climbing.

Elisabeth's eyes were on Paul Horvat—on the outline of his pectoral muscles under the mail shirt, on the mail shirt creasing slightly as he drew back the bowstring.

Beyond the battlements was chaos and confusion. On the parapet was the panic of people running this way and that, fear in their eyes. Women came up the steps with coals held in their skirts to pick them out and drop them in the braziers. Boys came up with quivers full of arrows to deposit them at the feet of the archers on the walls.

But there was Horvat—standing silent like a statue, not looking at the target yet somehow knowing where it was. His whole body was taut. The bow was part of his body, tough and sinewy. His eyes were not on the burning tip of the arrow but going through the flame into the blackness that lay beyond.

Whoosh.

A burst of flame fizzed through the night, dropping over the battlements.

Then it had gone.

Elisabeth stepped towards the battlements, but Horvat's firm hand on her shoulder stopped her.

"I need to see what's happening!" Elisabeth protested.

"We know where the enemy is," Horvat said. "Why do you need to look?"

"Because—"

"They hide in the trees; you won't see anything." Horvat had already pulled another arrow from his quiver and lit the end of it in the brazier.

The smell of burning was in the air. Were the arrows hitting the sow or was she smelling the smoke from the brazier? Elisabeth stepped forwards, hiding behind a battlement and then suddenly pushing her head forwards to get a glimpse of the sow at the bottom of the wall with arrow shafts protruding from it like spines on a hedgehog.

Could she make out metal glinting in the starlight? How many men were below? She screwed up her eyes, peering into the darkness. There was a rush of wind as an arrow sang past her ear. She stepped back.

Horvat was leaning forwards, poking the tip of his arrow into the brazier. Then he straightened up, his spine straightening as the bow bent. The arrow rested on his thumb.

Wheesch.

A ball of fire rippled through the air and dropped out of sight beyond the battlements.

FitzRoland's head came up through a round hole cut into a wooden bench.

Using his back and legs to brace himself against the walls of the sewer, he lifted the bench off the shaft. It clattered onto the floor with a loud thump.

FitzRoland tensed for a moment. Had he been heard? Too late now to worry. Then he was wriggling and stumbling his way into the privy.

Campbell came next, hauling himself out of the hole, his sword clanking as he rolled across the floor.

"Where's your dagger?" FitzRoland asked.

Campbell put a hand to his belt. Then he looked back down the hole. "Damn!" he hissed.

Too late now.

Campbell walked to the door.

"Wait!" FitzRoland hissed at him.

"We can't wait," Campbell said.

"Wait for me to put my shoes on." FitzRoland was untying the string and pushing his feet into his shoes.

Campbell quietly drew his sword and waited.

His dagger in one hand, FitzRoland went to the door and slowly raised the latch. The wooden door swung open. He took in the faint smell of tallow; the fluctuating candlelight revealed a passageway with wooden panelling and candles on a shelf at head height.

We turn left and follow the passage and then turn left again, FitzRoland was thinking. The passageway turned at a right angle. He walked slowly, holding his dagger in front of him. The dagger was shaking slightly in his hand.

Then he was around the corner, and another long passageway stretched out in front of him. The diversion was doing its job; everyone had been drawn to the other end of the castle.

There was a hand on his shoulder. FitzRoland jumped around. The point of his dagger caught on the metal mail shirt. Campbell jumped backwards.

"Careful!"

"Don't do that," FitzRoland hissed.

"*What?*"

"Don't touch me like that."

"You're shivering."

"It's cold."

"It's not that cold." Campbell was going to say something more, thought better of it, and swallowed his breath. "You're going the wrong way."

"We go halfway down here, and the door should be on the right."

"Get on with it, then."

FitzRoland turned and walked a few paces. He was holding the dagger in his right hand. A wooden door appeared on the right. FitzRoland fumbled with the latch, and then the door swung open.

FitzRoland went in, and Campbell went in behind him. A windlass—a chain wrapped around a wheel—told them they were in the portcullis chamber.

They stood on either side of it, ready to turn the handles, when Campbell's attention was caught by tousled black hair. "Who are you?" he asked.

Frightened blue eyes and a white face stared at him from the corner of the chamber. It was a boy, maybe ten years old, sitting holding a drum.

"We won't hurt you," Campbell said and sheathed his sword.

"Raise the portcullis!" FitzRoland said to Campbell. He turned to the boy. "Give me the drum." Two strides took him across the chamber, where he punctured the drum with the point of his dagger.

Campbell pulled on the handle, trying to turn the windlass, but the iron portcullis was stuck in its grooves and would not move.

There was a scuffle; the boy made a dash for the door, and FitzRoland grabbed him by the neck.

Campbell bent his knees, pulling at the heavy iron handle with his thigh muscles and his arms. His stomach was tense, and the muscles were straining across the whole of his back.

Then FitzRoland had his hands on the handle on the other side of the winch. The wheel was turning and the chain slowly rising. The portcullis slowly scraped upwards through the grooves.

"That's enough!" FitzRoland said and let go. "Hold it still," he commanded and pushed a rod through a link in the chain to act as a brake and stop the portcullis.

When he had finished, Campbell drew the sword from its sheath. A rope around a second wheel held up the drawbridge. He swiped at it with his sword; the rope shuddered and frayed but held firm. Wishing he had a saw, Campbell cut at it with a sawing motion. More and more strands of rope frayed off.

There was a creaking noise and then a loud crash and the vibration of a thud under their feet.

"The drawbridge is down!" Campbell said. He stepped across the floor to the door where FitzRoland had left the young boy lying. Only now did Campbell realise that blood was spreading across the wooden floor from the boy's slashed throat.

"You cut his throat?"

"What did you expect me to do?"

"You didn't have to cut his throat!" Campbell barked at FitzRoland.

"I couldn't have him running down the corridor, shouting out or banging on his drum."

"He was just a frightened boy, hiding where he thought he was safe."

"He was going to give us away."

"And the drawbridge collapsing isn't going to give us away?"

"I had to do it. I had no choice."

Running footsteps came down the passageway. There was no time to argue. Campbell pressed his shoulder against the heavy wooden door. There was a thud and the whole door shook. Campbell felt the vibration through his whole body, but the door held in place.

The drawbridge had dropped with a crash.

Elisabeth had wanted a bow; suddenly she found one being thrust into her hand. Paul Horvat lifted the mace from his belt and began running along the battlements and into the tower.

Then he was running down the corridor to the portcullis chamber. The door grew bigger and bigger until it was upon him. Taking the mace in both hands like an axe, he swiped at the door.

The door shuddered but remained shut. Inside, he could hear the screeching grinding of the portcullis being raised through the grooves in the stone.

Horvat swiped at the door again. Someone was beside him—he did not know who—bringing his mace down on the door. The wood cracked and splintered, but still the door held. The screeching and grinding continued, and Horvat knew from the shouting below that someone had got into the courtyard under the portcullis.

Horvat lifted both hands, his eyes on the latch. The man beside him was battering the door again and again, but Horvat kept his eyes on the latch and brought the mace down on it as hard as he could.

The door burst open, swung backwards, and then hit something and swung forwards again. Horvat put a hand on it and pushed it open. He got a glimpse of a figure exiting the portcullis chamber, shutting the far door behind him. Horvat ran forwards, dropping his mace on the floor and grabbing the windlass. There was a rod jammed in the chain. He pulled, leaning backwards and taking the weight on his legs. The rod jumped free, and Horvat went staggering backwards into the wall as the portcullis came crashing down with a screech and a scream.

FitzRoland, with Campbell behind him, had run out of the far door and onto the winding stairs. Their ears were full of the screech of the metal scraping through the stone grooves and a man screaming.

They came out into the courtyard, expecting to see soldiers rushing through the jammed portcullis. A few had gotten in, but the heavy portcullis had come down on top of one man, piercing his armour the way the point of a knife would break an egg and turn it to mush.

Now the archers were coming down the stone stairs to shoot their arrows through the bars of the portcullis. Campbell turned around in one movement, not knowing why. Both his hands were on his sword, holding it before him like a shield. There was the clash of metal hitting metal, and the whole sword shook in his hands. Then he instinctively turned the other way, the heavy sword sliding easily through the air, until there was the mincing noise of metal slicing into flesh and a man folding in half.

He let go of his sword and made a sprint for the portcullis, jumping around dead bodies that lay scattered on the ground. His foot stood on a boulder, and then he realised it was a man's head. Then he was climbing the portcullis, his feet and hands using the bars as steps. Up and up he went, his back to the courtyard. With every step, every handhold, he expected an arrow in this back.

Elisabeth drew back her bow. White arrow shafts were shooting through the portcullis. She watched the man climbing the portcullis, aiming for the centre of his broad back. She began to release her grip, but the arrow shot away too early, hit the iron portcullis, and bounced back.

Up and up, Campbell went. The portcullis was built to keep men outside the castle; it was not designed to keep someone in. Above him was the narrow slit through which they dropped and raised the portcullis. Turning his head to the side, flattening his shoulders against the metal gate, he squeezed himself through the opening.

The rough stone scratched the side of his head and then scraped the skin from his ear as he pushed himself upwards. His head surfaced in the portcullis chamber, and the stone was pressing hard against his chest, pressing and pressing, till he felt his ribs would break. He was stuck. He could not breathe. And his ribs were breaking. The stone had him in its jaws, crushing and crushing him.

Oh, Jesus, get me through, get me through! He pushed and pushed with his feet, forcing his body through the narrow space. His chest was going to burst, and he was going to die there in that hole. Then, all of a sudden, he was through and lying gasping on the floor. The portcullis chamber was empty; everyone had rushed to the courtyard. But already he could hear the sound of feet on the stairs as they came back this way.

The door at one side was broken. He stood up, staggering through the door and unfastening his belt as he went. Was he going back down the sewer or into moat? He pulled off the loose-fitting mail shirt and dropped it on the floor.

The far door to the portcullis chamber burst open, but he was out of the portcullis chamber now and climbing onto the empty battlements like a monkey. With one jump, he was off the battlements and falling freely through the air till the cold crash of the water in the moat hit him. He scrambled about in the water, feeling his way to the bank and climbing out. He was shivering with cold, and he had lost his sword and his armour. If the archers could see him from the battlements, he was a dead man.

He looked around, suddenly realising he was on his own. Where was FitzRoland? He hesitated, looking up at the stone wall. A head appeared above the battlements and then a flash of orange and the burning tip of an arrow.

Campbell burst into a sprint, running for the trees and the cover of darkness they offered. Then he stood, pressing his back hard against a tree, out of sight of the castle, breathing hard.

He was out of danger now. He could walk, unseen, through the woods to the camp. He took a step, feeling the soft, mossy undergrowth against his foot. Suddenly, his foot felt sore. He looked down, only realising now that both feet were scratched and bleeding.

And his shoes were in the sewer.

CHAPTER 3

"She's on the toilet!" Isabella shouted out.

"Not so loud," Catherine hissed through the curtain.

"The queen wants to see you."

Catherine Douglas was crouching over an iron grille with the hem of her dress bunched around her thighs. She stood up, letting the folds of material drop and drew back the curtain.

Isabella skipped across the floor. "You're in trouble again."

Catherine stepped out of the privy.

"You're always in trouble."

"Almost as much as you," Catherine said, looking down at ten-year-old Isabella. They walked through Sheona's bedchamber and then Catherine's own bedchamber and then the nursery.

Nobody had any privacy in this place; there were no corridors. The only way to the royal bedchamber was through the other bedchambers. Nobody could sneak up on the king unsuspected, but there was always someone blundering their way into the ladies' chambers.

Like Isabella.

"The queen received a letter this morning from your mother."

"How do you know that?"

"I heard the horseman shout out that he was carrying a letter from Lady Douglas."

Catherine grimaced and then forced the grimace into a smile. "That doesn't mean I'm in trouble."

"It usually does," Isabella said knowingly.

Was she being recalled? Or maybe her mother had found another gruesome suitor for her?

Isabella skipped ahead, running into the royal bedchamber where Jean Lockhart was plaiting the queen's hair.

"Here she is!" Isabella announced as if she was delivering a captured prisoner.

Catherine took a deep breath and walked in slowly. "Good morning, Your Grace."

"That will be all, Jean," Queen Joan said.

"I'm not finished."

"You can come back and finish it later."

"As you wish." Jean let go of the long, brown hair.

"I received a letter from Lady Douglas," Queen Joan said to Catherine.

"The Formidable Lady Douglas," Jean said.

"Be more respectful," Queen Joan said.

"Jamie has a dead mouse he wants to show you," Isabella said to Jean.

"Marvellous," Jean said as she left the room.

Queen Joan stood up. "I hate sitting on that wooden chair," she complained.

And Jean hates plaiting your hair, but she can never say so. Catherine waited expectantly.

A Savonarolan chair[2] sat underneath the stained-glass window. The queen went over to it and sat down.

Catherine remained standing.

"Please sit down," Queen Joan said.

Catherine sat on the wooden chair.

"Not on that one—take the other chair by the wall."

A second Savonarolan chair had been pushed up against the wall. Catherine went over to it and sat down, sinking into its softness.

"We will be going to St John's Town[3] next week," Queen Joan said.

"Yes," Catherine said.

"You have a friend who lives there?"

"You mean Margaret?"

"Margaret FitzRoland."

---

[2] A chair with an X-shaped frame that had been in use since Roman times
[3] Perth

"Yes."

"Yes," the queen said. "Your mother—Lady Douglas—sent me a letter." Then she paused.

Catherine took a deep breath.

"Alexander Lovell is a young man with good prospects." The queen shot Catherine a glance. "He will be attending court in a few days." The queen's voice trailed away. "But that's not why I called you here." Her tone changed. "Alexander Lovell is importing wine from Lubeck. Well, that's not important. What he discovered was that a berth on the ship has been taken by Sigismund."

Catherine knew immediately what this meant. Her heart began to race.

"Alan FitzRoland has been serving in Emperor Sigismund's army. It looks like he's coming home." The queen smiled. "You must tell Margaret when we're in St John's Town."

"I don't think." Catherine hesitated. "I don't think she wants to see him again."

"Then you should tell her and give her time to get used to the idea." That was Sheona Crockett's voice.

"Thank you for that contribution, Sheona," the queen said with narrowed eyelids.

Sheona strode confidently into the room. "A shipment of wine has arrived from Hamburg, courtesy of Alexander Lovell." She winked. "Catherine's boyfriend."

"Don't you start," Catherine growled.

"Some of us would be happy to have a man who's never around."

"And you wonder why you never have any suitors?"

"Thank you, Catherine," Queen Joan said curtly. "You can tell Jean to come in and finish plaiting my hair."

"You were in the portcullis with Mr. FitzRoller?"

"I would like a cup of wine." Sean Campbell spoke slowly, carefully enunciating his words in German. He was sitting on a bench covered with a piece of cowhide in a large, round tent and casting his eye over the empty copper cups that sat on the wooden table.

Stibor stood above him, his arms folded, resting his back against the tent pole. He frowned.

"Wine," Campbell said.

"We do not have any."

"A cup of water?"

Stibor frowned.

"Vaa-ter." Campbell said slowly.

"We do not have any."

"We are camped on a river; we must have water."

"We are packing up and moving; have you not noticed, Sir Schon?"

"Sean."

"That is what I said."

"I will go and get some water myself," Campbell said. He stood up and then thought better of it, remembering how sore his feet were.

"Not yet." Stibor waved a finger at Campbell.

"I need shoes and a cup of wine."

"You tell me what happened."

Campbell shook his head. "I do not know what happened. We were in the courtyard. You were too slow getting your men underneath the portcullis."

"You were too slow raising the portcullis."

"You were too slow."

Stibor slowly shook his head.

"We raised the portcullis."

"Not high enough."

"You did not get your men through in time which meant—which meant we were trapped. So we climbed up the portcullis and back into the portcullis chamber."

"Impossible."

"Everybody else had come down the stairs and into the courtyard. So we got onto the battlements and jumped into the moat."

"Where was Mr. FitzRoller?"

Campbell shrugged helplessly. "I thought he was behind me."

"You did not look?"

"We got in, and we got out."

"*You* got out."

Campbell gritted his teeth for a moment. "We got in, raised the portcullis, and got out. We did our job."

"And what do I tell my liege Sigismund?"

"You tell him you did not get your men under the portcullis until it was too late."

Stibor glared at Campbell through narrowed eyelids. "We employed you because we trusted you to do the job."

"Because no one else was stupid enough to do it," Campbell muttered to himself. He looked up at Stibor. "Maybe it is time I went home."

"Yes. Go back to England."

"Scotland."

"You are not much use here. We are paying you good money, but you are not doing much to earn it."

"Then give me Alan's share, too, and I'll take it back to his widow."

Stibor frowned.

"Give me FitzRoland's share." Campbell was speaking slower, more loudly. "I will take it back to his widow."

"His widow? You are saying he is dead?"

"He's not coming out of there alive."

The tent flap opened; a gust of wind immediately blew out the candles. Someone's head and shoulders poked into the tent. Stibor stepped outside. There was a muffled conversation, and then he came back in. "We are going south to Prague," he announced.

"That is where Zizka is going?"

"No." Stibor shook his head. "Zizka is coming here. He is one day's march away."

"I need a pair of shoes!"

But Stibor had already lost interest and left the tent.

"Where were you, Alan? Where were you?" she shouted in anger.

Margaret FitzRoland walked back and forth across the garden. She could not sit down. It was not the hardness of the ground or the coldness that stopped her sitting down. She could not sit inside, either, could not rest by the side of a warm fire. Here she was, walking back and forth across her garden, behind a stone wall that sheltered it from the wind but failed to keep it warm under the weak winter sunshine.

She walked, arms folded in front of her chest, as she had done yesterday and the day before.

Walking and walking, she passed a heap of newly dug earth where the grass would not grow. she passed two sticks of wood bound together with twine to make a cross and the letters *A. FitzRoland* carved on them with a knife.

"Why couldn't you have come home, Alan?" she asked.

Then she turned around and gasped. The dark figure of Catherine Douglas, with long brown hair cascading down a brown kirtle that was, perhaps, a little too low-cut, was standing at the top of the ladder.

The kitchen door, like the front door, was on the first floor. The way into the house was by climbing a ladder, which was withdrawn at night. There were windows (no glass) on the ground floor and shutters that could be shut and then bolted tight.

"Oh!" Margaret gasped.

"Jeanie let me in," Catherine shouted down.

"Catherine!" Margaret cried out, perhaps feeling a little self-conscious. "You should have spoken."

Catherine tried to smile. She turned around and, lifting the hem of her skirt with one hand, climbed down the ladder. Margaret walked to the bottom of the ladder.

"I didn't want to disturb you," Catherine lied. In truth, she had not known what to say. "How are you, Margaret?"

"I'm all right." Margaret ushered Catherine back towards the kitchen. "Let's go inside."

"Remember how we used to sit at the kitchen table breaking open pea pods and pulling out the fresh peas?"

"We used to eat them straight from the pod. Hardly any went into the soup."

"Fresh peas are always too good to put in the soup."

"That's what I always thought."

"But not your mother."

"No. I was always in trouble."

"Your mother wasn't so bad," Catherine said. "She was never as bad as my mother."

Margaret shivered slightly. "She was bad enough."

"You're looking well," Catherine said, changing the subject. "You've put on weight."

Margaret flinched. "Let's go for a walk."

"We could talk in the garden," Catherine said.

"No. Let's go for a walk."

"There's a cold wind coming off the river."

"Then we'll go to the woods! Like we used to do when we were children."

"We didn't walk; we always ran."

Summer days spent in the woods—days the boys spent climbing trees while the girls picked flowers, made daisy chains, and talked about the boys. Whole days spent outside, out of sight of parents or elders, finding mushrooms or berries to eat. Every stream was a river back then, no matter how small.

Days spent playing together or falling out about stupid things. And there was always a falling out, for they always went in gangs of five or six, boys and girls together; her mother used to say to her again and again to never, never, never walk through the woods on her own. And at night-time, her mother would tell her stories about Little Red Riding Hood and the wolves that lived out in the woods, and she would promise never to go near the woods on her own. And she kept the promise, even though everyone knew there was not a wolf to be found for miles around.

Sean Campbell was sitting in a tavern in Prague enjoying a breakfast of beer and cheese.

His shoes, taken from a soldier who had taken an arrow in the chest, were too big. They were no use for running and fighting. But so far, he had only had to walk or ride in them. He had a new dagger, too, taken from the same soldier, along with a leather sheath that he had tied to his belt.

He did not know what was going on. They had retreated to Prague; there were whispered reports that Zizka was nearby. He had been told to come to this tavern; he did not know why.

He sat on a broken bench at a splintered wooden table. A lantern hung from the rafters, swinging slightly in the breeze whenever someone came in the door. Campbell had been served a block of smoked Bavarian cheese and black rye bread. He cut a piece of cheese with his knife and broke off a piece of bread.

"Kam-bull?" a voice said.

Campbell looked up. A tall, heavily built man with greying hair was standing above him. "Do I know you?"

The man sat down, pulling out a knife and cutting off a chunk of cheese.

"Help yourself," Campbell said.

The man nodded to the innkeeper, who came over with a pewter cup of beer and set it on the table.

Campbell waited for the man to speak.

The man took a drink of beer and put the cup back on the table. He seemed to spend a long time studying the tabletop. Then he looked up at Campbell. "You are going back to Scotland."

Was it a question or an instruction? Campbell frowned. "You have not told me your name."

"My name is Ludwig."

"I do not know you."

The man shrugged his shoulders as if he did not care. He was stocky and slightly fat with a growth of hair hiding his double chin. "I was sent here to meet you."

"I am not ready to go back to Scotland."

"Sigismund does not have much work for a man who cuts children's throats."

"What?"

"You know what I am referring to."

Campbell hesitated for a moment. "No one saw us."

"No one saw you do what?"

Campbell's mind was racing. "We were in the portcullis chamber."

"We know where you were."

"Then you know we raised the portcullis."

Ludwig gave Campbell a long, hostile stare. "My lord Sigismund must think about his reputation. He has no use for you."

"I did not—" Campbell stopped himself in mid-sentence.

Ludwig gave him a quizzical look. "Did not what?"

Campbell whispered, "Cut the boy's throat."

"He cut his own throat?"

"I speak the truth."

A serving wench came up to their table, bending over to set a plate of cheese before them and displaying her large bosom. Then she went away again, coming back with two tankards of ale. The men watched her as she set the tankards on the table and then left.

The cheese looked old, being hard, cracked, and dry. Both men preferred it that way on account of it having a stronger flavour. Ludwig pulled out a knife from his belt and cut off a slice, putting it in his mouth and sucking it. "I have been told to give you five gold coins." Ludwig put a hand in his pocket and pulled out a small leather pouch. He passed it across the table.

Campbell took it and put it in his pocket without opening it. "Tell my liege Sigismund—"

Ludwig quickly spoke. "There is another job for you."

"What is it?"

"I do not know that."

Campbell frowned. "You must have heard something."

"No."

"These are Sigismund's orders?"

The man shook his head. "No, not Sigismund."

"Where is this job?"

"You must go to Cuxhaven. First, you ride north to Coswig."

"On my own?"

"From there, you take the High Road to Cuxhaven."

"I should get my horse shod."

Ludwig frowned. "You do not have much luck with shoes, Kam-bull."

"One of the horse's shoes is loose."

"Sell the horse."

"No. I need to get it shod. I need a blacksmith."

Ludwig shook his head. "Not in Prague. The horses here are only for show. They do not work hard. They carry fat nobles around town; that is all they do."

"My horse is a good horse. But it needs shod."

Ludwig shook his head. "You do not understand. City blacksmiths make shoes for horses that do not work hard."

"It's not important."

"You've never shod a horse?"

"Of course not. I'm a knight, not a smith."

Again, Ludwig shook his head. "You put the nail in too deep, it goes into the nerve, and the horse kicks you. City blacksmiths are cowards. They put the nails in shallow to avoid the nerve. They do not hurt the horse; they do not get kicked."

"So what?"

"So the nail is in shallow. After a while, it breaks, and the shoe comes off."

"Then tell me where there is a good smith."

"You learn to do it yourself. Go deep but not so deep that you touch the nerve."

"I don't have time for that."

"You ask for my advice; I give it to you."

Campbell decided to change the subject. "What do I do in Cuxhaven?"

"There, you will get your instructions."

"From whom?"

"Pat-riik Heb-bunn."

"Patrick Hepburn?"

"That is what I said."

Campbell frowned. "He will be in Cuxhaven?"

"He has a boat called *Mo-rag Dun-vey-gan*."

"Where are you sending me?"

"The boat sets sail in three days."

"What is the job?"

Ludwig shrugged as if he did not care. "Just make sure you are on the boat."

CHAPTER 4

"The queen thinks Alan's coming home," Catherine said.

There was a gasp. Margaret seemed to stumble slightly. "How does she know?"

"A man has taken a berth on a boat coming back from Lubeck."

Margaret frowned. "But that could be anyone!"

"It's a Scotsman who has been serving with Sigismund."

Margaret was walking with her arms folded tightly across her chest. Then she stopped and gave Catherine a wild look. "You must help me!"

———————

Tall buildings leaned outwards on either side as their wooden beams aged and warped. The street was narrow. Campbell stepped carefully around mounds of horse droppings and holes in the road where cobbles were missing.

A sign hanging from a rusty chain indicated there was a blacksmith's forge halfway down the street. Campbell led his horse towards it.

The sign, in which a man bent over an anvil with a hammer in his hand, grew bigger and bigger until it was hanging over Campbell's head. Peering into its dark recesses, he shouted, "Hallo!"

There was no response.

The sign hung from an awning which was supported by two posts on either side. Campbell took a length of rope from his saddlebag and tied the horse to it by the neck. He stepped into the blacksmith's shop, immediately feeling the warmth from the forge.

"Hallo!"

A dull red point of light appeared in the distance. It came towards him, slowly growing bigger.

"Servus?"

That was the blacksmith's voice. Suddenly he was standing in front of Campbell, a glowing poker in his hand. He was a stocky, bearded man wearing a leather apron.

"My horse," Campbell said. "One shoe is loose."

"You want new shoes?"

"No. One shoe is loose. On the right foreleg. Take it off; put it on again."

"Replace the shoes."

"No. Take the shoe off; put it on again."

"I understand."

Campbell led the blacksmith outside. He looked at the horse, bending forwards to pick up the hoof and study the shoe. He put it down carefully before going around the horse, picking up each hoof in turn and looking at it.

"I replace all the shoes."

"No." Campbell shook his head. "The shoe on the right foreleg is loose. Take it off and then hammer it in again."

"Two groschen."

Campbell held up one finger. "One."

The blacksmith looked away, muttered something, and went back into his shop. He came back moments later with a hammer and a chisel in his hands and holding nails in his teeth. He picked up the horse's hoof, held it between his knees as he bent over it, and prised the shoe off with a chisel.

He set the shoe against the hoof, took a nail from his mouth. and hammered it in. Then, quickly, he hammered the other nails in.

A leather pouch hung from Campbell's belt. He untied it, opened it, and pulled out a silver coin.

The blacksmith let go of the horse's hoof and stood up. Campbell pressed the coin into his hand. Then he was leading the horse back up the narrow street, heading north.

They were walking through the narrow streets of St John's Town together—a walled burgh on the north bank of the River Tay; the gates were always closed after dark. This was a safe place for her to wait for her husband to return home. Or that had been the idea.

Edinburgh, with four hundred houses, was the Athens of Scotland. But the royal burgh of St John's Town was little more than a cluster of houses. What gave the town its status was what lay outside the walls. To the south was Greyfriars Monastery. To the west was Whitefriars Monastery. And to the north was the magnificent Blackfriars Monastery, where the king stayed when he visited the burgh.

Blackfriars Monastery was on their left as they walked out of the North Port, the hems of their kirtles collecting dust as they went. Around them was the bustle of people going to the river for water or the hammer of metal on wood as coopers made barrels or buckets. Behind the burgh walls were small houses with thatched roofs on top of rickety wooden frames where mud or moss was used to plug the cracks and keep out the draught. There were stone houses, too, for the better off—a dull orange in colour where blocks of sandstone were held together with mortar.

Neither of the women spoke. Margaret walked with her head hanging down, her eyes on the road. Soon, the town was behind them, and they were out in the country. The trees were bare after the long winter, but they could hear the branches gently rustling in the breeze and the crows crowing above their heads.

"It looks different," Catherine said.

"Every year, men cut down trees and sell them to the navy. Every year, the clearings grow bigger. Every year, there are more fields and less trees."

The sun was setting, but its rays were weak. They followed the river as it turned inland. Soon they were leaving Blackfriars Monastery behind them, following an earthen road that had fields to the left and the river on the right. The land was flat and bare but rising slightly—glistening in the distance were the snow-topped Grampian foothills.

Catherine was waiting for Margaret to speak with growing impatience. "It won't be so bad," she said. "Alan will stay for a few weeks and then go off to war again. You know what the men are like."

"It's not that," Margaret said. She was looking down at her feet.

"What's Alan FitzRoland going to do in a place like St John's Town? He won't stay long."

"It's not that," Margaret repeated.

"What is it?"

Margaret looked down at her feet. "I was pregnant when Alan left."

The sky had gone from blue to dark blue and then to black as the stars slowly grew brighter. Campbell was following a dark earthen track taking him away from Prague where the streets were populated with taverns from which lanterns swung in the wind.

The road he followed was dark and getting darker. It was a thick black line against a dark background, but then the dark track would disappear, and he would be riding across rough country. Then it would reappear. But was this the same road or a different one?

The night was cold; he could see the horse's breath condensing in long plumes as it was expelled in snorts. He had to keep the North Star in front of him. Come morning, the sun would rise on his right-hand side.

On he went, into the blackness. But there was only blackness. To go back was to go back to a deeper blackness, back to a botched attack, a dead drummer boy and the accusing eyes of people thinking he had abandoned FitzRoland to save his own life.

On he went, through the night, always with half an idea he was travelling north. If he got through this, if he made his way home, he would meet FitzRoland's wife again. Wife or widow? And what would he tell her? Had a hand grabbed his foot as they'd climbed the portcullis? Had an arrow punctured his mail shirt?

Why was FitzRoland the one who got caught with a wife and baby at home? Campbell would have swapped places with him in an instant. To die, surrounded, hundreds of miles from home but fighting on to the bitter end! To die like Spartacus or William Wallace. To die with your name remembered—to be sung about by the minstrels.

This had been his chance to make his reputation, and already the chance had gone. Like all the other boys his age, he had spent his boyhood dreaming of fighting in the Holy Land, where he would ride on horseback with the reins held in one hand and a sword in the other, jousting with giants and always winning.

And it was a chance to stop paying rent to a baron for land sublet to peasants. The rent a knight paid was the hire of his sword, and he would ride at the lists while peasants tilled his fields.

And the war offered him a chance to make his name—a chance to make a better life, a chance to get away from small houses stacked on top of each other where everybody lived in everyone else's filth. It was a chance to get away from drunken, noisy, abusive wheelwrights, coopers, fletchers, potters, sawyers, thatchers, and masons; a chance to get away from dirty, ill-mannered children and their bad-tempered mothers shouting at each other all day long in the streets; a chance to get away from earthen roads that were used as sewers and lay covered in excrement, human and animal, till the hard rains came in winter. War was chance to get away from stinking streets that the women walked along with flowers pressed to their noses to block out the smell; a chance to get away from the filth that he trudged through on the way to market or to church and then brought back home clinging to his feet and shoes.

And it was a chance to get away from faces that never smiled and from the pain that lay behind every pair of eyes. A chance to get away from small children who would be playing in the streets one week and then dead the next, covered in black boils after a week spent lying on their floors at home fevered and delirious with their wailing mothers at their sides. A chance to get away from small bodies being tossed into deep pits outside the city walls and left there; a chance to get away from mothers standing over the pits and weeping or others, too tired to grieve, staying at home to cook their husbands' meals with ashen faces and a deadness in their dry eyes.

But for him, there was only infamy. To go home and say that FitzRoland had killed the drummer boy would look like he was putting the blame on a dead man who could not speak up for himself. He would be despised for it.

If there was one thing he could give Margaret now, it was a good memory of her husband. He died bravely, my lady, outnumbered and surrounded but refusing to give up. He died like a hero.

The drummer boy got killed but these things happen in war. And anyhow, your husband did not do it. His hands are clean. Somewhere out there, is a man with blood on his hands, but it is not Alan FitzRoland.

And if she asks, You were there, Sean. You saw what happened. Tell me who cut the drummer boy's throat?

And if I lie … what then? Yes, my lady, I did it. I cut the boy's throat, and then I left your husband in the castle to be hacked to pieces by furious Hussites while I jumped to safety.

If I lie, I'm a coward. If I tell the truth, I will not be believed. Either way, I will be despised.

Starlight caught his eye, sparkling silver wobbling on the surface of a grey river. He let the horse slow to a walk as he looked at the slow-moving water winding one way and then another as it slid forwards. Was this the Elbe? Whatever it was, it looked like it was moving westwards.

"He said he would be back to see the baby born," Margaret said. "He promised me. He promised." She looked up at the sky. "Why did I believe him?"

The women were following a path that was clinging to the side of the river, winding its way towards the distant hills. Blackfriars Monastery was behind them now, its monks quietly working in the large garden behind thick stone walls.

"He would make his name and come back a war hero. That's what he said." Margaret spat the words out like they were poison. "On one side was the Pope and the Holy Roman Emperor; one the other side was a blind commoner called Jan Zizka."

He had left in late summer, full of hopes to be back within a few weeks. But the summer turned to autumn, her belly grew large, and there was no sign of the army returning. Then winter came with frost on the roads and a chill in the air. Boats would dock at Leith with news, which was always the same; they had attacked Zizka and been driven back. The local taverns were full of men explaining how they would beat Zizka if they had command of the Holy Roman Emperor's armies. All it required was one cavalry charge—or archers to decimate the enemy lines. What were the commanders doing? They could not be any good.

But there was never any talk of Alan FitzRoland.

"I never knew if he was alive or dead," Margaret said.

"If he was dead," Catherine said quietly, "someone would come with the news."

"I couldn't understand," Margaret said, "why the army kept getting beaten. This Zizka—he was a commoner, and he was blind. How could he command an army?"

"He was possessed by the devil."

"Didn't we have God on our side?"

The women turned off the road and onto a path through the wood. There had once been a narrow path leading to a small clearing where they had played as children, but now the path was wide like a road and the clearing as big as a farmer's field.

"I thought they'd come back for the winter," Margaret continued. "Maybe they couldn't fight during the winter. And they'd march back in the spring."

"But they didn't."

"No—nor the next spring."

The two women walked on in silence. Soon it would be springtime again—the third springtime since Alan had left.

"I began to get angry," Margaret continued, "angry with Alan. He didn't have to go away like that. It was his choice. He went because he wanted to. Instead of being with me and the baby, he wanted to go up there and fight useless battles against blind men. I began to think maybe he didn't really love me.

"And I began to think how stupid he was. How stupid all the FitzRolands were."

"You're a FitzRoland."

"I'm ashamed of the name."

"You don't mean that."

"He'd see it as an honourable thing—fighting for years, hundreds of miles from home. His father would have done the same thing if he'd been alive. He'd want to be remembered as the man who captured Melnik Castle, not as the man who lost it. I could just picture him standing on the parapet and preening himself."

"Alan's not like that," Catherine said gently.

"Yes, he is. They all are. The last thing they think about is their families. Alan would rather get himself killed in some foreign country, leaving behind children he's never seen, than spend his life at home with me."

"He loves you."

"Huh!"

They had come upon the fallen trunk of a birch tree. The bark was smooth to the touch. The women sat down, Catherine looking at the trees and the grass struggling through the carpet of moss underneath.

"You never saw my baby," Margaret said.

"No."

"She was such a beautiful baby. When she was born, she kept staring at me and kicking her legs. I remember just holding her in my arms looking at her. I was so tired, Kate. But when I saw her, my tiredness vanished, and I just lay and held her. And I remember feeling so relieved.

"I'd been very scared—scared of the pain, scared I might die. I thought I might die and never see my husband again. I wanted Alan to be there and hold my hand. Then I wouldn't have been afraid. I wouldn't have been afraid if he'd been with me." She smiled. "I'm never afraid when he's with me."

Catherine tried to adopt as reassuring a tone as she could. "He'll be with you next time."

But Margaret just shook her head. "No, he won't."

Catherine picked up Margaret's hand and gave it a squeeze. "Your hand's cold," she said.

Margaret said nothing.

Catherine smiled. "Everything will be all right."

But Margaret shook her head again. "No, it won't."

CHAPTER 5

Margaret walked on in silence for a while. Then, suddenly, she started speaking again, the words coming out in a rush. "I never told you I nearly died."

"What?" Catherine shot Margaret a glance.

"I lost a lot of blood. I was in bed for weeks after the birth. I just felt tired all the time—tired and cold. It was the start of springtime, and I've never felt so cold. And Alan should have guessed because it happened before. It happened with our first one. She was stillborn, and I was so ill he nearly lost both of us.

"I was heartbroken, but he wasn't bothered—it was only a girl, not the son he needed to carry on the precious FitzRoland name."

"You know what men are like." Catherine tried to lighten the tone of the conversation. "They don't express their feelings."

"Pah!" Catherine snorted. "He was thinking of the money she'd cost if she lived—a young child to be fed and clothed, servants to look after her. And then there's the massive dowry he'd have had to pay out when she got married. No, no, no—he was glad she died."

The grass was damp. The bark on the tree was uneven; a thistle was growing up between Catherine's feet. She shifted her feet, and the hem of her kirtle caught a thorn. She tugged at it, and it snapped free, but a strand of thread began to unravel.

Margaret was speaking again. "So when my second one lived—well, part of me was delighted. And she looked so much like Alan—brown hair, green eyes. I mean, I knew it wasn't the son Alan was wanting. I'd wanted a boy to call Alan, after his father. But I had another girl, so I called her Anna. But even if she was a girl, she was still our child, and

I knew Alan would want to see her. I wanted him to see her. I wanted him to see our baby. But he didn't come back. He didn't come back."

Catherine squeezed Margaret's hand. "He'll be back." She smiled reassuringly.

Margaret looked away. "Alan still hadn't come back when Anna had her first birthday. He never saw her smile. He never heard her talk. He never heard her say Daddy. I just wanted him to see her because she was a beautiful baby."

Margaret halted. She was losing control over her voice. She was having to work hard to keep the voice under control, to keep the words coming out calmly and evenly. Then the tears flooded out, like a damn bursting all at once. "I taught her to say Daddy, and-and-and he never heard her."

"It wasn't his fault," Catherine said. But words were no use here. She put her arm around Margaret's shoulders.

"Yes it was his fault!" Margaret shouted. She pulled herself away.

A breeze was coming off the river. Catherine shivered slightly. Only now was she realising that the bark of the tree she was sitting on was damp. She wanted to stand up and start walking again even though the road was stony and uneven. But she knew Margaret needed to talk, so she remained where she was.

"She got smallpox," Catherine said. There was a pause; neither woman spoke. "I didn't let the servants near her. She was my daughter—it was my job to look after her. It didn't matter that there was no one to look after me. It didn't matter that my heart was breaking. I nursed her all day and all night for six days. I never left her side. I couldn't have lived with myself if she'd died crying for her mother and I hadn't been there to hold her hand. So I stayed with her, day and night." Margaret halted for a moment to look up at the sky. Then she shouted, "I needed you here, Alan. I needed you to be strong for me. I needed you to hold me and tell me everything would be all right. And if you'd been here, Alan, maybe I would have coped better. Because I didn't cope, Alan. I grew so tired I would just put her to bed and lie beside her, listening to her crying. Then I started wishing she would give me smallpox, and we could both die together. But I didn't get smallpox, and I had to watch her die on my own. I had to watch her die day by day, night by night.

In all my life, Alan, I've never needed you so much as I did then, but you weren't here. You weren't here."

The torrent had ceased. Margaret stood up and took a few steps into the clearing. She was shaking.

"You're cold," Catherine said. "I'll take you home."

"Two years," Margaret whispered.

"The sun has set," Catherine said. "We should be going back." She began to edge forwards, guiding Catherine towards the road.

"Two years! Two years of my life. Giving birth. Having a child and losing her. Two years feeding, carrying, coaxing. Two years, and all I have left is a couple of sticks and a mound of earth in the garden."

They came out of the clearing and back onto the road. The trees fell away, and they could see fields, where some boys were watching cattle as they grazed. Beyond them, the river wound its way back towards St John's Town.

"You'll have another child," Catherine said.

Margaret froze.

"Come along," Catherine tried to encourage her. "What is it?"

Margaret opened her mouth, but nothing came out. She hadn't come here to talk about Alan or losing the baby, and going back now was pointless. She couldn't go back yet.

"What is it?" Catherine asked again. Her tone was gentle and encouraging.

Margaret hesitated. There was something else she had to say. Something important. Something she needed to talk about.

"What is it?" Catherine asked for the third time.

Eventually, Margaret squeezed out the words, "There's something else."

"What?"

"I'm pregnant." Suddenly the words were out—words she'd thought she'd never be able to say. They had come out in a moment.

Catherine's jaw dropped involuntarily. There was a long silence. Then she said, "Who's the father?"

"Walter."

A DAGGER FOR CATHERINE DOUGLAS

"Walter *FitzRoland*?" Catherine's voice was a whisper.

———— † ————

Riding through the night, not even knowing why.

No, that's not right. You do know why.

You're the second son of a second son with nothing to inherit. Campbell of Loch Awe does not want you. King James does not want you. Emperor Sigismund does not want you.

You had your reputation, made by your sword. Whatever tiny amount of respect you had when you set sail from Leith, going east, has gone. Now you are the man who climbs up sewers covered in filth and murders defenceless children. By the time the story gets back to Scotland, you will have come out of the sewer smeared in faeces from head to foot. You will have killed over one hundred children and then cooked their bodies on spits and devoured them. There will be horns protruding from your head as, every night, you sacrifice another child to Satan.

And Janet MacRory—the gossips will be telling her that she had a lucky escape. Maybe they're right; my priorities were always all wrong. When we played games of handball on the pebble beach at Dunoon, I always played to win. It was important to me to show you how strong I was. I should have just knocked the ball towards you and let you hit it back.

"I was never any use to you," he said out loud, shaking his head. "I'm sorry, Janet."

They'd walked hand in hand along the beach at Dunoon under the summer sun, watching the ferry glide through the water, the oars dropping into the water in unison. Why didn't I take you in my arms and kiss you? Why didn't I take you off the beach and into the pine forest? We could have made love in the forest where the carpet of pine needles would have been soft on your naked skin.

Words like, "I love you." Why did I never say these things to you?

Suddenly, Campbell pitched forwards in the saddle as the horse stumbled. He pressed his knees into its sides to coax it forwards, but it was hobbling now and barely moving. Campbell jumped down from the saddle and took a look at the front hooves. He could see immediately what was wrong. The shoe was hanging off—the same shoe that the city blacksmith had put on.

Campbell looked up at the black sky, dotted with twinkling stars. Leading the horse by the reins, he walked northwards.

"Santa Maria, Mater Dei," Catherine said. Her eyes were on the setting sun. "How did it happen?" She immediately realised how stupid that sounded.

"Does it matter?" Margaret asked. She hadn't confided in Catherine just to be judged.

"Yes, it matters," Catherine said. "Do you love Walter?"

"I don't know."

"Do you love Alan?"

"I don't want to talk about it."

"Tell me what happened."

"You can't work it out?"

"You know what I mean."

Margaret smiled, but it was a weak smile full of sadness. When the baby died, she had thrown out the crib, the baby's clothes, and the blankets. She had thrown out everything that might have reminded her of Anna. She was punishing her husband, who had not been there to see her and never would now. But still the walls seemed to echo with her crying and the days were long and empty. And the table and chairs seemed somehow to smell of Anna, such that she couldn't bear to sit by herself in the house, and she would go for long walks in the country, not bothering to eat and not wanting to return.

It was when she was out on the road, going nowhere and having nowhere to go that she saw Alan. She saw him coming towards her with a spring in his step and a sword swinging from his belt. She gasped. Then she began to walk, quickly breaking into a run.

She could see him smiling. She could see his blue eyes twinkling and already had a hand on his soft brown hair.

"Margaret!" he called out.

And, immediately, she slowed to a walk. Then she stopped, watching him as he walked up to her. The voice was wrong. Something about the walk was wrong, too. The way he held himself—straight-backed and taking bold, confident strides. Yes, he was confident but not so confident as he should be.

"Hello, Walter," she said.

"Hello," he said, holding out his arms as he approached her.

She stepped forward, stepping into his embrace and putting her head on his shoulder.

"I came as soon as I heard the news," he said.

"It was good of you to come," she said.

"I can only stay a couple of days," he said.

"Yes," she said.

"Are you all right?"

"Fine."

"I'm sorry."

She smiled. "You're not going to be an uncle this year."

"Maybe next year," he said with a forced laugh.

"Maybe."

"Any news about Alan?" he asked.

She shook her head dumbly.

"He'll be all right."

"Yes," she said.

"If I know Alan, he'll find a way back home."

"Yes," she said.

He put a hand on her chin and lifted it up till he was looking into her eyes. "When did you eat last?" he asked.

"I don't know," she said.

"Then let's go home and have dinner!"

Suddenly Margaret was embarrassed. "We can't. I don't have any food."

"Then we'll go to a tavern!" he declared.

They linked arms and walked along the road, heading towards the town. She smiled and, for a moment, almost felt happy. She was glad he was here and grateful to him for doing the simple things—for linking arms with her to walk along the road and share a meal in a tavern. Glad, too, that he wasn't asking any questions to remind her of things she'd rather forget.

"Tell me what happened!" A voice, a harsh voice, shattered the silence.

Margaret looked at Walter and then at the fields and then at the town in the distance. But she did not speak.

"Tell me what happened!" the voice repeated. It was a female voice.

Then Walter disappeared and Margaret looked around to see Catherine standing beside her. It was Catherine she had linked arms with, and it was Catherine who was walking alongside her.

"We went to the Ram's Heid Inn," she said ashamedly. She was looking down at her feet, mumbling.

"Then what?"

She remembered eating a hare. They'd served it on a plate and laid it on the table between them. Walter had told her to help herself, and they'd both dug in. Soon her lips were greasy and her fingers dripping with fat. She hadn't realised how hungry she was till she started eating; then the hunger overwhelmed her, and she began pulling meat off the bone with her hands and devouring it ravenously.

A serving wench came up to the table with two pints of wine and set the tankards down. Walter thanked the girl and then turned to her and told her to *drink up!* So she picked up a tankard and began to drink. The wine was sour and sharp to the taste; neither refreshing nor warming, it was good for nothing but washing away the grease.

Then ...

"I took him home," Margaret said.

She had wanted to sleep with Alan. But Alan was not there. He was never there. She needed Alan's arms around her, but here she was in bed with Walter. She could not explain it. She could not try to explain it. It sounded awful whatever way she tried to explain it. All she knew was that the house was cold and dark when they got back to it and smelling of death.

She put her arms around him because the house was cold, and he was warm. And then she noticed how much he smelled like Alan, how much he felt like Alan. She looked up into his eyes, which were blue like Alan's and ran her fingers through his hair that was soft like Alan's.

And then he kissed her. It was a gentle kiss at first, more of a peck than a kiss, but soon she was feeling his warm tongue on her neck and on her ears, the hot breath on her skin sending a thrill up her spine. Soon he was unlacing her bodice and pulling it off and his hands were on her breasts, touching them, squeezing them. Then he was unlacing her skirt and his cold hands were on her skin, touching her thighs and her bottom.

"Let's go upstairs," he said. It was a statement, not a question, and she went with him up the stairs and into the bedroom.

She was needing to be loved, needing to be touched, and she lay naked on the feather mattress with her skin glinting in the faint moonlight. She was open to him, giving in to him, giving him everything, just to feel him above her, warm, strong, firm. She was overpowered with his desire, with his passion, with his love.

The women walked on in silence.

"What are you going to do?" There was a knot in Catherine's stomach as if she knew what was coming next.

"You have to help me get rid it," Margaret said.

A black hole was opening up in front of Catherine. She thought she might fall into it. "Give me a few days," she said.

"You said Alan's coming home." Margaret flashed Catherine a desperate look. "I need somewhere to go."

The black sky had turned to dark blue.

Sean Campbell shivered with cold. Clouds of condensing air were blowing from the horse's nostrils. Shapes began to emerge out of the darkness. The outline of a house was coming into view—a timber-framed house with a thatched roof. It had shutters at one end where people slept but not at the other where animals were kept.

The sound of splashing caught his attention. Beyond the house, Campbell caught sight of the naked back, buttocks, and thighs of a woman washing in the river. Her wet brown hair clung to the wet skin on her back.

He gently tightened his grip on the reins, pulling the horse's head downwards and making it halt. But his eyes were on the woman. He looked around for something to tie the horse to but could not see anything.

The horse let out a snort.

The woman turned around and let out a shriek, one arm over her breasts. "Trudbert!" she screeched.

"Hallo!" Campbell shouted.

"Trudbert!" the woman shouted.

An unshaven man, pulling a loose-fitting shift over his head, blundered out of the door.

Campbell pointed to his horse's bad hoof. "Shoe!" he said.

The man came forwards, looking at the hoof. He picked it up and bent over, holding it between his knees and studying it.

"Blacksmith," Campbell said.

Trudbert pointed down an earthen track that passed for a road. "Twelve miles," he said.

Campbell groaned inwardly. If he lost half a day or more hobbling to the blacksmith, he would not make it to Cuxhaven. He looked at Trudbert, wondering if he might strike a deal. "Buy horse?" he said.

"Your horse is lame," Trudbert said.

"Not lame!" Campbell protested. "She has lost her shoe."

"Lame," Trudbert said.

The woman was stepping out of the river, dripping wet. Campbell tried to avoid looking at her as she picked up her tunic from the bank. All of a sudden, he noticed a small rowing boat, drifting in the current, tied by a length of rope to a pole that had been hammered into the bank.

"I will buy the boat," Campbell said and pointed to it.

The woman pulled the tunic over her head. Her head disappeared as she fought with it, tugging at the material that was clinging to her wet skin. Then her head reappeared. There was a short exchange between the man and the woman, but they were talking too quickly for Campbell to understand.

"The horse for the boat," Campbell asked.

Trudbert pointed at the sword hanging from Campbell's waist. "The horse and the sword."

"No." Campbell shook his head.

The two men eyed each other warily.

Campbell patted the horse's rear. "Good horse," he said.

"Lame," Trudbert said.

"Not lame."

There was another exchange between the man and the woman.

"The horse and the saddle," Campbell offered.

"We need the boat." That was the woman's voice.

The woman came forwards. Campbell tried to avoid looking at the outline of her breasts against the dark blue linen tunic open at the neck.

"Small boat," she said.

Was she saying they had a small boat for sale? Campbell wondered.

"Come," Trudbert said, waving a hand.

The woman quickly took the reins of Campbell's horse. Campbell followed the man around the house, his feet getting wet in the long grass that was damp from the morning dew.

Then he saw it—a small, oval-shaped boat upturned and lying on the grass. "That's not a rowing boat; that's a coracle," he said.

Trudbert frowned. "Good boat."

"You want my horse for that piece of junk?" Campbell felt his heart sinking.

"Good boat," the man said.

He could sit in the coracle and the river would carry him westwards. He would get to Cuxhaven with enough time to find Patrick Hepburn. But what if he walked on? What then? Hepburn would have sailed by the time he reached Cuxhaven.

Did he want to go home?

Did he know what he was doing?

There was a rapid exchange between the man and the woman.

"The boat for the horse, and we give you breakfast." Trudbert smiled. It was an insincere smile.

The door to the house opened, and a young boy ran out, running to his mother, who took his hand.

A young boy with black hair and frightened eyes, running to the safety of his mother and hiding behind her skirt. That drummer-boy in Melnik Castle—where was his mother?

Who was his mother?

Suddenly Campbell just wanted to go, to get out of there. "I'll take the boat."

"Come," Trudbert said.

To sit in the house with that boy staring at him across the table? "I don't want breakfast," Campbell said.

CHAPTER 6

"Breakfast is served," a voice called out.
"Not yet."
The brush caught on a knot of hair. Catherine immediately stopped.
"All my ladies-in-waiting get married," Queen Joan said. "But not you."
"Did I hurt you, Your Grace?"
"Where is Jean?" The queen was sitting on a Savonarolan chair, looking out the window of her chamber in Stirling Castle. Catherine Douglas stood behind her, combing her long, black hair.
"She is in the nursery, with the children."
"She is better at combing my hair."
"I will fetch her."
"No," Queen Joan said. "She's better with the children, too."
"My only pleasure is in serving, Your Grace." Catherine had a comb in her hand with teeth made from bone. She began carefully working it down the queen's long hair.
"How is Margaret FitzRoland?"
Catherine stopped. Then she said, "She is well."
"You must invite her to court."
Catherine stopped combing again. "It is very kind of Your Grace to make the offer, but I regret she is going to Glen Esk to visit her cousin."
"She does not have cousins in Glen Esk."
"Friends."
"You have cousins in Glen Esk."
"Yes."
"So she is visiting your cousins?"
"Yes. That is what I mean to say, Your Grace."

"Soon it will be winter, and the glens will be blocked with snow. She will not be able to return before springtime."

"Glen Esk is very beautiful."

"She wishes to see it in the winter when the roads are blocked with snow?"

"The mountains are beautiful when they are white with snow."

"Alan FitzRoland returns after two years, and he learns that his wife is in Glen Esk and the roads are blocked with snow. Whose plan was this?"

"She does not know when Alan will return." Catherine began separating the queen's hair into plaits with her fingers.

"Is she fat?"

"What?"

"Is Margaret fat?"

"No!"

"Alexander Lovell visited His Grace the king yesterday for a game of royal tennis."

"They say he is a very accomplished player. I wish I had been able to watch."

"They talk while they play. I am sure I heard him say he had been in St John's Town and had seen Margaret. He said she was fat."

"Her baby died," Catherine said a little too quickly. "She has nothing to do but sit by the fireside and eat. She worries about her husband, so she eats."

"This is why she is fat?"

"Yes."

Queen Joan turned in her seat. Her hand took hold of Catherine's wrist. "You said she was not fat."

Catherine avoided the queen's eyes. "She will stop eating when she hears that her husband is returning."

"So she is fat?"

"It is of no concern to Your Grace."

"All my subjects are my concern."

"Yes, of course."

"I never thought Alan FitzRoland would be a good match for Margaret. But she wanted to get married."

"Alan is—"

"The kind of man who will spend long periods of time away from home."

"Margaret understood that."

"I doubt it. She eats because she is unhappy."

"Your Grace need have no concerns about Margaret. She will not be fat when she comes back in the springtime."

"You seem very sure."

"I only meant—" Catherine fell into silence. She had said too much. That knot was back in her stomach, tighter than ever.

"If one of my ladies ever needed my help, I would hope she would ask for it."

"Margaret does not need your help!" Catherine said vehemently. As soon as she spoke, she realised her bullish tone was inappropriate. She fell into silence, avoiding the queen's eyes.

Queen Joan knitted her brows. "Yes," she said quietly. "You are quite right." Her tone was insincere. She smiled. "Let us change the subject. I have some good news for you. The king has invited your parents to Stirling for Christmas."

A horrible feeling overcame Catherine. If only the floor would open up and swallow her! Was there a place where she could hide for forty days? She smiled a brave smile and turned her attention to the queen's long hair. "Let's get your hair plaited," she said with forced cheerfulness.

"Breakfast is served!" a voice shouted.

———— † ————

He used the paddle to push away from the bank. The tiny boat was wobbling in the water and then drifting downriver, and he was watching Trudbert turn his back and grow smaller as he walked away.

That horse is worth ten times the value of this boat, he kept thinking. He sat on the plank that stretched across the width of the boat and passed for a seat. He had thought he might get a rest if he travelled this way. Now he was thinking that the boat was too small to lie down in.

The trees on the right-hand side started moving forwards, and he realised the boat must be moving backwards. No—it was turning in the current! He leaned over the side, pushing the paddle into the water. The trees halted for a moment, and then they were moving backwards again.

Now he was in the middle of the stream and heading downriver. But if he tried to sleep in this boat, would he just get stuck on the bank? He tried to comfort himself with the knowledge that he was moving.

Nothing to do but sit in this boat. Plenty of time to think about things.

He had come to the continent to make a name for himself. For the first time in his life, maybe he could do something better than his brother. No one cared when he left; the favoured son was remaining in Argyll. They all gave each other knowing winks as he left; he would make a mess of it and come back in disgrace.

And here he was, coming back in disgrace. No point in saying, "FitzRoland cut the boy's throat," because that was not what they wanted to believe.

"I was married with a six-year-old child by the time I was your age," Catherine said. "That's the first thing she'll say, I guarantee it."

"Hold still," Jean Lockhart said.

"Married with a six-year-old and your little sister on the way."

"I said, Hold still."

"Jenny Soutar is married, and so is Mary Cameron. And both of them are younger than you."

"I told you to stay still."

Catherine was holding a yarn of wool stretched out between her two hands; Jean was slowly unravelling it to make a ball.

"If I wanted to be married, I would be married. Can't my mother understand that?"

"You mean if a man wanted to marry you, you'd be married."

"The right man."

"You haven't had an offer from any man."

"So it's all my fault?"

"You just need to relax a bit more."

"Relax! Have you ever spoken to my mother? Every time she speaks to me, she makes me feel like I've failed in my duty."

"I don't mean relax with your mother. I mean relax with men. Relax in the company of men."

"Like you do, I suppose?"

"I'm not scared of men the way you are."

"They never come near you." Catherine shot Jean a harsh stare. "What do you have to be scared of?"

"Och, don't worry. Christmas will be over before you know it."

"I'm dreading it."

"Don't. All you have to do is curtsey to him and take a walk in the palace gardens."

Catherine frowned. "I'm not going to curtsey to my father."

"No, I meant Alexander Lovell."

"What?" Catherine frowned. "Why would I curtsey to him?"

For a moment, Jean stopped winding the thread. Then she carried on.

"What's going on?"

"Maybe I heard it wrong."

"Heard what wrong?"

"Nothing. It will be a mistake."

"What's a mistake?"

"Nothing."

"You're not going to tell me that my mother wants me to marry Alexander Lovell?"

Jean's attention was on the strands of wool she was winding into a ball. "All right, then. I won't tell you."

"She thinks she'll sell me off like cattle?" Catherine growled.

"Look, I don't know. Maybe I misheard."

"Misheard what?"

"He's been discussing something with your father, that's all."

"He imports wine, doesn't he?"

"Yes, that's it. Your father will be buying some wine."

There was a brief silence. Then Catherine said, "Is my father bringing this man to Stirling for Christmas?"

Jean was silent.

"To meet me?"

"I told you. Curtsey to him and take a walk in the garden. Then he'll go away, and you won't see him again."

"He'll come back."

"You might like him."

"I guess I might."

"Well, then."

"My parents have given up on me finding a man by myself; now they're going to do it for me."

"Your father will have your best interests at heart."

"His own best interests, you mean. He'll have found someone who plays bowls in summer and curling in winter—someone his own age who visits regularly so they have an excuse to sit by the fireside, open jars of whisky, and talk about the old days."

"He'll have money."

"When did I say I wanted money?"

"You want to be poor?"

"You know what I mean."

"Look, well, you know your parents want the best for you."

"They want the best for themselves, you mean."

"Look at it this way. If you have to put up with your father's choice of man, you'll know you'll have a nice house and servants."

"Nice dresses?"

"That, too."

"Why can't I have a man who loves me?"

"A knight in shining armour who'll ride out of a fairy tale?"

"Just because you've given up on finding love doesn't mean I have to."

"Love?" Jean laughed. "Men don't love. They don't know how. All they're good for is going off and getting killed. Then, at least, you get some peace."

"I don't see them queuing up to court you."

"I've had boyfriends."

"When?"

"They go hunting while you're going through the agonies of childbirth; they go hunting while you look after the children. They expect you to be happy standing beside an iron pot hung over a fire."

"You haven't had children."

"I know people who have. And I and know people who're desperate to get rid of them."

Who was that comment directed at? Catherine said nothing.

"Look." Jean shrugged. "Meet this man."

"It sounds like a I don't have any choice there."

"Give him a chance. He has a big estate at Ballumbie."

"Where's that?"

"South of Forfar."

"I guess there's worse places to live."

"You won't have to live in Ballumbie. He's never there. He's always travelling around the country, trading. You'll never see him."

"You want me to marry a man I'll never see?"

"Those are the best kind. Besides, if he goes to Berwick on business, you know he's coming back." Jean hesitated for a moment. "My John went off to war," she said.

"*Your* John?" Catherine's eyebrows shot up.

"John Drummond."

"You're not going to tell me John Drummond was your boyfriend?"

"Not in so many words."

"Not in his words or anybody else's."

"We used to have great conversations in the kitchen."

"What was he doing in the kitchen?"

"He came to talk to me."

"Eye up the serving wenches, more likely."

"I liked John."

"He would have made a good husband, would he?"

"He might have done. If he could have stopped telling lies and stopped looking at other women. If he could have done that, he would have been perfect."

CHAPTER 7

He could not eat, could not sleep. The boat was pitching from side to side, and Campbell sat at the rear, using the oar as a rudder.

He had gone away to forget about home. Now, here he was thinking about it all the time. Janet MacRory, what was she doing? he wondered.

Five feet tall and perhaps one inch, Janet had long straw-coloured hair and blue eyes. She had nothing on her chest, but that had never put off the boys.

Especially Patrick O'Donnell, a big red-haired brute who had come over the sea to look for work with Campbell of Loch Awe—and got it. Argyll was never short of Irish thugs, disgraced at home, who came over to try their luck as mercenaries.

O'Donnell noticed that Ewan MacLean was taking an interest in Janet MacRory. Then Ewan was walking home one night, that's all he was doing, and he saw O'Donnell coming the other way. As they were passing, O'Donnell pulled a mace from his belt and smacked Ewan in the face. He left him with bruising, a broken jaw, and two missing teeth.

The next day, O'Donnell apologised to Ewan, and everyone thought maybe he wasn't so bad, after all. Maybe he had just been drinking that night he'd attacked Ewan MacLean. Then, coming out of Innellan Priory one Sunday morning, Janet turned and spoke to Nichol Wallace.

"It's a beautiful morning," she said, even though it was nearly midday.

"I'm going fishing on Loch Fyne," Nichol Wallace said.

"You must take me with you one day."

"You can come with me now, if you want."

"No, I cannot. I promised old Mrs Ballantyne that I would pay her a visit this afternoon."

"I will catch a fish for you."

"Please do that."

"You can cook it tonight."

That evening, as the sun was setting over the loch, Sean Campbell was waiting for Wallace as he rowed his boat onto the shore.

Wallace jumped out of the boat. "Do you want some trout?" he asked. "I didn't catch very many, and I promised one to Janet; I can only give you one."

"You need to be more careful," Campbell said.

"I am careful. I draw the oars in; the boat doesn't make any noise on the surface. That's not the reason I didn't catch more." Wallace pulled a basket of fish out of the boat.

"You spoke to Janet MacRory when you came out of the priory."

"What about it?"

"Patrick O'Donnell saw you talking to her. He says he's going to cut your throat."

"She spoke to me!" Wallace protested.

"You spoke back—that's enough."

"What was I supposed to do?"

"If you had ignored her, O'Donnell would be threatening to cut your throat because you had been rude to her."

Wallace put the basket down. Campbell helped him drag the boat up onto the beach, away from the rising tide. Then Wallace walked back to pick up his basket. "I said I would give her a fish tonight."

"You'd better not."

"I promised her!"

"Don't go up to her house."

"I must."

"I don't think you should."

"I'll just knock on the door, give the fish to her mother, and go away."

"Leave it for a few days. You can give her fish another time."

"I won't go into the house; I won't speak to her."

That night, O'Donnell waited for Wallace as he made his way home, beat him to a pulp, and left him in a ditch. Then he apologised to him a few days after like that made it all right.

Maybe you didn't go looking for her, Nichol, but she still spoke to you—and she never showed any interest in speaking to O'Donnell. That was the problem.

O'Donnell had everybody living in fear. If you spoke to Janet, the brute would threaten you. But if she spoke to you, that was worse; then he would come after you insane with jealousy.

Campbell watched the shadows swinging back and forth against the wall. You could not speak to Janet. Whatever you did or said was going to be wrong. There was nothing you could do.

"There's nothing for him to do here during the winter," Queen Joan complained. "He eats and drinks all day. We need to get him down to St John's Town where he can keep fit playing royal tennis."

"I don't want to go to St John's Town." Isabella's wavy golden locks appeared in the doorway. "I like it here!"

"We will come back," Queen Joan said.

"St John's Town is disgusting."

"We're not going until Saturday."

"Saturday is a disgusting day."

"Where is your brother Jamie?"

"I hate St John's Town. Why do we have to go to St John's Town?"

"Because," Catherine said, trying to be helpful, "the people in St John's Town, they all want to see the king."

"What about the people in Stirling?"

"They get to see him too."

"What about the people in Berwick?"

"Go and look for your brother Jamie," Queen Joan said.

"What about the people in Elgin? We never go there."

"Find out what your brother is doing."

"What about the people in Dunbarton? They never get to see the king."

"I see the Lady Catherine has been teaching you geography." Queen Joan shot Catherine a sideways glance. "A little too well."

"What about the people in Brechin? They never get to see the king."

"Go and look for your brother!" Queen Joan shouted.

"On you go!" Catherine said.

Isabella turned and scampered out of the room.

"She goes when you tell her," the queen said.

"I didn't listen to my mother when I was that age."

"You still don't."

Catherine knitted her brows. "I should go and look for Jamie," she said. "It took you long enough to have a boy; you don't want to lose him." She turned, walking through the royal apartments where the white walls were stained with smoke from the log fires that were kept constantly burning in every room. A blast of wind outside forced some smoke down the chimney; the flames in the fireplace shivered as a cloud of grey smoke blew out into the room and then floated upwards to spread itself across the ceiling.

There was no corridor in the royal apartments that an assassin could stealthily creep along at night. In the centre was the royal bedchamber, buttressed by courtiers' bedrooms, dining rooms, and meeting rooms like defence works built outwards from the keep. The door from the royal bedchamber led into the nursery. On the other side of the nursery were the bedrooms of the ladies-in-waiting, like Catherine Douglas and Sheona Crockett. On the other side of their bedrooms was a supper room, and only beyond that was the king's presence chamber, where he would meet with his councillors, his chancellors, or his chamberlain.

Sheona was in the nursery, cradling Annabella in her arms as three-year-old Eleanor was busy trying to break a clay saucer by hitting it against the wooden floor.

"Where's Jamie?" Catherine asked.

"I thought he was with you."

"What?"

"He'll be with the little princesses."

"And where are they?"

"Nothing's going to happen to them here."

"Where are they?"

"In the courtyard. They are organising a wedding for two of Margaret's dolls."

Catherine pushed open the door to her bedchamber and went through it and into the next bedchamber and through that into the king's presence chamber, enjoying the feel of the thick carpet under her bare feet. The large tapestry of a unicorn looking regal in a green forest slowly passed by on her right-hand side. On her left, King James was sitting in a chair on an elevated wooden platform; two men were in discussion with him. One was grey-haired, but the other was younger and black-haired.

As Catherine passed, she realised that the men were remonstrating with the king and perhaps not showing the deference that might have been expected.

After a few moments, Catherine recognised the older man as Walter Stewart, Earl of Atholl. "Robert Graham has all the experience Your Grace might ask for," he was saying.

But King James was impatient, butting in, "Nicholas Balmyle studied in St Andrews and in the Vatican."

"Your humble servant Robert Graham is well-respected by earls and the clan chiefs. He has the confidence of the people."

Catherine came out of the king's presence chamber and was descending the narrow winding stairway, designed to be defended by one doorman at the bottom.

She came out into the courtyard, wishing she had shoes on her feet, carefully stepping across the frozen cobbles. The air was sharp; the stone battlements were encrusted with snow. Smoke was blowing down into courtyard after being funnelled upwards and into the air from the roaring log fire in the castle kitchen.

The three princesses were throwing bones onto a bonfire that someone had started for them. Wincing, Catherine walked over to them, her bare toes peeking out from under the hem of her kirtle. The girls skipped around the fire, their feet warm in leather boots.

"Your feet will be cold," Isabella said.

"No." Catherine grimaced.

Young Jamie was sitting astride a cannon. Catherine walked over to lift him off, knowing that his father encouraged him to take an interest in cannons. Their explosions were deafening; they might misfire or break apart with broken pieces of metal flying in all directions. But a king was expected to command armies and oversee sieges, so young princes were allowed to play on cannons, and ladies-in-waiting were not expected to say it was dangerous.

She was standing beside the bonfire, moving her weight from one foot to another to allow her to always have one foot held up to the flames.

"The chamberman's watching you again," Isabella said.

Catherine looked up. Robert Stewart was watching her from an upstairs window. "Chamberlain, not chamberman," she said to Isabella.

She put both feet back on the ground. How long had he been watching her like that, looking down her cleavage while she pulled up her kirtle and showed a bit of bare leg?

Jamie had crawled over to the end of the barrel and was leaning forwards, holding his head, upside down, over the mouth.

"Jamie!" Catherine shouted.

"He likes cannons," Isabella said.

"The boys all like to play soldiers," Catherine said.

"The cannon makes a loud noise."

"Only when the fuse is lit."

"Jamie will go deaf."

"Gunners go deaf," Catherine explained patiently. "The men who fire and reload the cannons go deaf."

"Jamie will go deaf."

Catherine smiled. "I don't think so."

But Isabella insisted. "He will go deaf."

"He might fall and hurt himself, but he won't go deaf."

"He's on a horse," Mary said.

"Yes," Catherine smiled, admitting how much it looked like that. She knew she should lift him off the cannon before he fell but he was well-balanced, his legs astride the cannon as if he was riding a horse and the curl of smoke from the rear resembling a horse's tail.

Trail of smoke?

Suddenly Catherine was running across the courtyard to roughly grab Jamie in her arms. He was clinging onto the cannon, but she ripped him off and then jumped to the side. There was a loud explosion, and she slipped on some ice and crashed onto the cobbles, twisting her body as she fell so that the child landed on her. Something whacked her on the back of the head, and then stars were flashing amid the blackness.

When she opened her eyes, Queen Joan was looking down at her, her long brown hair cascading across her face.

"Where is Jamie?" Catherine asked.

Through a sharp ringing, she heard the queen reply "He's with Sheona."

Pains shot up her back as Catherine sat up. Her head was pounding.

"You're shivering with cold," Queen Joan said.

"Jamie is all right?"

"Come," the queen said, and she led Catherine back across the courtyard. "What happened?"

Catherine looked at the fire burning on its own with no children around it. "I don't know."

They went into the royal apartments, where King James was coming down the stairs. Robert Stewart was beside him. Catherine was immediately aware of Robert Stewart looking down at her and instinctively folded her arms across her bosom.

"How's Jamie?" King James barked.

"He's all right," Queen Joan said.

"What happened?"

"A spark from the bonfire lit the cannon," Robert Stewart said from behind the king's shoulder.

King James seemed unconvinced.

"I saw it," Stewart said. "I saw the spark fly across the air."

"Luckily, Catherine was there," Queen Joan said.

"Jamie is all right?" the king asked, seeking reassurance.

"Yes."

"You need a cup of whisky," Queen Joan said to Catherine. She led Catherine through the king's presence chamber and into the great hall.

The two men remained where they were. Catherine could hear a murmured conversation continue between them, quietening and quietening with every step she took away from them.

"You're shaking like a leaf," Queen Joan said.

The great hall was too big to be heated easily, and there were no stools which could be placed by the fireside. Catherine sat on one of the long benches next to a table while the queen stood over her with arms folded.

"How's Jamie?" Catherine asked.

"Alive," Queen Joan said.

Catherine was waiting to be told to pack her bags and go home.

The clump of the king's angry footsteps could be heard next door. "Whenever I make an appointment, I create one ingrate and ten malcontents," he complained as he stepped into the room. His eyes turned to Catherine. "How did it happen?"

Catherine was still shaking. "I-I don't know."

"Did you see a spark?"

"No."

"Something lit the fuse."

Something or someone? Catherine did not know what to say. "Maybe."

"So what my chamberlain says is correct; you were not paying attention?"

"What?"

"Did you see anything or didn't you?"

"I … eh … I saw Jamie playing on the cannon."

"You were warming your feet by the fire."

"I was watching the children."

"You're paid to see things."

"Don't be hard on her," Queen Joan said.

"The chamberlain saw you with a tinderbox."

"That was yesterday!" Catherine protested.

"So you admit you have a tinderbox?"

"I was showing Jamie how to use it."

"Why would you do that?"

"He asked me!"

"He asked me that, too," Queen Joan interjected. "He's fascinated by fire."

"So it was a spark?" King James persisted.

"I don't know," Catherine said. As soon as she said the words, she realised how feeble they sounded.

"If you were doing your job properly, you would know."

"She's had a fright," Queen Joan said.

"So it was a spark that caused it. And the fact that Atholl's children take the throne if mine are killed, that has nothing to do with it?"

"You see enemies everywhere!"

"You're going to tell me I don't have any?"

CHAPTER 8

"I had been married for six—no—seven years when I was your age."

"Yes, Mother," Catherine said.

"Both you and your sister had been born."

"Yes, Mother."

Lady Douglas swept forwards, the hem of her gown trailing along the floor. She put a finger on Catherine's cheek. "You have a spot."

"I hadn't noticed."

"You never look in the mirror?"

"No."

"You should wash your face in the morning dew."

"It's cold in the mornings."

"That's what I had to do at your age. I had to walk to the river before dawn every morning to collect a bucket of water. I always washed my face on the dew in the long grass."

"Yes, Mother," Catherine said quietly as she bent down to pick up Arabella.

"What are you doing?" Lady Douglas screeched, all of a sudden.

"What?" Catherine asked, immediately on edge.

"You can't hold the baby's head like that!"

"What?"

The baby was wrenched from Catherine's arms.

"You support its head like this!"

"*Her* head."

Lady Douglas had the baby in her arms with her palm supporting the back of the head. "Who's the wet nurse?"

"Queen Joan is feeding her."

"Oh, I don't approve of that."

"The queen wanted to feed her. She insisted."

"She should have a wet nurse."

"Mairi will do it when the Queen is away."

A young girl came running into the room.

"She wants to hold the child," Catherine said.

"Does she hold it the way you hold it? Does she support the head?"

"Let her hold the baby. She finds it comforting."

"Then she should ask."

"This is Princess Joan."

"Then she should be taught to show respect and ask politely."

"She can't ask."

"What's this? A shy princess?"

"She's deaf and dumb," Catherine said, taking Baby Annabella from her mother and passing her down to the young princess, whose face broke into a smile as she held out her arms.

Princess Joan ran out of the room.

"You're not going after her?"

"She's going to the nursery; she's very good with the baby."

"What will the queen say when she comes in?"

"Nothing."

"I wouldn't have left you in the care of a six-year-old."

"Princess Joan is eight years old."

"She's too young."

"You left me to look after my sister when you were going to market."

"Not very often."

"You did it all the time."

"That was different." Lady Douglas's eyes scanned the room until they settled on a woollen blanket lying across a sack of feathers. "Aren't you going to finish making your bed? You don't want the queen to see your bed looking like that."

"I have finished making my bed."

"I hope you don't make the queen's bed like that."

"I don't make the queen's bed."

"I'm not surprised."

Sean Campbell walked along the quayside, passing the boats that were tied up. Grizzled, hairy men stared down at him.

He came to the bow of a ship, reading the golden letters that stood out against a black background—*M rag CF Dunvega*.

A rope bridge led up to the ship. Grasping it with both hands, Campbell made his shaky way over it while a man looked down on him, smirking.

Campbell stepped onto the deck. "Captain Hepburn?" he asked. "I am Sean Campbell."

A stoutly built, grey-haired man with a weather-beaten face strode confidently over. "Come."

Campbell followed him into the captain's quarters. There was a table and a stoneware bottle. On the one side of the table was an armchair. On the other side was a three-legged stool. Campbell sat down, leaning both elbows on the table.

"You are late, Campbell," Hepburn said. "I wanted to sail yesterday, on the high tide."

"You can sail now."

"I must wait for the tide." Hepburn poured some brandy into a silver quaich[4] and passed it to Campbell. "How was your journey?" he asked.

"Uneventful," Campbell said. He had traded his horse for a coracle that he would never see again. After days drifting with current, never able to find a comfortable seat, never able to sleep, he had tied it to a jetty. Then he'd walked away, knowing it would not be there when he went back. But it was worth it just to straighten his spine and stretch his legs.

"You will be in Leith for Christmas Day," Hepburn said. He spoke as if everything had already been agreed.

Campbell frowned. "What do I do when I get there?"

"You go to a tavern called the Black Swan."

---

[4] A broad and shallow drinking vessel

"And then?"

Hepburn shrugged. "That is all I have been told."

Campbell frowned a deeper frown. So much secrecy—it was not a good sign. If you did not know who was giving the orders, you could not give anyone away when you were caught—no matter how much they tortured you. "How much do I have to pay?"

Now it was Hepburn's turn to frown. "Pay whom?"

"Pay you—for the journey."

"Nothing. Your journey is paid for."

"Who paid you?"

Hepburn shrugged. "A man gave me some money in a leather pouch. I did not ask his name."

"Is that the way you normally do business?"

"It depends on the business."

"I did not say I wanted to go to Leith."

Hepburn let out a snort. "What else are you going to do?"

"Stay here."

Hepburn laughed. "Nobody wants you."

"I could go back to Prague."

Hepburn laughed even more loudly. "There's no work in Prague for men who cut boy's throats."

Campbell winced involuntarily. "Who says this?"

"Your fame as preceded you."

"I do not cut throats."

Hepburn shrugged. "Do not say that too loudly, Mr Campbell. Then there will be no work for you in Leith, either."

"What's this job?"

"My job is to take you to Leith; that's all I know."

"Who told you I cut the boy's throat?"

"You took a slow boat up the river. Other people travel faster."

Sean Campbell felt his shoulders sag.

There was a knock, and the door opened.

"Thomas!" Hepburn announced. "Take Mr Campbell to his quarters."

Campbell stood up and followed his guide down some steps, which took him below deck. Lanterns swung from the beams, shadows rose and fell, and everywhere was the smell of sweat and urine. Then he was going down again, where there was not enough room to stand upright and where the smell became a stench.

He felt like he was on the way down to hell.

--- † ---

"My Lady Catherine?"

She had only just got away from her mother, and now Bishop Wishart was following her in his long black robes.

She stopped and turned. "I need to attend to Her Grace."

"I will not detain you for long." The old, splintered floorboards creaked under his weight as he approached. His smile made her shiver.

She remembered, as a child, all the touching as she had sat on the bishop's knee. His hand underneath her smock, on the small of her back. Another hand on her knee, moving slowly, imperceptibly, along her thigh.

"How is Margaret?" he asked.

"Princess Margaret is in France."

"No. I mean the Lady Margaret." He paused, smiling. "Margaret FitzRoland."

"I have not spoken to her recently."

"The king thinks the lady Margaret is very beautiful."

Was this a question? "I have heard him say as much," Catherine answered coolly.

"All the men say this."

Catherine frowned. "It is good they are all agreed."

"She is very beautiful," the bishop continued. "Her husband is away from home. And now she is fat."

"I did not say she had grown fat."

"You have seen her more recently than I."

"She was not fat when I saw her last."

"She has gone to Brechin?"

"Glen Esk," Catherine said.

"She should attend mass with the Bishop of Brechin."

"I am sure she will."

"Then she will return to St John's Town after the winter?"

"I expect so."

"Glen Esk will be blocked with snow. She will not be able to get out before the spring."

He was too close. Catherine involuntarily took a step back.

"She cannot get out; people cannot get up the glen to visit her."

"I will tell her to visit you on her return."

"There will not be much food in the glen."

"They have food," Catherine said. "They have mutton and salmon. And there will be kale."

"And whisky."

"Yes, whisky too."

"There is plenty food?"

Bishop Wishart put a hand on Catherine's shoulder. She stepped back. He stepped forwards. She stepped back; the back of her head cracked against the wood-panelled wall.

"I thought you were going to tell me that there was very little food in the glen and that she will not be fat when she returns."

The hand was on her shoulder again. Catherine was doubly trapped—trapped by the small space and trapped by this line of questioning. "She worries about her husband; she may not be eating much."

"She worries about her husband so much that she goes to Glen Esk where she cannot be contacted."

"She does not like being in the house. There are too many memories."

"If she is not fat when she returns, but you tell me there was plenty of food, then there must be another reason for her loss of weight." He was pressing his body against her, and the wall seemed to be pushing her towards him. His eyes were studying her face.

She looked away. "I told you; she worries about her husband."

"This family she is staying with—how many children do they have?"

How should she answer that? Concealment of pregnancy was a capital offence. And so was adultery.

"I must go and find young Jamie," Catherine said.

A young voice called out. "Lady Cat!"

"That's Princess Eleanor," Catherine said. "She calls me Lady Cat. I must attend to her."

"You said it was Jamie you should be attending to."

Without even trying to think of an answer, Catherine found the strength to push the bishop off. And, suddenly, she was running, relieved, into the adjoining room.

CHAPTER 9

"He's coming back here?" Sheona Crockett gasped.

"Yikes!" Jean Lockhart stabbed her thumb as she sewed one of the king's crimson shirts.

"This is why I like the colour red so much," Queen Joan said. "There's never any harm done if a chambermaid pricks her finger."

"You said FitzRoland was coming back." Sheona's tone was almost accusing.

"That's what we thought," Queen Joan said. "Maybe he's coming on the next boat."

"Cut-throat Campbell?" Jean stammered.

"He's not going to cut *your* throat," the queen said.

"Or ravish you," Sheona added. "So there's no need to act so disappointed."

"Surely … Surely the king is not going to make a man like that welcome at his court?" Catherine had come into the room with one child clinging onto her hip and another hanging onto the folds of her skirt.

"The man's a coward," Jean Lockhart protested. "Other men fight in the open, but he hides in the sewers."

"How could a man lie in the sewers all night?" Catherine asked.

"I don't think he washes very often," Jean said with a knowing air.

"When he's in the castle, you can smell him coming from three rooms away," Sheona said.

"When he was living in Castle Sween, they say he didn't wash from one year to the next."

Catherine shuddered involuntarily.

"He cut the drummer boy's throat!" Eleanor sang out.

There was a brief silence in the room, as if the women suddenly realised they should not be talking about this in front of a three-year-old.

Catherine felt her mother's intimidating presence behind her. "The drummer boy," Lady Douglas repeated, spitting the words out.

Annabella was stretching, clutching at the blue ribbon in Catherine's hair. Eleanor had let go of Catherine's skirt and was taking an interest in the needle in Jean's hand that was hovering over the king's shirt.

"They were catapulting dead cats and dogs over the walls to spread the plague," Lady Douglas said. She brushed past Catherine, dominating the room with her bulk—flat in the chest but large in the hips in a kirtle that always seemed too big with folds of material hanging shapelessly.

"It's raining cats and dogs," Eleanor said.

"Cats, dogs, mice, and rats."

"Cut-throat Campbell!" Eleanor sang out.

"He was beaten by a blind man," Jean Lockhart said. "As soon as Zizka arrived, Sean Campbell fled like the coward he is."

"Beaten by a blind man," Lady Douglas repeated, "a blind man."

"They say he is very handsome," Sheona Crockett said.

"They say that of the devil," Lady Douglas said.

"We'll find out when he comes to court," the queen said.

Lady Douglas let out a gasp. "He's coming to court?"

"I'm thirsty," Eleanor said.

"I'll get you a cup of milk," Catherine said.

Sheona stood up. "Maybe we could all have one?"

"I think Lady Douglas needs something stronger," Queen Joan said.

Sean Campbell had always liked Janet and had always known a confrontation was coming, especially since Janet never discouraged him. He smiled as he remembered, aged twelve years old, paddling in the sea at Cowal with Janet. He would scour the beach for flat stones. If you threw it just right, you could watch it skip across the waves—skip, skip, skip, skip. Then it would sink.

He got horrible sunburn on the back of his neck that summer. He remembered his mother scolding him as she rubbed butter onto it. But he had grown up with a quiet confidence that Janet was his girlfriend for the long term. He wondered what they would do when they were adults. She would stand over the fire with flecks of soot in her hair in their thatched cottage with its stone walls and cook the deer that he hunted.

Then O'Donnell, older, bigger, came over from Ireland, and everything changed. Campbell knew a fight was inevitable and decided the only thing to do was to act first. He challenged him to a duel before O'Donnell could sneak up behind him on a dark night. And he did it properly, slapping him hard in the face with a gauntlet, knowing the metal plates over the knuckles would leave red scratches on his cheek.

A duel on horseback with lances—Campbell had made the challenge, and they would do this his way, where he had the advantage. They would do it in front of Campbell of Loch Awe, where O'Donnell could not cheat. O'Donnell was bigger and heavier, but good technique was always more important.

But when O'Donnell rode at him, he did so with his lance held too high. The lance had to be aimed at the chest, and it would break if the rider stayed firm in his seat. But O'Donnell held his lance too high, aimed at Campbell's face. Campbell had to twist in his seat to avoid it, and the lance caught him on the shoulder. He was off balance and off the horse and on the ground, with everybody smirking and O'Donnell above him.

Days later, with no one in earshot, O'Donnell apologised to him.

Maybe I should go back to Cowal? Campbell wondered. I could push a knife in between O'Donnell's ribs and apologise to him afterwards.

"I wonder what you're doing now, Janet MacRory?" he said out loud. Married to Nichol Wallace? Unless he's been beaten to a pulp by Patrick O'Donnell.

Dulce Jesus Christus.

———— † ————

"That's watery milk," Isabella said.

"Maybe those cows have been drinking a lot of water," Catherine said.

"Tell her the truth," Sheona said.

"You'll put her off," Catherine said, putting her cup down. "Besides, you knew it was almond milk."

"What's almond milk?" Isabella asked.

"It's what happens when the cows eat lots of almonds."

"It's too bitter," Sheona said.

"Put some honey in it," Catherine said.

"What's almond milk?" Isabella asked.

"You crush the almonds," Sheona said, "and pour water over them. What you get is a white liquid that tastes like milk."

"It looks like milk, but it doesn't taste like milk," Catherine said.

"Why don't you just eat the almonds and drink the water?" Isabella asked.

"Because," Sheona explained, "the cows don't always produce milk. When they're not producing milk, we can drink almond milk." She cast a sly glance at Catherine. "Catherine's intended can import almonds from Persia."

"What?" Catherine growled.

"No, it's Constantinople," Sheona corrected herself. "He gets them from Constantinople."

"What's your intended?" Isabella asked, looking at Catherine.

"My intention is not to drink almond milk again," Catherine said.

"It quenches the thirst better than milk," Sheona interjected.

"So does water," Catherine said.

"When we say 'intended,'" Sheona said, looking at Isabella, "what we mean is that—"

"Queen Joan likes almond milk!" Catherine announced. She picked up the clay jug and left the room.

"Careful!" Sheona shouted. "Don't spill any on the carpet. It's a Persian carpet."

Catherine turned around, half in the doorway and half out. "You don't know if it's Persian or not."

"Your beloved said—"

"Do you want this almond milk poured all over you?"

"You'll spoil the carpet if you do that."

"Ballumbie took a carpet off a boat in Leith harbour," Catherine cut in. "If he says it's a Persian carpet, he knows he can add ten or twenty merks onto the price."

"What a horrible thing to say."

"Nobody in this place speaks the truth."

"Who's Ballumbie?" Isabella asked as she watched the tail of Catherine's gown disappear into another room.

Sean Campbell walked through the narrow street with the smell of rotting wood in his nostrils. High tenement blocks reached to the sky on either side.

A creaking sign was swinging in the breeze—"The Black Swan." Campbell stepped carefully over clusters of black flies feasting on the piles of horse droppings and over the gutter that ran down the middle of the road where human urine mixed with animal blood.

He pushed open the door and stepped into the Black Swan. Lanterns hung from beams above his head, casting the interior in a yellow glow. He walked across the uneven stone floor, where drinkers sat on benches at the wooden tables while others lay collapsed across the floor.

Barrels were stacked at the far wall, behind a long iron bar. Behind the bar sat the unshaven, beer-bellied bartender.

"A pot of ale," Campbell said.

The barman filled a clay tankard with ale; Campbell held out a silver coin.

The barman looked at him. "What's that?"

"It's an albus."

"What's that?"

"A white pfennig."

"What?"

"A silver penny."

"What am I going to do with that?"

"It's all I have."

Shaking his head, the barman gave Campbell the pot of ale and then took the coin from him. He turned around, picking up an axe, and placed the coin on the bar. He lifted the axe above his head and then brought it down suddenly.

There was a loud clang followed by a ringing in Campbell's ears. The barman brought the axe down on the coin again and again. Then then coin broke into two pieces, jumping up and dropping onto the floor behind the bar where they were out of sight. The barman quickly bent down and picked up the two pieces. He gave Campbell one piece, not letting him see the size of the other piece.

Campbell looked around the room. A strange, black-hooded figure sat on his own at one of the tables with only his nose and ginger beard visible in the lantern light. He walked over to that table.

"Sit down," the hood said.

Campbell sat down. "Who are you?"

"Robert Graham."

"Take your hood down."

Graham hesitated.

"Take your hood down," Campbell said, "or I'm leaving."

Graham reluctantly pulled down his hood to expose a head of thinning red hair.

Campbell eyed the rough wooden table for splinters and then carefully rested an elbow on it. He put the clay cup to his lips.

"You had a good journey?" Graham asked.

"Oh!" Campbell ejaculated suddenly.

Graham looked at him.

"In Germany, they make their ale with wheat," Campbell said. "You forget the taste of ale made from barley."

Graham knitted his brows. He had not come here for small talk. "You did not come here to tell me about your travels across Europe."

"No."

Graham nodded. "We have a job for you."

"We?"

"We should not be meeting like this," Graham said.

Campbell frowned.

"We never meet again," Graham said. "That is agreed?"

Campbell nodded.

"And if we find ourselves in the same place, we act like strangers who have never met."

"What do you want me to do?"

"King James is a tyrant. He does not respect the people. He lives in luxury; his queen dresses in silk. They eat fine foods imported from France while the people are starving."

Campbell's heart began to race. He knew what was coming next.

"The nobles are burdened with high taxes they cannot afford to pay; they toil while the king goes hunting."

"Tell me of a king in Europe who lives differently."

"King James has banned the playing of football.[5] Young men must practise archery while the king plays royal tennis."

"A king needs an army."

"Yes, he needs one to oppress the people. There can be no freedom in the land while this king remains on the throne. My clan—and yours—fought with King Robert the Bruce for our freedom. What we got instead was oppression."

"It is the same across Europe."

"Does that make it right? Because the people in Germany have no rights, neither should we?"

Campbell realised he was breathing heavily and sweating slightly. He took another drink of ale, the taste bringing back memories of summers spent by the shores of Loch Awe hunting boar. Then, afterwards, the smell of burning skin in the air as they roasted the boar by the lochside and, in the background, the soothing sound of the waters washing onto the shore. Then drinking ale as the loch sparkled silver in the moonlight and the pine trees whistling gently in the breeze.

A loud, crashing voice broke the peaceful silence. "The man who delivers us from this tyrant will be rewarded."

"How?"

"Goodly."

---

[5] James I, King of Scots, banned the playing of football in 1424; James II, King of Scots, renewed the ban in 1457—a ban that has never been repealed.

Campbell put his cup of ale down on the table. "How much will you pay?"

"Not I."

"Who is paying?" Campbell asked, but he already knew the answer. "The Earl of Atholl?"

"You will do this deed?"

"King James …" Campbell was thinking aloud. Did he want to kill this man?

"Is a tyrant. No one in the kingdom is safe while he remains alive. He will kill anyone who has a claim on the throne. You are lucky that your name is Campbell, and your family has no claim."

"I think I share that privilege with a few other families."

"But the kingdom will not be at peace while this king remains alive," Graham said more urgently.

"This job is dangerous."

"You got into Melnik Castle, cut the drummer's boy throat, and got out again."

"I—" Campbell opened his mouth and then hesitated. Was it worth saying that he did not kill the drummer boy? Would anyone believe him?

"You can get into Stirling Castle, cut the king's throat, and get out."

So that was the job. Campbell took another swig of ale, trying to give himself time to think.

"If the king is a tyrant, he must be removed."

"I am not Macbeth."

"This is for the whole country. For the people."

"How much will I be paid?"

"Ten gold lions."

"Twenty."

"Where else will a man like you earn ten gold lions?"

"Fifteen."

"Twelve."

"Agreed. Who pays me?"

"I do."

"Let me see the gold."

Again Graham hesitated, his eyes darting around the room. He put a hand in a pocket and pulled out a brown leather pouch. Undoing the string, he took out one coin and placed it on the table.

Campbell looked at the gold coin with a rampant lion on one side. He picked the coin up and turned it over. On the other side was an impression of Saint Andrew nailed to a wooden cross.

Graham quickly took the coin from Campbell's fingers and dropped it into the leather pouch, pulling the drawstring tight. "You get paid when the job is done."

"After the deed is done, what then?"

"You will have friends, my lord Sean."

"I will also have enemies."

"But you will have influential friends."

"I will also have bitter enemies."

"Your friends will be strong; your enemies will be weak."

Campbell took another drink; there was an uncomfortable feeling in his stomach. "How do I get into Stirling Castle?"

"You got into Melnik Castle."

"I'm being serious," Campbell growled.

"The Earl of Atholl has arranged an introduction for you." Graham put a hand into his doublet and then pulled out a sheet of paper that had been folded and sealed.

Campbell looked at the wax seal, recognising the arms of Walter Stewart, Earl of Atholl. "Where do I go once I have killed the king?"

"You take Prince Jamie to Lord Atholl."

"You want me to kidnap Prince Jamie?"

"My lord Walter will be regent. The young Prince Jamie is six years old. Tutors will be required to teach him about the unjust rule of his father."

"We are killing a tyrant; there is no reason to kidnap his son."

"This is not your concern."

"I do not hurt children."

"You did in Bohemia."

Campbell gripped the table, his knuckles turning white. "I do not hurt children," he growled. His mind was racing. Did it matter who sat on the throne? He was a misfit and an outcast. Here was a chance to make some money. Did it matter if the king was James the First or Second?

He had gone to Bohemia to make his name. But he was neither wanted nor needed there. Maybe it was Scotland that needed him. Was that why God had brought him back here?

"Kill the king; the nation will be grateful," Graham said.

Campbell was not sure what he was agreeing to. "When Lord Atholl becomes regent, what will be my position at court?"

Graham hesitated slightly. "Payment will be made at Blair Castle," he said, deftly changing the subject.

"What will be my position at court?"

"You must ask my Lord Atholl."

"When?"

"When the deed is done."

"And payment?"

"When the deed is done."

"Half in advance," Campbell said.

"You will find a horse in the stables. You can be in Stirling this evening."

"I just walk into Stirling Castle and kill the king?"

A look of alarm flashed across Graham's face. "Not so loud," he hissed.

"What reason would the king have to meet with me?"

"Your sword is for hire, isn't it? Ambitious young men on the make gravitate towards the court. The king will be expecting you."

"He won't be expecting me."

Graham smiled. "Your reputation has preceded you. The news will be in Stirling by now that you have arrived in Scotland. King James will be expecting you at his court." Graham stood up. "We do not talk again," he said. "If I meet you at court or in church, I do not know you, and you do not know me."

"My payment?"

"When the job is done," Graham said.

Campbell stood up. "I'll go tomorrow."

"You will go today," Graham said. "There is a horse in the stables."

"The seas were rough; I did not get any sleep during the crossing."

"You go now," Graham said. "You will be in Stirling tonight. By tomorrow evening, my lord Atholl will be expecting a courier to arrive at the gates of Blair Castle with news of the king's fate."

CHAPTER 10

"We're eating blancmange tonight," Lady Douglas said. "Alexander arrived this afternoon with the bags of rice."

"You mean Ballumbie?" Catherine asked. She had seen him coming through the gates in a saffron doublet and hose, his chest puffed up with pride, swinging one leg over the horse and jumping down. He saw Catherine watching him from the window; she turned away.

"What's blancmange?" Jean asked.

"White food," Catherine said.

"I can speak French," Jean retorted testily.

"It's chicken boiled in milk with rice and sugar," Sheona said.

"The rice is boiled in milk, not the chicken," Catherine said.

"Then how to they cook the chicken?"

"It has almonds in it, and cinnamon," Lady Douglas said. "I'm so looking forward to it. Alexander imported the almonds from Spain: he's so clever."

"Who's Alexander?" Sheona asked.

"She means Ballumbie," Catherine said. "He has a farm to the south of Forfar."

"Alexander Lovell of Ballumbie," Lady Douglas enthused. "Yes, he has some land in south Angus, but he's a merchant with properties in Edinburgh and in St John's Town." She winked at Catherine. "He exports wool and hides to Flanders and then imports all sorts of exotic and usual things—like the blancmange you'll be eating tonight."

"Not the whole blancmange," Catherine said. "He didn't import the chickens from Spain."

"You're so rude!" Lady Douglas scolded.

Catherine rolled her eyes. "I'm not rude, Mother. I'm just stating a fact."

"He's clever; he's rich. Your father has worked hard to get a good match for you. I hope you're not going to let us down again."

"I'll be nice to him."

"I should hope so. He's an exciting intelligent young man with excellent prospects. You won't get another opportunity like this."

"Catherine's a pretty young woman," Jean intervened. "She'll have no shortage of suitors."

Lady Douglas carried on as if she had not heard Jean Lockhart. "Alex has been all the way to Florence to get the rice you'll eat tonight."

"The sugar comes from Florence, not the rice," Catherine said.

"Must you contradict everything I say?"

"He didn't go there himself. He picks up sacks of rice at Leith," Catherine said.

Lady Douglas shot Catherine a hostile stare; Jean looked down at her sewing.

"I knew it was a mistake letting you come to court; you're getting ideas above your station. Your father and I, we worked hard to give you a good start in life, and this is the way you treat us."

Sheona tried to calm the situation. "Nobody's criticising you. All she said was that the sugar comes from Florence, and they pick up sacks of it at Leith."

"You make it sound like anyone could do it."

Sheona gave a shrug of the shoulders. "All you need is the money to buy a sack of rice and a horse to transport it."

"You don't have a good word to say about anyone; is this the way it is at court? I'm so glad I live in the country."

Catherine turned around and walked out of the room and through the next room, the queen looking obliquely at her as she passed. She went through the next room and the one after that, picking up Eleanor on the way. Then they were out in the courtyard; she shivered in the chill air.

"I want to look at the cannon," Eleanor said.

"No," Catherine said.

"Jamie gets to look at it."

"It's cold; we should go inside."

Catherine turned to go inside and found herself looking at Alexander Lovell. Where had he come from? "Good day, my lord," she said.

"My lady Catherine." Lovell bowed slightly.

Catherine curtseyed. "I do hope you enjoy your stay in Stirling."

"I regret that I cannot stay long," Lovell said. "There is a shipment arriving at Leith that I must attend to."

"Then perhaps we will see you another day."

"Oh, you will see me tonight."

Catherine groaned inwardly.

"I leave for Leith in the morning. Then I go to Berwick. I am looking for a storage facility—a strong room where I can store goatskins until I am ready to export them to Flanders."

"Uh, uh, uh." Eleanor was tugging at Catherine's hand.

"I hope you find one," Catherine said to Lovell.

"Well, that's the problem," he answered. "These border towns are always likely to be attacked. When a man is trading across continents, he has to think about things like that. You can have a warehouse full of skins, ready to ship to Flanders, and then the town gets ransacked and set on fire, and you've lost everything. If I export from Leith or St Andrews, there's much less risk."

Eleanor had lost interest in the cannon and was looking at a crow that had landed on the battlements. "Blackbird," she said.

"Crow," Catherine said.

"I want to start importing silk from Venice," Lovell said. "It gets shipped from Venice to London, but I have to pay extra if I want it brought up here. And the London merchants, they take the best silk. If there was a boat going to Hamburg, it could stop at Leith on the way. But then, you wouldn't take silk from Venice to Hamburg by sea when you could go by land."

The crow flew off, and Eleanor let out a howl.

"It will come back," Catherine said, but Eleanor was not comforted.

"The roads can be dangerous. But then so can the seas," Lovell said. "I could take out a bond and hire a boat to bring silk from Venice to Leith. But first, I need a place to hold it."

"Like birds," Eleanor howled.

"Let's go inside," Catherine said.

She turned, letting go of Eleanor's hand. Eleanor had wanted to go inside, but now she was wishing for the crow to return and would not move.

"Come along," Catherine cajoled her. "It's cold."

Suddenly, Eleanor turned and rushed ahead, skipping, into the royal apartments.

"Excuse me, my lord," Catherine said to Lovell as she hurried after Eleanor.

She kept half an eye on Eleanor as she made her way through the rooms, watching for the other children. Joan was always the one who worried her. Eight years old, deaf and dumb, she would express her anger by sitting on the floor with her back pressed up against a door to stop people going in and out. If she was still being ignored, she would bang the back of her head against the door, and then all the ladies-in-waiting would come rushing to her.

You could not shout to Joan; if you were looking for her, you just had to search the rooms. There was always the worry that she would take her frustrations out on herself and start banging walls or scratching her legs with a knife to get attention. If Catherine could not see Joan, she would ask Isabella, who always seemed to know where her sisters were and what they were doing.

She came into the nursery, scanning the room with her eyes, and was relieved to see Sheona kneeling on the floor with Joan. Joan was concentrating hard on the playing cards that Sheona was dealing out across the floor.

"You shouldn't be so rude to your mother," Sheona said without looking up.

"She's *my* mother."

"She's only thinking about you."

"Thinking about me? Hah!" Catherine snorted. "She's picturing herself wearing Venetian silk. In her head, she's already inviting the neighbours to Michaelmas and picturing herself in a silk gown. Then she'll make a point of talking about how nice Fiona MacNaughton looks in her green kirtle and then taking delight in examining the garment in detail and complimenting how goodly the repairs have been done in that poisonous tone of hers. And all the time, she knows that Fiona will have to return the compliment and comment on my mother's new silk gown. But, of course, my mother will delight in explaining it was made from silk imported from Venice."

"Maybe she's picturing herself looking at you in a fine silk gown."

Princess Joan picked up a playing card.

"You don't know my mother."

"You don't put it there; you put it here," Sheona said to the princess and pointed to a gap in the floor between the cards. She turned to Catherine. "Your mother will be the same as anybody else's mother."

"I might be more inclined to listen to you if I thought your mother had picked a husband for you."

"She did," Sheona responded with an air of superiority.

"You always told me that you married Donald for love."

"I'm not talking about him. My mother's choice was Duncan Hay, the younger son of Alan Hay of Belhelvie. He had a farm and half a dozen acres—and kept the inn at Balmedie. We would have had a comfortable life. But I knew better. I was swept off my feet by Donald MacDonald; he was tall and strong, rode a big horse, and could handle a sword. He was the sort of man you felt safe with." She was looking through the floor and into the distant past, seeing the deep blue of Donald's eyes and the outline of his muscles under the mail shirt. "He looked magnificent on his horse with a sword hanging from his belt."

"So," Catherine retorted, smiling, "you didn't listen to your mother. But you expect me to listen to mine?"

"The worst day of my life, up to that time, was the day when Donald left me. And it was superseded only by the even worse day when he came back."

"You told me you were happy."

"We were happy—when Donald wasn't getting drunk on whisky or getting into fights. He was such a good swordsman that no one wanted to take him on. So he was stabbed in the back a dozen times after an argument about cheating at a game of cards. Meanwhile, Alan Hay married Maureen MacWhirter; they've had three children and he traps hares during the day, and she cooks them and serves them in the inn."

"You wouldn't want to be skinning hares. You go faint if you're asked remove dead mice from the queen's bedchamber."

"Maybe you should be listening to your mother a bit more. She's still married after thirty years."

"Twenty-eight years."

"Then she knows something about marriage."

"Yes. She's always telling me how long her marriage has lasted even though she hasn't got a good word to say about my father and hasn't slept with him in as long as I can remember."

"A marriage is not only about sex."

"No. He used to go hunting because he could not bear to spend the days at home with her. But it had its compensations—we used to eat venison, boar, and pheasant all the time."

"But not blancmange?"

"No."

"When you marry Alexander Lovell, you'll be eating blancmange every day."

"Where did Eleanor go?" Catherine walked out of the nursery.

CHAPTER 11

The thatched roofs were glinting gold in the winter sun.

The street followed a straight line uphill to the castle. The doors of the Red Lion Inn swung open, and the dishevelled, busty barmaid threw a dead rat out and onto the street. A red kite watched from a rooftop with its wings tucked behind its red breast. It waited for Campbell to pass and then, suddenly, stretched out its wings, displaying the black-and-white marking.

Apprehensive and slightly nervous, Campbell dismounted and led the horse up the street. The red kite glided effortlessly down towards the earthen track, swooping to clutch the rat in both talons and then flying back to its perch on the rooftop, where it pecked on the rat and watched the comings and goings in the street.

With pale grey walls arising out of the rock at the top of the hill, the castle dominated the landscape. Below, the River Forth wound around the foot of the hill like a serpent. An iron portcullis lay on the other side of the wooden bridge. It rose slowly, the chains clanking, as Campbell crossed the bridge. A soldier, in chain mail and breastplate, came out of the castle and took the reins of the horse. He led it away, following the curve of the wall until he was out of sight.

Campbell walked through the entrance as the portcullis came crashing down behind him. He found himself in the guardhouse square or "murder hole." One portcullis was behind him, one in front, and two stone walls on either side. This was where enemies of the king could be shot with arrows from defenders on top of the walls.

Another soldier came out of the guardhouse.

"I am Sean Campbell of Argyll. I seek an audience with His Grace, King James. I have an introduction from the Earl of Atholl."

"Leave your weapons here."

Campbell pulled his sword from its sheath and the dagger from his sock. Putting them down, he pulled the mail shirt over his head and dropped it onto the ground. He walked towards the second portcullis that was slowly rising. Impatient, Campbell ducked underneath it as it rose to waist height and found himself passing a bowling green on his left. Then he was in the outer courtyard.

Imposing stone buildings with ornate windows stood in front of him. Another soldier came walking towards him.

"Come," he said. "I will take you to the king."

Campbell followed him into a large room that smelled of polished wood. A blue carpet interwoven with purple-headed thistles lay across the floor, and he wished he was standing in bare feet so he could feel the carpet against his skin. Against one wall sat an armchair on a raised platform. Against the opposite wall was a unicorn, which seemed about to leap out of the tapestry and thrust its horn into him.

Campbell stood in the centre of the room, not sure what to do next. The soldier remained in the room, his eyes never leaving Campbell.

A young girl, maybe eight years old, came running into the room. She stopped when she saw Campbell and stared at him, open-mouthed.

Sean Campbell looked at her bare feet that were standing on a thistle embroidered into the heavy blue carpet. "Be careful," he said. "You will hurt your feet."

The girl looked at him but did not speak.

"What's your name?" Campbell asked.

The girl did not answer.

"My name's Sean."

The girl did not answer.

"I have been besieging castles in the Holy Roman Empire," Campbell said.

The girl said nothing.

"The Holy Roman Empire is big, much bigger than Scotland."

The girl said nothing.

"The castles are big, too—much bigger than ours."

"She cannot hear you." A young woman with long brown hair had come into the room. "She's deaf and dumb."

Campbell was looking at her shape underneath the loose kirtle, at the blue material against her white skin and the hint of a cleavage. His eyes dropped down to see bare toes peeking out underneath the kirtle. The big toe was short and fat; the second toe was longer.

The young girl turned and ran back to the woman. She grabbed the loose folds of the woman's gown, as if for comfort.

Campbell lifted his eyes from the woman's toes. "You can tell her she's safe," he said. "I only cut boy's throats."

The woman looked at him with a cold expression on her face.

"That was a joke," Campbell said.

"Not in good taste," the woman said.

"I am waiting for an audience with the king," Campbell explained.

"Then you may be waiting for a long time. The king will see you at his pleasure, not yours."

Campbell looked around the room. "Where should I sit?"

"On your bottom."

"You have not told me your name."

"No," the woman said, "I have not."

Blue eyes were framed by brown hair. She was neither tall nor short. There was nothing exceptional about her appearance. And yet, and yet, Campbell was wanting to draw this conversation out and keep her in the room a little longer. "My name is Sean Campbell," he said, immediately disappointed that he had not found something more interesting to say.

But those words seemed to be very interesting. The woman took a step backwards. "We had heard you were coming," she said.

"You must tell me what they said." Again, he knew that was the wrong thing to say.

"Much of the time, there is nothing else to do at court but pass on gossip."

"Then surely you can share it with me?"

"You do not belong at court."

"I am here now."

"It was just idle gossip," she said defensively.

"I am waiting for an audience with the king," Campbell said. "That means I am idle."

"It was gossip—they described your physical characteristics."

"They did it well enough that you recognised me?"

"Yes," she said. "I knew you by your cloven feet, your tail, and the horns protruding from your head."

The young girl was tugging at the woman's gown and trying to lead her out of the chamber.

"She is bored," the woman said. "She wants to go to the nursery."

"Women have called me many things before, but never boring."

"I expect the king will invite you to dinner. You will get a chance to entertain us then."

The young girl turned and ran out of the room. The woman turned to follow.

"You will share a bowl of broth with me?" he said hopefully.

"I will bring a long spoon,"[6] the woman said over her shoulder.

Then she had gone.

The room was suddenly big, empty, and quiet. Campbell stood with his eyes on the doorway the woman had passed through.

"She didn't tell me her name," he said aloud.

"Forget about her," the soldier said.

Campbell looked around. He had forgotten there was a soldier in the room. "You could still tell me her name," he said.

The soldier looked at the tapestry of the unicorn and said nothing.

Campbell gave a shrug of his shoulders. He walked the length of the chamber with the soldier watching him intently. He turned and walked back. The soldier kept his eyes on him.

Campbell's eyes were on the carpet of thistles, all in flower. "I have never walked through field of thistles before," he said.

The soldier stared at the tapestry and said nothing.

"I shouldn't walk on a woollen carpet with these boots." Campbell bent down and untied the drawstring at the side of his ankle-length boots. He stepped out of the boots, putting one foot and then another on the carpet. He walked along the carpet, feeling the strands of wool between his toes. This was the luxury of life at court.

He turned around to find a man of medium height staring at him. The man had shoulder-length brown hair and brown eyes; he wore a red surcoat embroidered with gold thread.

---

[6] "If a man must sup with the devil, he should use long spoon" (old Scots proverb).

The man walked past Campbell and climbed onto the platform to take the only seat in the room.

Campbell dropped onto his knees. "Your Grace," he said and bowed his head.

"Rise," the king said.

Campbell stood up in his bare feet.

"Why do you attend my court, Sean Campbell?" King James asked.

"I have a letter of introduction," Campbell said. He pulled a folded sheet of parchment out of the leather purse that hung from his waist.

King James reached forwards and took the parchment from Campbell's hand. He broke the seal and read it. "The Earl of Atholl says you will make a loyal and devoted servant," he said.

King James passed the parchment back to Campbell, allowing him to read it.

Campbell quickly scanned it, reading complimentary lines suggesting that Sean Campbell would make an excellent addition to the king's bodyguard.

"How do you come to know My lord Atholl?" James asked.

He had not been told to expect questions! "He knew my father," Campbell said, a little too quickly.

"How did he come to know your father?"

"I was very young; I cannot remember."

But the king would not let up. "Your father must have spoken about him."

"He said they had gone on campaign together."

"Which campaign was that?"

"They were in France—at the Battle of Bauge."

"Your father was at Bauge?" James fingered his slight growth of beard, as if thinking to himself.

"Yes."

"But Atholl was not there."

Wasn't he? Suddenly Campbell's mind was racing. "I meant the Earl of Buchan," he said in a panicky voice.

"Ah, yes. Atholl's brother."

Campbell allowed himself a sigh of relief.

"Why does Atholl dislike you so much?" James asked.

"What?" Campbell scanned the letter again but could see only praise.

"Why does the earl want you dead?"

"What?"

"I fear you are not suited for the intrigues of court, Sean Campbell," James said.

"Your Grace," Campbell stammered, "I came here to—"

"To commit murder," James finished his sentence for him.

"No!" Campbell pleaded from the floor, his head bowed. It was only after he had shouted out that he realised he had dropped onto his knees. He was looking at the king's long and pointed leather shoes, like a jester's without the bells, and wondering why people at court wore such impractical clothes.

"A letter of praise from Atholl is a death warrant in my court," the king said.

"I came here in good faith," Campbell stammered. His words sounded so feeble. Could he think of nothing better to say?

"Rise," James said, "and look me in the eye."

Campbell stood up.

"If I and my family had been attacked and killed on my return to Scotland, who would be king today?"

Campbell grimaced slightly. "The Earl of Atholl."

"And who becomes king when I am dead?"

Campbell knitted his brows. "Your son."

"My six-year-old son."

"Yes, Your Grace."

"And a man turns up at my court who cuts boys' throats. How very convenient for Atholl."

Campbell's jaw dropped involuntarily. He shot a glance towards the door as if he expected half a dozen armed guards to come charging into the room. But nothing happened. "I did not kill the drummer boy," he said.

"I would expect you to say that."

"It's true!" Campbell pleaded.

"So who did?"

"FitzRoland."

"But we have a problem," James said. "Alan FitzRoland of Galloway is not here to speak for himself."

"I can only tell you what I saw," Campbell said tamely.

"You saw the guards rushing into the room, and you jumped out of the tower and left you friend to die."

"We were both trying to escape," Campbell explained.

"Did you try to help him?"

Campbell was silent.

"Sigismund is disgusted with you, so you come to my court to get some money."

"I have money!" Campbell said indignantly. He ripped the leather pouch from his belt, pulled it open, and tipped the contents onto the floor. A few silver coins dropped out.

"What are they?"

"White pfennigs."

"I have never seen one."

Campbell picked one up and passed it to the king.

The king noticed that one of the coins on the floor was broken. "What is that?"

"Half a pfennig."

"It is a small half."

"It bought me breakfast in Leith."

"An expensive breakfast." James looked at the coin in the palm of his hand. "It has an engraving of Saint Paul," he said. "Show me the broken one."

Campbell passed it to him.

"It's solid silver. I think they make them from copper now."

"They mix in lead and pewter so you cannot tell."

"So I have heard." All of a sudden, the king's tone changed. "How much is Atholl paying you?"

"Nothing!" Campbell protested.

James laughed. "Now you are telling the truth. Nothing is exactly what my Lord Atholl pays. When the job is done, you will get a dirk between your shoulder blades."

A picture of that bag of gold coins flashed in front of Campbell's eyes. And then how quickly it was taken back into the folds of Robert Graham's plaid.

"I assure you," Campbell stuttered.

King James cut him short with a wave of his hand. "You came here because you want a job at my court?"

"If it pleases, Your Grace."

"Why do you come bearing a letter from Atholl?"

"I thought I would need a letter of introduction to gain an audience with you."

"Why would I want to employ a stupid man?"

"I can use a sword."

"Yes," the king said. "We all know about that." He paused for a moment, thinking. "I have to decide whether to trust you or to kill you."

"Don't kill him!" That was a young girl's voice. "You will make a mess of the carpet."

Campbell looked to the side. Another young girl had run into the room.

"I like the carpet," the girl said.

"Yes, you're right," James said. "It's a Persian carpet. We do not want blood on it."

"That's not a Persian carpet," Campbell said. It was something he said instinctively, too quickly.

A chilly air seemed to blow through the room.

"Alexander Lovell assured me that this was a Persian carpet," King James said in a clipped tone.

"Emperor Sigismund had a Persian carpet. It looked nothing like this."

"What did it look like?" the girl asked.

"It had a different kind of pattern; it didn't have thistles on it."

"Does Sigismund live in a castle?"

"Oh yes, a big one—much bigger than this one."

"Isabella!" The woman in the blue kirtle was back in the room. She glanced at the king. "My apologies, Your Grace."

"Catherine will take you to the nursery," the king said to Isabella.

"I don't want to go to the nursery."

The woman grabbed Isabella's arm. "Come along."

Isabella shot an angry glance at the king. "Why did you have children when you treat them like this?"

The woman led Isabella out of the room. "You know you're not allowed to play in the king's presence chamber."

"I do not have as big a castle as Sigismund, nor even as big a carpet?" King James's piercing eyes turned to Sean Campbell. "You came to my court to insult me?"

"No!"

James glanced at the guard. "What do you think, Ranald?"

"He is arrogant. When Atholl was regent, he put such men in the stocks until they learned some humility."

"An assassin would feed me compliments to gain my trust and get up close." James's frown turned into a smile. "Whatever you are, Sean Campbell, you are not an assassin." Then he said, "I may have a job for you."

Campbell looked from the king to his bodyguard and back. Did they want him to cut Atholl's throat?

"Did you cut the drummer boy's throat?" the king asked.

"No."

"Do you speak the truth?"

"Always."

"Then you are no use to me."

What? Maybe the king was right; maybe he was not suited for the intrigues of court. "I came here to serve, Your Grace."

"Any of my subjects would say that."

"I have served Sigismund—"

"Badly." The king was looking over Campbell's shoulder at the tapestry as if he was reading the unicorn's thoughts. "How did you get into Melnik Castle?"

"We climbed up the sewer."

"You crawled through the sewer for Sigismund?"

"Yes."

"You would do that for me?"

"Yes!"

"Then I may have some work for you," James murmured. His eyes were still on the unicorn. "The queen will not approve," he muttered. Then he turned to look Campbell in the eye. "You must attend dinner; it will be your chance to impress the queen."

"I have been travelling all night and all day; first, I should take some sleep."

"There is no time. Dinner has already been prepared."

CHAPTER 12

"He's coming to dinner?" Sheona's loud incredulous voice carried across the great hall.

At the top of the room was a long table on a raised platform. There were seats only on one side so that the king and his family could get a good view of the diners while servants served them from the other side of the table. Two other long tables lined the other walls, with long benches against the wall for the diners. A log fire was burning in the centre of the hall, the smoke rising to a smoke hole high in the ceiling.

After the king and his family had seated themselves, the courtiers came in and took their seats. The clerks, all dressed in black with frilly collars, came out of the scriptorium and took their seats. Every diner had his or her back to a wall, which allowed them to see everyone else in the room as they ate.

Catherine had followed Sheona into the dining hall. She saw her mother and father were already sitting down and quietly took a seat on the other side of the room.

"They were cooking a swan in the kitchen," Catherine said.

"What happened to the blancmange?" Sheona asked.

"Maybe it's burnt."

A male voice said, "They were cooking a swan and blancmange."

Catherine turned to see Alexander Lovell sitting down beside her in his puffed-out saffron doublet and codpiece. "Surely you do not want to be sitting beside the ladies?"

"Nothing would give me greater pleasure."

"We are not well travelled. You will find our conversation boring."

"Not at all, my lady."

"There he is," Sheona hissed.

Sean Campbell had entered the dining hall. For once, the king was not the centre of attention, as all eyes immediately turned to him.

"A rogart shirt," Lady Douglas tutted. "Oh dear."

"He attends court wearing a rogart shirt[7] and coarse woollen hose!" Alexander Lovell was disgusted.

Catherine cast Lovell a sideways glance and then looked back at Campbell. She was comparing the outline of muscle under the woollen shirt with the puffy silk doublet that gave Lovell the appearance of a broad chest. She let her eyes drop to Campbell's strong legs and then shot a sideways glance at the saffron hose hanging loosely on Lovell's thin legs.

Sean Campbell bowed to the king and queen and then noticed a vacant seat at the far side of the room next to a large woman with grey hair tightly drawn back and tied with ribbon. He walked over and sat down, his attention taken by the piper coming into the hall. "Those are small pipes," he said quietly to himself, not intending the royal table to overhear.

"They're reel pipes," Lady Douglas scolded in a loud voice. "They're not monstrous Highland pipes."

Campbell felt Queen Joan's eyes upon him. He smiled uncomfortably.

"He sat down beside Lady Douglas," Sheona whispered, relieved.

"The Formidable Lady Douglas will be a match for him," Jean whispered.

"Not so loud!" Catherine hissed.

Potage was served first, mainly kale and barely boiled in animal bones. They supped it from silver bowls with horn spoons.

"I will be most interested to see how the blancmange turns out," Lovell said. "I can get rice from Venice, Aragon, or Alexandria. The rice in Alexandria is more expensive but—they say—is higher quality."

Lovell's voice was carrying across the room as if he wanted to make sure the king and queen could both hear him. Catherine turned her head away.

---

[7] A rogart shirt was a made from two rectangles of cloth stitched together with a slit cut at the top for the neck. Two more rectangles of cloth were stitched on to make sleeves.

"The climate is dry in Alexandria," Lovell was explaining. "That's why it's easier to preserve food. So it's worth paying a little extra if the rice is in better condition."

Catherine's eyes were on Sean Campbell. He picked a bone out of his bowl and threw it onto the fire. The bone sizzled and sparked. Then he dipped his spoon in his bowl again, only for Lady Douglas to grab it with a horrified expression on her face and snatch it from his surprised fingers.

The king and queen had stopped eating; everyone else put down their spoons. The servants came in and took away the empty bowls.

A murmur of conversation arose as they waited for the servants to bring the next course. Sean Campbell turned to speak to Lady Douglas but found himself looking at the back of her head as she turned to speak to her husband.

"Not salmon again!" Sheona protested as the servants brought in roasted salmon on silver plates and set them down at the tables. Then came golden roasted swans with crispy outer skin and their heads and beaks still attached.

"Here it is!" Jean announced. A long silver platter was making its way to the royal table.

"That's the blancmange?" Catherine guessed.

"It's a bit shapeless."

"It doesn't look like anything."

"It's just a pile of barley on a plate," Jean complained.

"It's not barley; it's rice," Alexander Lovell said, "imported from Alexandria. It's served with fowl, but also almonds, cinnamon, and sugar—all boiled in milk."

"It's a bit colourless," Sheona said.

Blacmange was followed by a roasted hog with its skin turned red and an apple in its mouth. Then came fruit tarts—apple and raisin—in slightly burnt pastry and served with jugs of cream. Afterwards, the guests drank wine and chatted while the piper played.

All that Campbell could feel was his tiredness collapsing in on him. He would have gratefully lain down on a stone floor and gone to sleep. But here he was at court—allegedly a privilege—where everyone waited on the king. A guest could not begin eating before the king; nor could he leave the table.

On his left was the broad back of Lady Douglas, her head turned away from him. His folded arms on the table made an inviting pillow. He rested his head. He felt his eyes closing.

"My lord Campbell!"

A hand shook Campbell's shoulder. He opened his eyes to find himself looking at a bearded man in a silk doublet with a frill collar. He sat up, realising the room was empty; the piper had gone, and the servants were clearing away the dishes.

"You fell asleep in the King's company," the man said, suppressing a smug smile. "You'll never be invited back to court."

"Oh."

"Queen Joan and Lady Douglas were horrified."

"Oh."

"Nobody falls asleep at the royal table."

"Oh."

"You don't know how to behave at court."

Campbell stood up. "Who are you?"

"Alexander," the man said. "You're sharing a bedchamber with me tonight." He smiled haughtily. "The king asked me to take you to my chamber, since you needed the sleep. Oh, but you should have seen the look on his face. No one has done that to him before."

"I'll know better next time."

"There won't be a next time. You don't get a second chance at the royal court."

———— † ————

"He's so uncouth," Jean Lockhart said.

"He came with a reputation." Sheona laughed. "He did not let us down."

"He didn't know what to do with the blancmange. Did you see him picking at it with his fingers?"

"Blawminge," Isabella said.

"Blaw—mawnge," Catherine said.

"One thing's for sure—the queen will never have him back at court," Jean said.

"He scales castle walls and cuts throats," Sheona snorted. "The king always has a use for a man like that."

"He didn't scale the wall; he climbed up the sewer."

A stern voice said, "We know that, Annabella."

Catherine flinched, feeling the dreaded presence of her mother in the doorway. She turned around. "This is Isabella, not Annabella."

"You contradict everything I say. You should show me more respect."

"Annabella is the baby," Princess Isabella said.

"I'm so disappointed in you, Catherine. Your father and I have worked hard to give you a good upbringing. You should be more grateful."

"Next time you get the name of the princess wrong, I won't tell you."

"See what I mean?" Lady Douglas asked, looking to Jean and Sheona for support. "This is what I have to put up with."

"You don't have to put up with it," Princess Isabella said. "You can go home."

Sheona suppressed a smile.

"We got you an appointment at court and a good match, and this is how you repay us."

"What have I done now?" Catherine sighed wearily.

"We get the agreement of the king for Alexander Lovell to accompany us here, and then you sit all night with your back turned to him."

"I didn't have my back turned to him."

"You spent the night talking to Mistress Crockett."

"So if Sheona speaks to me, I'm not supposed to speak back? I can be rude to the other ladies-in-waiting but not to your friends?"

"You know what I'm talking about, Catherine. You were able to cast surreptitious glances at that uncouth, uncourtly, ill-mannered, rude, loutish brigand who's turned up at court. I've never been so affronted. I've worked hard, giving Alexander a good impression of you, and you behave like that! What am I supposed to say to Alexander now? And your father, well, let me tell you that your father is furious."

"All I did was eat my dinner."

"That was a chance for you to make a good impression. I don't know when you'll get another one. The king's going to St John's Town; Alexander is going to Venice."

"He's not going to Venice." Catherine groaned. "He picks up the silk at Leith or Berwick."

"He's in contact with traders in Venice."

"No, he's not."

"There you go again, contradicting everything I say. All I've ever done is to want the best for you, and this the way you treat me."

"Alexander won't have left yet," Sheona said. "You can go and speak to him before he leaves and wave goodbye."

Catherine gave Sheona a hostile stare.

Sheona turned to Isabella. "Do you want to help Catherine find Mr Lovell?"

"Is that the yellow man?"

"Saffron," Lady Douglas said. "He was wearing saffron."

Sean Campbell opened his eyes to find himself looking at a flat wooden ceiling. After a few moments, he realised he was looking at the floor of the room above.

He felt strangely comfortable; the floor beneath his back was soft. He pulled himself to his feet and discovered that he had slept on a sack of feathers. His boots lay beside his bed. Had he taken them off or had someone else done that? he wondered.

He pulled on his boots and walked out of the room, the leather soles scuffing quietly on the wooden floor. He came out into a corridor and took the first winding stone stairway downwards.

When he saw a stone floor, he knew he was on the ground floor. He worked his way through the labyrinth of rooms till he was outside and in the fresh air. A soldier saw him come out of the royal apartments and watched his every move across the courtyard.

He could hear male voices, laughter, and clapping coming from the bowling green.

"How did you sleep, my lord?"

Campbell turned around to see a woman approaching. She was wearing a blue kirtle that matched her blue eyes; her uncombed brown hair fell about her shoulders.

"Goodly."

The woman smiled. "We know that."

"I fell asleep at dinner."

"Queen Joan has never been so affronted."

"I was tired."

"The king's company bores you?"

"I had been awake all night. I had not slept for several days or nights."

"Stop boasting about your sex life."

He ignored that playful remark. "Come with me up to the battlements. You can show me the Valley of the Forth."

"I am not wearing shoes," Catherine said.

"I like your feet."

"Only my feet?" she asked.

Isabella came skipping across the cobbled courtyard. "He's playing bowls."

Campbell shot a glance towards the bowling green, where a man dressed in yellow stood beside a man dressed in red and gold. Two men wearing black stood a respectful distance away.

"The king is winning!" Isabella announced.

"There's a surprise," Catherine said.

"You must tell me your name," Campbell said.

"No one has told you?"

"They told me not to touch."

"They did not tell you not to speak?"

"No."

"They will."

"Then you must tell me your name while you are still allowed to."

"Her name is Catherine," Isabella said.

Catherine shot Isabella a glance, scolding her with her eyes.

"Catherine Douglas," Isabella said. "Her mother is Lady Douglas."

"I was sitting at the same table as Lady Douglas during dinner," Campbell said.

"We call her the bossy woman," Isabella said. "My mother calls her Lady Godiva."

"Why does the queen call her that?"

Catherine cut in. "It's a joke. She doesn't mean anything by it."

"It's because she thinks she's important, but she has no clothes," Isabella said.

"That's enough, Isabella," Catherine said.

"She wears the same brown kirtle all the time. It's hard to see dirt on brown clothes."

"That's enough, Isabella!"

"That's good trick," Campbell. "Maybe I should do that?"

"You can have one of my kirtles," Catherine said.

"I meant maybe I should wear brown."

"You look nice in that green shirt," Catherine said. "It brings out the green in your eyes."

"But I'm at court. Everybody dresses to impress. This is the first time I've felt poor as a church mouse."

Catherine smiled. "You find other ways to make an impression."

"Why do they call you Cut-throat Campbell?" Isabella asked.

"I said that's enough, Isabella" Catherine hissed.

"I'm a barber," Campbell said.

"Barbers cut hair."

"Sometimes you miss the hair and cut the throat by mistake. Do you think I should cut Lady Catherine's hair?"

Isabella shook her head vehemently.

A burst of clapping broke out. The men were walking away from the bowling green. A soldier was bringing a horse through the castle gates. Isabella seemed about to run over to the horse, but Catherine grabbed her wrist.

The man in yellow shot a sideways glance at Catherine. She immediately curtseyed, holding out the folds of her blue gown.

The man bowed his head. Then he was climbing onto the horse and exchanging words with the king.

"I'm in trouble now," Catherine muttered to herself.

"Why?" Isabella asked.

"Because I'm speaking to Mr Sean when I should be waving goodbye to the yellow man."

"Then let's go and speak to the yellow man."

"Too late now."

Lovell turned the horse around and rode out of the castle gate. The other men started walking towards Catherine and Isabella.

"Catherine!" the king called out as he approached. "Take Bella indoors."

"Yes, Your Grace." Catherine said.

"I want to ride a horse," Isabella said.

"Your horse is in the nursery," Catherine said. "But I'm going to ride it before you."

"No, you're not."

"I'll race you."

Catherine and Isabella raced across the courtyard, their gowns billowing like sails in the wind.

The king approached; the two men in black kept their distance.

"Sean!" the king announced. "You had a good sleep?"

Campbell winced slightly. "Yes, Your Grace."

"Let me show you the battlements."

Campbell followed James across the courtyard and up the stone steps that had been cut into the side of the wall.

"I come here every morning to enjoy the view," James said, looking out across the Valley of the Forth to the distant Ochil Hills.

"You are very safe here," Campbell said.

James cast him a sideways glance. "Everywhere I go, I am surrounded by smiling faces who would love to take my throne and try it out for themselves."

"Your Grace! Your Grace!" A man dressed in black was walking hurriedly across the courtyard with a scroll in one hand. He held the scroll up. "The charter—you asked to read it as soon as it was finished."

"I shall read it in the scriptorium," King James said with a tired air.

The man did not move.

"At my pleasure," James said.

The clerk bowed and turned around, walking back across the courtyard.

James turned his brown eyes upon Sean Campbell. "The Earl of Atholl thinks he should be king. But he has to content himself with the title of earl."

"I am not in the service of the Earl of Atholl." The words came out naturally, instinctively. Campbell was surprised when he realised what he had just said.

"Tell me why you came to my court," James said equally quickly.

"Sigismund sent me away."

"Men who speak quickly are not thinking about the correct answers to give. Such men can be trusted." James smiled. "I like a man who speaks before he thinks."

"What about a man who insults you?"

"Don't make a habit of it."

"You said you might have some work for me?"

James was silent for a moment, as if thinking. "You broke into Melnik Castle?"

"Yes."

"I hold council meetings in Glasgow, Stirling, and in St John's Town. But the king must be everywhere. I must be in Aberdeen and Inverness, in Portree and in Irvine." James paused. He seemed to be deep in thought. Then he was speaking again. "I'm safe in Stirling Castle. But I'm vulnerable when I'm on the road."

"You need a bodyguard?"

"I have a bodyguard," James cut in. "When I am in St John's Town, I stay in Blackfriars Monastery. I want you to visit the monastery and tell me how secure it is. Imagine you were going to break into the monastery; then tell me how you would get in."

Campbell felt uneasy. "A monastery was not built for defensive purposes. There will be many ways in and out."

"Then you must tell me what they are."

"You fear for your life, Your Grace?"

"A king has few friends but many enemies."

"When do you go to Blackfriars?"

"I hold council there in February."

A long journey on the open road and then a few nights spent in a monastery with only monks to defend him? A worried look flashed across Campbell's face. "Atholl is attending?"

"Yes."

"So he knows when you will be travelling and when you'll be staying in Blackfriars?"

"Yes."

"Then it will be very easy for him plot your assassination."

James winked. "But you will tell me how to make the monastery secure."

CHAPTER 13

"Mistress FitzRoland has gone to Glen Esk for the winter."

The wooden house, with its door high above street level, was quiet and dark. There was no ladder leading up to the closed main door. Sean Campbell was talking to a middle-aged woman. They stood on the cobbled street, looking up at the house.

"She will not return before the spring." The woman walked on, down the street.

Sean Campbell remained where he was. Some flakes of snow landed on his shoulders. He shivered as a blast of cold wind came off the river. Before he visited Blackfriars Monastery in St John's Town, he had promised himself that he would visit Margaret FitzRoland. So here he was. But where was she?

He turned away, slightly relieved. There was no need, now, to explain who had cut the drummer boy's throat or how it had happened. No need to explain how he'd left her husband to die in Melnik Castle.

A rat was drinking from the gutter where a trickle of blood flowed from the slaughterhouse. A woman was coming towards him, carrying two buckets of water from the river and hurrying to keep herself warm. Campbell stepped aside to let her pass and became conscious of a hooded figure on the other side of the street.

Campbell let his eyes follow the woman as she brushed past him and made her way down the street. Her fingers, tightly clutching the handles of the buckets, were red with cold.

The hooded figure had stopped. Campbell waited; the hooded figure did not move.

Suddenly, Campbell started marching quickly. He was marching away from the monastery, not knowing where he was going, and found himself walking to the river. The hooded figure, in its peasant-like tunic and hose, rapidly increased its pace.

Campbell came to the bank of the River Tay. There were women on their knees slapping garments against the surface of the water and then wringing them with their hands. A man was rowing a small boat upriver, towards the bridge. Campbell watched, one hand on his belt. Then, in one movement, he turned around. A dagger had appeared in his hand.

The hooded figure halted abruptly.

"Who are you?" Campbell asked.

The man pulled his hood down. It was Robert Graham. "What are you playing at, Campbell?" he asked.

Sean Campbell put the dagger back in his belt. "I didn't know who it was."

Graham pulled his hood back up. "I mean," he hissed, "what are you playing at here in St John's Town?"

"What business is it of yours?"

"The king is in Stirling, but you are in St John's Town. I think it *is* our business. Very much so."

A cold breeze came off the river, blowing some loose strands of thatch along the street. Campbell shivered involuntarily.

"Do you have cold feet?" Graham asked menacingly.

"It's cold," Lady Douglas said.

"It will get warmer," Queen Joan said. "The heat from the kitchen comes up through the floorboards."

"Mairi!" Lady Douglas shouted. "This wine's too sour. Bring us some honey!"

"It gets like that once the barrel has been opened."

"Then bring us some honey."

A young woman with long black hair turned and hurried out of the room.

"Where's Catherine?" Lady Douglas asked. "I haven't seen her all day!"

"She's in the nursery."

"They're all in the nursery?"

"Maybe they don't want to disturb us."

"I take the trouble to travel to Stirling in winter, and I barely see my daughter!"

Queen Joan picked up a bell that sat on a small wooden table and rang it.

"There's no need," Lady Douglas said. "If my own daughter doesn't want to see me—"

A tall broad woman, also with long black hair, appeared in the doorway.

"Tell Catherine to come through," Queen Joan said.

"Certainly," Jean Lockhart said.

"I do my best for her. And look at the way she treats me," Lady Douglas said. "That Alexander Lovell, what a nice man he is. He's always so smartly dressed, and his manners at court are impeccable."

"He did his best to make a good impression."

"And Catherine sits with her head turned away from his all through the dinner. This is what I have to put up with."

"A lady doesn't want to look too eager. It sounds like you taught her well."

Catherine appeared in the doorway. A young girl holding a baby in her arms stood next to her.

"I always see you with other people's children, never with any of your own," Lady Douglas said.

"You wanted to speak to me, Your Grace," Catherine said to the queen.

"Come and sit with us."

Catherine looked around the room. Her mother was sitting on one of the Savonarolan chairs and the queen on the other. She sat down on the floor in one movement, her legs crossed.

"Please have a chair," the queen said, looking at the empty wooden chair that was next to Lady Douglas.

"We don't mind sitting on the floor, do we, Isabella?"

"Of course not." The girl with the baby in her arms sat down beside her.

"Does Annabella need to be fed?"

"She's sleeping," Catherine said.

"Then put her to bed."

"She will wake up again. She likes being cuddled."

"I like cuddling her," Isabella said.

"As you wish," Queen Joan said and smiled. She turned to Catherine. "I was complimenting your mother on how well she has trained you. An eligible bachelor turns up at court, and you showed a lot of restraint."

"She spent more time talking to that cut-throat."

"Where is Mr Sean?" Isabella asked.

"He's in St John's Town," Queen Joan said.

"He made one appearance at court, and the king sent him away," Lady Douglas said.

"He didn't bow for very long," Isabella said.

"It was enough," Catherine said.

"He just walked straight into the dining hall, didn't bow properly, and then fell asleep. I've never been so affronted!"

"He'd been travelling all day," Catherine said.

"Black affronted, I was."

"I think it's for Her Grace to decide if we should be affronted," Catherine said.

"Honey, Your Grace?" Mairi had reappeared in the room with a pot and a horn spoon.

"It was for Lady Douglas," Queen Joan said.

Mairi spooned some honey into Lady Douglas's cup and stirred it.

"Do you want some honey?" Catherine asked Isabella.

Isabella shook her head. "It gets my fingers sticky."

"I will wipe them."

Isabella shook her head again, more vigorously this time.

"Thank you, Mairi. That will be all," Queen Joan said. She watched Mairi leave the room and then turned to Lady Douglas and winked. "We will invite Ballumbie back to court. Catherine will get the opportunity to meet him again."

"Who's Ballum-bee?" Isabella asked.

"The yellow man," Catherine said.

"Now, Catherine, be more respectful," Lady Douglas said.

"He looks like a bee," Isabella said.

"He doesn't have any black stripes," Catherine said.

"We should get him some," Isabella said.

"Show more respect," Lady Douglas said.

"Father doesn't like him," Isabella said.

"No, he didn't say that," Queen Joan said hastily.

"Yes, he did."

"No … well … what he meant was … he just finds his conversation a bit boring."

"Father likes Mr Sean better."

"What?" Lady Douglas gasped. "That uncouth cut-throat?"

"The king spends so much of his time in the company of false friends. It's refreshing when he meets someone—"

"Uncouth," Lady Douglas cut in.

"Honest." Queen Joan shot Lady Douglas a sideways glance. "If a man goes to sleep at the dinner table—"

"It's an insult."

"It means he's not plotting anything. He's not watching the others in the room. He's not trying to make himself look good."

"So why did father send him away?" Isabella asked.

"Because he has no manners," Lady Douglas said.

"St John's Town isn't so far away," Catherine said.

"I can visit St John's Town if I wish to," Campbell said. They had come to the end of the street and were standing on the riverbank. A boy was sitting on the wooden bridge, dangling his legs over the side.

"You got fifty groats and a horse," Graham said.

"You said I had to return the horse."

"You know what the job is," Graham hissed. "Why are you taking so long?"

"It's not easy to kill a king."

"I agree with you there," Graham said. "If you're in St John's Town and he's in Stirling, it's not going to be easy."

"What happens to the boy?"

"What boy?"

"The king's son. Young James."

"Not so loud," Graham hissed between bared teeth.

"What happens to him?"

"That is not your concern."

"You kill the boy after I have killed the king?"

"No one is going to kill the boy. The plan is to kill the king.".

"And I have to plan out how I will do it. That takes time."

"How much planning does it take to stab the king while he sleeps?"

Campbell shuddered slightly. "I am not Macbeth."

"There we are in agreement," Graham said. "Macbeth would have the deed done by now."

"When do I get paid?"

"You have been told all this." Graham was beginning to lose his patience.

"It's not good enough."

"You made an agreement."

"The earl has not paid me."

"The earl will keep his word."

"His word to whom? He hasn't said one word to me."

"I have told you—"

"I don't know anything about you."

"You went to fight for Sigismund. What did you know about him?"

"I knew he would pay me."

"You want the earl to pay you now so that you can take a boat to Norroway[8] with the earl's gold in your pouch?" Graham was getting agitated, spitting the words out. "Do the job, and you will be well rewarded."

"You want me to cut the king's throat while he sleeps?"

"It's your choice how you do it."

"I don't cut throats," Campbell said.

Graham frowned. "What?"

"You have the wrong man."

"The king has turned you?"

"Nobody has turned me," Campbell barked. "I don't cut throats."

---

[8] Norway

"Do not speak so loudly." Graham's eyes darted up and down the riverbank. A woman was washing clothes a few yards upriver, but she paid no attention to him as she put the wet clothes back in a wooden tub and walked away with her with rolled-up sleeves displaying her nicely muscled arms.

Campbell's eyes were on the woman.

"Lord Atholl is most displeased by the delay," Graham said.

"I have not had the opportunity."

"There is an opportunity every night when the king is asleep."

"I don't cut the throats of sleeping men."

"Only drummer boys?"

Sean Campbell's fingers gripped the handle of his dagger. "I don't have to listen to that." He quickly turned away from Graham and began to walk towards Blackfriars Monastery.

He quickened his pace, not looking back. His eyes were on the thick stone walls of the monastery. He thumped his fist against the heavy oak doors. He waited and then thumped again. He waited some more and then thumped again. He turned to look down the street, but Robert Graham had gone.

The key turned in the latch; the door slowly opened. "Benedicamus Domino," a monk said.

"May I speak with Abbot Henry?" Campbell asked. "I have a letter of introduction from King James."

"Abbot Henry will attend to you during meridian."

"When is that?"

"After sext."

"When is that?"

The monk stepped aside. "Come this way."

Standing in the cloisters, looking out over the atrium, the powerful silence was broken by the scuff of sandals on the stone floor. Abbot Henry was approaching.

A monk sat on a stone bench in the atrium under the weak winter sun. Bare toes peeked out from under the folds of his heavy habit. He seemed absorbed in the silence, completely at peace with himself. There was no plotting here and no intrigue, no ambition and no jealousy.

Just for a moment, Campbell felt envious. Life was so simple; you were on your own path to God. And maybe you would get there and maybe not, but it was no one's business but your own.

"How may I help you, my son?" That was Abbot Henry's voice.

"King James sent me—"

"You wish to look at the royal apartments?"

The abbot walked on, and Campbell found himself following. Except that the abbot did not walk; he glided like a ghost along the cloisters, the black hem of his outer cloak brushing the stone floor. The stone pillars were like his armed guard—standing to attention and silently saluting him.

The royal apartments had a large dining room, where three long tables lined the walls in a U shape with a large space in the middle for attendants and musicians. Next to it was a royal tennis catchpule,[9] which the abbot proudly showed Campbell.

Finally, they went into the bedrooms. In the king's bedroom was a four-poster bed with a cradle at its foot. But it was the floor that took Campbell's interest.

"What is underneath the floorboards?" he asked.

"The sewer," Abbot Henry said.

"Is the end blocked?"

Abbot Henry gave Campbell a curious glance. "Why would we block a sewer, my son?"

"If someone climbs into the sewer, it will lead them straight to the king's bedroom?"

"Beggars look for shelter in strange places, but no one sleeps in the sewer. And," the abbot added, as if by afterthought, "if we found a beggar sleeping in the sewer, well, we would—"

"Give them a bed in your dormitory?"

---

[9] Court

"The Thrissil[10] Inn has stables, which the king uses when he visits. That is where we send the beggars. There is plenty of hay; a man can sleep comfortably in the stables."

"Yes, of course."

"A stable was good enough for Our Saviour."

"Yes, of course."

---

[10] Thistle

CHAPTER 14

The royal train, brightly coloured carriages and wagons pulled by horses, could be seen in the distance as it lumbered down the high road.

Suddenly there was panic on the North Inch—a broad expanse of grass on the banks of the River Tay where cattle were often at pasture.

It started with Alan Gow, the smith, running down the High Street and shouting. Then others noticed and the children who were playing football on the North Inch stopped and looked up.

"Get that ball out of sight!" Alan Gow shouted.

A boy picked up the ball—an inflated sheep's bladder with goat hide stitched around it—and ran off. The rest of the boys looked at Gow with bemused faces.

"That's not fair," a boy said. "We were winning."

"Habbie[11] always wins."

"We were going to win this time."

"Go and get targets," Gow said. "Get them erected quickly."

"Why?"

"You're practising archery."

"Do we have to?"

"Yes—for as long as the king is here."

Shoulders sagged. Grumbling, the boys trudged off to collect targets and bows.

The royal carriages made their slow way down the High Street. The king and queen had arrived in St John's Town. Horsemen with swords dangling from their saddles were shouting out orders. In the

---

[11] Halbert

streets, young children came out of their houses to gaze at the brightly coloured wagons.

Catherine's carriage jolted to a halt outside Blackfriars Monastery. Isabella was first to open the door and jump down with glee. Catherine hesitated, looking down at the uneven cobbled street.

"Jump!" Isabella shouted.

A voice said, "I will bring you a step, my lady," and a man ran towards the wagons.

"Jump!" Isabella goaded her.

A tall dark-haired man dressed in tartan came into view and stood in front of her. He was challenging her with his eyes to jump.

"Jump!" Isabella shouted.

Some cobbles were missing from the road to the man's left-hand side. Perhaps the muddy ground would make a softer landing? Suddenly, Catherine jumped.

The man stepped forward, not jumping out of the way but jumping into her path. Then she was in his embrace with both of his arms locked around her waist. She waited for him to let her go, her hands on his shoulders.

He did not move. She avoided looking into his eyes—those hazel eyes that were sometimes green, sometimes brown. She could feel the tension in his pectoral muscles pressed against her breasts. She was fighting an urge to plunge her lips onto his.

Held, suspended—the moment had dragged on too long.

Not long enough.

One hand moved across her buttocks as he gently lowered her to the ground. Then both his arms were away, and he stepped back. That hand was off her buttocks. She felt the release of tension and the cool breeze on her chest now, instead of his warm muscles. She looked up at his eyes, knowing it was the wrong thing to do. She did not move, did not want to move, but stood still as if inviting him to hold her again.

"Let's go inside!" Isabella exclaimed, running to the door of the monastery.

Catherine could still feel the imprint of his fingers on her buttocks. "Yes, of course," she said to Isabella.

Sean Campbell watched Catherine turn away and walk to the door. He remained where he was, turning his attention the monastery's thick walls. He was looking at an ornate stone arch built into the wall. Out of it gurgled a tiny steam.

"This is the monks' lavatorium," King James said.

Campbell suddenly realised that the king was standing beside him. "We need to put iron bars across it."

"Nobody could get into that hole," James said.

"If you can get your head in, you can usually twist your shoulders and get them in too," Campbell answered. "Once you're in, you can almost stand up straight. There's quite a lot of space in there."

"I'm always losing tennis balls down that sewer," James said. "Can you block it up so that I don't lose any more tennis balls?"

"I would need to see where you play tennis."

"If you lose a ball in the middle of a game," James continued, "it's really annoying."

Two young girls came running along the side of the wall. "Can Mr Sean play a game of royal tennis with us?" one of them shouted out.

"No, Isabella, Mr Sean must go to the blacksmith's shop," the king said.

"Mr Nicholas can do that," Isabella said.

"No, Mr Sean must go."

"Mr Nicholas pays the money. He can go."

"Yes, he will go with Mr Sean."

"They don't *both* have to go."

"No ... but—"

"Mr Sean can play until the blacksmith gets here."

"The blacksmith's shop is not far away."

"Please!"

"There isn't enough time for a game."

"We only want a quick game."

"A quick game then." James found himself agreeing.

The girls each grabbed one of Campbell's hands and began dragging him back through the monastery gates with a sense of urgency. They took him into the royal apartments and then into the royal tennis catchpule.

High walls surrounded them on three sides. On the fourth side was a gallery for spectators. There were two clock faces—with only an hour hand. A net straddled the court, five feet high at the sides but dropping to only three feet in the centre.

"The yellow man plays tennis with my father," Isabella said.

"Maybe I will be allowed to watch," Campbell said.

Isabella rolled her eyes. "If he knows you're here, he will challenge you."

"Oh," Campbell laughed. "I think your father will win."

"Not my father, the yellow man."

"I can play him, too, if he wants."

"Are you going to let him beat you right in front of Lady Cat?"

"Well ... I don't think—"

Again, Isabella rolled her eyes. "He will beat you, and then you'll look stupid right in front of Lady Cat."

"I can make myself look stupid without playing tennis," Campbell said.

"Don't you like Lady Cat?"

"Eh ... yes."

"Don't you want her to like you?"

"I'm not sure that—"

Again, Isabella rolled her eyes. "We will help you," she announced. She made a hand signal to Joan who ran into the spectators' gallery and stood beside the clocks.

"The clocks don't work," Isabella explained. "We use them for keeping score." She made another hand signal, and Joan threw two leather gloves onto the court. Isabella ran over and picked them up. She held one up to Campbell. He put it on.

Joan threw a ball onto the court. It bounced slightly and then rolled to Isabella's feet. Isabella picked it up and ducked underneath the net.

"Put your glove on," Isabella said. "You hit the ball with the palm of your hand."

Campbell put on his glove. It was more like a mitten; it had a thumb but no fingers.

"I hit the ball, and you hit it back."

"I'm ready."

"Tenez!" Isabella shouted. She hit the ball; it came up and over the middle part of the net. Campbell swiped at it, and it spun off his glove, hit the net, and dropped to his feet.

"Quinze to l'oeuf!" Isabella shouted.

Joan pushed the hand of the first clock forward to show one-quarter of an hour.

"Fifteen to egg?" Campbell queried.

"That's the score."

"You've only scored one point. How can you have fifteen points?"

Again, Isabella rolled her eyes. "I have one point; you have nothing. That is the score."

"You said fifteen to egg."

"That's the way they count the scores. When you score one point, the clock goes forward by a quarter."

"Then the score would be one quarter to egg."

"Fifteen minutes," Isabella explained.

"Oh."

"Tenez!" Isabella shouted. She hit the ball over the high part of the net, where it dropped onto the ground.

"Trente to l'oeuf!" Isabella shouted out.

Joan moved the hands of the clock forward.

"You hit the ball to the other side of the catchpule," Campbell protested. "I'm standing here, not over there."

"You're standing in the wrong place."

"You didn't tell me."

"You move every time a point is scored."

"Tenez!" Isabella shouted and hit the ball over the net.

Campbell swiped at it, and this time, it went back over the net.

Then Isabella hit it onto the roof of the gallery. It rolled along the roof and dropped onto the ground. Joan moved the hands of the clock again.

"Quarante-cinq!" Isabella shouted. "That's my score," she added. "Your score is nothing."

"You hit the ball onto the roof," Campbell said.

"You didn't hit it back," Isabella explained.

"Play on," Campbell said.

"Tenez!" Isabella shouted. She hit the ball up in the air.

This time, Campbell kept his eyes on it and carefully knocked it back over the net.

Isabella hit the ball over the high of the net. It scuffed off the wall and dropped onto the ground.

A burst of clapping broke out in the gallery. "Good shot!" Catherine shouted.

Campbell shot a glance at the gallery. How long had she been there? he wondered.

"Soixante to l'oeuf!" Isabella called out. "I win the game."

Joan put the hands of the clock forward.

"You hit the ball to my left," Campbell complained.

"I know that."

"I only have a glove on my right hand."

Isabella gave him a disdainful look. "Are you going to try harder if we play another game?"

"I will play you." Catherine stepped into the catchpule. "Mr Sean is a very busy man. He has important work to do for the king."

Almost with relief, Campbell pulled the glove off his hand and passed it to Catherine.

"The score was soixante to l'oeuf!" Catherine said to Isabella. "Do you think I can do better?"

"Sixty to egg," Campbell grumbled. "I guess I've learned something today."

"Surely it isn't the first time a woman has left you with egg on your face?" Catherine winked to him.

Campbell slowly walked into the gallery, looking for the exit.

"Are you going to marry the yellow man?" Isabella asked Catherine.

Campbell instinctively stopped and looked back.

"I like Mr Sean," Isabella said.

Campbell turned away, walking quickly along the passageway.

"Ballumbie hasn't asked me," Catherine said.

"Your mother says you will marry him."

"When did my mother say that?"

"Yesterday—before we left Stirling."

"We don't always do what our mothers say."

There was a pause. Isabella knitted her brows. "So why do you tell me I always have to do what my mother says?"

Catherine quickly bent down. "I have the ball," she announced. "Tenez!" she shouted and hit the ball over the net.

The virgin snow was compacting under the weight of the horse's hooves.

Crimp, crimp was the sound it made.

Robert Graham had ridden up Glen Garry, a thickly wooded ravine made treacherous by the snow and ice. The winding River Garry at its bottom was a demon waiting to swallow the souls of innocent travellers who slipped and tumbled down the hillside. On the other side of the river was Schiehallion, shining white in its purity like a saint but a frozen murderous demon to any poor fool who tried to climb it in winter.

His hands were red and sore with the cold. He clenched them and released them repeatedly, but he had to keep his numb fingers on the reins. What passed for a road was a narrow track that disappeared into a muddy quagmire in wet weather, re-emerging later. Or it would vanish into a stony scree that the horses would have to pick their way across carefully.

Big and imposing, glimpses of Blair Castle flitted through the trees. This was a castle fit for a king—majestic against the snow-capped mountains with the river at its foot. Sitting at the fireside in the great hall with a quaich[12] of whisky in his hand was the man who thought he should be king—fifty-five-year-old Walter Stewart, Earl of Atholl.

"I meet my guests in the great hall of my castle," he complained. "King James meets them at the High Altar of Blackfriars Monastery, where they bow to him as if they are bowing to Christ."

---

[12] A broad but shallow cup, often made with silver.

The statue of Christ looked over the walled garden at Blackfriars, supervising the growth of the kale and beans under the shelter of the apple trees. Sprigs of lavender sprouted from the stony paths, and their flowers and bracts were scattered around the lavatorium, where the monks washed.

The children were never encouraged to play here and told not to disturb the monks or trample across flower beds that provided food for the bees. But this was a place where the queen liked to walk.

She was looking at the kale, its dark green leaves sparkling in the winter frost. In the corner of her eye, she saw a man in a purple cloak walking towards her. He was walking at a brisk pace as if something was on his mind.

"Good afternoon, Your Grace." She smiled.

"Have the pair of you cooked this up together?" King James asked.

"You think we should have kale broth tonight?"

"You know what I'm talking about."

"I do?"

"Why am I hearing that Walter FitzRoland will be riding this way from Berwick with Alexander Lovell?"

"I am not responsible for Ballumbie's choice of travelling companion."

"When FitzRoland arrives at Blackfriars, I will tell him that he does not have permission to enter the royal apartments."

"If such is your will, Your Grace."

The king paused for a moment. "Unless the queen has already granted permission."

Queen Joan looked away. "The journey from Berwick to St John's Town is a long one."

"There are inns and alehouses in the town."

"It would be ungracious if—"

The king cut in. "It would be most ungracious if you invited Walter FitzRoland to stay in the royal apartments knowing that Sean Campbell was also here."

"I did not invite him."

"Then, pray tell, why is he coming?"

"Lady Douglas said—"

"I might have known she would have something to do with it."

"She didn't have anything to do with it!"

"No?"

"Ballumbie will pass through her estates on the way north from Berwick."

"And that's why he wanted to go to Berwick. It gives him the excuse to visit Lord Douglas."

"He went to Berwick on business."

"So he passes Tantallon on the road north, and coincidentally, Sir Walter will be there. Then he invites Sir Walter to be his travelling companion?"

"Why should they ride alone when they can ride together?"

"I don't want Sir Walter FitzRoland in my court."

"What kind of court is this? We accommodate cut-throats but not knights?"

"Sir Walter is not coming here as my guest."

"That would be most ungracious, Your Grace."

"Then I shall be ungracious."

"The roads are dangerous for a man travelling on his own. I merely said to Lady Douglas that you would wish Ballumbie a safe journey north."

"You mean Her Shapelessness wishes Ballumbie a safe journey north? So she has arranged for him to have the company of Sir Walter FitzRoland?"

"You travel with a train of swordsmen."

"You have designed it so that Sean Campbell will have an enemy in my court—an enemy who bears him a grudge." The king's eyes flashed with anger. "Is this the way you clear the path for Ballumbie to marry Catherine?"

"It is not my business who marries Catherine."

"I cannot stop FitzRoland travelling to St John's Town, but he will not enter Blackfriars while I am here."

"Surely Your Grace would wish to ease his discomfort after such a long journey?" Queen Joan smiled. "They will respect the customs of your court."

"Indeed they will," James said, glaring at her. "And they will also respect my wishes outside of court."

"Whatever do you mean?"

"Does Walter FitzRoland blame Sean Campbell for the death of his brother?"

"I cannot say, Your Grace."

"You think he will challenge him to a duel? With a bit of luck, they will both kill each other, and there will be nothing standing between Ballumbie and his marriage to Catherine Douglas. Is this what you planned with Her Shapelessness?"

"Give her her proper name."

"The Shapeless Lady Douglas."

"Stop it!"

"The Formidable Lady Douglas."

"You wouldn't call her that if she was in your company."

"I don't talk about Cut-throat Campbell, either."

"Try to see it from a woman's point of view."

"Sean Campbell doesn't wear a codpiece. But then he doesn't need to."

"Some of us are more interested in what's between the ears."

"And you got a man with as much between his ears as he has between his thighs. You knew a good thing when you saw it."

"Yes, and I can see why Catherine is attracted to Sean Campbell. Who wouldn't be?"

"You wouldn't be, I hope."

"We've all been young and stupid."

"I remember being young once; I'm not so sure about the other bit."

"These knights—they have their duty to the king, and their duty always comes first. What's Sean Campbell going to do but break Catherine's heart one day?"

"But Ballumbie won't break her heart because she has no feelings for him?"

"Ballumbie has money."

"You may find that Catherine has higher aspirations."

"My mother warned me against you so many times."

"And no wonder. You're her social superior now. She must curtsey to you when she visits. How she must hate that."

"How do you think she will feel when she learns that you're blocking up sewers to stop assassins crawling up them?"

"I am blocking up the sewer because I keep losing tennis balls down it."

CHAPTER 15

A young woman came into the hall, the hem of her loose-fitting kirtle trailing the floor. She was holding a quaich, filled to the brim with whisky.

She bent forwards, knowing the loose material would fall forwards, and held out the quaich. She was aware of Robert Graham's eyes on her chest as he took the quaich in his trembling hands.

Walter Stewart, Earl of Atholl, stared at a flame as it followed a crack in one of the logs in the fireplace. Blue, yellow, red—the earl watched the different coloured flames merge one into another. "Sean Campbell could be sitting here with a cup of whisky in his hands. Instead, he kneels before King James like he is kneeling before Christ."

"King James thinks he is Christ." Graham put the quaich to his chapped lips. He took a sip of the whisky and then another sip.

Atholl shot a glance at Graham. "Can we trust this man?"

"He asked for twenty gold lions; I offered twelve."

"Tell him he can have one hundred. He doesn't get any of it until I hear the news that James is dead."

Graham hesitated for a moment. Then he said "Maybe he thinks you will not pay."

"Of course I'm not going to pay if the job's not done," Atholl roared.

"Give him five now and the rest later."

"Five!" Atholl shifted uncomfortably in his seat.

"It is not easy to kill a king, my lord. He has to wait for the right moment."

"Macbeth did it in one night." The earl was still staring hard into the fire. "We need another plan." He shot Graham a glance. "James is holding a great council in St John's Town in February. That is when we will strike."

"I will tell Campbell."

"No," Atholl said. He took a slow sip of whisky. "If we have two plans, maybe one of them will work." He winked. "A monastery is not a castle. Pick six men and do it at night when the monks are asleep."

"What about Campbell?"

"If he does it before then, so much the better."

"We kill him afterwards?"

"Yes. We can tell the people we are avenging the king he murdered." He shot Graham a glance. "Then you bring the boy to me."

"The queen will still be alive."

"Then you kill her and blame it on Campbell." A smirk crossed Atholl's face. Then he suppressed it. "Draw up a guest list."

"What for?"

"I want a lot of people here when the courier arrives with the news that the king has been murdered. They will witness my shock—my outrage."

"You will be in St John's Town, my lord."

"Not when the murder is committed." Atholl gripped his quaich with both hands. "That man … that man"—he was spitting the words out—"that man would not be king if I had not brought him back to Scotland."

The quaich was shaking. Graham was watching droplets of whisky spatter onto the floor.

"I put James on the throne," Atholl shouted. "I rode to Berwick to meet him and give him safe passage to Scone."

"He owes you," Graham said.

"He owes me," Atholl shouted. "He owes me a debt!"

———— † ————

The man kneeling at the high altar stood up and walked down the nave. The only sound in the church was the scuff of his leather soles on the stone floor. Campbell waited for a wave from the king and came forwards, head bowed.

"We need more iron bars for the sewer. If you need the money," the king said to Campbell, "you can ask my chamberlain, Robert Stewart." The king waved a hand, and Stewart came over.

"We have enough iron bars," Campbell said. "No one can get in the sewer."

"What are you talking about?" James barked. "I want iron bars over the sewer so I stop losing tennis balls down it." He looked at Robert Stewart and smiled. "You find it annoying when a tennis ball drops into the sewer?"

Stewart bowed his head slightly. "Yes, Your Grace."

James turned to Campbell. "My chamberlain is a very good player."

"Not as good as you, Your Grace," Stewart said.

"The blacksmith will need to be employed; Sean will need more money."

"Yes, Your Grace."

"Attend to it, now."

"Yes, Your Grace," Stewart said and walked off.

James took hold of Campbell's elbow. "You must show me how the work is progressing."

"Certainly, Your Grace."

James's eyes followed Stewart as he went behind a pillar, opened a wooden door, and then vanished. "This way," he said quietly, turning towards the royal tennis catchpule.

"Not much has been done, yet," Campbell said.

"Whenever I speak to someone in the royal apartments, I feel that Robert Stewart is always listening."

"Why do you give him a place at court?"

"He is my chamberlain. He is also the grandson of the Earl of Atholl."

"I know who he is, Your Grace."

King James rolled his eyes. "I am beginning to see why you were beaten by a blind man."

"Zizka had one good eye," Campbell retorted.

"All the great nobles expect to be represented at court," James explained. "If I send Robert Stewart away, Atholl will send someone else in his stead."

"Then you send him away, too."

"If I know who he is." James paused for a moment, as if thinking. "If you treat an enemy like an enemy, he remains an enemy. If you treat him like a friend, you can fool him into thinking he is a friend. Then, when the time comes, you act."

"Robert Stewart will tell Atholl about your movements. A king on the road is easily ambushed."

"If Atholl listens to him." James smiled a brief smile. "I tell Robert Stewart I am going to Linlithgow. Then, at the last moment, plans are changed, and I go to Dunfermline. If I know what Robert Stewart knows, then I also know what information goes to Atholl."

"It sounds to me like you have a viper in the nest."

"Court is a vipers' nest," James said.

CHAPTER 16

"You cannot enter the monastery," the monk said.

Alexander Lovell had arrived at Blackfriars. But what was concerning the monk was the man next to him, who wore a mail shirt. A sword hung from his belt, and the handle of a dagger protruded from his right boot. The two men, on horseback, dwarfed the monk.

"You can take custody of my weapons until I leave," the other man shouted down to the monk.

"Absolutely not!" the monk said. "This is a house of God." He smiled kindly yet stood with a quiet defiance, his back to the door, which he showed no intention of opening. In his right hand, he had a firm grip of the large, heavy iron key.

"Tell King James that Alexander Lovell of Ballumbie is here."

"I will tell Abbot Henry," the monk said. But he showed no signs of moving.

"We can go to the inn," Sir Walter FitzRoland said.

"A very good idea," the monk said.

"We should stable the horses."

"A very good idea," the monk said.

"I will come back to seek an audience with the king," Lovell said defiantly.

The monk did not seem so sure that that was a good idea. "Men come here to commune with God, but you may take the king's counsel if you wish," he said.

"Come on," FitzRoland said. "You can talk to the king in the morning."

Lovell turned his horse around and slowly rode away.

"Wake up!" Eleanor had run into the bedchamber.

James was looking up at the roof of his four-poster bed where a spider was clinging to the top of the bedpost. *I hope Joan hasn't noticed it*, James thought.

"Yes, we should get up," James groaned. "Before that sycophantic turnip arrives."

Queen Joan, half-awake, turned her face to his. "Turnip?"

"He's the same colour as a turnip."

"You haven't told the servants to cook turnip again?" Eleanor complained.

"I'm not talking about turnip," James said.

"Yes, you are," Eleanor said.

"I'm talking about Ballumbie."

"Has the yellow man brought us a shipment of turnips?"

"He looks like a turnip."

"No, he doesn't," Eleanor said.

"The flowers on a turnip are bright yellow."

"I'd better not buy you a saffron coat then," Queen Joan said.

"Please don't."

"We ate turnip yesterday. We have it all the time," Eleanor said.

"Not all the time, only in winter," James said.

"Leave us alone, Eleanor," the queen said.

"I don't like turnip."

"Your father was talking about the yellow man."

"He was talking about turnips."

"Turnip is very nice with mutton," James said.

"I like blaeberry[13] tart."

"Go and find out if Sheona is awake," Queen Joan said to Eleanor.

"I like raspberry tart, but blaeberry tart is my favourite."

"Find out if Sheona is awake."

---

[13] Bilberry

Eleanor went running out of the room. A loud grunt came from the room next door.

"I tell her not to do that," James said. "She likes to wake Sheona up by jumping on her stomach."

"It's because she's fat; Catherine is too bony."

"Catherine's not bony," James said, picturing the way her gown always seemed to cling to the contours in her body.

"You always said you liked a bit of flesh on the bone."

James sat up in bed, letting the rough woollen blankets drop down his shoulder. Joan looked at the pectoral muscles, flabby from lack of use and fat from overeating.

"You used to have the body of a knight."

"You wish I looked like Sean Campbell?"

"You did when I met you."

"He's available, if I'm assassinated."

"Don't talk like that."

"You want to get Catherine married off to Ballumbie; Campbell will still be unattached if something happens to me."

"I told you not to talk like that," Queen Joan scolded him. "Besides, you've outsmarted me for once."

"Only once?"

"There's a first time for everything."

"You and Lady Douglas, you'll work out a way to get Catherine and Ballumbie together."

"You have Campbell in the monastery, and Ballumbie's stuck outside."

"I asked him to take a look at the monastery's defences, that's all."

"And he says you should block up the sewer?"

"I'm always losing tennis balls down that sewer; I don't know why I didn't think of this before."

"So we have got Catherine in Blackfriars, and purely by accident, Sean Campbell is also here. Well done."

"What of it?"

"What will Lady Douglas think? After working so hard to get a suitable match for Catherine." Joan paused, before delivering the coup de grâce. "Besides, her father will never allow her to marry a man like Sean Campbell."

"Who's talking about marriage?"

"Do you want to see Catherine spending next winter in Glen Esk?"

"She's a sensible woman."

"Not if her head gets turned by love. Look what happened to me."

"You married a king."

"You were king of nothing when I met you; you were a homeless vagrant."

"And all the more attractive for it." James laughed.

"He was king of nothing. I was the man who brought him back to Scotland. Now look at the way he treats me." Atholl's loud voice reverberated down the corridor.

The wooden shutters were closed to keep out the cold wind; tall, thick candles ran down the middle of the long table. Robert Graham was sitting on the wooden bench.

"He owes me," Atholl shouted. "I brought him back here."

"You brought him back here to kill him," Graham said and immediately regretted it. It was a tired remark, but then he was having the same conversation with Atholl every time they met, and he was growing tired of it.

Atholl shot Graham a hostile stare. "For twenty years, I was doing the work of the king," he barked, "and getting no thanks for it."

"Eighteen years."

A woman came into the hall, holding a pot of porridge in both hands. She placed it on the table, picking up a spoon and serving the Earl of Atholl first.

"Are you drinking whisky?" Graham asked.

"What of it?"

"Where's mine?"

Atholl nodded to the woman, who spooned some porridge onto Graham's plate and then left the great hall.

A small bowl of cream sat next to Graham's larger bowl of porridge. He took a spoonful of porridge and then dipped it in the cream before putting it in his mouth.

"Why did he have a country to return to and a throne kept warm for him?" Atholl shouted. "Because of me!"

"And all that time he was hiding in the English court—"

"And all the time, I couldn't touch him. The throne was so close. So close ..." *But still so far away.* Atholl slurped at his quaich of whisky. He did not seem interested in the porridge. "I can't let him go back to Stirling Castle."

"What?"

"He holds a great council in St John's Town and sleeps in the royal apartments in Blackfriars Monastery." The earl paused, as if thinking. Then he said. "It's easier to do it in the monastery; I can't let him go back to Stirling Castle."

Graham heard footsteps at his back and turned his head instinctively.

A woman had come into the great hall with a jug in her hands. "Whisky, Sir Robert?" she asked.

CHAPTER 17

"The king told you not to go down there!" Catherine shouted. Isabella was running through the laundry. A middle-aged monk was standing with his bare feet in a large tub and his habit bunched around his waist, trampling clothes. He gasped and let his habit drop to cover his bare knees.

Catherine crossed herself. "Ave Maria, gratia plena." She pushed open the oak door and caught a glimpse of Isabella's white gown vanishing into the lavatorium.

"Dominus tecum." Catherine marched quickly through the laundry, her eyes fixed on the floor. "Benedicta tu in mulleribus."

Isabella was in the lavatorium now, running along the stone slabs that made a walkway next to the channel of water. Then she skipped down the stone steps that led to the sewer and out of sight.

"Et benedictus fructus ventris tui Iesus." Catherine reached the stone steps. "Sancta Maria, Mater Dei." She went quickly down the steps. "Ora pro nobis peccatoribus."

The corridor grew darker and darker as they descended into the sewer. At the end of the corridor, the yellow light from lanterns, like the fires of hell, reflected off the walls and sparkled on the water.

"Mr Sean! Mr Sean!" Isabella shouted.

Two men, both with their feet in the water, were standing at the end of the sewer. One was holding an iron bar across the aperture, and the other was pressing a coarse mixture into the small hole where the end of the bar entered the wall.

Sean Campbell turned around. "Keep out of the water," he warned Isabella as he stepped up onto the walkway.

"He's standing in it." Isabella pointed to the other man.

"Oh, you don't want to smell like him," Campbell said.

"Nunc et in hora mortis nostrae." The figure of a woman in a blue gown came out of the shadows. "Amen," she said and crossed herself again.

"The yellow man brought a man with him," Isabella shouted urgently to Campbell. "He's wearing armour, and he has a sword."

"Maybe he doesn't have any other clothes," Campbell said.

"They're going to kill you!"

"It's Walter FitzRoland," Catherine said. "He thinks his brother's dead because of you."

"Alan went to Melnik on Sigismund's orders, not mine."

"You left him there."

"He would have left me."

"That's not the way his brother will see it."

"You'll kill him, won't you, Mr Sean?" Isabella said.

"Nobody's killing anybody," Catherine said. "I'll talk to Sir Walter."

Isabella noticed a long iron bar lying on the stone walkway. "You could hit him with that," she said, pointing at the bar.

"That's mine," the other man said. "And we're blocking up the sewer with it."

"This is Alan Gow," Campbell explained. "He's a blacksmith."

"Why are you blocking up the sewer?" Isabella asked.

"Because the king keeps losing tennis balls down it," Campbell said. "He's not a good tennis player like you."

Catherine took Isabella's hand. "These men have work to do," she said. "You're coming with me."

"Mr Sean doesn't have a sword!"

"We're in a monastery," Catherine said. "Nobody has a sword."

"The yellow man's friend does."

"But he's not in the monastery," Catherine said. "And we will tell the king not to let him in."

"I don't care if you let him in," Campbell said. "I'm not scared of him."

"Oh? You're going to fight an armoured knight with your bare hands?" Catherine shook her head in disbelief. "You men are all the same."

"You could go to Stirling, Mr Sean," Isabella said.

"No," Campbell said. "We have to finish our work."

"I'll do it," Catherine said.

"Do what?" Campbell asked.

"I can hold up an iron bar. What's so hard about that?"

"It might be a little bit heavy for you."

"You're only going to hold it there until the mortar sets."

"Then we do the next one," Campbell said. "They're too heavy, and you're not standing in the sewer, either."

"How long will you be here?" Catherine asked Campbell.

"The rest of the day," Alan Gow said.

"Let's go," Catherine said to Isabella. She began to lead her away. "I must go and find Walter FitzRoland."

"No," Isabella said. "You can't fight him."

"There are other ways to weaken a man; you will learn that when you are older." Catherine winked to Isabella.

They walked back up the passageway. Catherine noticed a man standing still, dressed in black. He was barely noticeable in the darkness.

"What are you doing here?" Catherine challenged him.

"I ... well ... I came down to—"

"You're always following me around," Catherine said.

―――― † ――――

Campbell had watched Catherine's blue gown disappear into the shadows with Isabella skipping ahead. He could hear her speaking briefly to a monk, but her voice was quiet, and he could not hear what she was saying.

He turned back to the sewer.

"These bars won't stop tennis balls drifting down the sewer," Gow said. "Look at the gap! That won't catch a tennis ball."

"It's not meant to."

Gow furrowed his brows. "Then what are we doing here?"

"Carrying out the king's orders."

"I'm a professional man," Gow pointed to his chest. "I do good quality work. That's what my reputation is based on. I can't have people laughing at me because I blocked up a sewer to stop the king losing tennis balls and then everybody sees the balls coming out and rolling down the High Street."

"The king has young children. We're telling them he's putting the bars up to stop losing tennis balls." Campbell let out a long, tired sigh. "The real purpose is to stop anyone crawling into the monastery this way."

"Who's going to crawl up a sewer into a monastery?"

"An assassin might. Now let's get on with it." Campbell said. But something caught the corner of his eye as he bent down to pick up an iron bar from the floor. He stood up quickly. "I thought you were a monk," he said.

Dressed in black doublet and black hose with black shoes, Robert Stewart took an involuntary step backwards. "I came to speak with you."

"Proceed," Campbell said.

"Alone."

Campbell splashed forwards a few steps. "What is it?"

Robert Stewart turned his back on Alan Gow, casting a long shadow across the black water in the yellow lantern light. He began to walk down the sewer, taking Campbell with him.

"You have noticed that King James takes prayers at the altar every morning," Stewart whispered, "after the Latin Mass?"

"It is morning for the king, midday for the monks."

"But you have noticed?"

Campbell frowned. Was this an invitation to kill the king or a warning that he was vulnerable? "You think the king should be better guarded?"

"The king likes to be on his own when he is in prayer," Stewart said cryptically.

"Then we must advise him to post a guard at the door," Campbell said. "Excuse me, Sir Robert, but I must get on with my work." He turned around, making the reflections of the lantern light sparkle on the surface of the water as he splashed his way back towards Alan Gow.

Catherine let the large, heavy double-doors close behind her and stepped into St John's Town High Street. Head down, avoiding eye contact with the beggars and the thieves posing as itinerant chapmen, she marched up the street. If her eyes were downcast, her ears were alive to the sounds of the street—the idle conversations, the bargains being concluded, the whispered remarks directed at a woman on her own, and the footsteps behind her.

She turned around to see Robert Stewart following her along the street.

"What are you doing?" she challenged him.

Stewart halted and then took a step forwards. "The king told me to watch out for you."

"I didn't tell the king I was leaving Blackfriars."

"I meant the queen. It was the queen who told me to make sure you were all right."

"I didn't tell the queen, either."

"She saw you leave."

"Go back to Blackfriars," Catherine said.

"Where are you going?"

"Go back to Blackfriars," Catherine repeated. Then, without waiting for an answer, she turned around and marched quickly up the street to the Thrissil Inn.

As soon as she pushed open the door, a hush fell. Her eyes scanned the room until they fell on Walter FitzRoland. He was sitting on his own with a pot of ale in front of him. His eyes had been on the serving wench, the belt drawn tightly around her stomach to pull down her shift and expose her cleavage. The public house was busy with customers shouting their orders at the serving wench from their seats. The woman was carrying pots and jugs back and forth from the tables to the bar, good-humouredly pushing off the grasping hands that slipped around her waist when she approached a table.

Suddenly, no one was looking at the big-breasted serving wench. Catherine walked across the floor in complete silence. She sat down at Walter FitzRoland's table.

"Hello, Walter," she said quietly.

The public house was still silent; everyone was looking at this young woman. FitzRoland's eyes were wide with surprise.

Catherine gave him a hostile stare. "What are you doing here?"

"I was told to wait here; maybe I'll be summoned to the court."

Catherine waited for a moment or two. "You're not going to ask about Margaret?"

FitzRoland winced. "Maybe I should visit her."

"You're a bit late, thinking about that now."

"What do you mean?"

"Don't pretend you don't know."

"I don't know," FitzRoland stammered.

Catherine gave him a long, hard stare. "Somebody got her pregnant."

FitzRoland broke off eye contact.

"You can go and visit her in Glen Esk; maybe it's not too late."

"Too late for what?"

Catherine glowered at him. "Before it's too late to stop her doing something you might both regret."

"The road will be blocked with snow."

"How convenient for you."

"Look." FitzRoland's tone was placatory. "Whatever you think—"

"I think you're a swine."

"Whatever it looks like," he was still avoided her eyes, "I was always very fond of Margaret."

"We know that," Catherine hissed at him. "Much too fond of her."

FitzRoland seemed to wince again.

"Go to Glen Esk," Catherine pleaded, "while there's still time."

"The thing is … What I mean is … We have to think about Margaret's reputation."

"Yes!" Catherine exclaimed. "That's exactly what we have to think about." Catherine turned and walked quickly out of the Thrissil Inn, going through the door and walking down the dark street.

"Lady Catherine."

A black figure emerged from the shadows, and she realised it was Robert Stewart. She broke into a run, the hem of her kirtle billowing as she fled across the cobbles. The monastery appeared on her left-hand side, its heavy oak door tall and austere. She pushed it open, running into the royal apartments—running through the king's presence chamber and down the passageway and past the dining hall.

She pushed open a door and stepped into a small room. A fire was crackling in the fireplace; a wooden tub sat in the centre of the floor.

Sitting in the tub was Sean Campbell. He looked up. "Working down in the sewers has its compensations," he said. "Nobody asks any questions if you say want a bath."

Catherine shivered involuntarily.

"You're cold?"

"It's Robert Stewart," Catherine said. "He makes me feel unclean."

A young man came into the room with a bucket of warm water, brushing past Catherine and emptying the bucket into the tub. He turned to go, pausing for a moment as he looked at Catherine. Then he left.

Catherine quickly pulled the kirtle over her head and let it drop onto the floor. She stood for a moment, letting him look at her.

Her eyes were all over him—his wet hair clinging to his shoulders, his wet skin glistening in the firelight. She put one leg into the tub and then the other, her thigh brushing past his shoulder and her pubic hair almost touching his nose. She lowered herself gently into the water, her breasts catching bubbles of air, which broke on the surface as she submerged.

Then there was just her head above the surface, her back against the tub, and her legs entangled with his. She touched his chest, her hand going down across his firm stomach, down and down till her fingers were folding around the iron rod that lay underneath.

CHAPTER 18

"He took you down to the sewers and you don't see the irony?" Queen Joan said.

"It was my choice."

"Other men bring their women flowers or take them swimming in the river. You go to the sewers."

"His Grace trusts him," Catherine said.

"His Grace trusts the juggler to entertain us at dinner; he does not expect you to marry him."

"You sound just like my mother."

A burst of clapping broke out. "Good shot, Your Grace," Robert Stewart shouted out from the gallery.

"Yes, good shot," Alexander Lovell said.

"Men like Sean Campbell," the queen said, "have their duty to the king, and their duty always comes first. They don't make good husbands."

James stepped over to the ball, which had rolled to the side of the catchpule. He picked it up; Lovell steadied himself.

"Tenez!" James hit the ball low over the net.

Lovell knocked it back. Then James hit it over the high part of the net. The ball ricocheted off the wall, changing direction, before dropping to the ground.

"Excellent shot!" Robert Stewart shouted.

"Game!" Isabella shouted.

"Your Grace is too good for me today," Lovell said.

"And every other day," Catherine said quietly.

James pulled off his glove. "Perhaps Sir Walter will play?" He strode into the gallery, tossing his glove to FitzRoland and then taking his seat beside the queen.

FitzRoland picked up the ball. "Tenez," he shouted. He hit the ball over the net.

Alexander Lovell, who had been slow and lethargic when the king was playing, suddenly became lithe and agile. He looked like a wasp in his saffron doublet and black boots, and now he was moving like one. Every ball that FitzRoland hit over the net came back at a faster speed, always angled away from him. Now Lovell was a blurred streak of yellow, jumping up high and then diving down low or leaping to his right and then to his left.

Catherine became aware of a figure in a green rogart shirt standing at the back of the gallery. Queen Joan noticed him, and then others were casting surreptitious glances.

Lovell made as if to hit the ball to his left but, with a subtle flick of the wrist, sent it over the net to his right. Caught flat-footed, FitzRoland watched it drop onto the ground and then roll to a halt.

"Game!" Lovell called out.

But this time, there was no applause. Everyone was looking at FitzRoland and Campbell as if they expected the two men to rush at each other with swords drawn.

FitzRoland came walking towards the public gallery. He pulled off his glove and threw it to Robert Stewart. "Perhaps you will make a better opponent for Mr Lovell?" Then he bowed to King James. "Your Grace, you must allow Mr Campbell to tell me about the siege of Melnik Castle?"

Catherine reached for Isabella's hand, but it was not there. She turned and wove her way through the spectators, all the time searching the gallery with her eyes. She heard the King James saying "Robert, you should play Ballumbie!"

"Sir Walter will want to know what happened to his brother," the queen interjected. "The two of them will have much to talk about."

Whispered mutterings darted around the gallery. Catherine had caught up with Isabella, who was standing next to Campbell; she put a firm hand on her shoulder. But her eyes were on Campbell's as she whispered, "You will not let him take you outside the monastery."

"I can look after myself."

"Are you listening to me?" Catherine hissed under her breath. "You stay in the monastery."

Robert Stewart had taken his place on the other side of the net from Alexander Lovell. Catherine felt FitzRoland brush against her shoulder.

"Tenez!" Lovell shouted.

"The monks will be at prayer," Campbell said to FitzRoland. "We can talk in the cloisters."

James twisted his neck, looking from Campbell to FitzRoland. "Very well," he said, "but you will respect the fact that you are in house of God."

FitzRoland bowed; the king turned his attention back to the tennis. Queen Joan watched Campbell lead FitzRoland out of the gallery and into the cloisters. The weak winter sun was obscured by clouds as the two men walked slowly under the stone arches. Eventually, Campbell said, "It was all my fault. We climbed the portcullis to get onto the battlements. I should have looked back to see where he was, but I didn't."

"Alan was always too rash; he never thought about his own safety. First in and last out—that's the way he was."

They stepped out from underneath the arches and into the square. FitzRoland sat on a stone bench. They were surrounded by silent statues. Campbell also sat down, shivering slightly at the touch of cold stone under his hose.

"The drummer boy." FitzRoland let out a sigh. "That was Zizka's fault, not yours. Zizka put him there."

Campbell was looking at the dry fountain in the centre of the square, where a statue of the Virgin Mary stood with hands clasped in prayer.

"If that had been a sentry on the battlements and you'd cut his throat, we'd all be saying you did the right thing. But because it was a boy …"

Campbell was looking at the statue's flowing robes and the tight waistline under the bust.

"There's something I know," FitzRoland said, "something these weak men who attend court will never understand. If you hadn't cut the boy's throat, my brother would have done it. You don't know if he's got a knife hidden in his clothes; if you wait for him to scream out, it's too late. You can't take the risk." He shot Campbell a sideways glance. "They don't understand what it's like. You have half a second to take a decision. If you take the wrong decision, you're a dead man."

Campbell nodded.

"I understand," FitzRoland said. "You cut the boy's throat because you had no choice. Then my brother gets caught in the castle, and they take their revenge on him."

"I thought he was behind me. I didn't realise—"

"I never blamed you for his death," FitzRoland said.

"Everyone else does."

FitzRoland shrugged. "Me and Alan—we weren't that close."

Campbell decided to change the subject. "I sometimes think about Alan's widow," he said.

"Not as much as I do; I think about her all the time."

"I went to visit her."

"She's not in St John's Town."

"You should go to visit her."

"What use would I be to her?"

"I went to speak to her. I didn't know what I was going to say, but I felt I had to go. But she wasn't there."

"She's in Glen Esk."

"She'll be back in the spring."

"Maybe it's better if I'm gone by then."

"Maybe." Campbell nodded briefly. "She can meet someone else. Start afresh."

"My brother." Suddenly FitzRoland seemed agitated, wringing his hands. "He was better than me at everything. Better at handling a sword, braver, better at attracting women." He stopped himself as if he had suddenly realised he was in a monastery.

Campbell waited for FitzRoland to continue.

"What I'm trying to say is … what I mean is … he was always going to go off and get himself killed one day. It was always going to happen." FitzRoland shot Campbell a sideways glance. "Alan trusted you like a friend."

"We were friends."

"That's what I meant."

"I wasn't afraid going into that sewer. I knew Alan was in front of me."

"And he knew you were at his back. So he wasn't afraid, either." FitzRoland held out his right hand.

Campbell grasped the hand. "No one will understand if we become friends."

"They expect us to settle this matter like gentlemen?"

Campbell grunted. "No one will ever think I'm a gentleman."

"Maybe we should play chess?" Robert Stewart suggested. He had already taken off his glove to show that the game of tennis was over.

"King James only has wooden chess pieces," Alexander Lovell said, his voice carrying out of the catchpule and into the public gallery.

"The pieces were carved from Indian rosewood by Scrimgeour the Sculptor and painted by Thomas Boyd," Queen Joan said.

James stood up. "Let us go inside," he said.

"King Eric VII of Denmark has ivory chess pieces," Lovell said. "They are made from walrus tusks."

"What's a walrus?" Isabella asked.

"It's a seal with tusks," Catherine said.

"Like a unicorn?"

"A unicorn has a horn, not a tusk."

"I could get ivory chess pieces in Copenhagen," Lovell said. "I don't know what the price would be, but you can always get a good deal if you take the time to haggle."

"How long are you going to keep that man at court?" Queen Joan whispered to James asked as they walked away.

"People don't know how to haggle," Lovell said. "They don't know how to strike a deal."

"I could ask him to get some ivory chess pieces," James said. "That will get rid of him for a while."

"I'm not talking about Alexander Lovell."

"Who are you talking about then?"

"The sewer rat."

"He's doing some work for me."

"We go to Linlithgow next; I suppose you'll say he has to come with us?"

"I am rebuilding Linlithgow Palace."

"And it's a palace—not a defensive fortification."

"Which is all the more reason for Sean Campbell to take a look at it."

Alexander Lovell had caught up with the royal party. "We should have one chess set in ivory for the king; the others can be made from wood."

"Chess is boring," Isabella said.

"Mistress Catherine could have an ivory necklace," Lovell said. He turned to look at her. "It would look nice around your pretty neck."

"I already have a silver necklace." Catherine smiled politely.

"But not ivory?"

"I have a necklace."

"Only one?" Lovell smiled back. "A lady at court should have more than one."

Two men were approaching.

"Mr Sean!" Isabella shouted out. "Let me show you the statues in the cloisters." She ran forwards to grab Campbell's hand. "You come too, Lady Cat."

"Don't make a noise," Queen Joan said.

"Promise!"

"Maybe Mr Sean has seen the statues," Catherine said.

"I want to show him something."

"You need not go," Alexander Lovell was saying to Catherine. "One of the other ladies-in-waiting—"

Catherine turned to Isabella. "What is it you want to show Mr Sean?"

"Oh." Isabella made a face. "Just something."

The rest of the royal party was making its way to the royal apartments, where wine, sweetened by honey, would be flowing freely. Catherine found herself alone with Isabella and Sean Campbell. Isabella skipped ahead.

"I have seen the statues," Campbell said quietly.

"She wants to take you away from Alexander Lovell and Walter FitzRoland."

"What does she think I'll do to them?"

"Don't joke."

Isabella pointed to a door. "That's the monks' toilet."

"No, it's the laundry," Catherine said.

"It smells of pee."

"That's how they wash their habits."

Isabella frowned. "Why don't they go to the river?"

"Maybe they don't like to."

They followed the arched corridor; Isabella skipped out of it and into the atrium.

"I like to come here," Catherine said. "It's always so quiet; you can hear the monks singing in Latin. I could sit here all day, just listening to them."

"Is Mr Sean going to Stirling?" Isabella asked.

"No," Catherine said. "He's going to Linlithgow."

"I want to go to Linlithgow."

"There's nowhere to sleep," Campbell said. "The palace doesn't have a roof."

"Are you going to put a roof on it?"

"Maybe."

Isabella turned away, running across the atrium.

"The children are going back to Stirling," Catherine said. "They will stay in the castle, but the king and queen will return to St John's Town."

"Good," Campbell said quietly. "The king and the children will be in different places. We should not make life easy for the king's enemies."

Catherine had become aware of someone walking behind them. She turned around. "Are you still here?"

"I … eh …" FitzRoland stammered.

"He's here at the king's invitation," Campbell said.

Catherine shot Campbell a warning glance. "You keep out of this." She turned back to FitzRoland. "It's not too late."

"Shhh."

"You could try thinking about her, for a change."

"I'm thinking about her reputation."

"I'm thinking about her life," Catherine said, "and the baby's life."

"You're talking too loudly."

"She could come back here, after the winter, with a husband and a baby and a chance to start again."

"Alexander Lovell promised me an introduction to court. I can't insult him by leaving now." Then, as if by afterthought, he added, "I can't offend the king, either."

"You can destroy Margaret's life, but you can't offend Alexander Lovell?"

"I'm not proud of myself."

"Then what are you going to do about it?"

"You're talking too loudly," Campbell hissed.

"Keep out of this," Catherine warned him.

"Do you want the whole town to know about it?" That was Queen Joan's voice.

Catherine looked around to see the queen standing at the end of the public gallery, her arms folded under her bosom. The point of her shoe was protruding from the hem of her gown and tapping the floor in irritation.

CHAPTER 19

"I hate scratchy kisses," Sheona Crockett said.

"Or tickly kisses," Jean Lockhart said.

"When I see a man approaching, and I know he's going to kiss me, I just shudder. If I want to scrape my cheek along a gravel path, I can do it for myself."

"When the hair gets a bit longer," Jean Lockhart said, "it's still stubbly, but it gets a bit softer. It's tickly."

"It makes you feel like you've got a rash on your cheek."

"They hold you in a cuddle; and then they're offended if you push them off."

"What happens to a man when he turns twelve years old?" Sheona complained. "They're adorable. Then, all of a sudden, they turn scratchy."

"They start drinking beer and whisky," Jean said. "If they don't get killed in a fight, they get bloated and fat."

"You're letting them do that?" Catherine had come into the nursery; James and Eleanor were busy rolling a die along the floor.

"They're only playing," Sheona said.

"He's teaching her to gamble." Catherine picked up the dice. "Where's the skipping rope?" she asked.

"We're playing dice," Prince Jamie said.

"I can't play dice."

"I'll teach you."

"Oh no. It's too hard."

"I'll get you soft dice."

Catherine shot Jean a pleading look that said, *Please help me out here.*

"Dice is too difficult for Catherine," Jean said.

A DAGGER FOR CATHERINE DOUGLAS

Catherine shot Jean a murderous stare.

"You like whittling," Sheona said to James.

"I don't want him playing with knives," Catherine said.

"He has to learn some time."

"He made a sword," Jean said.

"A sword!" Catherine exclaimed.

"Go and get your sword," Jean said to James. "Show it to Catherine." James ran out of the room.

"What do you think?" Sheona asked.

"I think we should teach them to play chess," Catherine said.

"That's just another war game," Jean said.

"I was asking about men," Sheona said. "If only they stopped growing at twelve years old, then they'd just be perfect."

"She won't know what you're talking about," Jean said. "Her man goes to the barber every week."

"My man?"

"Alexander Lovell," Jean continued. "He gets his hair cut and his chin shaved every week."

"I would take a cuddle from a man if I thought his chin was smooth," Sheona said.

"Smooth as a baby's bottom," Jean said. Then she added, "Or, like Alexander Lovell, smooth as the silk shirts he wears."

"Silk shirts scented with crushed rose petals," Sheona said.

"You don't know how lucky you are, Catherine."

"I tried marrying for love," Sheona said. "Next time, I'm doing it for money."

Eleanor was prodding at a burning log in the fireplace with a poker. Catherine was watching her carefully.

James came running back into the nursery with the branch of a tree in his hands which he was holding proudly. He had whittled off the bark to create a handle and flatten the blade. "It's Robert the Bruce's sword!" he said.

"You won't impress Lady Catherine with that," Sheona said. "She likes men who wear silk shirts."

"And keep title deeds in strong rooms," Jean said.

"What's a strong room?" Eleanor asked.

"The nursery is a strong room," Sheona said.

"Because it holds up other rooms?"

Jean pointed to the ceiling. "That's where Lady Douglas sleeps when she visits."

"It must be a very strong room," Eleanor said.

"The monastery has strong rooms," Sean Campbell said.

Walter FitzRoland looked doubtful. "How strong can a monastery be?"

"It has thick walls of stone; the rooms can be bolted."

They were sitting with their backs to the wall in the Thrissil Inn, talking to each other but also watching the comings and goings in the inn.

"The walls provide the monks with silence. They weren't built for defence."

At the table in front, a man had been picking the flesh off a salmon with his fingers. He stood up and walked to the door.

"Goodnight, Elshender!" the innkeeper called out.

The man raised a hand as he walked out the door. Campbell watched him go.

"You're not in Melnik Castle now," FitzRoland said. "You can relax a bit more."

Campbell's eyes fell on the pot of ale that was sitting in front of him. "It was easier in Melnik Castle," he said. "You knew your enemies were inside the castle, and your friends were outside." He shook his head. "You come to the Scottish court, you don't know who your friends are—or your enemies."

"You think Sigismund's court is any different? You never got high enough up to find out."

"Life was simple in Sigismund's court. You were told what job to do, and you did it. Then you got paid."

"And you wasted your money on women of ill-repute. You have a shot at something better here."

The door to the Thrissil Inn slammed shut. The man turned into a narrow lane, where there was barely room for two people to pass. There were no cobbles under his feet, any more, just an earthen track. The smell of rotting wood was in his nostrils; his feet stood on something wet.

"Elshender."

"Did you have to meet me here?" Elshender snapped angrily.

"Not so loud," a voice said.

Elshender looked at Robert Stewart in his leather boots with his warm cloak pulled around him. "You can afford a change of clothes. I can't."

But Stewart did not want to get bogged down in an argument. "What were they talking about?"

Elshender shifted from side to side. The thin soles of his shoes were cold on the freezing ground. "They were talking quietly; I couldn't hear properly."

"What did you hear?"

"They were talking about defending the monastery."

"Defending it against who?"

"I don't know. I told you I couldn't hear properly."

Somebody started coughing farther down the lane. Stewart quickly stepped out of the lane and into the High Street. "You must go to Blair Castle and tell the Earl of Atholl."

"What? The roads are blocked with snow."

"Go by river."

"How do I do that?"

"In a coracle."

"I can't."

"You go up River Tay and then up River Tummel."

"I know how to get there. What I mean is, I'll be paddling against the current."

"Then you had better leave right away."

"You win again," James said.

Queen Joan pulled her gown over her head and threw it on the floor. She gave her head a shake, letting her brown hair cascade around her bare shoulders. James looked at her golden skin, glistening in the candlelight, the body spreading outwards at the hips and the collapsed breasts.

"You have all the chambermaids to look at and you look at this body?"

"Then tell them to come through."

"You wouldn't know what to do with them." Holding her hands across the slack skin on her stomach, Queen Joan walked the up to the bed.

"Take your hands away."

"What do you want to see?"

"You used to enjoy undressing in front of me."

Joan lifted the woollen blankets and dived into bed.

James let his hand drift down to her stomach, feeling its softness and its uneven tracks. "This is the body you have; you should let me look at it."

She pushed herself towards him, pressing her lips onto his and squashing the softness of her body against his. They lay together, enjoying the warmth. James turned his head away to look up at the roof of the bed.

"You win again," he said after a while.

"What do you mean?"

"You have Ballumbie in the royal apartments in a bedroom that's only a short distance from Catherine's."

"He won't go near her bedroom."

"He doesn't have the courage."

"He's a gentleman," Joan retorted. "Besides, you couldn't have your guest—"

"*Your* guest!"

"You couldn't have your guest staying in Thrissil Inn."

"Walter FitzRoland is."

"He'll enjoy it there."

"And Ballumbie won't?"

"He'd just get robbed—if he didn't get his throat cut first."

"This is the man you and Lady Douglas want to look after Catherine?"

"Catherine can look after herself."

"It's just as well."

"There's more to a man than the muscles on his chest." Her head was on his shoulder, her hand was on the king's thigh. It moved across to his penis, the fingers closing around it and moving the foreskin up and down as it swelled and hardened.

James winced slightly.

"You don't know what Ballumbie is hiding down there."

"Not much, judging by the size of his codpiece."

"They weren't all built like you."

"He certainly wasn't."

"And we don't all get to marry kings. Ballumbie will be a good match for Catherine."

"You're talking like this has already been agreed."

"It has."

"Between you and Lady Douglas."

"I was a young woman once. I remember some of the stupid things I did."

"You scratched your face in the garden at Windsor."

"Who hasn't done that?"

"You were looking up at me, you couldn't take your eyes off me, and you walked into the yew tree."

"I was looking up at you because you were leaning out of the window in the tower."

"You were always staring at me."

"I was thinking, is that idiot going to fall out that window? You used to hang out of it just to get my attention."

"It looks like I succeeded."

"I was thinking, he needs a woman to look after him."

"Then your mother told you not to walk in the garden, but you did it anyway."

"The garden at Windsor Castle was a dangerous place to me in those days. I would walk in it knowing this strange, wild man was looking at me; it was exciting." She laughed quietly. "That's how young I was. We weren't all born old, like you."

"Maybe you should just let Catherine be young and stupid."

"She's already done that, hasn't she?" Queen Joan's tone changed, becoming more serious. "You can make a mistake once and get away with it but not a second time. Catherine's had her mistake. She needs to be careful, now."

"Maybe she could settle down with Sean Campbell?"

"It's not worth thinking about."

"Your mother wanted you to marry the Earl of Leicester. You gave up everything to come to Scotland with me."

"I think she was glad to see the back of me by then."

"You're always telling me you had to fight your mother to marry me."

"My mother wasn't Lady Douglas."

"The Formidable Lady Douglas."

CHAPTER 20

"Why do you want an appointment at court?" Catherine asked. "It can't be any worse than Sigismund's court."

He was looking at her, wanting to stroke her brown hair but doing nothing about it. Wanting to wrap his arms around her waist but keeping them firmly by his side. Wanting, wanting, wanting to press her body close to his.

"Put that down!" Catherine scolded.

Eleanor had picked up the poker and was stabbing a log in the fireplace. There was a flicker of fire as if the log had been roused from its slumber.

"That's dangerous!" Catherine scolded again, louder this time. "Put the poker the down."

Eleanor angrily dropped the poker onto the floor with a clatter.

"I've told father to give him a job!" Isabella announced.

Sean Campbell turned to look at her. "A job doing what?"

"Mother said you could clean the sewers."

"Isabella," Catherine said, "go and find out what Princess Joan is doing."

"Where is she?"

"Go and find out!"

Isabella turned and ran out of the room.

"Everybody wants to be at court," Catherine said. "But when you get here, you realise that it's a vipers' nest."

"That's what the king says."

"Nobody has any friends at court. You only have enemies. If the queen smiles at you, the other ladies are all jealous. But if the king smiles at you, that's worse; then the queen is jealous."

"I don't think the queen will be jealous if the king smiles at me," Campbell said.

"You don't know what it's like," Catherine said. "I'm scared to make myself look pretty by wearing ribbons in my hair because Jean or Sheona might think I'm making eyes at the king." She leaned towards him, her hair falling forwards across her face. "Take me away from here," she whispered, barely audible.

"What?"

"I'd love to see Loch Awe and Loch Fyne. I'd love to see the Highlands." The mountains, shimmering white in winter and sprinkled with blaeberries all summer. The men hunted stags or fished for salmon while the sun shone every day. In the towns, you could never see the sun for the tall buildings and the smoke in the narrow streets. You had to walk with your hands holding your skirt around your shins while you stepped over the horse droppings. You had to pretend not to see men urinating against walls or the blood from the slaughterhouse that ran down the street and collected in gaps between the cobbles.

"It's a hard life in the Highlands." He was picturing her swathed in green and blue tartan, a knee and bare shin protruding from the folds of material.

She looked at him, pleading with her eyes. *Take me away from here. Take me away from the intrigues of court, away from my matchmaking mother. Make love to me in the heather under the shade of the birch trees.*

"Yes, I'll take you," a male voice said. After a while, Campbell realised that that was his voice. But this was a stupid idea for a woman brought up at court. All the summer had to offer was long hours of hard work. All the winter had to offer was freezing temperatures and a front door blocked up with snow if you dared to go outside.

Catherine was smiling.

"Yes," Campbell was saying.

Yes.

Yes, I'd love to take you to the mountains. You can wear a ribbon in your hair every day. Wear a ribbon as you milk the cows; wear a ribbon as you pick kale. Wear a ribbon as you lie down beside me every night.

Princess Joan came running into the nursery, agitated. She was making hand signals to Catherine.

"Where's Isabella?" Catherine asked but then realised that Isabella had run off in another direction.

"Stay here," Catherine whispered to James and Eleanor. She shot a glance at Campbell. "Watch them for a moment."

"What do I do with them?" Campbell asked, slightly flustered.

Catherine rolled her eyes. "Play with them!"

Taking Princess Joan by the hand, Catherine walked out of the nursery to the bedroom that Jean shared with Sheona Crockett. The bedroom door was closed. "I don't want you to close any of the doors," she said, casting a glance back over her shoulder at Campbell.

"I didn't close any doors."

"Then who did?"

"You know how it is; they blow shut in the wind."

"It's easy to see you've never lived in the royal apartments. We have glass windows. We open the shutters but never the windows."

Campbell stepped forwards.

"Go back and watch over James and Eleanor," Catherine reprimanded him. "If you get me the sack, you'll have no choice but to take me to Loch Awe."

Campbell turned around, walking out of the room and into the nursery. Eleanor was holding a poker in both hands and prodding the logs in the fireplace.

Joan was gripping Catherine's hand tightly and pointing to the heavy wooden door that led to the children's bedroom. The last time she had done this, there was a dead mouse on the floor. Isabella was scared of it and had shut the door so that she did not have to look at it.

Catherine put her hand on the latch and pushed it down. The door swung open slowly. She stepped into the room.

"What is it?" Catherine asked, turning to Joan. She held her arms out with the palms upwards.

Joan pointed to the king's bedchamber. This door was also closed. That usually meant the king and queen wanted privacy, but they were in the dining room with Alexander Lovell, who was keen to impress with wine he had imported from Aquitaine. In winter, the queen liked to spend a long time over the breakfast table eating oatcakes spread with honey and enjoying the attention from her courtiers. The children would get bored and run off, which gave Catherine the excuse to run after them.

Motioning to Joan to stay where she was, Catherine slowly walked to the door. She put a hand on the handle and then hesitated, trembling. A moment of doubt paralysed her. What if Sheona Crockett was inside? She had taken a male servant in there more than once, knowing that no one would disturb them if they were in the royal bedchamber.

Then she plunged the handle down and, with the flat of her hand, pushed the door open a little. She poked her head into the room.

The hunched figure of a monk in his black habit, carefully sweeping the floor, came into view. Catherine relaxed. "It's only a monk!" she announced to Joan. Then she clasped her hands together, to show Joan that this was a friend.

Joan shook her head vigorously.

The door swung open; the monk straightened up.

"There's no need to sweep the floor," Catherine said. "The servants will do that."

The monk nodded respectfully.

Catherine held out a hand. "I'll take the broomstick. I'll give it to my mother; she can fly home on it."

But the monk held onto the broom and began to make his way out of the room.

"You'll be late for Mass," Catherine said.

The monk quickened his pace slightly, his leather boots peeking out from the bottom of his habit.

Didn't the monks at Blackfriars usually wear sandals? "Wait!" Catherine barked, surprising herself at the vehemence in her voice. "Why aren't you in the transept?"

The broom dropped onto the floor with a clatter; Joan turned and ran out of the room. Stars exploded in Catherine's head as the wall rushed forwards and crashed into her. The monk's coarse black habit was all over her; there was a hand over her mouth and a blade at her throat.

His left hand was on her long hair, twisting it tightly till she could not move her neck. The blade in his right hand was cutting into her throat. She couldn't scream, he would cut her throat, and she would be dead without warning the king and queen. The knife was shaking; both his hands were on it, and his other hand had a strong grip of her hair.

His other hand?

Then she was being pushed violently, and the wall shot past her as the room turned upside down. Something hit her hard on the back, and she was looking up at the ceiling. She quickly got up, dizzy, not knowing what to do, and found herself looking at Sean Campbell's broad back. He had got himself in between her and the monk and had a hand on the knife, forcing it backwards.

Catherine looked around for something to pick up—a stick, a broom, even a doll if it was hard enough.

Campbell pushed the monk backwards, and they both fell over with a thump.

A finger went into his eye, and suddenly he could see nothing but stars exploding in the vastness of space. Then they were rolling on the floor together as they fought for the knife.

Catherine picked up the broom, holding it like a spear. She jabbed it downwards, suddenly, the way a poacher might lance a salmon. She aimed for the monk's eyeball, but his head jerked to the side, and she caught him on the cheek. There was the sensation of something giving way, as if she had dislodged a tooth.

The monk's arm was sticking up at an awkward angle and Campbell twisted it back on itself, using his body weight to push downwards. There was a horrible snap, and the arm hung limply at the monk's side, broken at the elbow.

The knife had dropped onto the floor. The monk twisted his shoulders to grasp at it with his good hand. Catherine kicked it across the floor.

Campbell was grasping the throat and squeezing, squeezing, squeezing and the monk was punching him again and again. There was a sudden, sharp pain in his ribs, but he had both hands on the monk's neck now. He could hear the monk gasping, and he knew that he had only to hold on, hold on, and keep holding on. But a knee went into his groin and his whole body was paralysed by crippling pain, and he wanted to be sick, to let go and just be sick, but he held on as the monk writhed this way and that, kicking, scratching, punching as they rolled across the floor.

He was compressing and compressing that squishy neck, his fingers digging into the throat. Both thumbs were on the Adam's apple, pushing it deeper and deeper into the neck.

Something went *pop*. The neck caved in under pressure from Campbell's thumbs.

The knife was on the floor. Campbell picked it up and pushed it through the black habit, into the monk's stomach, and then pushed it further in and twisted it and pushed again to push it even further in. The monk was shaking, retching, and there was blood on the floor now as Campbell twisted the knife again, pushing it up and up till his whole hand had disappeared into the monk's habit. Then the monk was lying still on the floor.

"You killed a monk!" Prince Jamie said.

Catherine looked at the young prince. When had he come into the room?

"That means eternal damnation!" Jamie said.

"I think my soul was damned a long, long time ago," Campbell said wearily.

"My sword!" Jamie exclaimed.

A toy wooden sword lay on the floor. Campbell picked it up and passed it to Jamie. "Thank you, Jamie."

"You killed him with my sword," Jamie said proudly. He held it up. "Look at the blood on it!" He turned and ran out of the room, eager to tell everyone that his wooden sword had killed a man.

Catherine was still holding the broom like a spear.

"Put that away," Campbell said.

Her whole body was trembling. She rested the broom against the wall, turning to grasp Campbell's hand. Then she was pulling him towards her, and her head was on his shoulder. She could not speak. She closed her eyes and took a deep breath. Campbell's hand was wet with sweat. She smiled to herself. These strong men—they felt fear just like the rest of us.

"We should tell the king," she said.

"I suspect Prince Jamie will already have done that."

"Even so." Again, she smiled. "We can't let them catch us alone in a bedroom together. What would my mother say?"

She let go of his hand. The sweat, red like blood, was dripping onto the carpet. Suddenly, she shrieked. "You're bleeding!"

"He did have a knife."

"Get a bucket of water and cloth!" Catherine barked at a surprised-looking Isabella, who had come into the room. "A clean cloth!"

"Is that the man who Jamie killed?" Isabella was looking at the body on the floor.

"Get a bucket of water and a cloth!" Catherine grabbed Campbell's elbow and marched him out of the royal bedroom. She took him through the nursery and then into the ladies' bedrooms.

"Sit down," she said.

"On the bed or the chair?"

"Don't push your luck." She glowered at him. "Now sit on the chair."

There was a Savonarolan chair against the wall. Campbell sat down on it, holding his injured hand firmly and trying to keep the blood from dripping onto the chair.

"Not on that chair!" Jean Lockhart had come in with a bucket of water and a cloth.

"Leave him alone!" Catherine scolded. She turned to Sean Campbell. "Now let me see your hand."

Jean Lockhart set the bucket down at Campbell's feet.

"Is that a wound in your side?" Catherine was staring hard at a wet patch of red emerging on Campbell's left side.

"The king wants to know what happened," Jean said.

"Let me dress his wounds first," Catherine barked.

"A man puts on a monk's black habit and pulls the hood over his head," Campbell said. "He can walk straight in here, and no one asks any questions."

"You only brought one cloth!" Catherine upbraided Jean.

"Isabella said you only wanted one."

"Couldn't you use your common sense for once in your life?"

Jean turned around and went out.

"Let's get your clothes off." Catherine started unravelling his plaid.

"All of them?"

"I need to see where you've been stabbed."

He stood up, pulling the rogart shirt over his head and dropping it on the on the floor. Then he was standing there in tightly fitting woollen hose. But there was a scratch in the material and a wet patch.

"Take those off, too." Catherine dipped the cloth in the water.

"A man should be careful what he wishes for."

"What do you mean?"

"Here I am, undressing in your bedchamber." He rolled the hose down to his knees.

"It's not my bedchamber." Catherine put the cold, wet cloth against the wound in his side.

Campbell winced slightly.

"Hold that there!"

Campbell took hold of the cloth.

Catherine got down onto her knees. Ignoring the dangling, twitching penis, she pressed her palm against the score in his thigh. "Get me another cloth!" she shouted to whoever could hear.

Isabella went running off.

Campbell gasped.

"Is it sore?"

"The things a man has to do to get into a woman's bedroom."

"Oh, be quiet."

CHAPTER 21

"Be quiet!" he whispered, bringing his lips to her ear.

"Oh," she gasped. "Oh, oh, oh."

He was inside her now, his chest pressing against hers, his stomach on hers. Strong arms carrying his weight. She was sweating; he was sweating. She felt him glide across the slippery surface of her stomach.

A bubble of air was caught between her stomach and his. She giggled, feeling it move.

He was going faster, now, faster and faster and not in control and not caring anymore who heard them. Not caring about the head of brown hair and wide, staring eyes that appeared in the room and then vanished. Not caring about the journey or even where he was but only wanting to get to the end. He was a snowball rolling downhill, getting bigger and bigger and going faster and faster towards the crashing oblivion that lay below.

Catherine squealed. That bubble of air—it was tickling, being pushed up her stomach towards her heart. Then it burst as he burst with it, collapsing onto her.

Collapsing into her softness. She was softer than a heather bed. His skin was alive with sensitivity; he was twitching at the touch of her hands on his back. The perfume of her scent was in his nostrils, the wild strands of her hair glinting red in the firelight.

Hard men and hungry women were all he knew from the marches, the sieges, and the battles fought across the continent. Here was something different—nurturing, life-giving femininity. He lay beside her, rolling onto his back and staring up at the ceiling. In these moments, hours could pass like seconds.

Catherine ran her hand across the skin on his stomach, feeling the muscles. She felt surface tension, prodding the firmness of the muscles and feeling the resistance. Then her hand was moving around to the side, where the skin was rough and uneven.

"You have a scar."

"That's what happens when you don't wear a mail shirt."

"You're not wearing one now."

"Why do you think I grabbed the knife?"

Then her hand was moving up to the pectoral muscles. The muscles were soft yet strong—soft with an underlying hardness. She was enjoying the contrast where softness and strength came together in a perfect fusion—like his eyes, where green and brown came together seamlessly.

All these contradictions came together in perfect harmony. Where was the rose without its thorns? she wondered. Beautiful to look at and soft to touch. But those thorns prevented you grasping its stalk and breaking it. It was the thorns that allowed the rose to flower with impunity.

And Sean—his strength gave him his beauty. It gave him that air of confidence he carried. He did not need to brag about the land he owned or the money he had; he was a rose in a field of dandelions, standing tall and elegant with thorns that were never used in aggression and never spoken of but that waited imperiously in silence to impale anyone who attacked it.

Her arms were around him now, and her head was resting on his shoulder. She knew they had stayed too long but was hanging onto this moment, hanging onto him. Eventually she said sadly, reluctantly, "We should be moving."

"Yes."

"Before we are seen."

"Yes," he said. "We're lucky it was young Joan."

Catherine frowned and pushed her head up. "What was young Joan?"

"It was only young Joan who came into the room."

"Young Joan saw us?" Catherine jumped out of bed.

Campbell felt that cold draught where her warm body used to be. "Only for a moment; she came in and then went straight out again."

"Why didn't you tell me this before?"

"She cannot tell anyone."

Catherine was picking up her gown, which had lain, cast aside, on the floor. "She can make herself understood when she wants to."

"You sound like you have been talking to Sean Campbell," King James said.

"You are vulnerable when you are on the road," Queen Joan said.

"My people must see me visit their towns. How else will they know who is their king?"

They were in the dining hall, sitting on the same side of a long table with their backs to the wall. A tall clay jug sat on the table. Alexander Lovell picked it up and filled his cup from it. He looked hard at the wine, sniffing it carefully. "What is this that Your Grace is drinking?"

"It's dandelion wine," King James said.

"It's what the monks drink," Queen Joan said quickly.

"What happened to the shipment of claret I docked at Berwick?"

"It went to Stirling Castle."

"You will be in St John's Town in February?" Lovell asked.

Princess Joan ran into the room on her own. She stood in the centre of the room, where the fire was burning and looked at her mother.

"What is it?" Queen Joan said.

"She can't hear you," James said.

"She understands."

Young Joan took a step forwards, towards the table.

"Go and find Catherine," Queen Joan said.

The princess stopped and looked down at her feet.

"Cath-rinn," the queen said slowly and deliberately.

"There you are!" Catherine rushed into the room, her hair uncombed. She took Joan by the hand and turned to go. "Let's go and look for Isabella!"

"Catherine, your feet are bare!" That was Queen Joan's voice.

Catherine looked down at her bare toes protruding from the hem of her gown.

"You'll catch cold!" Queen Joan scolded her.

"You'll help me find my shoes, won't you?" Catherine said to Princess Joan. "Then we'll go and look for Isabella."

Queen Joan watched Catherine lead the princess out of the room.

"You will be in St John's Town in February?" Alexander Lovell asked again.

"What?" James said.

"You're coming back here in February?"

"I am holding a general council. I have no choice."

"So your enemies know where you will be, with plenty time to prepare," Queen Joan said.

"The king must hold councils and parliaments."

"King Henry holds them in the Tower of London and makes his subjects come to see him."

"Which explains how unpopular he is. Besides," James added, "I want to see my kingdom, not hide in a tower."

"If Your Grace remained in Stirling Castle," Alexander Lovell protested, "you would not be drinking dandelion wine from a clay cup."

"But we are enjoying the hospitality of the monks."

"He likes dandelion wine," Queen Joan said to Lovell.

"But what of your guests? What of Lord Gordon or the Earl of Mar? Let the monks drink their dandelion wine. Your Grace should be impressing his guests with the finest French claret served to him in a silver jug."

"I wish to speak with Your Grace."

Everyone looked around; Sean Campbell had entered the room.

"If a man puts on a black habit and pulls the hood up," Campbell said, "he can walk in here, and no one will stop him or even look twice at him."

"The main door is locked at night," King James said.

"Then it can be locked during the day, also."

"This is a House of God. The monks will say that it is always open to those who seek salvation."

"They must look after the king, their guest. The door can be locked when there is royal business to be done."

"And how would that stop a man dressed in a black habit walking in? A loose habit that can easily hide a weapon?" King James gulped down a couple of mouthfuls of wine. "I have already decided," he announced. "We must have locks on the royal apartments."

"A lock fitted on every door." Lovell frowned as if deep in thought. "I'm sure I could get that done for Your Grace at a good price."

"There's not enough time," Campbell interjected. "This place must be secure on February 4."[14]

"If the job must be done quickly, that would obviously influence the price," Lovell said.

"We don't need locks," Campbell said. "The doors to the royal apartments can be bolted with bars of wood. All you need is an iron stay—a slip rail bracket—to fix the bar to the door and to the wall. You slide the bar through the brackets, and you have a very strong lock."

"The king should have mechanical locks and his own keys," Alexander Lovell said.

"This could be done very quickly," Campbell said. "A carpenter's workshop is always full of wood; he only has to cut some bars to the right length."

"He should use oak," King James said. "Oak is strong."

"A blacksmith can make brackets that the bars can slide through."

"Good," King James said, looking at Campbell. "You will have this done when I am in Linlithgow?"

"It will be done."

"What will the doors look like with rudimentary metal brackets nailed to them?" Alexander Lovell complained. "A decorative iron lock, inscribed with thistles, would be much more fitting for the royal apartments."

"This is a monastery," King James said. "We should respect that."

---

[14] A great council was held in St John's Town (Perth) on February 4, 1437.

"He feels safe because he's in a monastery." Atholl snorted. "Monks will not defend the king."

Blair Castle was a castle without a moat—that was provided by the gurgling River Garry below. Elshender Rutherford had travelled up Glen Garry where the heavy snow and ice had stilled the violent waters. He had made his way uphill to the castle on all fours—his flat-soled leather boots could not get a grip of the hard, icy hillside.

Shivering with cold, Rutherford now stood before Atholl.

"There's a stool by the fire," Atholl said.

But the fire was burning hot, too hot to go near. Rutherford took one step towards the stool and then pulled it towards him. He sat on it, still shaking and shivering. His red hands were numb and stinging with the cold.

"Get him a whisky!" Atholl shouted to a man who was standing at the back of the great hall. The man left quietly, brushing past Robert Graham as he entered.

"What is it?" Graham asked. He came forward, sitting on the bench at the long wooden table.

"Sean Campbell is treacherous."

"What?"

"This is Elshender Rutherford," Atholl said. "Robert Stewart sent him here."

"What of it?"

"He overheard Sean Campbell talking about defending the monastery."

Graham stared hard at Rutherford. "What did you hear him say?"

Atholl waved a hand dismissively. "I can tell you later. First, we must decide what we're going to do."

"He might still be intending to kill the king. I need to know what he said."

"Then you can go to Blackfriars and ask him yourself." Atholl glowered at Graham. "We cannot take any chances here."

A man came in carrying a jug and a quaich.

"Thank you," Graham said, snatching the quaich.

The man looked at Atholl.

"Go and get another," Atholl said wearily.

The man set the jug down on the table and left.

Atholl was thinking aloud. "The monks must all be asleep by nightfall so they can rise early in the morning. The king sits up late in the evening, drinking wine and listening to music."

"He often plays music himself," Graham said.

"He will have some attendants but not many." Atholl smiled as if he thought he had had a brilliant idea. "So that is when you will do it."

Graham looked at him. "*I* will do it?"

"Campbell cannot be trusted."

"You have not given him any money."

"He has not done the deed; why should I give him money?"

"Maybe King James has promised him more."

Atholl continued as if he had not heard that. "The King's Council meets in St John's Town," he said. "The weather will be cold; the roads will be blocked with snow. The king will probably stay in Blackfriars awhile."

"The royal party—"

Atholl cut him short. "Is made up mainly of women and children. The king does not have sentries posted at the doors of a monastery. We only need a small group—four or five men. You get in after midnight, and you go to the royal apartments. There will be no one to stop you."

"The walls are made of stone; the doors are made of oak reinforced with iron."

"The doors will be open."

"All of them?"

"My nephew will make sure of it."

"But Sean Campbell will be there," Graham said.

"You'll have four or five men with you. You can't take on Campbell?"

"What better way to warn the king than by attacking his courtiers?"

"Are you afraid of Campbell?"

"We want this done quickly and quietly."

Atholl hesitated for a moment, as if thinking to himself. Then he said, "Campbell will not be in St John's Town when the King's Council meets."

"How are you going to make sure of that?"

CHAPTER 22

"How do I look?" Queen Joan asked.

Jamie whacked his sword against the carpet.

"Don't do that," the queen said.

Sheona was looking at the queen's lilac gown stretched tightly across her expanding stomach. The young queen had had a fuller bosom. Maybe some material could be taken from the bosom and moved down to the waist? she wondered.

Whack! Whack, went the wooden sword against the carpet.

"Put your sword away."

Jamie swung his sword; the tip of it scratched the queen on the leg.

"Put it away!"

Jamie ignored his mother, slashing at imaginary opponents.

"I'll put it in the fire!" Queen Joan threatened.

Jamie paused, looking at the long wooden sword he was holding and then at the fireplace. "It's too big."

"Put it away, or I'll put it in the fire."

"He's right. It's too big," Catherine said with a giggle.

Joan glowered at Catherine through narrowed eyelids. "Haven't you got something else to do?" She turned to Isabella. "Go and show Lady Catherine the flowers in the garden."

"It's winter; there are no flowers."

"Then show her the statues."

"She's seen them before."

"She wants you to show them to her again," Joan said. She turned to look at Catherine. "Don't you?"

Catherine stood up. "I need the exercise," she said to Isabella, "and the fresh air."

Isabella took Catherine by the hand and led her out of the royal apartments and into the cloisters.

A monk was brushing the stone floor.

Isabella and Catherine sat down on a stone bench. They were looking at a statue of an angel with long hair and wings extended.

"Why doesn't she have pupils?" Isabella asked.

"What?"

"The angel—she has eyes but no pupils."

"That's because she can see everything," Catherine said.

Isabella thought about this for a moment. "Why do you make me go to confession?"

"To tell Jesus about your sins."

"But if He can see everything, He already knows."

"Yes, but you ask His forgiveness."

"But Jesus is all-forgiving; hasn't he forgiven me already?"

"It's polite to ask," Catherine growled.

"Jamie's playing hide-and-seek." That was the queen's voice.

Isabella turned around to see Queen Joan approaching.

"Go and find him!" the queen said.

Isabella jumped down from the stone bench and ran off. Catherine stood up.

"Please sit down," Joan said and sat down on the stone bench. She immediately shuddered. "The bench is cold!"

"I know." Catherine sat down.

"How do the monks put up with it?"

"Let's go inside."

"Not yet." Joan was looking at Catherine.

Catherine groaned inwardly; she could sense what was coming.

A monk was edging his way towards them, carefully brushing the stone floor as if every sweep of the brush was an artist's stroke across canvas.

"He's a very handsome man," Joan said.

"The monk?" Catherine shook her head. "I don't think so."

"Sean Campbell."

"Yes."

"Handsome, tall, strong."

"Yes."

"More handsome than Alexander Lovell."

"Yes."

"But you love Alexander?"

Catherine hesitated. How to describe the tingle she felt on her spine whenever she saw Sean Campbell come walking towards her? The excitement when he was in the same room, her eyes continually being drawn towards him? Wanting to sit next to him, her thigh caressing his but nobody noticing? When he touched her, she felt it through her whole body; when he looked at her, he looked straight into her soul.

Those hazel eyes—sometimes green, sometimes brown. Something she could not pin down. Ballumbie's eyes had no sparkle in them. Did she even know what colour they were? Did she care?

"Alexander is as handsome as Sean?" Queen Joan was prodding, probing.

"Not as handsome."

"Wait till Sean goes off to war and comes back with scars all over his face."

"Why should that make a difference?" Catherine said. But she knew immediately she had spoken too quickly, too spontaneously.

Queen Joan eyed Catherine suspiciously. "You have a chance to make a better life for yourself," she said, "a chance to correct the mistakes of the past." She paused for a moment. "Don't make a mess of it."

The monk had disappeared behind a pillar.

"Marry for money, not for love," Catherine muttered. She avoided the queen's eyes.

"You forget the company you keep," Queen Joan said.

"I am never allowed to forget that."

"I should listen to my children more often," the queen said. "They always know what's going on." She gave Catherine a long, hard stare. "They all like Sean Campbell."

"They're wise enough not to listen to the gossip and rumours of court."

"You like Sean Campbell?"

"What of it?"

"My children all tell me that you like him."

"We should be polite to him for as long as he attends court."

"Why are you so fascinated with this man?"

Because he makes me feel alive. "Can we talk about something else?"

"Your mother will have concerns."

Catherine shot Queen Joan a sideways glance, her mind racing. "You're fond of telling us that the king was a homeless pauper when you met him."

Joan took a breath. "He was not my parents' choice. He had many enemies and few friends when I met him."

"But that changed when he became king?"

"What you have to understand"—Joan paused, as if searching for the right words—"is that parents want the best for their children; you will understand this yourself one day."

The monk had reappeared on the other side of the pillar, always edging closer. Catherine shot him a desperate glance. "Brother Gillespie," she called out.

Queen Joan cut in. "Have you no respect? You must not speak to the monks." She turned to the monk. "You must forgive her, Brother Gillespie."

The monk stood erect, holding the broom in one hand like a weapon. "We do not take an oath of silence at Blackfriars," he said. "My Lady Catherine may speak if she wishes."

"We do not wish to interrupt your work," Queen Joan said.

"My child, everything I do is an act of prayer."

"Should a daughter always obey her parents?" Catherine blurted out.

The monk carefully rested the broom against the pillar, as if taking care neither to dent the broom nor scratch the pillar. "We should respect our parents," he said.

But that was not an answer to the question, and all three knew it.

The monk continued. "If Jesus had obeyed his corporeal father, he would have become a carpenter. Sometimes, there is a higher calling."

"Catherine has made a promise," Queen Joan said.

"My mother made the promise," Catherine said.

Queen Joan frowned. "You have a chance to make your parents very happy," she said to Catherine, "a chance to show your gratitude for all the sacrifices they have made."

Catherine shuddered involuntarily.

"Think about your parents for a moment. Think how disappointed your father will be if you do something foolish again."

Again. Catherine knew what she was referring to. You let your parents down once; don't do it again.

The monk was silent, as if thinking.

Catherine looked at him, waiting for him to speak.

"Everything you do should be done with love," the monk said. "If you make a promise, make it with love. If you keep a promise, keep it with love. If you cannot keep it with love, then break it with love."

"How can you break a man's heart and call it love?" the queen scorned.

Now the monk turned his attention to the queen. "Because he will not want to break your heart in the name of love."

"The promise has been made," Queen Joan said.

"Did you obey your parents when you married King James?" Catherine asked.

Now it was Queen Joan who winced.

"You came here to help an exiled king regain his throne; your mother will be proud of you," the monk said.

"She has not seen me since that day—"

"You will not meet in the afterlife?" Brother Gillespie smiled a knowing smile. "What is ten years set against eternity? What is one hundred years? There is no parting. There is no parting for any of us, at any time."

Queen Joan knitted her brows, thinking about future meetings with her mother. Who would get to say *I told you so?*

"I had my duty to consider," Queen Joan answered. She was trying to think of a way out of this. "I had my duty to the kingdom—my duty to two kingdoms."

"You asked for my advice; I gave it," the monk said. He turned away and picked up his broom.

Queen Joan watched the monk's back and shoulders moving as he reverently brushed the floor. The realisation was slowly dawning on her that she had been dismissed by this man.

Catherine suppressed a smile.

Queen Joan stood up, the anger rising in her chest. "I'm cold," she said, masking her irritation. "We should go inside."

Catherine stood up.

"Men like Sean Campbell," Queen Joan said. "Men like that have their duty to the king, and their duty always comes first. What's he going to do but go off on an adventure one day and get himself killed?"

"I should choose a life entertaining my husband's guests by wearing gowns of silk and serving claret in silver goblets while he talks of trade deals he has struck in Aquitaine or Norroway?"

"He's a burgess; what do you expect him to talk about?"

"I want a man who makes my heart beat faster!" Catherine suddenly blurted out.

But the queen made an unsympathetic audience. "Your father will never give you permission to marry Sean Campbell," she said. "It's not worth thinking about."

"He's getting too big for his boots," Robert Graham said.

"Who?"

"Lamont of Cowal."

"Ambitious men can be useful," Atholl said. "Dunoon Castle stands there, on territory Cowal thinks is his. It's a fishbone stuck in his throat. Every day, he watches the Campbell galleys go up and down Loch Fyne to remind him of his impotence."

"He won't take on Campbell of Loch Awe."

"He might."

"He'd have to be stupid."

Atholl smiled. "Ambitious men are stupid. They are easily bought." He winked to Graham. "Cowal will attack Dunoon if he thinks he has the support of the king."

"King James?"

"Walter the First, King of Scots."

There was a short silence as Atholl waited for Graham's reaction.

"We haven't got you on the throne yet."

"My grandson, Robert Stewart, attends the royal court. He knows what to do."

"He's going to kill the king?" Graham's tone was incredulous.

"Of course not." Atholl gave Graham a cold stare. "You are going to do that."

Graham twitched slightly. "With Campbell there?"

"What of it?"

"Campbell knows me; he knows who I am."

"St John's Town is in the east; Campbell's family is in the west. If he visits his family, you will have plenty time."

"He's not going to visit his family."

"He might have reason to."

Graham knitted his brows. "You will attend the council?"

"Yes."

"You can bring one hundred men—"

"Absolutely not," Atholl cut in with a wave of his hand. "Nothing will happen while I am in St John's Town. I will attend an unremarkable, peaceful session of the King's Council. Afterwards, the citizens of St John's Town will see me take the road to Blair. Only when everyone knows that I have gone will you take action."

A panicking expression passed across Graham's white face.

"No one will suspect that I am involved in this," Atholl said. "But Robert Stewart will help you. Tell him what you need, and he will give it to you."

CHAPTER 23

The stink from the tannery was in his nostrils as he came out of the blacksmith's shop and walked down the earthen track that passed for a street.

He saw her standing in the middle of the road, the hem of her gown trailing in the dirt. He smiled, quickly walking up to her. "We have oak beams three inches thick and six inches broad!" he announced excitedly. "The blacksmith is making slip rail brackets. All the royal apartments will have them. When you need to lock the door, you slide the bolt along the bracket. To open it, you slide it back." He smiled. "All the bedrooms can be locked from the inside."

"If I want to listen to a man tell me how clever he is, I can sit with Alexander Lovell," Catherine said bluntly.

Campbell frowned. "What is it?"

"You do not ask why I am standing in the street?"

No, he had not thought about it. Now he realised how unusual it was to find her in the street without either the queen or the children.

"I was waiting for you to tell me," he said lamely. But this was not true, and he was already feeling guilty.

"We're going back to Stirling," she announced.

"The castle is secure; you will be safe there," he said. As soon as he said the words, he knew he had said the wrong thing.

"Yes."

"I must stay here and oversee the fitting of the bolts to the bedrooms in the monastery."

"I know."

"But you will come back to Blackfriars?"

"If the queen so commands."

Was she saying goodbye to him? Campbell suddenly felt uneasy. "You will be in Stirling," he said with bravado. "I can ride there in a day."

She took a deep breath. Then she said, "My parents have asked for the use of the royal chapel."

"They cannot pray in North Berwick?"

"I am to marry Alexander Lovell."

The ground under Campbell's feet moved slightly. He felt giddy; his heart was racing. His whole body was tense; there was a knot in his stomach.

Catherine looked at him, pleading with her blue eyes.

Suddenly the attack on Melnik Castle seemed easy compared to this. His palms were sweaty. "I will speak to your father."

"No, please don't."

"I will speak to the king."

"My father has the ear of the king."

"The king has two ears," Campbell said. Again, he knew it was the wrong thing to say.

"Goodbye, Sean." Catherine turned and began walking back to the monastery, her eyes downcast.

Campbell grabbed her elbow and pulled her back to him, knowing he was being too rough. "I will ride to Stirling," he said.

"And carry me away?"

"If I have to!"

"My father will never allow it."

"I'll give up everything!" he found himself saying. He did not know what he meant by it. All he knew was that he did not care about anything, any more, except having this woman at his side.

"You can't buy silk in Venice and sell it in Edinburgh."

"I can dig a trench in the ground and plant barley." That was also a stupid thing to say, and he knew it.

She shook her head. "I don't think that's the kind of future my father has in mind for me."

"I will ... I will," he stammered, trying to think of something to say.

"I must get back," she said. "The queen will be wondering where I am."

"I will come to Stirling," Campbell said.

"When?"

"After I finish my work in Blackfriars." He let out a sigh. "The king wants me to go to Linlithgow."

"They're keeping us apart."

"I'll come to Stirling."

"After I am married?"

"No!" he shouted.

She stopped in her tracks, looking down at her feet. "Everybody tells me to—"

"Go to Stirling," he said. "Marry Alexander Lovell. That won't stop me."

"You're going to ride into town on a white horse and carry me away?"

"I have a brown horse. I'll come and get you. I don't care who you're married to."

"You'll get yourself killed."

"Take this." Campbell took Catherine's hand and pushed something into it.

Catherine looked at the wooden handle and short, broad blade. "What's that?"

"It's a *sgian achlais*."

"I know that."

"Then why do you ask?"

"Other men give their women flowers. Or jewellery."

"I was going to give you an amber cairngorm in a gold ring. It belonged to my grandmother."

"Is this some kind of farewell gift?"

"Of course not!"

She looked at the knife in her hand and then at him. "What am I going to do with it?"

"You hide it in your gown."

"That's not what I mean."

"Hide it—and tell no one you have it," Campbell pleaded. "I'm staying here to put bolts on the doors. I won't be around if something happens. If you have a knife, at least I know you have something."

Catherine frowned. "How do I hide a knife?"

"Hide it in your armpit. Tie it to your arm with string."

"You want me to stab Ballumbie?"

"I cannot protect you if you go to Stirling."

"Protect me from Ballumbie?"

"From an assassin who might attack the king."

She was looking up at him with moist blue eyes, deep like the waters of Loch Fyne.

"When this is over, I will come for you with my grandmother's ring and take you to Argyll. You'll like Argyll—there are lochs, mountains, and the sea on the west coast. It's much more beautiful than Stirling or St John's Town."

"I would like that," Catherine said quietly.

"In summer, you can eat blaeberries as they ripen on the mountainside. You can go swimming in Loch Fyne. In the evenings, we can sit on the beach and look up at the stars as we roast fish over an open fire."

Robert Stewart had come out of the monastery and was walking along St John's Town High Street. He walked hurriedly, nervously, looking around as if he thought someone might be watching.

He went into the Thrissil Inn and ordered a pint of wine at the bar. A man wearing a habit like a monk's with the hood still up sat on his own at one of the tables. Stewart took his tankard of wine and sat down next to him.

"The council will be held on February 4, in the royal apartments," the hooded man whispered.

"I know that," Stewart said. "All the earls have been invited." He took a long drink of wine. "Take your hood down," he said. "Nobody cares who you are."

The man took his hood down. "The king is fitting locks to the doors in the royal apartments."

"Bolts, not locks. He's fitting bolts."

"Then it will be your job to make sure the bolts do not work."

"What?"

The man was speaking very quietly. "This is what Lord Atholl says."

"But Sean Campbell is—"

"Sean Campbell will be called away," the hooded man said. "Then you will disable the locks."

The King had breezed through the royal apartments, telling everyone in a loud voice to get ready for the journey to Linlithgow Palace. The real destination was Stirling Castle, but if anyone was planning a surprise for the royal party, they would find themselves waiting on the wrong road.

Catherine was carefully folding up her clothes to pack them into her chest. The chest served as a seat for the small number of guests who were allowed into her bedroom. Her father, puffed up with pride, had paid a carpenter to make it for her when he heard she had been appointed to serve in the royal court.

The chest had travelled with her from Tantallon to Linlithgow and then to Stirling and St John's Town and back again. When her father had presented it to her, the chest had smelled of linseed oil, which had been rubbed into the wood to preserve it. Now, when she looked at it, she saw only the dents and scratches made when courtiers had thrown it up and onto wagons and then down and onto the ground. The chest was always on the move from Linlithgow to Stirling or from Stirling to Linlithgow; it was always being picked up and then thrown down again.

"What's that?" Jean Lockhart screamed in horror.

The knife that Campbell had given Catherine sat on a pile of clothing on her bed. "It's only a sgian achlais." Catherine let out a sigh of relief. "I thought it was a mouse from the way you were shrieking."

"I can see what it is."

"Then why do you ask?"

"Who gave it to you?"

"Why does it matter?"

"Sean Campbell," Jean announced.

"If you already know, why do you ask?"

"Alexander Lovell will give you silk gowns scented with saffron; Sean Campbell gives you the dagger he cut the drummer boy's throat with."

"Don't you have packing to do?"

"What's your mother going to say about this?"

Catherine gave Jean a harsh stare. "Nothing—because you won't tell her."

"If you were fifteen years old, I might understand this. But you're not—you're a grown woman! Catherine, you're twenty-five years old."

"I'm twenty-four."

"Why do you think your parents sent you to court? It was to meet a man like Alexander Lovell."

"Everybody else knows what's best for me. Nobody ever asks me what I want."

"Do you want a man who crawls up sewers? A man who's going to ride off and get killed one day? A man who doesn't have any land or any money to leave you when you become a widow?"

"Don't you have packing to do?"

"He's not the kind of man to stay at home; he'll get bored with you and ride off looking for adventure, telling you that he'll return with gold in his pockets. Then, one day, he'll return with a wooden leg and an eyepatch and his arm in a sling."

"I'll help you with your packing."

"If you marry that man, you're going to spend your future holding out a begging bowl to the passers-by."

"You haven't folded your kirtles."

"I can hear your mother saying I told you so."

"Have you packed the children's things?"

"What do you think I'm doing in here?"

"Spying on me."

"I'm looking for Jamie's wooden sword."

"I haven't seen it."

"No—you have something much better."

Catherine turned away, avoiding eye contact and putting her attention back on folding her clothes.

"Someone needs to knock some sense into your head; that's all I have to say."

Catherine carried on folding her clothes, her back turned to Jean.

"You'll end up pregnant again, and then you'll get the news that Sean Campbell's lying dead in a ditch somewhere in Flanders." Jean turned around and walked out of the bedchamber.

Suddenly Catherine found herself thinking about Margaret. She wished she had Margaret to talk to.

Margaret would understand.

And maybe now, Catherine was beginning to understand Margaret. Sometimes you meet someone who everyone else thinks is completely inappropriate, completely wrong for you.

Because they're thinking about a house with stone walls and shuttered windows, about dining rooms with a table, chairs, and silver plates. They're thinking about a warm house, about venison cooking over the fireplace and the smell of pine logs burning.

They're not thinking about the dread in your heart when your husband returns home or the relief you feel when he goes away on business. They're not thinking about the loneliness you feel in a house that is full of people.

Maybe now I understand you, Margaret. Yearning to be loved, needing to be loved, wanting to be loved. Then a man comes along and takes all the pain away.

Then, next morning, the man has gone, and the pain is back. But he still gave you an evening when the pain was not there. The loneliness, the fear—none of these things were there. For one evening, his body merged into yours. His heart was your heart; your heart was his heart. Your breath was in his mouth; his breath was in yours.

Afterwards, you meet with tutting disapproval and gossips discussing your folly behind your back and secretly enjoying the prospect of your fall from grace. But they don't understand the pulsing throbbing sensation and the tingling pleasure rising and exploding in your head. When he left in the morning, he left a part of himself inside you.

How judgemental was I? Catherine wondered. How did I speak to you, Margaret? Did I roll my eyes like I knew better? Why didn't you tell me that, for twenty years, you had been dead, but for one evening you had discovered what it was to feel alive?

Why didn't you explain that to me?

Or maybe you did but I didn't listen?

Nervous, excited, uncomfortable, unable to settle, Catherine lay awake in bed with her eyes wide open. The room was dark, lit only by the solitary candle burning slowly at the bedside.

The minstrels had stopped playing; the king and queen had retired to bed. On the pretext that she had a headache, Catherine had excused herself to take a walk along the battlements in the cool night air.

It was cold outside; her breath condensing in front of her. The town was quiet; the faint sounds of drunken singing in the inns drifted through the air and along the streets. Having stepped outside, she turned to look behind her. On seeing that no one was following, she took off her shoes and stepped back into the royal apartments in her bare feet.

Instead of going back to the Dining-Hall and then to her own bedchamber, she turned in a different direction and pushed open a different door. She made her way silently along a narrow passageway and pushed open another door. She pulled off her gown and let it drop onto the floor.

Naked, shivering, she lay on top of the blankets, turning first onto her right side and then onto her left. But it was more than the freezing temperatures that kept her awake, more than the eerie dance of the shadows on the walls.

It was more than the certain knowledge that Sheona and Jean would be gossiping about her behind her back: Where was she tonight? How long was that walk along the cloisters for some fresh air under the night sky? How many times can you go around the cloisters?

The blankets felt rough against her skin, and she turned onto her back and looked up at the rafters, studying the strands of cobweb that dangled downwards and drifted from side to side. Then she smiled to herself and looked down at her belly, picturing it growing larger every day, running a hand over it and prodding the skin that was soft and springy.

Then she heard noises—the creak of the door opening and the dull thud of a bolt being pushed into place and footsteps on the floorboards. She watched the door attentively. It swung open, and he stood there, his face pale in the candlelight. "What are you doing here?"

She drew back the blankets, inviting him to join her. "I couldn't sleep; I went for a stroll along the cloisters."

"Like that?"

"Sheona and Jean will be asleep when I go back; they'll never know how long I was away."

He pulled the shirt over his head and stood in front of her, the sweat on his skin glistening softly in the candlelight.

She reached out her arms for him as he clambered onto the bed. He put a hand on her belly, stroking it gently.

One day that belly would be carrying his child.

He brought his lips up to hers, kissing her softly and then bringing his mouth up to her nose. She closed her eyes, letting him kiss her cheeks, her nose, her eyelids, her brow.

His lips were warm. And they were wet, beautifully wet. She smiled, enjoying the lightness of his touch. His rough, unshaven chin was caressing her cheek. Lying on her back, she kneaded his pectoral muscles with her fingers—soft to touch with that underlying firmness.

His body was over hers, resting his weight on his elbows and his knees. Her hands worked their way round to his back; his lips were on hers now, and his tongue was in her mouth.

Take this used body, this bruised heart.

She gasped as he entered her. Then she was holding him tight, their bodies moving together rhythmically. His hands were in her hair, his sweat on her chest, and her sweat on his.

"Oh," she gasped, the words ejaculating from her mouth and shooting up towards the roofbeams.

"Oh," he said.

"Oh, oh, oh."

She might be overheard; she might be seen going back to her bedchamber. *Oh, but I would give up the rest of my life for one night here with you.*

CHAPTER 24

"Now we will have some time for silent prayer," Abbot Henry said. Then he added, quietly, "Until His Grace returns."

Two monks were walking through the cloisters towards the gardens at the back. Also coming through the cloisters with a heavy wooden bolt on his shoulder was Sean Campbell.

Sean Campbell stopped for a moment, turning to the monks. "The royal party has left?"

"Yes. How peaceful is the monastery is now!"

"They didn't wait for breakfast?"

"They have had breakfast."

There was a loud clatter as Campbell dropped the bolt and ran through the royal apartments, running through one empty room after another.

He came out onto the High Street where the train of carriages and wagons was already in the distance and bumping along the road.

He had wanted to stroke her hair and then pull her towards him to give her one last long kiss, not caring who saw them. Instead, here he was watching the back end of a wagon grow smaller and smaller with horsemen on either side of it.

He held up a hand to wave, but who was he waving to? He watched, hoping Catherine would push her head out of the window and look back.

He ran after the wagon, not knowing what he was doing, till the wall of the monastery was behind him and the road curved behind some trees. One by one, the carriages and the wagons disappeared behind the trees. Still he stood there, his eyes on the trees, watching. He watched the trees without seeing them as other travellers rode up and down the road with horses and carts; he watched the trees' shadows shortening and the sun rising into the sky.

"Stop wasting time," a voice said.

Campbell turned around to find Walter FitzRoland standing behind him.

"We have work to do," FitzRoland said.

"Yes."

With FitzRoland beside him, Sean Campbell walked back into the town, never feeling more alone in his life.

A man was kicking a football down the street; the archery targets in the North Inch were being taken down.

Campbell turned and followed FitzRoland into Blackfriars Monastery and then into the royal apartments.

"You'll have to tell me where we're going," FitzRoland said.

"The king and queen's bedchamber."

They passed through the nursery and the ladies' bedchambers and then the children's bedchamber till they were in the royal bedchamber.

"I couldn't sleep in a bed like that," Walter FitzRoland said. "Could you?"

Campbell looked at the heavy, four-poster bed enclosed by curtains. "You're not going to tell me you prefer the open air and a bed of heather?"

"They draw the curtains when they go to sleep. You're sleeping in total darkness. Anybody could approach you during the night; you'd never know."

"You'd rather lie on the floor with a drawn sword at your side?"

"I couldn't sleep in that bed with the curtains drawn," FitzRoland said. "I wouldn't want to sleep on the floor, either; the wood smells damp."

"That's not the wood you're smelling; that's the sewer underneath."

FitzRoland look at the large carpet spread across the floor with a long, broad cross on it against a background of red and yellow squares. "Is that a Persian carpet?"

"That's what Alexander Lovell says."

"Let's get on with this," FitzRoland said. "What are we meant to be doing?"

"You've never fixed a bolt to a door, before?"

"I'm not a carpenter."

"A blacksmith made the bolts, not a carpenter."

"You mean the blacksmith made the brackets to hold the bolts?"

"Oh, let's get on with it," Campbell said. He picked up one of the iron slide rail brackets that was lying on the carpet.

Campbell held the bracket against the door. It had small holes at the top and bottom, and FitzRoland carefully placed a nail against the hole and then tapped it several times with the hammer, nudging the nail into the wood. Then he took one hand off the nail so that both his hands were on the hammer and hammered it into the door with ringing blows.

They did the same with another nail, fixing the bottom of the bracket to the door. Then Campbell picked up a second bracket and set it against the wall, parallel to the first. Again, FitzRoland hammered it into the wall with ringing blows.

They picked up a wooden beam and threaded it through the brackets. Then they stood back and looked at it, pleased with their handiwork.

"Now the king can sleep easily in his bed with the curtains drawn," Campbell said. "Nobody's getting through that door."

"How's he going to get dressed in the morning?" FitzRoland asked. "His personal dresser comes through with his hose, his doublet, and his cloak."

"Then he will just have to wait."

"That's all they do, anyway—stand around all day and wait for the king."

"They call it a privilege—waiting around for the king to change his underwear."

"It's a bit easier than scaling the walls of castles."

"And better paid."

"Maybe the joke's on us?"

But Campbell was in no mood to joke. "Let's get the other rooms done," he said.

"Other rooms?"

"We're doing all the rooms in the royal apartments."

"You didn't tell me that before."

"I'm telling you now."

"Where are the brackets and bolts?"

"The blacksmith is making more."

"Oh." FitzRoland groaned.

"He will bring a cartload down when he is ready."

"We could go to the smithy to check on his progress?" FitzRoland suggested.

"And pass the Thrissil Inn on the way?"

"You're so lucky, Catherine!" Lady Douglas said.

The wagons had rolled into Stirling Castle; Catherine had gone to sit on a wooden bench in the royal chapel. She looked around to see the imposing figure of her mother standing in the doorway.

"So lucky," Lady Douglas said. "Getting married in the royal chapel at Stirling Castle by the Bishop of Dunkeld!"

Catherine had come to the chapel to be alone for a few moments. But the moment was ruined; she stood up.

"That's right. You won't be standing there. That's where I will be sitting."

Catherine stepped into the aisle; she could feel her heart sinking into the stone floor.

"You're so lucky!" Lady Douglas enthused. "I was married by a priest in Tantallon Castle—not by the Bishop of Dunkeld in the king's own chapel."

"Catherine!" That was a different voice.

Catherine turned around to see Jean Lockhart standing in the doorway.

"She's thinking about her big day!" Lady Douglas announced. She turned to Catherine. "You don't need to worry, my darling. You don't have to do anything, either. You don't even have to get dressed; the courtiers will make sure you do that."

"Her Grace wishes to see me?" Catherine asked hopefully.

Jean took a step into the chapel. "No … eh … well … not right away."

"Won't she look nice in red?" Lady Douglas asked Jean.

"She's wearing a red wedding dress?" Jean asked.

"Yes!" Lady Douglas enthused. "And red, well, it's so expensive. They make the dye from the root of the madder plant. Alexander imports it from Venice."

"He gets it from Berwick," Catherine said.

"And how does it get to Berwick? It comes from Venice."

"Marseille," Catherine said.

"Do you have to contradict everything I say?" Lady Douglas turned to Jean Lockhart. "She'll have a red gown with the shoulders bare—this is what they wear in Venice." She turned back to Catherine. "You're so lucky, Catherine! When I got married to your father, I didn't know what they were wearing in Venice. And if I had, well, I would never have had the courage to ask for it, because I know what my mother would have said."

"I've never seen you wearing red," Jean Lockhart said to Catherine.

"She'll look beautiful in red; the colour will match her hair."

"I don't have red hair."

"I didn't say you had red hair; I said it would match your hair."

"I like wearing green."

"She looks nice in green," Jean Lockhart offered.

"She can't wear green. Teuchters[15] wear green. My daughter is only getting married once in her life; she can't have a colour like green. What will my cousins think? What will the Lennox Stewarts think? What will the Lindsays or Ramsays think, when they hear my daughter got married in green?"

Catherine shot pleading eyes at Jean Lockhart. "We should not keep the queen waiting."

"You don't realise how lucky you are," Lady Douglas continued. "A lot of young women would give their right arms to have a life like yours."

"You're right, Catherine," Jean said. "Maybe we should go and see what the queen wants."

"You said Her Grace didn't want to see Catherine," Lady Douglas said.

"Not right away. Not immediately. But she does want to see her."

---

[15] Peasants

"That doesn't make any sense. Does Her Grace want to see my daughter or doesn't she?"

Jean hesitated for a moment. Then she said, "Yes, she does."

"Then let's go now."

"No … em … it was only Catherine she wanted to see."

"Why didn't you say this when you came in?"

"I did."

"No, you didn't."

"I'm going!" Catherine announced, relieved to know her mother was not following her as she walked out of the chapel. "This is what I used to have to do at home; work was the only way I could get away from my mother," she said to Jean as they stepped into the court.

A light rain was falling. A spot hit Catherine on the nose.

"When I got dressed in the morning, I always had the wrong kirtle on. I dreaded going down to breakfast because there was no escape from her. The whole family would sit and eat together. My kirtle would be wrong, my hair would be wrong. If I tried to make myself useful by working in the kitchen, everything I did would be wrong. I always had my mother standing over my shoulder, watching what I was doing. If I was plucking a pheasant, it was never done properly. But how would she know? She's never plucked a pheasant in her life. That didn't stop her telling me how to do it, though. And hanging the bird afterwards—it was always too high or too low or too near the fire. But I could work in the stables. Mother didn't go near the stables, but father liked the idea. Maybe he thought I'd go hunting with him when I grew up. But I just liked being with the horses."

They turned into the royal apartments and made their way through the rooms. Isabella was skipping with a rope.

"You should do that outside," Jean said.

"Where's your mother?" Catherine asked.

Isabella stopped skipping. "She's teaching Jamie how to play chess."

"Why aren't you playing?"

"It's a silly game."

Catherine carried on, walking to the nursery. Queen Joan was sitting on the floor with Jamie; a chessboard lay between them.

"Did you want me, Your Grace?" Catherine asked.

Queen Joan looked up and frowned. "Well, yes, but not right at this moment." She looked over Catherine's shoulder. "Didn't I make that clear to you?"

"I thought—" Jean stammered.

"Not clear enough, obviously." Queen Joan turned back to the board. "No, you can't move that piece there."

"You said the bishop could move two squares," Jamie said.

"Two squares diagonally," Queen Joan said.

"There's a king, but there isn't a queen," Isabella said. "That's not fair."

"The king has a counsellor," Queen Joan said.

"Father has lots of counsellors," Isabella said.

"This king only has one."

"He doesn't have a queen?"

"No."

"He must rule a very small country if no one wants to marry him," Isabella said, "and he only has one counsellor."

"When Father holds Council meetings, hundreds of people are there," Jamie said.

"What's the bishop doing there?" Jean asked.

Isabella rolled her eyes. "He moves diagonally."

"Two squares diagonally," Jamie said.

"No. What I mean is, How's a bishop going to kill someone?" Jean asked. "He doesn't have a sword."

"The piece looks like a bishop's hat," Queen Joan said. "That's why we call it a bishop."

"The chariot looks like a tower," Isabella said. "How can a tower move up and down the board?"

Queen Joan stood up. "Lady Jean will teach you chess," she said to Jamie. "Catherine, come with me."

Catherine followed the queen out of the nursery and into her bedchamber. The bed had been made carefully, with the heavy curtains tied to each of the four pillars. Two wooden Savonarolan chairs with ornate thistles carved into their arms sat by the wall. Queen Joan motioned to Catherine to sit on one.

The two women sat down.

"His Grace and I must return to St John's Town for the great council," she said. "The children will remain here."

Catherine nodded.

"One of the ladies-in-waiting will come with us."

Catherine waited expectantly.

"Jean is very good with the children; they are all very fond of her. She should stay here."

"Yes, Your Grace."

"Sean Campbell will be in Blackfriars," Queen Joan said.

"Yes, Your Grace."

"Your parents have worked hard to give you this opportunity."

Catherine frowned. "To gain employment in court?"

Queen Joan shook her head. "You know what I mean."

Catherine felt her heart sinking. "Is Your Grace referring to Alexander Lovell?"

"Your parents have found a good match for you."

"He's a burgess; my father is—"

"A very disappointed man," Queen Joan cut in. "Your father expected you to marry the youngest son of the Earl of Lennox." She paused to take a breath. "But he is married to the youngest daughter of the Earl of Buchan."

"I know what happened, Your Grace."

"All that work your parents did, providing you with a suitable match—"

"I didn't like the look of him—or the smell."

"It was a match that would have secured your future if you hadn't …if you hadn't—"

"I was fourteen years old," Catherine said.

"If you hadn't lost your maidenhood." Queen Joan shuddered. "To this day, your mother cannot bear to talk about it."

"Iain MacDougall was—"

"Completely inappropriate for you." Queen Joan shook her head. "Completely inappropriate."

"My mother—"

"Was mortified."

"You are fond of telling us you married for love."

"Yes, I was young once. But now I'm a parent, and I understand how parents think. We think about our children; we think about what's best for them."

"I suppose my parents were thinking about me when they shut me in Tantallon Castle?"

"They were protecting you."

"They shut me away because I was an embarrassment to them."

"You should be more grateful."

"Grateful?" Catherine gasped. "They never let me see my daughter again. They took her away from me as soon as—"

"That was for your own good, for your own reputation."

"I spent years spinning cloth in Tantallon Castle wondering what happened to my baby."

"They found a good home for it."

"Her. They found a home for *her*."

"It was better that you didn't see it again."

"They kept me in Tantallon for years."

"They had to wait until everybody forgot about what you did."

"All I did was fall in love."

"You fall in love, you fall out of love; these things are not permanent. Alexander Lovell has land. The land was there before you were born; it will be there after you die. Land makes a much better basis for a union than whimsical feelings of love." Queen Joan smiled, her tone softening. "We were all young once, Catherine. When you are older, you will understand these things."

"I spent the best years of my life behind the walls of Tantallon Castle."

"And what you don't understand—what you don't understand—is that your parents are always trying to do their best for you. Look at you now—you're a lady-in-waiting who's going to marry a wealthy burgess. You should be more grateful, my lass. Not everyone gets a second chance."

A second chance to do what? Catherine wondered. A second chance to be miserable? A second chance to feel trapped?

"I'm surprised no one has told him about your past. A man like that will catch the eye of other families. There are always plenty of fathers of unmarried daughters seeking to do their best for their children."

"Yes, Your Grace," Catherine said quietly, her head bowed.

"Now go back to your bedchamber and prepare for your return to Blackfriars."

"We have only just got here, Your Grace!"

"Yes." Queen Joan smiled. "We said we were going to Linlithgow Palace, but we went to Stirling Castle instead. Now we are going back to Blackfriars Monastery. My Lord Atholl will not know what to think."

Catherine stood up and walked out of the queen's bedchamber, passing through the children's bedchambers till she got to her own. She stripped her bed back to the network of ropes that criss-crossed the empty wooden frame like the rigging on a ship. On top of the ropes lay the feather mattress. On top of the mattress lay the knife, the sgian achlais, that Sean Campbell had given her.

"What's this?" Sheona's loud voice demanded.

Catherine turned around. Sheona had come into the room and was standing with hands on hips and a horrified expression on her face.

"You know what it is." Catherine picked up the woollen blanket and spread it over the mattress.

The knife was something to sleep with every night, her hands on the leather sheath. Underneath the firm sheath was a steel blade. It reminded her of him—strength and firmness underneath the soft exterior.

She envied male bodies—all that smooth skin but, underneath it, firm muscle. The female body collapsed after childbirth. When her father's roving eye strayed to other women, her mother always blamed her. "You gave me this stomach," she would say as if it was a debt Catherine had to spend the rest of her life repaying.

How unfair it was that the male body kept its shape. The pectoral muscles, the stomach—everything was soft to touch yet with an underlying hint of hardness. Soft and smooth on the outside but hard underneath. If she squeezed, her fingers encountered deeper and deeper layers of firmness. He seemed to get stronger and stronger the further she probed.

Her hands on the sheath were like her hands on his hard penis; she could squeeze it and feel the underlying resistance like it was a rod of iron. She could lie in bed, drawing back the sheath like she was drawing back his foreskin.

Wringing wet clothes as you washed them, twisting them and squeezing them and feeling the cold water gush through your fingers—the cloth gave way as the water poured out, but then the water was gone and there was nothing left to give, and the roll of material lay tough between your fingers. This was the male body—softness and strength. Giving way like an oak bending in the high winds till it could bend no more and it remained there unmoved, untouchable, as its awesome, imposing, comforting, protective strength was revealed.

"Other girls sleep with their dolls," Sheona said.

"We're all a bit old for that, aren't we?"

"So why are you sleeping with a knife?"

"It's none of your business."

"It reminds you of him?"

"Why are you asking if you already know?"

"I was hoping you were going to tell me something different."

To have it in the bed with me, my fingers closing around it. It's his penis I am holding onto.

CHAPTER 25

"Shouldn't it have cinnamon in it?" Bishop Wishart asked.

"Mainly almonds, perhaps a touch of cinnamon," King James said.

"Chicken, rice, almonds—all boiled in milk," Queen Joan said.

Bishop Wishart fingered the sticky substance. "So this is what they eat in the French court?"

"They eat it in Denmark, too, and in Venice."

"But the French gave it the name *blancmange*," Bishop Wishart said. "I wonder what they call it in Denmark?" He was sitting with his back to the wall and looking down the room as if the answer lay hidden in one of the tapestries that hung from the walls.

King James motioned to a servant. "Give the bishop more wine."

"Ah, yes, the blood of Christ."

The servant came over with a jug and poured some wine into the bishop's cup before bowing and stepping back.

Bishop Wishart put the cup to his lips. He frowned. "Is there some honey to sweeten the wine?"

King James shot a glance at one of the servants, who quickly disappeared.

"You are returning to St John's Town, Your Grace?" Bishop Wishart said.

"Yes," King James said.

"But you are not taking the children with you?"

"No."

"A sensible idea. They will get bored on the long journey."

"They like the journey," Queen Joan said. "They get bored in the castle."

"But you are not taking the ladies-in-waiting."

"Only Catherine."

King James gave Queen Joan a sideways glance. "Jean is your favourite."

"I don't have a favourite," Joan said.

"I always thought—"

"What?"

"Between you and Catherine, there's a little bit of tension."

"Maybe I see something of myself in her," Queen Joan said.

"Who will dress you in the morning?"

"You enjoy undressing me; maybe you should dress me for a change," Joan said a little too quickly. Then she remembered Bishop Wishart was sitting on the other side of her husband.

Bishop Wishart decided to move the conversation on quickly. "Lady Catherine is promised to Alexander Lovell," he said.

"He does not really have her status," James said. A piece of chicken had caught in his teeth.

"Catherine should not worry about his status," Bishop Wishart said.

"Lord and Lady Douglas are very pleased with the match," Joan said.

"Catherine is happy?" Bishop Wishart asked.

"Catherine respects her parents and wishes to make them happy," Joan said.

"Catherine does not have feelings for another?" Bishop Wishart asked.

"Who told you this?" James asked.

"You're the king, and you don't know what's going on under your own nose?" Joan let out an exasperated sigh. "What would you do without me?"

"Are Catherine's parents respecting her wishes?" Bishop Wishart asked.

"Did Catherine come crying to you in the chapel?" Joan asked.

"Catherine is part of my flock, as is Your Grace."

"We all know what it's like to have our heads turned by love," Joan said. "Sometimes you meet someone who is inappropriate, completely wrong for you, but you just want to go for it!" Joan picked up her cup of wine. She had uttered the words instinctively, unconsciously, without even realising it.

James gave the queen a curious stare.

"Wasn't someone bringing honey for the wine?" Joan said as she gulped from the cup.

James nodded to another servant, who quickly left the room.

"Once, there was a carpenter and an emperor. Who did Our Lord choose to be his mortal father in earthly flesh and blood?"

"I know, I know. The burgess is the equal of the knight," James said. "But please don't say that in front of any of my knights."

"What is important is what's in your heart," Bishop Wishart said.

"You don't understand," Queen Joan said.

"Alexander Lovell does not have a heart?" the bishop asked.

"What I mean is, what you have to understand is, Catherine let her parents down once before—let herself down, I mean."

Bishop Wishart spoke slowly, carefully. "Would it not be more sensible to make sure she stays in Stirling?"

"I'm a woman; I understand how she feels." Queen Joan smiled weakly. "We have all been in love."

"Sean Campbell is in St John's Town," James said. "Do you want Catherine to be spending next winter in Glen Esk like Margaret FitzRoland?"

There was sudden silence. James had spoken too quickly, and he knew it.

"What do you mean by that?" the bishop asked.

"He means I should keep watch over her until her marriage," the queen said, coming to the rescue.

"It is for her own good. Alexander Lovell is a burgess," the bishop said.

"A very successful one," James said. "He is wealthy."

"Catherine is—" the bishop began.

"Very lucky," the queen cut in.

"And so is Alexander Lovell," James said. "He will gain status and influence. This marriage is a good business transaction for him."

"Does Alexander Lovell love Catherine?" Bishop Wishart asked.

Queen Joan spotted a servant entering the great hall. "Ah!" she exclaimed. "The bishop wishes some honey to sweeten his wine."

A servant approached with a piece of honeycomb on a plate. He cut off a piece with a knife and stirred it into the bishop's wine.

"Merchants," the bishop said, answering his own question, "they come into the chapel with silver in their pockets and take their seats close to the high altar as if they think the Almighty cannot see those who sit at the back." He leaned forwards, so that he could make eye contact with Queen Joan, who sat on the other side of King James. "You were the great-granddaughter of King Edward III when you met your husband."

Joan smiled at the memory.

"How many times have you told me that he was a penniless refugee?"

James looked at Joan. "You told him that?"

Joan looked down at the tabletop, avoiding his eyes.

"Other suitors had land," Bishop Wishart continued, "huge estates with tall towers and forests for hunting. King James gave you a poem.[16]"

"She still reads it," James said.

"It was a beautiful poem," Joan said quietly.

"I had a desk in my room in the tower," James said. "I used to sit at the window, writing that poem as I looked down at the people walking in the garden at Windsor Castle."

"I was the only one you looked at," Joan said.

"Some of the milkmaids were very attractive," James said.

"They never walked in the garden. You never got near any of them."

"They brought the milk into the dining hall."

"And they served King Henry first. They didn't notice you."

"They were looking at me while they served Henry."

"You were the only man wearing rags."

"He was handsome?" Bishop Wishart asked.

"He still is," Joan smiled.

"And strong?"

"I was the only person who spoke to the king like an equal."

"This is King Henry V?"

---

[16] *The Kingis Quair*

"Everyone else bowed or curtseyed to him and waited for him to speak before they spoke back. They agreed with everything he said. I was the only one who told him the truth. He respected me for it."

"He couldn't understand your accent," Joan retorted. "If he'd known what you were saying to him, your head would have been on a pole outside the Tower of London."

Bishop Wishart persisted. "You could have had the hand of an English noble with vast estates," he said to the queen. "Instead you chose banishment with a pauper."

"Banishment!" James protested. "This is the most beautiful country in the world."

"And the coldest."

"You're a queen, now; what were you before?"

"Warm."

"A marriage between a king and queen is usually a treaty between nations," Bishop Wishart said. "He had nothing when you met him; you came up here with nothing. It's beautiful."

"She knew she was going to be Queen of Scots," James said.

"If someone didn't thrust a dagger between your shoulder blades," Joan said.

"If His Grace wished to reclaim his kingdom, he would have been goodly advised to marry the daughter of a Scottish noble and build alliances that way. Instead, he came north with the woman he loved."

"He needed someone at his side he could trust," Joan said. "When we were in the English court, nobody had anything to gain from his murder. We come up here, and all I see are nobles looking at his throne and picturing themselves upon it."

Bishop Wishart smiled. "You came up here with him to help him reclaim what is rightfully his. Life would have been easier for you if you had stayed in the English court. But you did not take the easy path. Something else was driving you."

"Lust," James said.

"Lunacy," Joan said.

The children were in bed; the King and Queen were entertaining Bishop Wishart. Catherine came out of the royal apartments and walked across the courtyard, the *crimp, crimp* of the snow compressing underneath her feet. She felt the sharpness of the air, her breath condensing in front of her eyes, and watched the bright stars in the black sky. Above her head was the Plough with its beam and coulter was ready to carve a furrow through the constellation Perseus.

She walked carefully, her heavy mantle pulled around her. In front of her lay the battlements crusted with snow—a light topping on the grey stone like the top layer of pastry on a blaeberry pie. In summer, she might have leaned against the stone and rested her chin on her folded arms as she gazed across the Valley of the Forth where the river wound its way through the boggy flatlands under the gaze of the thickly wooded hills to the north. Tonight, she approached the cold stone battlements warily and stopped more than a foot away.

Her leather shoes were wet in the inch-deep snow. Her feet were cold. "Catherine, come inside!" she could hear her mother saying. She was always being told to, "Come inside!" like she was an embarrassment, something to be hidden from view. Even in summer, she'd be called in. Taking shelter under the oak tree in the gentle rain, she'd listen to the rhythm of the raindrops against the oak leaves and let the rain massage her hair. She'd lean her back against the tree's rough bark, its protective branches above and on either side like they wanted to embrace her.

Then her mother's hectoring voice would sound from the portcullis: "*Catherine, come inside!*"

She shivered. Was she shivering from the memory or from the cold? Or from both? Everybody else knew what was best for her—her mother, Queen Joan, and even Sheona Crockett. Nobody trusted her to take her own decisions.

She would come out onto the battlements during those winter nights at Tantallon when the others were asleep or getting drunk in front of the raging log fire. Here she was again with the Seven Sisters, sparkling white against the dark sky. Zeus had turned them into white doves to fly out of reach of the predatory Orion; and there they were now, above her head, shimmering in their purity.

Purity.

Something she did not have.

"I used to enjoy throwing snowballs." A male voice crashed through the silence.

Catherine turned to see a dark shadow approaching against the night sky.

"I used to make snowballs and stack them up like they were cannonballs. Then I would throw them over the battlements, imagining they were cannonballs."

The voice belonged to Robert Stewart, the king's chamberlain. Had he followed her out here?

"I can't do it now," Stewart said. "It's unbecoming. That's what the king says. I might hit someone." He drew closer to her. "Who am I going to hit? The traders at the *mercat cross*[17] are too far away. A few beggars might approach the castle, chancing their luck if they know the king's in town. But who cares about them?"

He was standing beside her now.

"Nobody's allowed to enjoy themselves in King James's Court," he said. "Nobody's allowed to play football; we all must spend our spare time at archery practise."

"The king and queen are entertaining Bishop Wishart; should you not be in attendance?"

"They don't care about me."

"I should go inside," Catherine said.

"Wait a moment."

"I can't."

His hand gripped her elbow through the mantle.

"I'm cold," she said.

"The chapel's never locked. We could go in there."

"The chapel's cold."

"I'll keep you warm, Catherine." Now he had a firm grip of both her elbows, his fingers digging into her flesh. "This is your last chance to sleep with a man before you marry that peacock."

"Let go of me!"

"He'll never know. And even if he does, he'll never do anything about it."

---

[17] Market Cross

"I said let go of me!"

He pushed her backwards. She stumbled slightly. Her mantle was flapping open.

"I'll scream!" she threatened.

Her smooth leather soles were slipping on the snow. If she fell backwards, he would be on top of her. He was too big for her and too strong; he was turning her sideways as if he was manoeuvring her towards the chapel.

"Your Grace!" she shouted into the night air.

He had one arm around her waist now and a firm grip on the wrist of her right hand.

"Bishop Wishart!" she shouted, louder this time.

Her arms were free, he had let go of her, and she punched him hard on the jaw with her left arm.

He did not move, did not flinch.

"King James won't always be here to protect you," he said.

She turned away, stumbling and running across the snow. Her right foot slipped, and her whole body thumped into the snow and the hard stone floor that lay underneath. Then she was up on her feet again and running into the royal apartments.

The king's presence chamber was empty, and she stopped running, looking behind to make sure no one was following. Her shoes were gripping the carpet now, and she could walk more easily. She passed through the dining hall where a cluster of servants attended to the king and queen. who were still talking to Bishop Wishart.

"Catherine, you're shaking!" Queen Joan said.

"I've been outside. It's cold."

"You've scraped your nose."

"I slipped on some ice."

"Have a seat by the fire and a cup of claret."

"Thank you, Your Grace, but I think I should go to bed."

"As you wish."

"Goodnight, Your Grace." Catherine curtseyed to the queen, king, and Bishop Wishart.

"Goodnight."

She pushed open the oak door and walked through the nursery and through Sheona and Jean's bedchamber.

Catherine took off her mantle, folded it and carefully placed it on the Savonarolan chair that sat at the bottom of her bed.

"What did he mean by that?" Catherine wondered aloud.

"What?" Sheona had wakened up and was standing by the door.

"I was talking to myself; I thought you were asleep."

"You're shaking. Where have you been?"

"I've been outside; it's cold. I slipped and fell."

"What did who mean by what?"

"What?"

"You said, 'What did he mean by that?'"

Catherine sat down on her bed.

"You shouldn't do that; you'll make the ropes sag."

"Yes, I know." Catherine stood up again.

"So?"

"So what?"

"What did who mean by what?"

Catherine pulled her kirtle over her head and folded it and placed it on top of her mantle. "It's probably nothing."

"What's probably nothing?"

"He said King James won't always be here to protect me."

"Who said that?"

"Robert Stewart." Catherine pulled on a thin linen shift.

"The chamberlain?"

"Who else do you know called Robert Stewart?"

"There was a boy in Aberbrothock[18] with that name."

"You know what I mean."

"You're marrying Alexander Lovell. That's all he means. Once you're married …" Sheona screwed up her face. "Hmmm."

"What is it?"

"I wouldn't want to be depending on Alexander Lovell to protect me from … well, anybody. Look, I'm sure everything will be all right."

"Do you think I should tell the king?"

"Tell him what?"

---

[18] Arbroath

"What Robert Stewart said!"

Sheona looked at Catherine; the candlelight was showing the contours in her body underneath the thin nightgown. "You're not going into the dining hall dressed like that, not when Bishop Wishart's there," she said. "Now blow out the candles and let's get some sleep."

CHAPTER 26

"I heard he was shaking with fear." Robert Graham was sitting at a dirty splintered table in the Thrissil Inn.

Across the table from him was Walter Stewart, Earl of Atholl.

"Who told you this?" Atholl asked.

"It's what I heard."

"He stands on the beach in January. What do you expect?"

"He said it's a difficult castle to attack."

"How many castles has he seen?"

"Campbell got in and out of Melnik Castle; maybe we should have stuck with him."

Atholl glared at Graham. "It looks worse than it is. The hills make it look impregnable."

"The sea and the river are never blocked with snow. When the news gets to Loch Awe—" Graham was picturing the galleys coming down the coast very quickly, water dripping from the oars that rose out of the river in unison and then slipped silently back in. They would come into the Firth of Clyde with Campbell of Loch Awe's banners fluttering in the wind and armed men standing on the prow ready to jump ashore.

"Cowal wants Dunoon Castle; he will pay anything to get it. When a friendly monarch sits on the throne in Stirling Castle, well, he will have nothing to fear from Campbell of Loch Awe."

"To attack Dunoon." Graham was thinking aloud. It was a dark castle. A black castle built high on a mountainside. Worse than that, it was built on the bend of the river so the defenders could look eastwards along the River Clyde and south to the sea. With hills behind it and sea in front of it, the only approach was from the south along the shingle beach in full view of the defenders.

The door to the Thrissil opened; a blast of cold air shook the lantern above Atholl's head.

Robert Stewart's eyes nervously scoured the public house. He saw Atholl and came quickly over. "I should not be here!" he hissed.

"I know. The weather is cold; you should be giving the king a mantle to wear."

Stewart glowered at Atholl. "I'm the chamberlain, not his dresser."

"He will be wanting his hair combed."

"I don't comb his hair."

"Then what are you worried about?"

"I could be seen with you."

"Who's going to see you?"

"Word could get back to the king."

"He's still in Stirling."

"I know where he is."

"And you're in St John's Town making preparations for the great council. Everything looks normal."

"Sean Campbell is still in town. Campbell will see me here."

"You are meeting the Earl of Atholl," Graham said. "And he has come here to attend the great council. What is there to tell the king?"

"Campbell—"

Atholl cut in. "Will be called away."

"What?"

"After the great council, the king will retire to the royal apartments. You will make sure that His Grace is comfortable. There is plenty of claret?"

"I have not counted the barrels."

"Count them."

"There should be enough for the servants and the bodyguards also," Graham said.

"The king is a generous host," Atholl said. "He will expect there to be plenty of wine."

"Then at midnight, when everyone is asleep, we make our move," Graham said.

"We?" Robert Stewart said. "My job is—"

"To make sure the king is comfortable," Atholl said. "And to make sure nothing impedes his servants or any courtiers who wish to attend to his needs."

"Sean Campbell has fitted bolts to the doors in the royal apartments."

Atholl frowned. "How can his servants attend to his needs if the doors are bolted? How can courtiers pay their respects to the king?"

The tone of Robert Graham's voice dropped slightly. "You must make sure that nothing impedes anyone who wishes to attend the king."

"I can't believe you're doing this," Sheona Crockett said.

She had come through the Royal Apartments, hoping she would find the queen alone.

Queen Joan was sitting on a Savonarolan chair, enjoying the warmth from the log fire. "Please sit," she said.

Sheona looked around the bedroom—at the four-poster bed with curtains, at the shuttered windows and the tapestries hanging from the walls and the Persian carpet. There was one empty chair in the room—another Savonarolan chair, which the king usually sat on. Sheona had sat on it many times, as had Jean Lockhart, but only when the king and queen were both absent.

Sheona pulled her kirtle up to her knees and sat, cross-legged, on the floor.

"Sit on the chair," Queen Joan said.

Sheona picked herself up and sat on the chair.

There was a long silence.

Eventually, Sheona said, "You're sure you won't regret this, Your Grace?"

"I know I will regret it; I feel it in my bones."

There was a surprised silence.

The Queen Joan said, "Well, no, I don't."

Sheona waited.

"I was young once. I was in love, once." Queen Joan smiled a weak smile.

Still Sheona waited.

"You are to tell me you have taken ill," Queen Joan announced, the words all coming out in a rush. "You cannot accompany me to St John's Town."

Sheona frowned, confused. She opened her mouth as if to speak, but no words would came out.

"We cannot say you have a fever," Joan continued. "You have a bad stomach; that is what we will say."

"As Your Grace wishes."

"You like mushrooms; we will say you ate some mushrooms. Maybe one of them was bad."

"As Your Grace wishes."

"The children will remain here," Joan continued. "But Catherine will accompany me to St John's Town."

"You're going to let her go to St John's Town?" Sheona could not hide the surprise in her voice.

"I will keep an eye on her," the queen said.

"Sean Campbell is in Blackfriars."

"I know that." The queen took a deep breath.

"All that work her parents have put in—you're going to throw it all away?"

"I made a promise to Lady Douglas," Queen Joan butted in. "I cannot be seen to be going back on my word. Therefore, you will take ill, and I will say to her that I had no choice."

"Catherine—"

"Does not understand how lucky she is. Or how much her parents have tried to help her."

"Your Grace, you don't need to be doing this."

"What I say to Lady Douglas and what I do. What I do and what I say. I am the queen. I do not have friends. I must think about everyone." Queen Joan was looking deep into the tapestry as if she was walking through the forests of oak and searching for the hermit's cave so he could give her the benefit of all his wisdom. "My mother did not want me to get too friendly with the king. Well, he wasn't a king in those days." Joan smiled a sad smile. "So I used to walk in the garden at Windsor Castle, knowing that he was watching me from his window in the tower. I would stand underneath his window, knowing that the top of my kirtle was unlaced."

"Your mother—"

"I behaved stupidly for love, once. Maybe I can allow Catherine to do the same. She will accompany me to St John's Town."

"Your Grace is very generous. Catherine will be—"

"My advice to Catherine will be to tell Sean Campbell that she is ending her friendship with him. But it will be her choice."

"Have we sent a courier to Loch Awe?" Janet MacRory had followed Nichol Wallace onto the battlements at Dunoon Castle.

"You shouldn't be coming out here in your condition." Wallace was looking her expanding belly, which was only partially obscured by the loose-fitting mantle.

Ewan MacLean put his fingers to his lips. "Shhh," he whispered, his face serious. "And don't move." He pulled back the string on his crossbow and took a bolt from his pocket, placing it carefully in the bow and then slowly lifting the bow to suddenly turn and shoot. Janet got a brief glimpse of a seagull gliding regally above the castle before it squawked and plunged down into the castle courtyard.

MacLean laughed, proud of his marksmanship. Then he left the parapet, walking down the winding stairway in the tower. He stooped to pick up the bird, pausing to look at it. It was warm and soft in his hands, wet with the blood that was soaking into its white feathers. He ripped out the bolt, wiping it on his sleeve and then putting it in his pocket.

"We should send a courier," Janet MacRory said.

A long way below, through the treetops, two men could be seen coming along the shingle beach wearing mail shirts with swords hanging from their belts. It was cold on the battlements. Janet pulled her mantle close around her.

"You should go inside."

"I have my own portable oven."

"Even so, you should go inside."

"I know, but—"

"There is nothing to see out here."

"I just think—"

"Don't look at them; it's what they want. They're trying to frighten us."

"They're succeeding."

"Cowal knows, if he as much as touches us, Loch Awe will come down on him like the Angel of the Lord on Sennacherib."

Janet was silent for a moment. Then she said, "Ewan MacLean was going to get some skins from the tannery in Grianaig."[19]

"What about it?"

"He could go today."

With three tall towers in its high stone walls, Dunoon Castle dominated the River Clyde. From here, an army could sail east along the Clyde to Glasgow or north up Loch Long and Loch Goil to Balquhidder or Inverary. Like Cerberus guarding the gateway to Hades, it was ready to spit fire at any unfriendly ships that attempted to pass.

"Look how calm the water is," Nichol Wallace said. He was watching a tiny rowing boat rise up as it rode the creamy white ridge of water where fresh water met salt as river and sea collided. "This is a good day to go."

"Yes."

"I will tell him."

"Maybe he should wait for darkness?"

"And lose more time?" Nichol Wallace had already turned away and was soon running down the stone stairs.

Janet remained on the battlements. Yes, someone should go. But would he get through? "You can't see anything for the trees," she muttered to herself. Then a thought popped into her head. Was this not the way they attacked Macbeth?

When Birnam Wood doth come to Dunsinane.

---

[19] Greenock

CHAPTER 27

"Wake up!"

Catherine opened her eyes to bright shafts of sunlight coming in through the latticed windowpane.

"You're going to St John's Town on your own," Jean said. Her head was framed by sunlight like a halo. "Get up and get ready!"

"What?" Catherine's eyes were on Jean's uncombed hair, on the strands of brown hair glinting red in the sunlight.

"Sheona's taken ill; you're going to St John's Town today."

Catherine cast a glance towards Sheona's bed. "Where is she?"

"She's in my bed; she came through in the middle of the night."

"She was all right yesterday evening."

"She ate too many mushrooms. I've told you before not to touch the tippler's bane."

"We ate field mushrooms cooked in butter; that was all."

"They all look the same."

"I could have sworn—" Catherine pulled back the woollen blanket. "I'll go and see how she is."

"Your duty is to the queen," Jean said. "Sheona will be all right; I'll make her a preparation with wormwood and mint. But it means she can't go to St John's Town, and neither can I."

"Do we have wormwood?"

"I've sent a servant out to get some."

"Oh." Catherine was out of bed now, her bare feet on the carpet and the hem of her shift hanging around her shins.

"Get yourself dressed," Jean said, "before the king sees you like that."

"He won't mind."

"It's the queen I'm thinking about. She won't want him seeing you like that."

Catherine pulled the shift over her head and threw it onto the bed. "That's not quite what I meant."

Catherine scanned the bedroom with her eyes. "Where did I put my kirtle?"

"And when you get to St John's Town, be careful."

Catherine flashed Jean a hostile glance. "I'm a fully grown woman."

"That's what I'm afraid of."

"There's nothing to be afraid of—that's what you said!"

Nichol Wallace felt Janet MacRory's accusing eyes upon him.

"Did you watch him take a boat across the Clyde?"

"Nobody saw a thing."

"Was anybody looking out for him?"

"You never listen to me! I said nobody saw a thing."

"Was anybody watching for him?"

"I saw him push off." Wallace's mind was racing. "Look, he could have been held up in Grianaig, for all we know."

"We have to get a message to Loch Awe."

"And tell him what? That Ewan MacLean is buying leather in the tannery?"

"I'll go to Loch Awe," Thomas Ogilvie offered.

Nichol Wallace shot him a sideways glance. Was he doing this to impress Janet?

"Good," Janet said. There was a flicker of hope and relief in her eyes. And the tone of her voice resonated with respect.

When does she ever speak to me like that? Nichol Wallace wondered. Or turn to me with that look in her eyes?

"I'll leave after sunset," Ogilvie said, seizing upon his sudden advantage.

Nichol Wallace looked at Ogilvie. He looked at the smirk on his face and his chest now puffed up with a new-found sense of his own importance. "Wait another day," he found himself saying. Why had he said that? he wondered. But he knew why. Whenever he said something, Ogilvie would say the opposite. And now he was doing the same.

"Will you be ready by sunset?" Janet asked.

"I'm ready now," Ogilvie said.

Nichol Wallace looked from one to the other. That look in her eyes—she was looking at Ogilvie as if he was a mythical Greek hero like Achilles. Achilles got himself killed, but everybody forgets that. "Wait till dark," he said.

The wagon juddered to a halt on the bumpy road.

In her head, she could hear Isabella shouting, "Jump!" Catherine looked out, judging the distance to the ground. Her eyes scanned the street for the outstretched arms of Sean Campbell. She wanted to leap out of the carriage and then be caught in his strong arms, her body being pressed into his, his firm pectoral muscles against her chest.

Catherine jumped. The ground came rushing towards her, and her knees bent on impact. This time, there was no warm body holding her close and no warm breath in her ear. No arms wrapped around her like she was a precious jewel.

She stood up straight. "Where is he?" she wondered aloud.

The king's carriage came to a halt behind her. A courtier opened the door and placed a wooden box on the ground for the king to step onto. Robert Stewart appeared from nowhere.

The king came out and then the queen, stepping onto the box and then onto the ground, with Stewart explaining to them that it was market day.

King James made an unsympathetic audience. "Surely the royal apartments are properly provisioned?"

"You don't want salt?" Queen Joan began walking down St John's Town High Street. She ushered Catherine to follow.

Stallholders were selling sturgeon and pike, capon, and wood pigeons. The smells of spices and newly tanned leather were in the air.

"It's wintertime; we can always use salt," Queen Joan said.

"We don't need any more salt, Your Grace," Stewart said. "Besides, the cellars are cold; the food does not go off."

"Coal then?" King James suggested.

"We have stacks of logs in the coal cellar."

"Do we have coal in the coal cellar?"

"There is some."

"Coal burns longer—and hotter."

"Yes, Your Grace, and the embers are easily rekindled in the morning."

"You don't rekindle the embers," Queen Joan interjected.

"I like to consider those who do," James said. "Besides, why should I welcome my guests with fires of logs when I could have coal?"

"I don't like the smell of coal," Joan said. "It fills the room and makes me cough."

James shrugged. "You heard Her Grace," he said to Robert Stewart.

"There is cockerel and wild boar."

King James looked at Queen Joan, who nodded.

Stewart gestured to a courtier, who ran up the street towards the market.

Where is Sean? Catherine was wondering. Then she saw him. She smiled, but he did not smile back. He was walking hurriedly, a worried expression on his face. She watched him walk past her and go straight to the king.

He stopped, bowing quickly. "Dunoon Castle has been attacked," he blurted out.

King James nodded. "I had heard that. The news came to Stirling two days ago. We shall discuss it at the great council."

"Let me go to Dunoon, Your Grace."

"Lamont of Cowal shall stand trial in Edinburgh. My chamberlain has written the arrest warrant."

"Yes, Your Grace," Robert Stewart said.

"One month from now, when the glens are free of snow," James said, "we can march on Dunoon if Cowal has not submitted to my mercy."

"Loch Awe has a fleet of galleys," Queen Joan said. "He can sail up the Clyde and put an end to this very quickly."

"It's the king's navy which should put an end to it," James said.

"Loch Awe cannot sail without the permission of His Grace," Robert Stewart said.

"Cowal did," Campbell said. He was looking at the king. "You must let me go now."

"The council must meet in St John's Town; I have summoned it. Some are here already; others are on their way. But I will tell the lords who assemble that we shall march to Dunoon on the ides of March."

"Do I have Your Grace's permission to go to Dunoon?" Campbell asked.

James hesitated.

"His work in Blackfriars has finished," Robert Stewart added with what seemed undue haste.

"What of Linlithgow?" the king asked.

"I will attend to Linlithgow upon my return," Campbell said.

"He can attend to Linlithgow on his return," Robert Stewart said.

"Very well," King James said.

Campbell bowed and turned to go. He saw Catherine looking at him and, for a moment, hesitated.

"May God be with you," Catherine said.

He took a couple of steps towards her. "I'll be back," he said.

Catherine tried to smile, but her face muscles did not seem to be working.

"Wherever you are, I'll find you," he said.

Then he was away—striding quickly up the High Street to the stables.

CHAPTER 28

All the bedchambers, and the nursery, had bolts—heavy wooden bars that would slide through iron brackets.

How empty the nursery seemed now—and even her own bedchamber. Every morning, the children would come clattering through the door to wake her up, always an hour too early.

Now there was only silence.

Already, Catherine was missing Isabella. She even missed Princess Joan, who would sit on the floor with her back pressed hard against the door when she was in a bad mood. She would stop anyone else entering or leaving the room. But if someone still did not give her attention, she would lean forwards and then throw her head back to bash the door with a loud thump that everyone could hear.

Now she was immersed in the silence of a monastery; how strange it sounded. It was silent apart from the sound of footsteps and the rusty hinge creaking open. Robert Stewart came into the room.

"What do you think?" he asked. He pushed the heavy door shut. "We did a good job?"

"Sean did a good job."

A heavy wooden beam lay propped up against the wall. Stewart picked it up, threading it through the iron brackets.

"There!" he said. He stood back, turning to Catherine and smiling. "The room is secure."

Catherine took a step towards the door. "I should be attending to Her Grace."

Stewart immediately stepped forwards, putting a hand on the bolt. "No one can get in, without the king's permission."

"Let me try the bolt," Catherine said.

He stood in front of her, looking at her, not moving.

"Remove the bolt and let me put it back."

"It is heavy."

"Let me feel its weight."

Still he was not moving. His body was between hers and the door. "A bolt like this could keep out a whole army. The king and queen will sleep safely," he said.

"His Grace will be assured," Catherine said calmly.

"Indeed." His eyes were on her breasts rising and falling underneath the kirtle.

Catherine stepped forwards to put a hand on the bolt. She felt Stewart's hand come down on top of hers.

She heard the murmur of voices and footsteps on the other side. "Your Grace!" she called out.

"Catherine?" That was the queen's voice.

"I am coming!" Catherine shouted through the door. "The chamberlain is showing us the new bolts on the doors."

There was a moment's silence. Robert Stewart did not move.

"Robert will let you in," Catherine shouted.

Robert Stewart slid back the bolt. Catherine took hold of the handle and pulled the door open. Queen Joan came walking into the room.

"Look how big the bolt is," Catherine said.

"Nearly as wide as Lady Douglas?"

There was a moment's silence.

"I can say these things." Queen Joan smiled. "You cannot."

Nothing in his life made sense any more.

You respected the king; you respected the earl. Knights rode on horseback, rescuing damsels imprisoned in towers and showing off their skills at the lists. A man went to the continent to make his name in combat and come back a hero. This was the way he had been brought up.

Nobody said that you would come back from the continent in disgrace or that the damsel's parents would arrange for her to marry a burgess. Nobody said that the earls plotted to kill the king and take his crown. Nobody said that you had no friends at the king's court, only secret enemies seeking the king's favour at your expense.

Campbell had come down St Thenew's Gait,[20] named after the mother of St Kentigern—not that there were many indications that saints had once lived in this narrow street with buildings piled so high on either side that the street surface was always in shadow. In the Highlands, the land devoured the filth dropped by animals. But not so in the city, where the excrement lay on the stone cobbles, thick with flies in summer and frozen in winter.

Stepping carefully to avoid the filth, Campbell noticed a unicorn on a wooden board swinging from a single chain. Years ago, perhaps, one of the chains holding the sign had rusted and snapped, and now the sign swung squint with nobody seeming to notice or care. The tavern itself was small and neglected, with latticed windows so filthy they neither let light in nor out.

He stepped inside, looking for a table to sit at and hoping he would not have long to wait. A lantern hung from a roofbeam, casting a yellow light around the room. Barrels of beer, wine, and whisky lay at the far end, protected by a long iron bar. Sitting on a stool behind the bar, a bearded man was watching him carefully.

"A pint of wine and a piece of cheese, please."

The innkeeper roused himself from his stood.

"My name is Sean Campbell. Has anybody been looking for me?"

"Sean Campbell?" The barman seemed to recognise the name and nodded. "Gillespie Campbell comes in every day at midday and asks for you."

Midday? It was about mid-morning. Campbell spotted an empty table and sat on the long wooden bench. The barman cut a piece of cheese and poured a tankard of wine; a woman placed them on a tray and took them over to Campbell's table. She bent over, giving him a view of her cleavage as she put the wine and cheese on the table. "Where are you from?" she asked.

"St John's Town."

---

[20] Trongate in Glasgow

She looked confused for a moment. "But you have a Highland accent."

"You asked where I have come from, not where I grew up."

She gave him a contemptuous look as if she thought him too clever for his own good, turned, and walked back to the bar.

Campbell picked up the tankard of wine.

He had gotten to the bottom of his second pint of wine when the door opened amid a blast of snowflakes and a short thick-set man came in. The man's eyes scanned the room till they came to Campbell.

"Sean!" he announced. "You haven't changed a bit!" He strode over to Campbell's table and sat down.

"You were expecting to see a man with one eye and a scar down his cheek?"

"Something like that."

"Plenty time for that."

"I guess so."

The maid had appeared at Gillespie's shoulder.

"Beer and bannocks,"[21] he said, putting a coin on the table.

"You can have some of my cheese," Campbell said.

The maid went away.

Gillespie gazed at her retreating back, imagining her round bottom underneath the loose kirtle. "She usually chats a bit more than that," he said.

"I annoyed her."

"That was quick, even by your standards."

"Can we get down to business?"

"Cowal has attacked Dunoon Castle."

"I know that."

"Are you just going to interrupt everything I say?"

"Sorry."

"You have a reputation for breaking into castles..."

"And other things."

Gillespie shot Campbell a hostile glance. "What did I say to you?"

"Sorry."

---

[21] A large, round oatcake

"Loch Awe needs more time. The mountain passes are blocked with snow—"

"It's winter in the Highlands; what else do you expect?"

"Here's an idea." Gillespie jabbed a finger at Campbell. "You let me speak two sentences in a row without interruption."

The maid was back at their table. She placed a tankard on the table and a very small coin.

"We want you to load a boat up with supplies—"

"And run the blockade?"

"All right. One sentence will do. Let me speak one sentence without interruption." Gillespie paused to take a swig of his beer. Then he carried on. "You tell them that Loch Awe is on his way." He paused again for another drink of beer. "Your job is to make sure morale is high; make sure that they have plenty food and that they know we're coming."

"Who's in command?"

"Inside the castle?"

"Yes."

"Nichol Wallace."

"Not Patrick O'Donnell?" Campbell asked. The relief in his voice was evident.

"I don't know where he is or what he's doing," Gillespie said.

"With a bit of luck, Cowal's men have killed him."

"We wouldn't be that lucky."

Campbell moved the conversation on. "What about the well?"

"What about it?"

"Do I check that it's not drying up?"

Gillespie rolled his eyes. "The well in Dunoon Castle never dries up."

"What if it's frozen?"

"Then they can gather snow from the courtyard and melt it."

"I could take a barrel of beer..."

"You're taking oatmeal, barley, and whisky."

"Wait a moment." Campbell raised a hand. "Dunoon Castle is up a hill."

"It's the same as Melnik Castle—on a hill overlooking a river."

"It's hardly the same."

"No. There won't be any drummer boys."

Campbell winced visibly. "One more remark like that, and I'm riding back to St John's Town."

"Sorry."

"How do I carry bags of oatmeal up a hill?"

"Hide them."

"Where?"

"Bury them."

"The ground will be frozen."

"Are you saying that the man who can break into castles can't dig up a bit of frozen ground?"

"How am I going to hide a boat?"

Gillespie rolled his eyes. "They won't be looking for you. They'll be looking out for a fleet of galleys coming up the Firth of Clyde. A small boat sailing from Gourock after dark—they won't notice it."

"You have a boat for me?"

"A small rowing boat."

"Where is it?"

"Gourock," Gillespie said. "We thought about Cloch Point because it's nearer. But a boat in the harbour at Gourock won't look suspicious. Nobody will notice it."

Campbell nodded his head.

"Look for a man called Gilchrist Muir." A hand disappeared into Gillespie's doublet. When it came out, it was brandishing a roll of paper. "This is your introduction."

Campbell looked at the scroll, closely scrutinising the seal of Campbell of Loch Awe. "I push off after dark?"

"Yes."

"Do they know I'm coming?"

"Nobody knows."

Campbell hesitated for a moment. "The people in the castle—they might mistake me for the enemy."

"They might."

"How do I get in?"

"If it was that easy, Cowal wouldn't be laying siege to it, would he?"

"So I have to get around Cowal's men and break into a defended castle?"

"Yes."

"If Cowal's men see me, they will try to kill me. And if the defenders see me, they will try to kill me?"

"Yes."

"I can see why no one else wants this job."

"No one else has your skills."

"No one else is so desperate to repair his reputation."

"You're lucky you have a reputation to repair," Gillespie Campbell said. "Nobody knows who I am."

CHAPTER 29

"Wake up!" a voice shouted.

Catherine opened her eyes, groaning to herself.

"Wake up!"

There it was again. A male voice.

Catherine vaguely remembered entertaining the king and queen the previous evening. The harpist played; King James and Robert Stewart played chess. Queen Joan was full of questions. How was Margaret? Had she heard anything? Catherine responded by asking about Sheona. How was she? She and Catherine had eaten the same food, but Catherine was not ill.

The hour had grown late and then later still. Catherine's cup had been continually refilled with claret. King James had picked up a lute and begun to play. Everyone had sat in silence and listened attentively.

To fall asleep was unforgivable; Catherine listened with eyes wide open, enjoying the music and praising the king.

At length, Queen Joan had announced she was sleepy and would retire to her bedchamber. The king had put down his lute; the harpist had left the room. With relief, Catherine had stood up. She'd followed the king and queen through the royal apartments to her own room. They'd gone on into their bedroom; Catherine had listened to the bolt sliding into place on the other side of the door.

Now she could relax! She'd pulled her kirtle over her head, hung it on a chair, and collapsed onto the bed.

"Wake up!"

Catherine pushed aside the scratchy wool blankets and stood up, immediately sensing the cool air against her skin.

Had she slept like that? Naked under wool blankets? She looked around the room. A white shift lay on the floor. Catherine picked it up and quickly pulled it on.

She went to the door, pulling back the heavy wooden beam. It moved a little; she pulled it again, and it moved some more.

The man on the other side knocked loudly.

"Patience," Catherine growled. The bolt was long and heavy. It was made of oak, as if it was designed to stop a charge from a mounted knight. She slowly slid the bolt out of the brackets, but the end grew heavier and heavier until it dropped onto the floor with a thump. Catherine stood it on its end, holding it with both hands, and leaned it against the wall.

The door opened, and Robert Stewart walked in.

"You wait for me to open the door," Catherine said.

"The bolt is too heavy for you."

"I am tired; I did not sleep well."

"We should remove the bolt and replace it with a lighter one."

"There is nothing wrong with the bolt."

"I will speak to the king about it."

"No, you will not."

His eyes were all over her—on the contours of her body, on her breasts under the thin shift, on her uncombed hair cascading around her shoulders and caressing her cleavage. He had been looking into her eyes at first but then his eyes had dropped down, as they always did. His eyes were studying her neck, her shoulders and trailing down to her bare feet and ankles before coming back up but stopping as they reached her protruding nipples.

"You are too early, my lord," Catherine said. "The king and queen are still resting."

"You should take breakfast with me."

"I shall come to the dining hall."

"Now?"

"When Queen Joan is ready."

Stewart cast a glance at the shut doors on the other side of the room. "It was late when they retired."

"After the king beat you at chess, he played the lute."

"I wanted to check that the building was secure; I walked around the perimeter."

"You were walking for a long time. You did not return."

"The grounds are large."

"Sean Campbell has made the building secure."

"It never does any harm to check."

"Tonight, you should stay and listen to the king play on the lute."

"I will be delighted to, if I do not have any other pressing duties."

"There are others who can check the perimeter."

"The king trusts me to do it."

"There are others he trusts," Catherine said pointedly. She had almost added "more" but had stopped herself. She attempted to push the door shut, but it came against Stewart's foot.

Stewart did not attempt to move.

"You may leave, now," Catherine said and, gently but firmly, pushed on the door.

"These bolts—they were not fitted for women to use."

"I told you; I am tired. That is why I dropped it."

"We should replace them with lighter ones."

"No," Catherine said. "There is no need." This time, she pushed harder; Stewart reluctantly stepped back. Catherine closed the door.

"Keep the river on your right-hand side, and you cannot go wrong," Gillespie Campbell had said, somewhat unnecessarily.

The ride to Gourock was an easy one—thirty miles, following the River Clyde westwards.

But not so easy in winter.

The journey could be made in a day—if you knew your horse. Slowing to a walking pace before it got tired, walking for a while and then trotting again—that was the way. You had to know the horse better than it knew itself. It would run till it was tired and then demand a rest or a leisurely nibble at the grass by the roadside.

You could not wait for signs of tiredness; you had to anticipate them. You had to love the beast until it became an extension of yourself and you understood every snort. Then you would find yourself pulling on the reins and coming down to walking pace because it felt right. It felt natural. No, it *was* natural. The horse's fatigue was your fatigue.

Campbell had left before sunrise, shivering in the cold night air. His breath was condensing in front of his eyes; his whole body was shaking. He rode through the empty streets, the sounds of hooves on the cobbles muffled by the carpet of snow.

He came to the West Port—a stone archway with locked doors. He waited while the bailie came out with the keys. The doors opened, and then he was riding out of Glasgow and taking the road to Greenock. It was a broad road soon turning into a narrow earthen track. The sun rose behind him, throwing the horse's shadow onto the road and making the branches of the trees sparkle with frost. The frozen surfaces of puddles crunched under the horse's hooves.

Before there was even a hint of irregular breathing, he jumped down from the horse and walked with it. They trotted, sometimes walked, with the river broadening all the time. Campbell had put some oatmeal and water into a leather bag, which hung from the horse's saddle. The heat from the horse and its movement slowly cooked the porridge.

"Have some cream with your porridge," Queen Joan said. She pushed a small bowl across the table towards Catherine.

"Thank you, Your Grace." Catherine scooped some porridge onto her silver spoon and dipped it into the small bowl of cream.

A loaf of bread sat on a silver plate in the centre of the table; the smell of roasted boar was wafting through from the kitchen. A servant was pouring a cup of claret for the king.

Robert Stewart stirred some honey into his cup of wine. "The bolts are too heavy," he said. He cut a chunk of bread from the loaf with a knife. "My lady Catherine dropped the bolt," he said to the king.

"Only because I was tired, Your Grace," Catherine said quickly.

"She was lucky." Stewart turned to look at her. "She might have broken a toe if it had landed on her foot."

"I will be more careful next time."

"I can have the bolts replaced," Stewart said.

"There is no need," Catherine said.

"You are too polite." Stewart smiled an insincere smile.

King James turned to Queen Joan. "Do you think the bolts are too heavy?"

"They are heavy"—Joan hesitated—"but not too heavy."

"King James can draw the bolt for you," Robert Stewart said. "My Lady Catherine must do so on her own."

"I can manage," Catherine said.

"They were chosen because they were strong."

"A lighter bolt can also be strong," Robert Stewart said.

"I can discuss this with Sean Campbell when he returns," King James said.

"Yes," Catherine said. "A good idea, Your Grace."

"Sean Campbell is not a carpenter," Stewart said.

Catherine threw him a quizzical look. "And you are?"

CHAPTER 30

His horse had picked its way slowly along the hard frozen riverbank, pausing repeatedly as it searched for safe spots to place its hooves.

He was thirsty, and he was surrounded by snow. It was so tempting to jump down from the saddle, scoop up a handful of snow, and eat it. But a handful of snow turned into only a few drops of water in the mouth. And not before it chilled the mouth and then chilled the stomach. It was better just to endure the thirst; at the end of the journey was a pot of beer and a seat by a roaring log fire—better just to think about that.

On the other side of the river, Dunoon Castle was obscured from view by the pine forest where the frozen branches of the trees were crusted with snow and the needles hung with icicles. If a traveller made it across the wide river without being seen—if he made his way up the hillside where the ground underfoot was frozen without slipping and falling back into the freezing waters below, if he came through the pine forest where the branches of the trees were like the arms of soldiers barring his way, if he did all that, he was confronted with high stone walls frowning down upon him and snow on the battlements sparkling in the winter starlight.

Urgent knocking shook the whole door.

Gilchrist Muir stood up.

Tam Beaton's boy, whose name was also Tam, pushed his sooty face into the room. "Someone's coming!"

"I've told you before—wait outside till I open the door."

"There's a man on a horse!"

Muir turned to his wife, who was sitting by the fire. Some salmon lay across a griddle, which hung from a roofbeam by chain. "Keep the door shut," he said. He stepped outside.

Tam and his father had their eyes on a horse and rider approaching from the east. Young Tam beat on his drum.

Muir looked at the approaching rider. He knew this was their guest by the mail shirt and the sword hanging from his belt and by the fact that this man rode alone. The earl's tacksmen[22] never rode alone.

They watched as the man dismounted. He was scanning the village with his eyes, sizing up the cluster of boats on the beach and the cluster of houses beyond the tideline.

Gilchrist Muir did not move but let the man walk towards him.

"Good day," the man said.

"Good evening."

There was a moment's silence as they both looked at each other—one in a mail shirt and hose and the other in broad green tartan, held around the waist by a leather belt and fixed to the shoulder by a plaid brooch. Campbell was thinking back to the days when he used to wear a tartan plaid and how much warmer it was in weather like this.

"I am Gilchrist Muir."

A young boy with black hair thumped his drum.

Sean Campbell jumped instinctively. That young boy in Melnik Castle with the frightened eyes, where was his father? Maybe the boy was frightened of his father? Maybe he'd hidden in the portcullis chamber thinking he was safe there? *But he came across us instead.*

"You're going to Dunoon Castle?" That was Gilchrist Muir's voice.

"What?" Campbell asked.

"You're going to Dunoon Castle?"

Campbell nodded.

"You want us to look after the horse until you come back?"

If you come back seemed like a more appropriate choice of words. Muir looked at the horse—big and brown with strong-looking legs. He was picturing himself riding to Grianaig on market days.

---

[22] Rent collectors

"Loch Awe will come in the spring with a fleet of galleys," Tam Beaton said.

"Yes," Campbell said. "That is the message I must take to the castle."

"Cowal's men are everywhere. They will see you crossing the river."

"I will travel by night. Is the boat ready?"

"Yes."

"I'll go tomorrow."

Muir nodded. "Better to make the journey after a night's rest. Do you like salmon?"

———— † ————

"Salmon?" King James complained. "Commoner's food?"

"What should I wear?" Queen Joan said to Catherine.

"His Grace says that your blue kirtle matches the colour of your eyes."

"I can't wear blue for a great council."

"We can't have salmon after a council," James complained. "We don't want salmon, do we, Joanie?"

Queen Joan turned to the king. "I don't mind."

"The Tay is full of salmon; stalls are loaded up with it every Friday at the mercat cross; what will they think if the king serves them with salmon?"

"The Earl of Atholl likes salmon," Robert Stewart said.

"He eats like a peasant."

"He is a peasant," Queen Joan said.

"What about brown?" Catherine suggested.

King James shook his head. "We don't want brown trout."

"Her brown kirtle," Catherine said.

"It's too dull."

"Your Grace could present a modest image to the council?"

"That's not modest. That's … that's … demeaning," James said.

"It's unbecoming," Queen Joan said. "Brown is unbecoming."

"Purple?" Catherine suggested.

"Purple is good," Robert Stewart said. "The Roman emperors wore purple."

"Too ostentatious," King James said.

"I didn't bring my purple kirtle."

"Let's go to your chamber and look through your kirtles," Catherine said.

"Don't you know what you packed?"

"Sheona packed them, not me."

"Oh."

Joan turned to James. "If you'll excuse us, Your Grace." The women began walking away.

"We should accompany them," Robert Stewart said.

"They don't need us," King James said. "Besides, we haven't finished. Did we agree on venison?"

"The bolts don't fit properly," Robert Stewart said. "How will Her Grace bar the door?"

"I can do it when I come through," the king said.

"The bolts work well enough," Queen Joan called out as she walked away. "Besides, we won't be locking the doors."

"The bolts are too heavy for the women," Robert Stewart insisted.

"I think I saw Jean pack your red kirtle," Catherine said.

"Red would be good," Queen Joan said.

The men's voices grew fainter. "Blancmange would be good," the king said. "Let's have blancmange."

"We could whittle down the size of the bolts."

"Do we have all the ingredients for blancmange?"

"We have chicken and cinnamon, but we need rice if we are to serve blancmange," Robert Stewart said.

"We don't have rice?"

"It's hard to get."

"I thought Alexander Lovell brought in a shipment?"

"That went to Stirling Castle. We don't have any rice in Blackfriars."

The women entered the royal bedchamber. Catherine quietly closed the door behind her.

"Red wouldn't be too bold, would it?" Queen Joan asked. "The business of the council must be attended to. One wishes to set the right tone."

"All the men will be looking at you."

"That's what I mean."

"Your dark red kirtle might perhaps be more becoming?"
"Did Sheona pack it?"
"Let us find out."

A blast of smoke hit Sean Campbell in the face as he stepped inside Gilchrist Muir's cottage.

Lit by yellow light through grey smoke, Campbell could see a woman standing over a griddle.

A hot bannock straight off the griddle and smothered in butter—Campbell suddenly felt hungry.

"Bring out the whisky!" Gilchrist Muir said.

There were no windows in the stone walls. The only light came from the fire in the centre of the stone floor. Smoke from the burning peat filled the room, drifting up to the roof and filtering out through the thatch.

A sideboard had been pressed up against the wall. Muir went over to it, opening it and pulling out a stoneware bottle. He set two quaich on top of the sideboard and poured out two generous measures of whisky.

A table had been pushed against one wall and a bed against the far wall. There was only one bed. Sean Campbell unbuckled his belt and set his sword against the farthest wall from the door.

After a plate of fish and oatcakes, a cup of water, and a quaich of whisky and then another quaich of whisky, the stone floor did not seem so uncomfortable. They set some straw down for him; Sean Campbell took off his mail shirt.

A pile of ash lay in the corner of the room—the remains of yesterday's fire. Seonaid Muir shovelled some up and carefully smothered the fire with it. The orange embers disappeared; the room was plunged into darkness. A speck of dark red light remained where the fire had once been. Campbell watched it for a while.

"Did you bolt the door?" Seonaid Muir's tired voice drifted through the darkness.

Gilchrist Muir grunted.

"Go and bolt the door."

"What?"

"Go and bolt the door."

"What are you worried about? If someone comes in, it's my job to do something about it," Gilchrist Muir said.

Campbell glanced towards the door; a faint whisper of cold air was brushing against his cheek. Gilchrist Muir snorted and then began to snore.

If someone comes in, it'll be my job to do something about it, Campbell thought to himself.

The speck of light where the fire was turned from orange to red to a dull red. Then it disappeared.

The next thing Campbell was aware of was a blast of cold air as Gilchrist Muir opened the door and went outside. The half-light of dawn cast the room in shadow. Muir came back in, shivering, with some sticks in his hands. He hurriedly put them on the ashes. His wife was already kneeling by the fireside with bellows in her hands, blowing the fire back into life.

A burst of flame, a flicker of yellow light, and the smell of smoke. "We'll make porridge for breakfast," Muir said. "You can take some with you."

No roasted fish and whisky for dinner tonight then. Just a handful of cold porridge before I step into the boat. "Thank you very much," Campbell said.

"You'll need three hours, maybe four, to row to Dunoon," Muir said. He was looking at Campbell, sizing up his fitness.

"I'll leave at dusk."

"You have to get across the river, hide the boat, and get into the castle."

"There's enough time."

"I'll show you the boat, and we can load it up. It won't matter who sees you; you're among friends here."

"Let our guest have his breakfast first!" Seonaid Muir scolded her husband.

Drammach for breakfast—a handful of oatmeal soaked in cold water. Janet MacRory looked at the greyish-white slops sitting in the wooden bowl. She stood up. "I'm going to take a wash," she said.

"Have your porridge first," Nichol Wallace said.

"Later," she said, knowing that time would wear on and she would get so hungry she'd be grateful to eat it. "After I have bathed in the river."

"Don't," Wallace said.

He was always telling her what to do: *Eat your porridge. Don't bathe in the river. You should go to bed.*

Without speaking a word, Janet walked the length of the great hall and into the tower, going down the winding stairway—round and round and down and down.

You got into bad habits during a siege, like not bothering to wash. Washing was a problem—you couldn't afford to waste drinking water on it. So the only way to wash was by making your way down the winding path between the trees. Lucifer's Stairway, they called it, because the descent was treacherous in the cold weather, and one wrong step on the frozen ground could send you shooting down into the sea.

And it was cold. The waters came off the snow-covered mountains to the north with no time to warm up before they joined the river and were passing Dunoon. So you would chill yourself to the bone in the freezing temperatures with a bracing sea breeze always whisking its way along the surface of the water. It was good to come back into the castle smelling of salt, not sweat, but it was never long before the fresh smells dissipated, and the stale smells returned.

Then there was that other problem. What if the enemy attacked while the seaport was open, and you were sitting naked on the stony beach with your clothes on a rock? *Not that I ever had anything worth looking at.* Janet laughed. *Nothing on my chest and nothing on my bottom either.*

But that did not stop the men on the parapet watching her. All the time, they were claiming to be watching out for the enemy. It was for her protection, they insisted. So why were they always watching her rub her wet thighs down with a towel or shake the droplets of water from her breasts?

The water was cold—it did not make you shiver; it put you into shock. So you would plunge in quickly because, if you didn't, you would never go in. You would splash around quickly with your arms and kick with your legs. Then you were out and rubbing yourself down, knowing that, from the battlements above, the men's eyes were always on you and never on the enemy they were supposed to be looking out for.

Then picking up her kirtle and holding it close to her body, she ran up Lucifer's Stairway to the Seagait Port[23] hoping that some debauched and depraved prankster was not laughing heartily because he had let the portcullis drop.

But the portcullis was open today, and she passed underneath it, pulling on her kirtle as it slid shut behind her. The second portcullis rose slowly. She had made the mistake of undressing once before she went out. They'd let her back in through the first portcullis and then let her wait there, naked in the murder hole, while they gaped at her and slowly raised the second portcullis.

Now she always took her kirtle with her when she went to bathe in the river. She had to leave it on the rocks where it might get wet or stained with seaweed, but a kirtle and a mantle around her shoulders was always the quickest way back through the portcullis.

The second portcullis had risen to her shoulders, and she ducked underneath it. She had shaken herself warm with her shivering. Already, she was thinking about breakfast of a bowl of drammach in the banquet hall.

Catherine woke to the smells of bread being toasted over an open fire and pheasant roasting.

The doors to the nursery were open. But beyond them, the doors to the royal bedchamber were shut. Catherine slid back the bolt in her own bedchamber. Setting it upright, she leaned it against the wall before she opened the door.

---

[23] The gate at the seaward side of the castle

She liked going to the cloisters in the early morning. It was peaceful, and she could faintly hear the monks singing in Latin. The statues of the Virgin Mary and the angels watched her benignly. She sat down on a frozen bench, not noticing the temperature.

This was the silent centre of the monastery. She liked coming here to absorb the quietness. She liked to speak to the monks too, tapping into their wisdom, but always felt guilty about disturbing their silence.

Under the watchful eye of the Virgin Mary, she prayed for a while. Then she sat, her mantle pulled around her, watching her breath condense as it left her mouth. She might have sat here a long time, even in the cold morning air, but she knew the queen would be looking for her.

She stood up, walking out of the cloisters and past the royal tennis catchpule to the royal apartments.

She noticed Robert Stewart walking the other way, carrying a wooden beam over his shoulder.

"What are you doing?" she asked.

"I should whittle down the bolt," he said.

"Put it back," she said.

"The bolts are too big, too heavy."

"Put it back," she repeated.

"It's you I'm thinking of," Stewart said. He smiled insincerely. "I don't want you to hurt yourself again."

"Put the bolt back," Catherine said firmly.

Stewart gave a slight bow. "As your lady wishes."

Catherine walked past him and into the royal apartments.

CHAPTER 31

Nichol Wallace came down from the battlements to find Mary MacLean sitting cross-legged on the ground, leaning her back against the wall. She was whittling from a block of wood, and white shavings lay scattered across the floor and across her lap.

"What are you doing?" he asked.

She looked up. "What?"

"I asked you what you're doing."

"What does it look like? I'm making more arrows."

"Leave that. I want you to boil up a pot of lard."

Mary looked blankly at him. "We don't have enough wood."

"Then find some."

"Where?"

But Wallace was already walking away.

"I'll boil some lard, and then he'll say we don't have enough arrows," she muttered.

———†———

"Is it true that the king lives in a palace with glass walls?" young Tam Beaton asked.

"It's not a palace," Sean Campbell said, momentarily distracted by a woman collecting seaweed from the foreshore. "I should push off from here," he said.

"They would see you," Tam Beaton said. "And they would see you loading the boat; they'd know you were coming."

"They can't see us now?"

"Two men on horseback riding along the beach at Cloch—that's not going to worry them," Tam Beaton said.

"Three men." Young Tam said.

"Yes," Tam Beaton said to the boy. "Three men on two horses."

"Is it a castle?" Tam Beaton's son asked.

"Is what a castle?"

"Where the king lives."

"Sometimes."

"Does the castle have glass walls?"

"It has glass windows."

"People can see inside?"

"Yes, but people can also see outside. If your house had glass windows, you could see the street."

"But I know what the street looks like," young Tam Beaton said.

"Strangers can look into your house?" The elder Beaton shuddered. "I don't like the sound of that."

"How do glass walls hold up the roof?" young Tam Beaton asked.

"I don't see anyone," Campbell said.

"You can't see anything for the trees," Tam Beaton senior said.

There was a strip of grey-blue water, ruffled by the wind. Beyond it, the hills of Cowal rose out of the sea with glimpses of the stone turrets of the castle among the pine trees. "It's very quiet."

"It will get noisier once they see you crossing the Firth."

"The journey's a lot shorter from here."

"They would see you."

"Glass walls won't hold up the roof," Tam Beaton's son said.

"They're not walls; they're windows."

"Holes in the walls?"

"Glass holes."

"They don't break?"

"Nobody throws stones at them."

"Our house has proper walls," young Tam said.

Campbell turned to Tam Beaton. "I'll push off after dark."

"From here?"

"I must have twice the distance to go if I'm pushing off from Gourock."

"It's more than twice the distance," young Tam said.

"They'll be looking to the south for a fleet of galleys coming up the Firth of Clyde. They won't notice a small boat crossing from the north-east."

"The current's not very strong," Tam Beaton said. "You'll get over very easily."

"It gets stronger in the middle," young Tam said. "That's what Davie Burness says."

"He exaggerates all the time."

"Davie says, if you're not careful, you'll get pulled south towards Donald Macintyre's farm at Innellan."

Campbell groaned inwardly. "So I have to row north-west to take account of the current?"

"Not at all," Tam Beaton said. "The wind coming off the Atlantic neutralises the current."

Janet MacRory noticed the door to her bedchamber was half-open as she came along the corridor. "What are you doing?" Janet asked, but her horrified tone suggested that she already knew.

Nichol Wallace was working the point of his dagger in between the panels of wood that lined the walls in the room.

"What are you smiling about?" Janet asked. "You're stripping all the wood from the walls," she said, answering her own question. "It's going to be freezing cold in here, now. And you're smiling about it?"

"That's not what I'm smiling about."

"Then what are you smiling about?"

"Oh, I was just thinking …" Nichol Wallace seemed about to say something but stopped himself.

"Thinking about what?"

How many days, how many months, have I spent thinking about being with you in your bedchamber? Just me and you in your bedchamber with the door shut, of course. And here we are.

"Thinking about nothing," he said. He looked at her standing there with her expanding belly hidden by the folds of the loose mantle. *You'll need a man when this is over.*

"How am I going to sleep in here?" Janet wondered.

"You still have a bed."

The wooden panelling was insulation; take it away and there were only cold stone walls left, walls the same temperature as the freezing winds outside.

"How am I going to keep warm in here?"

"I have a bedroom."

She eyed him suspiciously, hands on hips. "And where are you going to sleep?"

Nichol Wallace stopped scraping at the stone for a moment to look at her.

"You don't have the energy to keep me warm all night." Janet turned and stepped out into the corridor, walking to the winding stairway and up to the battlements, where she found James Duncan standing on his own looking out over the River Clyde. Today, the river seemed deep like the sea, cold and grey, its surface frothing in the breeze. But if the river was cold, the wind was much colder; Duncan's lips were cracked and dry, his hands numb and his feet cold.

"He's taking the wood panelling from my walls," Janet MacRory said. The wind swept along the surface of the river, chilling all in its path. It was sharp and painful, like arrows shooting through her chest, arms, and legs.

Duncan turned to look at her. "Auld Nick?"[24]

"He's not so old."

"He's older than you."

"What of it?"

"He took the wood off my walls a couple of days ago."

"How did you sleep?"

"Eventually, you shiver yourself warm. Then you sleep."

"I should tell him I'm sleeping in his room."

---

[24] Satan

"Maybe that's his plan."

"He will see Campbell of Loch Awe first?" Atholl spat out the words.

"This works to our advantage," Robert Stewart said. He was bending forwards slightly, wringing his hands.

"He will see Loch Awe before me?" Atholl made no attempt to suppress the outrage in his voice.

The two men were sitting in an upstairs room of the Pleuch and Harra Inn.[25] A stoneware bottle of whisky sat on the scratched surface of the wooden table.

"Loch Awe will be needing to get back to Dunoon quickly."

"I brought him back to Scotland. He wouldn't have a kingdom but for me. He owes me." Atholl's fingers gripped his quaich fiercely.

"Loch Awe intends to leave for Dunoon with the king's warrant in his hands."

"He thinks he can be seen before me?" Atholl growled, his voice getting louder. "Before me?"

"We don't want Loch Awe in St John's Town a day longer than necessary," Stewart said.

"I don't want to be in St John's Town a day longer than necessary." Atholl put the quaich to his lips and drained it. He put it down and refilled it from the stoneware bottle. He did not offer any to Robert Stewart.

"King James will see you at the High Altar in Blackfriars Monastery immediately after Campbell of Loch Awe," Stewart said emolliently.

"After Loch Awe." Atholl shook his head in disbelief.

"Then Loch Awe will leave, and we can act."

Atholl gave Stewart a sharp look. "I cannot be seen to be involved in this."

"What I meant was"—Stewart smiled placatory—"we shall act once you have left St John's Town."

---

[25] The Plough and Harrow

"Once I have returned to Blair Castle," Atholl corrected him. "No one will be able to say I was in St John's Town on the day of the event." He shot Stewart a glance across the tabletop. "The monks all go to bed after vespers."

"Compline."

"What?"

"They go to bed after compline."

"The king stays up late drinking and playing music. The monks will be asleep. There will be no one there apart from the queen and her ladies."

"I'll be there," Robert Stewart said.

"Yes."

"What about—"

"What about what?"

"Well … what if the ladies get in the way?"

"It would be just like James to hide behind his ladies."

"What do we do if they're in the same room?"

"I don't care about the ladies."

"You don't want people saying that the women got hurt."

"Then they should have known better than to get in the way. Besides, who respects a king who hides behind his ladies?"

"We want this to be clean and quick."

"I told you; I don't care about the ladies. When James is dead, you bring the boy to me."

"Not me?" Robert Stewart looked horrified. "I'm the king's chamberlain; I can't have people saying I had anything to do with this."

"You know what I mean. Graham"—Atholl took another slurp of whisky—"Robert Graham brings the boy to me."

———— † ————

Nichol Wallace pointed over the tops of the trees.

Janet MacRory had come out onto the battlements. She came forwards, standing next to him. "What is it?"

One dozen stones the size of heads jumped over the treeline as if being catapulted towards them. Janet instinctively ducked as the stones flew overhead. Some spots of rain hit her on the cheek and the forehead.

The stones dropped behind her, rattling around the courtyard. They bounced against towers and ricocheted against walls. The boulders were soft and damp, with matted hair, and spots of moisture sprayed from them when they hit the hard stone walls. Nichol Wallace slowly raised his head above the battlements to look out.

Janet let him look. If she stood up, he would flap his arms and shout, "No, no, no!" He had to look first; then he would turn to her and ask her if she could see anything.

The boulders had slowly rolled to a halt on the cobbled stones of the courtyard. Jock Brodie, the porter, marched out into the courtyard with a sack and began putting the boulders in it one by one.

"Are you all right?" Wallace had turned to look at her.

"Yes," Janet said. She had seen it all before. She was not brave; she was just tired.

"There's blood on your cheek."

Janet put a hand to cheek where the spots of rain had landed on it. When she pulled her hand away, the fingers were smeared with blood.

Down below, Brodie picked up one boulder by its brown hair and then held it up, dry and dusty like a puppet. He was staring hard at it as if trying to make sure that it really was the head of Ewan MacLean with its dead eyes and open mouth.

CHAPTER 32

He could hear the ripple of the waves as they spread across the beach, which was quiet except for the soft *scrunch, scrunch* of his feet on the pebbles. He walked slowly, calmed by the ripple of the waves and the moonlight dripping on the water like honey.

Such a peaceful scene. Campbell clambered into the rowing boat and sat down, picking up an oar in each hand. Gilchrist Muir and Tam Beaton bent forwards with their hands on the stern.

A blur of orange flashed across the night sky on the other side of the river. A ball of burning pitch had just been launched at the castle.

Campbell nodded to Muir; the men started pushing hard with their arms outstretched and their heads down. The boat slid along the pebbly beach, and then it was sinking and wobbling on the surface of the water.

Two other men came running forwards with a dead sheep, one holding its forelegs and the other holding its hind legs. They came splashing into the water.

"You'll capsize me!" Campbell protested as the sheep was heaved onto the boat, making it rock from side to side.

Tam Beaton threw Campbell a rope. He caught it and tied it to his seat. Beaton tied the other end of the rope to a ladder. As if the boat was not heavy enough, he would now be towing a long, heavy wooden ladder.

A bag of oatmeal, a bag of barley, and a barrel of whisky—that was what Loch Awe said he would be carrying. Whatever happened to that? Did Loch Awe's word count for nothing, here? There was always another sack, another barrel, coming out of the cottages and onto the boat.

"You never know what they might need," Tam Beaton had said.

Or how long it will be before the glens are clear of snow and Loch Awe's men can make their way across the hills to Inveraray where his galleys will be waiting.

The boat was sitting very low in the water now. It was harder to spot but also easier to sink if it was spotted. Sean Campbell dipped the oars into the water and leaned back, pulling on them. The men on the beach turned their backs and walked away.

He pulled on the oars again and then again. The boat was gliding out into the river. He was watching the small stone houses with their thatched roofs get smaller and smaller.

He rowed, getting into a rhythm, not thinking about the time. The river broadened out. He rowed with his back to the castle, continually pulling the oars in and letting the boat glide so he could turn and look at the castle. It was easy to begin with, the outline of its turrets visible in the moonlight. But as he rowed, the treeline got higher and higher, and the trees grew bigger and bigger until they obscured the castle.

The water was black like the night sky above him. It was strange how there could be such deep peace in the middle of the river. The smell of salt was in the air as the current met the incoming tide, throwing up waves and froth. The oars slipped silently under the surface and out again. The heavy load made the boat easier to row; it cut a clean path through the water, untouched by wind or waves.

The ladder bumped against the stern of the boat. Another fireball streaked across the dark sky, its tail dissipating as it travelled. Campbell watched it drop over the castle walls.

Sounds came floating across the surface of the river—the quiet *schhoop!* of another missile being launched and then the shuddering of the catapult. Another blaze of flame drew a line across the sky. Then it had gone.

The castle was built on a piece of land jutting out into the river between two bays. They would see the boat if he landed on either bay—better just to aim for the castle hoping the trees would hide him.

He could hear shouts and clashes. Nobody knew he was here amid the chaos. Campbell leaned forwards and drew hard on the oars.

Hard and pulling harder. Underneath the castle, the hill plunged directly into the river with trees growing out horizontally where the bank was undercut by the river and spreading their branches across the water. The canopy of twisted branches reached out towards him, forming a roof over his head.

The bow thudded against the bank. Campbell put one foot over the side and then the other. He was up to his thighs in freezing water, his testicles chilled and numb.

He pulled himself onto the bank on all fours, finding fingerholds and knee holds in the hard ground. He had a length of rope in his numb fingers; he wound it around a tree.

The boat drifted downriver till the rope grew taut; then it was pulled into the bank with the ladder in its wake. The boat and its cargo would be safe for a while—long enough, maybe, for him to get up to the castle and come back down with some men to move the sacks and barrels.

His feet were slippery on the icy ground. His leather boots with their flat soles could not grip. He made his way up through the trees, one step at a time and always reaching out with either hand to grab the frozen branch of a tree. The exposed roots of the trees acted like steps, creating a narrow path that wound its way up the hill—Lucifer's Stairway, they called it in winter.

Every step in the snow with his wet boots was treacherous. His feet were numb; he could not move his toes.

The ground rose gradually above him. A stone wall, barely visible in the starlight, emerged through the trees. Were they still using the sluice gate? he wondered. It would be on the seaward side of the castle. Could he stand outside and wait till dawn and then walk into the castle amid a deluge of excrement?

He looked above him and saw half a turret bulging out from the wall with the metal bars underneath. This was the garderobe[26]—not at ground level or discharging into the moat but higher up and out of reach.

There would be no way in through the toilet this time. But it might make for a useful murder hole to shoot arrows out of if someone inside mistook him for the enemy. Arrows, bolts, boiling oil—all manner of

---

[26] Toilet

things could come out of it and down on his head. Perhaps even arrows with their tips dipped in excrement.

He followed the wall for a few steps, feeling the stone with his fingers. The weak points were the places where traffic went in or came out—the entrance, the sluice gate, the toilets. To go round to the entrance was to come in sight of Cowal's men.

What about the ladder? It was floating on the surface of the river, soaked and heavy with water. Could he climb back down to the boat, untie it, and drag it back uphill through the trees? Could he weave it through the trees, his feet slipping on the frozen ground? If even if he managed to drag the ladder up through the trees, what then? He needed a firm base he could drive it into—not a slippery, frosty steep slope. And he had no one to hold it firmly against the wall while he climbed up.

And if the defenders saw a man on a ladder, would they take him for the enemy and shoot an arrow straight into his face with him stuck on the ladder and nowhere to go? He put a hand on the smooth stonework, feeling for a weakness. He took a step to his right, but the ground was icy, and he found his foot slowly sliding downhill. He fell forwards onto his face, putting his arms out to break his fall.

The sound of something dribbling caught his ear. He turned too quickly, and his foot slipped on the ice. His leg gave way underneath him, and he crashed onto the frozen ground.

A squirt of urine dropped out of the toilet and burned a hole in the snow underneath.

Crawling on all fours, finding fingerholds, footholds, handholds, he made his way back to the bulge of the garderobe coming out of the wall above him. The whistling wind cut through the trees, making him shudder.

Welcome to Lucifer's Stairway.

He stood up, slipped on the ice again and fell. Putting a hand against the wall for balance, he got up again. "Charaid,"[27] he shouted up at the grille.

Another jet of water squirted downwards.

---

[27] Friend

"Charaid!" Campbell stepped underneath the iron grille. The ground under his feet was soft and damp, not cold and hard like the rest of the hillside.

There was silence.

"Charaid!" he shouted again.

Then a voice shouted back, "Who's there?"

"Sean Campbell."

"Stay there," the voice said.

And where else am I going to go? Campbell wondered. His feet were cold; his toes were stinging. He clapped his arms against his chest and stamped his feet in the squidgy ground. His breath was coming out in clouds.

A different voice this time. A female voice. "Sean, is that you?"

"Yes!"

"Go to the sluice gate."

Far below, the sea was rising and falling against the rock. Seaweed and algae clung to the rock, making it slippery and treacherous. A wind was blowing—strong enough to send a man plummeting to his doom if he lost his footing.

Clusters of seagull droppings told him he was near the sluice gate.

There was the scraping of metal on stone and a portcullis slowly rising; the porter leaning back, groaning as he used his body weight to turn the handle; and the gate slowly lifting through the grooves cut in the stone.

Sean Campbell watched the iron gate rise up to his chest and then stop. The smell of rotting innards hit his nostrils as he bent down and passed underneath the portcullis. It quickly crashed back down behind him. In front of him was a second portcullis.

Here he was, trapped in the murder hole. The floor sloped downwards. Dried blood filled the cracks between the paving stones. Fish scales and pieces of skin lay scattered around. He waited for the second portcullis to lift up, but nothing happened.

Silence.

Then there was the scuff of feet on the stone steps. Suddenly, he was looking at a woman on the other side of the portcullis.

"Sean!" she gasped.

Straggly blonde hair, a flat chest, and a mouth that was a little too big. If you described her features one at time, you could not make her sound beautiful. And yet, those same features came together in a way that gave her both beauty and elegance. "Janet!" he said.

"You're shivering."

"I'm all right."

"Your hands are red."

But the first thing that had caught his attention was the swollen belly. "Who's the father?" he asked. No smiles, no warm greetings, no protestations of how much he'd missed her. Just a direct question.

"Patrick," she said.

"Patrick O'Donnell?"

"Yes."

His coldness forgotten, he felt a sickness rising in his stomach. And, with it, anger came up. *You were better than that, Janet.*

"Where is he?"

"He left to bring help."

Relief. At least you don't have to talk to him. But other thoughts were in his head now—O'Donnell's mouth on Janet's, his tongue down her throat, his naked body lying against hers, his seed in her womb.

"You must be freezing!" She tilted her head back and shouted upwards. "Raise the portcullis," she shouted. She turned back to Campbell "Where have you been?"

"You haven't heard?"

She hesitated. "I heard you cut a drummer boy's throat."

"Everybody seems to have heard that story."

She tilted her head again. "Raise the portcullis," she shouted once more, more urgently this time. She brought her head down to look at Campbell. "It's good to see you."

Could he say the same thing? *You've gotten yourself pregnant to a bully who'll sleep with other women and never think anything of it—a man who won't shirk his responsibilities because he doesn't understand what his responsibilities are.* "It's good to see you, Janet," he found himself saying.

"What are you doing here?"

Suddenly, Campbell remembered there was a boat full of supplies tied to a tree. "I'll need someone to help me carry bags of oatmeal up this hill," he said.

"If there's whisky, there won't be any shortage of volunteers."

CHAPTER 33

Sliding down the hill on his bottom, he felt the way with his feet and his hands surfing the ground. There was the boat, rising and falling on the surface of the water and the ladder trailing behind it.

Sticking out his legs, he would aim for a tree trunk, collide with it, and then push himself off it and be sliding downhill again. His bottom was wet and cold; his feet were numb. The black river came rushing up towards him, and he plunged into it, gasping when the cold hit him. He was up to his thighs, the water chilling his legs and freezing his testicles.

"What are you doing with that?" A man on Campbell's shoulder was pointing at the ladder.

"I thought I might need it to get over the wall."

"We could use it for firewood," the man said, wading forwards with his dagger drawn to saw at the rope attaching the ladder to the boat.

Campbell grabbed a bag of oatmeal with two hands, lifted it up, and dumped it on the bank. Other men were coming down the hill now, some on their feet and some on their bottoms. He grabbed the branch of a tree and pulled himself onto the bank with one hand. He took a step with his right foot, but these flat-soled leather shoes had no grip. He took a step with his left foot. Then he took a step with his right foot, feeling for a firm footing on the icy surface. Then his leg was pulled away from him and the ground came flying upwards to hit him in the face. There was nothing to grip, and he slid downwards into the water. He stood up, up to his waist in water, grasping the branch of a tree and pulling himself back onto the riverbank.

His whole body was shaking. He held onto the branch.

James Duncan was looking at him, hands on hips. "You unload the boat," he said. "We'll carry the bags uphill."

I stand here, in the cold water, with freezing testicles? Why do I get all the good jobs? Campbell lifted the sacks from the rowing boat and laid them on the bank. He watched the men carry them back uphill in pairs with dry bottoms, dry legs, and dry feet.

Men with bare feet and bare knees scampered up the slope, gripping the snow with their toes. Campbell watched the swinging pleats of tartan vanish into the trees. He was suddenly remembering walking with bare feet along the beach, enjoying the feel of the snow crumpling under his weight while making sure to bend the foot and toes to keep the blood circulating. To walk along the beach making footprints in the snow and then watch the snow retreat under the rising tide, his skin tingling in the cold, cleansing air. A man was invigorated, more alive, in weather like this.

He shook his head. When did I get so soft? he wondered.

Then he was bending into the boat to pull out the last sack and dump it onto the bank. He pulled himself out of the water, the cold, wet hose clinging to his legs. He was watching the other men climb easily and quietly back up that hill. They moved slowly, leaning into the hill, careful where they put their feet. Behind them, Campbell squelched his way up the hill one step at a time in his soaking hose and boots.

They went in through the sluice gate and up the stone steps, Campbell leaving a trail of wet footprints behind him. He followed a long passageway and then went up more steps until he found himself in the castle courtyard.

"The kitchen!" Nichol Wallace was shouting. "Take it all into the kitchen!"

And there was Janet, smiling, looking up at him the way she used to. "You'll join me for a cup of whisky?"

"Certainly." Campbell took a step towards the kitchen.

"Up there." Janet pointed to the battlements. "I want Cowal to see us."

Campbell was enviously eyeing the others scamper into the warmth of the kitchen, but a flurry of arrows, thick like the rain, came showering down into the courtyard bouncing against the cobbles. Campbell grabbed Janet with both arms and threw her against the wall; he pressed himself up hard against her, protecting her with his body.

White arrow shafts against a black sky, pattering onto the stonework like heavy rain.

Her nose against his, the way they used to shelter under the trees during a heavy rainstorm. Her body squashed between him and the rough stone wall. He could feel her taut belly against his—a belly that had once been flat and soft.

"Are you all right?" she asked.

Wasn't he supposed to ask her that? "Yes," he found himself saying.

She could not move; his hands were pressed against the wall on either side of her. She looked up at him. "Wasn't this always the way you wanted me?"

Or was it the way she had always wanted him? Campbell wondered. But that was another time and place. He turned away from her, looking across the courtyard.

"Morag!" Janet gasped.

A woman lay on the floor of the courtyard with arrows protruding from her chest, arms, legs, and stomach.

Another woman with long hair like straw was bending over Morag. She pulled an arrow shaft out of Morag's chest and looked at the tip, which was only a little blunted. "If you sharpen it, we could use it again." She passed the arrow to a man who was standing beside her and then pulled another one from the corpse.

Mary MacLean gathered up an armful of arrows that lay scattered across the courtyard and took them into the tower, running upstairs. Janet took Campbell's hand as another flurry of arrows came over the wall, running for the kitchen. They ducked into the doorway, flinching as arrows fell all around.

"Thanks," she said, gratitude in her eyes.

"Thanks for what?"

"For coming."

"It's nothing."

"It's everything." She smiled.

A barrel of whisky stood on the floor, where Nichol Wallace had left it. The stopper was still in it. Campbell looked around for an axe.

"Not now," Janet said. "In the morning. We'll drink it up on the battlements where Cowal can see us."

So I'll still be here in the morning? There's a woman in St John's Town, or maybe she's in Stirling. I need to go back and see her.

"Unless you have to take a message to Loch Awe?" Janet said.

She was offering him a way out. Get in the boat and row away with a message for Campbell of Loch Awe. Run away with respectability.

The man who didn't do the job properly in Melnik Castle and then cut and run when he had the chance in Dunoon—that's what they'll say.

"I'll drink your health from the battlements tomorrow morning—when Cowal can see us," Campbell said. And, in that moment, the die was cast.

To leave these people now, to climb back into his boat and row away seemed like such an act of cowardice. Already he could hear the gossips—the man who cut the boy's throat in Melnik, the man who rowed away from Dunoon when the fighting got too tough for him—Cut-throat Campbell, Cowardly Campbell, Cold-hearted Campbell.

If he could help them hang on a few days, a few weeks maybe, the failure of Melnik would be forgotten. Catherine did not care about his reputation, but other people did. If he could ride back to Blackfriars as the hero of Dunoon, maybe then her parents would give him their blessing.

She would be happier if he could marry her with her parents' acceptance. You want to make the woman happy, don't you?

Like you never did before.

He was looking at Janet. "Where do I sleep?"

"There are plenty empty rooms," she said. Then she added "The rooms are cold; some men are sleeping together in the kitchen to keep warm."

His feet and fingers were numb; his insides were chilled. How he wanted a warm body to sleep with—a warm woman's body. "I'll take a room," he said.

"There are no fires burning in the rooms."

Did she think he had gone soft? "I'm so tired, I could sleep anywhere."

"I can give you a wool blanket."

"Thank you."

"One blanket," she added, rather hastily.

He walked up the winding stairway and along the dark passageway with its burnt-out candles, feeling his way by trailing a hand against the wall.

A door was half-open; he stepped into a cold, empty room. The furniture had been removed, as had the wood panelling on the walls. The shutters had been left, thankfully, to prevent a gale blowing in through the window.

He lay down on the wooden floorboards and drew the blanket over him. He closed his eyes.

Catherine Douglas came up the stairs with a candle in one hand, standing in the doorway with her bare feet protruding out of the hem of her gown—her beautiful bare feet with the second toe longer than the big toe.

"Good morning!"

He opened his eyes. Janet MacRory was standing in the doorway, and there was no candle—only bars of sunshine coming in through the slats in the shutters.

"Are you awake?" That was Janet's voice.

"Yes," he mumbled.

"Come downstairs."

Then her feet were on the stairs, going down. Those bars of sunshine were in his eyes, lighting up the room the way they had lit up Catherine's hair as he lay underneath her in the bedchamber at Stirling.

Strands of hair sparkling red like rubies in golden rays. She was on top of him, sunshine lighting her head like a halo. He was looking through her hair at the rays of sun coming in through the slats in the shutters.

Her smooth stomach, her floppy breasts hanging forwards with the nipples pointing downwards. She was on top of him, leaning forwards with her hands on his shoulders and mischief in her eyes. Her hair cascading forwards, lowering her mouth onto his. Campbell reaching up, searching for her with his lips, as he thrust upwards and upwards, the sensations rippling through her body; she was gasping for breath, or was it gasping in pleasure?

She was pinning him down and leaning over him, and he wanted to give the whole of himself to her—to give her everything of himself till there was nothing left. He wanted to give and give and give, thrusting into her with her body erect and above his till she sighed and gasped and came collapsing down onto him wet and warm and soft and sweaty, smothering him in her softness and her love.

"Catherine," he breathed. She was with him in the room. She was in his arms.

"Wake up!" A man's brutal voice crashed into the room.

Sean Campbell opened his eyes again as a man he did not know unbolted the shutters to let in the weak winter sunshine.

The man walked out.

"You have not got up, yet?"

That was a woman's voice. Mary MacLean was standing in the doorway, leaning an elbow against the door frame. Her long, black hair obscured most of her face.

"I'm getting up."

"We're toasting the king's health from the battlements this morning—remember?"

"You can toast the king's health without me."

"Come on."

"Nichol can do it."

"If they see Nichol, they'll think it's a bluff. We want them to see you, so that they know we're getting supplied."

Exhausted, sore, he pulled back the blanket and stood up.

"You sleep like that? With a mail shirt on?"

"What else should I do with it?"

"You must be uncomfortable. And cold."

"You get used to it."

"We must give you a plaid." She winked. "Janet says the tartan brings out the green in your eyes."

He followed her out of the bedchamber and into the corridor and down the winding stone stairs and across the courtyard and into kitchen. A large iron pot hung by a chain over a fire that quietly smouldered.

The long wooden table had no food on it—only arrow shafts and a knife to sharpen them with.

Janet put two silver goblets on a silver tray and set them on the table. "Cut me a leg of mutton," she said.

Campbell took the knife from his belt. The carcass of a sheep lay on the floor, its dead eyes looking up at him. It had taken two men to drag it by the hoofs up Lucifer's Stairway. Now here it was on the floor.

Strange it was—the things that became weapons of war. Campbell cut around the top of the foreleg with his knife. Then, with one foot on the carcass and two hands on the foreleg, he twisted it and then twisted it again and pulled it off.

He was about to strip the flesh from the bone when Janet stopped him.

"Don't do that!" she protested.

"We're eating the skin?"

"I want them to see what it is."

The two goblets were full of whisky. A stoneware bottle sat on the tray next to them. "Let's go," Janet said.

"Where?"

"The battlements."

He followed the hem of her skirt brushing against the stone steps as they made their way back up the winding stairs. They came out of the tower and onto the battlements as a dying arrow flew past, dropping down into the courtyard. Campbell instinctively ducked.

"Stand up straight," Janet said. "I want them to see us." She put the tray down on one of the broad bays in the battlements. She picked up her cup and put it to her lips. "Slainte."

Campbell picked up a cup. "Slainte." Then he turned, theatrically, towards where he thought Cowal was. There were pennons fluttering between the bare branches of the trees and the glint of armour in the sunlight. Farther back were tents and horses.

There was a big tent in the distance. That was probably Cowal's. He held the cup aloft and then put it to his lips.

Another arrow shot over their heads, coming out of the trees, its trajectory taking it up and then down into the castle courtyard.

"Have a bit of mutton."

"It's raw."

"Pass me a bit."

He was resting the leg against his shoulder, holding it with one hand. He gripped it with both hands, twisting the joint till it snapped. He passed her the lower portion of the foreleg.

"I meant a portion for a lady."

"You want them to see you, don't you?"

She took the leg from him. She leaned an elbow against the wall, holding the mutton joint high up.

"You're not going to eat that, are you?"

"No. You are." She passed it back to him.

"I should have brought a boiled ham."

"You always liked mutton."

"When it's warm and greasy, served with boiled kale."

Janet put the cup to her lips and drank. "I used to dream about days like this."

"Eating raw mutton?"

"Having a castle all of my own. Living in it with you."

"I was never going to inherit a castle."

"A cottage can be a castle; it's how you see it."

He frowned. What was she saying to him? "You didn't wait for me," he said, glancing at her swollen belly.

"I'm supposed to wait for years, only to hear that you're lying dead in a ditch somewhere?"

"I was trying to make my name."

"You certainly did that."

He winced visibly.

"I was faithful to you for a long time, though I got no credit for it. I didn't know where you were or what you doing."

"Where is O'Donnell?"

"Paddy went to get help."

Paddy. How could she speak so affectionately of him? With luck, Cowal's men will have come across him by now. With just a little a bit of luck, we'll see his battered corpse floating down the River Clyde any day now.

"I used to lie in my tent outside Melnik Castle thinking about you."

"Men only think about making their names on the battlefield. You cut a boy's throat to make your name."

"You don't think I did that, do you?"

"You were so far away; we heard all sorts of stories."

"I didn't cut his throat."

"All that matters to you is what other people think of you."

Another arrow came over the wall. Janet turned to look outwards, holding up her cup and drinking from to it. "Let them see the mutton," she said.

Campbell held up the leg of mutton, touching it with his lips.

"Take a bite. Let them see you eat—and enjoy it."

He grimaced, touching his lips to the hairy hide. "I prefer my mutton hot."

"Get on with it."

Cold, hard, tough, chewy, tasting foul, Campbell bit into the leg. Then he passed it to Janet who hesitated for a moment and then reluctantly bit into it.

Down below, Nichol Wallace came running up the steps. "What are you doing?"

"I'm thirsty," Janet said. She took a sip of whisky.

"That's such a stupid thing to do!"

"We'll break their will," Janet said.

"You're telling them we can hold out till Loch Awe gets here."

"That's the idea."

"You're trying to impress this cut-throat?"

Campbell flinched instinctively. "They'll go home now."

"They know they're beaten," Janet said.

"They know they can't starve us out," Wallace said.

"Exactly."

"So they have no choice, now; they will attack tonight, before Loch Awe gets here."

CHAPTER 34

An iron pot sat next to the well, unsteady on a wobbly iron grate. It was half-full of lard, melting under the medium heat from some burning sticks.

Janet MacRory went over to the pot with a handful of arrows and leaned over on tiptoes, stretching her arms, careful not to touch the side of the pot. She dipped the arrows into the lard one at a time and then lit them on the fire and carried them, smouldering, up to battlements to hand to the men.

Nichol Wallace drew back his bow with a trail of smoke rising from the tip of the arrow. He was never given any respect when they were growing up; he could not fight with his fists or with a sword. But he could shoot an arrow and hit his target every time. He drew the back the string, pausing with the bow bending and the string taut. He let the arrow go. The arrow fizzed over the wall, a blur of orange, and dropped on the other side.

Alison Gow, tall and thin, always thin, but even thinner now, came along the battlements with more arrows. She passed Wallace as another flurry of arrows, thick like the geese that flew south every winter, came shooting over the wall.

"Nick!" Alison shrieked.

Wallace's bow was stretched tight, the string cutting into the three fingers of his right hand. His left eye was shifting from the burning tip of the arrow to the target beyond; then it was focussed only on the target. Then he let go, and the arrow left his bow with a rush, fizzing over the wall.

"Nick! You've been hit!" Alison shouted, looking at the arrow shaft in his shoulder.

"Another arrow!" Wallace shouted.

"Stand still!" Alison Gow shouted at him. "Stand still!" She had one hand on the arrow shaft and a cloth in the other, ready to stem the flow as blood as she pulled the arrow out.

"Get back!" Wallace shouted at Alison Gow. "Take cover!"

Alison seemed not to notice the arrows falling all around her. "Stand still," she said.

Wallace wrapped his good right arm around Alison's thin waist and lifted her off her feet, carrying her along the parapet and into the shelter of the tower. He let her down and she immediately gripped the arrow in his shoulder. "Brace yourself," she said.

The arrowhead came out, blood spurting out along with it. Alison pressed her hand against it. "Don't move!" she shouted in his ear. She took the scarf from her head and wound it around his shoulder.

"Get into the keep!" Wallace shouted at her as he came out of the tower, the strip of woollen tartan around his wound already having a red patch on it. Another volley of arrows came over the wall.

Alison went back down to gather more arrows and whittle them sharp, arrows falling all around her as she came out into the courtyard. She got down on one knee and picked up a bow that was lying on the floor, not knowing whose it was, and picked up a stray arrow that had fallen onto the cobbles. She could hear somebody shouting, "Take cover in the keep!" But whether the shout was aimed at her or not she knew not.

On the battlements, Nichol Wallace had gone down onto one knee. He did it when an arrow hit his thigh, and his leg began to tremble as he lost control of the muscle.

Alison Gow came running back up the stairs, standing over him and suddenly looking very tall. Here he was before her, on one knee, the way she had always wanted him. But she had never said anything.

She put down the arrows in her hand and carefully looked at the arrow in his thigh.

"I'm all right," Wallace said. But it was himself he was trying to convince.

Alison lifted up her gown, exposing the white linen petticoat underneath. She took the dagger from James Duncan's belt and punctured the petticoat with the tip. Then she cut downwards, hearing the material rip, and took a long strip from it, tying it around the wound in Wallace's thigh.

"There! That's better!" she said and smiled.

"Get more arrows." Wallace was already picking up the next one to load into his bow.

Alison rushed down the stairs and into the courtyard, picking up the fallen arrow shafts that lay scattered around. If she could collect enough, she could sit with him, sharpening them as he shot them from his bow. The two of them would defend the castle together, shoulder to shoulder amid the chaos while the walls collapsed before an enemy howling at the gate like a pack of wolves. They would stand together hand in hand against the furies like David and Bathsheba or Anthony and Cleopatra.

Wallace drew back his bow, his attention on the tip. He was aiming at his target, trying to anticipate where it was moving. Then he took his attention back to the arrow till there was only the arrow and the hand at his ear and the string stretched tight. The bow was part of his arm, part of him. Then he let it go effortlessly, without strain, without thinking.

He turned away, not looking at the result of his shot, not interested. He was looking for Alison coming out of the tower, but she was still in the courtyard.

She was lying on her stomach, her arms spread out and an arrow protruding from her shoulder-blades. Wallace dropped his bow and stumbled down the stone steps, his wobbly legs no longer under control.

"Alison!" he shouted, bending over her and pulling the arrow out and then realising he had nothing to bind the wound with. But there was not much sign of the wound bleeding, and so he got his arms underneath her and carefully and gently turned her over.

Something smacked into his side, just above the kidney. But he was not interested in that, didn't care about that. "Alison!" he said to her, but she was looking at him with faraway eyes.

Another shower of arrows came over the wall and fell all around, like rain. "Alison!" Wallace shouted, and he gripped her hand. But there was no strength in her fingers; she did not return his grip.

Wallace crawled around her till both his arms were under her armpits and tried to stand up. Her body lifted, but the pain in his leg was excruciating. He took a step towards the chapel and then another, his face twisted in agony. The war was forgotten; the battle was forgotten.

Cowal could have the castle. What did he care? He had to get Alison into the chapel and bind up her wounds.

Suddenly he was angry with himself. All that time he had spent fighting and ignoring her! Why had he made her wait so long, this angel of a woman? If he loved her, he would have said to them, to hell with your feud! He would have taken her out of the castle and deep into the Highlands, out of reach of feuding armies.

He took another step towards the chapel and another. His leg was buckling, but he was not going to let it buckle, not going to let it. He was taking her to the safety of the chapel, and he would dress her wounds. Let them come through the gate; they wouldn't harm anyone who was in the chapel. And, anyway, he was finished with this feud.

Another flurry of arrows came over the wall and hung in the air above their heads. He did not have time to get Alison under cover; he was moving too slowly, and the arrows were dropping down too fast. He lay her body on the ground and threw himself on top of her.

There they lay, like lovers, as half a dozen arrows thudded into Wallace's broad back. One hit him in the kidney while the other landed higher up, piercing his lung.

"We'll tear his shirt into strips. Hold him steady while I pull out the arrow." That was Mary MacLean's voice.

A head appeared in front of Wallace's eyes. "You're going to feel some pain, Nichol," the voice said, "but it will only be for a moment."

He opened his mouth to say *I understand*, but the words did not come out.

Suddenly they were pulling at him, pulling hard at his chest. They were pulling at his ribs like they were going to break each one and wrench it from his chest. His eyes were filling with tears; he was in pain—his whole body was breaking apart. He shouted at them to stop but no words came out. What was wrong with his voice? They were going to burst open his whole chest and leave him there to die, a bloody mess of entrails and gore, lying on the table like a goose carved open for the feast.

Why was he lying on the kitchen table, staring up at the ceiling? How did he get here? They had stopped pulling. Was that good or bad?

There was no pain now. Or was it just that there was no pulling? He could think of nothing but his tiredness. He was too tired to feel pain.

A face appeared in front of him again. He could not recognise it. Then he did; it was Mary, her long black hair falling in front of her face and hiding it. There were so many questions to ask. Had anyone else been hit? Or was he the only one? He opened his mouth. "Where is Alison?" he asked. Why was no one answering him? Could they not hear?

The face had seen him mouthing silent words. "Can you speak up?" the face asked.

Nichol Wallace opened and closed his mouth, but nothing would come out. Then he sighed, a long, tired sigh, and closed his eyes. *How is Alison?* he wondered.

He had failed to get her out of here—failed even to get her out of the courtyard. He'd failed to be a leader.

"Alison," he said.

All the men liked Janet—Janet, with her blue eyes and blonde hair. She was beautiful and elegant. That was it. Elegance.

Why had he never noticed Alison before? Well-meaning, ignored, neglected Alison. All those things I should have said to her. I'll look after you when all this is over.

Or maybe we'll get away from hills and castles and clans fighting with each other and rival chiefs always trying to gain the king's favour—just you and me on a small patch of land, you and me, your belly growing bigger all summer long.

I never said to her, Alison, let's get out of here. Let's go to the Carse of Gowrie. The land's fertile there and flat like a bowling green. A man can make a good living on a small patch of land. You don't have to be a good farmer; the rain comes every spring, and the oats and the barley grow tall in the summer sun.

I never kissed her.

Not once.

"I need a bucket of water." That was Mary MacLean's voice. "A bucket of water!"

I'm not thirsty. I don't need any water.

All that time chasing Janet MacRory, but it was Alison who was with him now. Alison—always in the background. Honest, hard-working Alison—she was a bit too tall, clumsy, always ignored, dull, plain, serious. She didn't make the boys laugh.

But it was her hair he could feel brushing his cheek now, her cold hand in his.

You're hand's too cold, Alison. We'll have to get you in front of fire. Get a big fire roaring and hold you in front of it.

Above his head, the walls were beginning to spin. Or was it the floor spinning? Why was the floor shaking like a table with a broken leg?

Like that table in the kitchen that nobody had fixed. He could feel the rough wooden surface under his fingers. Why had they taken the table out of the kitchen and into the courtyard?

Or had they taken him into the kitchen? Where was Alison? Why could he only see Mary MacLean's black hair?

Alison.

He wanted to reach out to her. All those times I ignored you. All those years you carried your pain around with you, hiding it behind a mask. Why could I never see that before? All those things I never said to you.

I'll do things differently now.

He could feel himself going round and round—round and round. Like they were dancing together. Round and round with their arms locked together and a bright fire burning under the night sky.

With a detached sense of disbelief, he watched the walls moving, spinning—spinning slowly at first but getting faster.

There must have been a hole in the ceiling because he could see the sun shining through. The room was full of white light. White light poured in through the hole in the ceiling. And he was floating upwards—upwards and upwards towards the white light.

The table had stopped shaking now. Why was he looking down at Mary MacLean's dark hair? He could see her head over his, her hand in his.

She was sobbing.

Why are you sobbing, Mary?

Sobbing over a fool like me?

I wasn't worth it.

"Nick!" a voice whispered but the voice was faint. The voice was on the floor and out of the light. It was beneath him and far away. Already it was calling to him from a long way off.

CHAPTER 35

"Give me those arrows." Sean Campbell held out his free hand.

"I've never seen you shoot an arrow in your life," Janet MacRory said.

"How difficult can it be?" Campbell had picked up Nichol Wallace's bow.

Mary MacLean had been dipping arrows into hot oil before she'd dropped them on the courtyard, running over to help Nichol Wallace. Now Janet had picked them up. "I'll give them to Baldred," she said.

"Give them to me."

"If Baldred uses them, there's at least a chance he might hit something."

"You're bound to hit something if you shoot into the crowd."

"Archers are cowards who stand a safe distance from the battlefield." Janet gave him a critical look. "That's what you used to say."

Campbell flinched slightly. Yes, he had said that. He had spent his whole life breathing contempt for the archers who would go through a whole military campaign and never get hurt. They didn't go home with missing legs or arms or scars across their cheeks. Archers were a lower class of life who did not understand chivalry or the concept of giving a man a fair fight. "Just give me the arrows," he said.

"To have you waste them all?" She shook her head. "I don't think so."

Baldred MacDuff had come down from the battlements and had gone over to James Duncan, who was lying face down on the cobbles. MacDuff put a foot on his back and plucked the arrows out one at a time. Duncan let out a feeble groan. MacDuff ran back to the tower and put the first arrow into his bow. Above his head, he could see Mary MacLean run along the walkway with head bowed beneath the battlements.

He came up the winding stair, and Mary dropped the bundle of arrows at his feet.

"You take one," he said, having picked up two bows that were stationed by the battlements.

Mary was about to protest that she had never loosed an arrow from a bow in her life, but MacDuff had already turned away from her to take aim. Mary loaded an arrow on the bow, pointing the tip to the floor like she had seen the archers do. Then she lifted it up in one movement. Her arms were strong from carrying pails of milk, but pulling back the tight bowstring was difficult; the string fought against her and cut into her fingers. She let go too early; the string snapped forwards and the arrow shot over the wall. Whether it hit anyone or not, she could not tell.

"Not so hard," Queen Joan said.

The comb was tugging at a knot of hair. "Sorry," Catherine said.

"Jean's never rough with my hair the way you are."

Catherine picked carefully at the knot with her fingers.

"Alexander Lovell should be here soon." Queen Joan said. "I was expecting him to arrive a few days ago, but the roads are bad at this time of year."

"Yes," Catherine said. Her voice was tense.

"He has expectations. Once he marries into the Douglas family, he expects to receive a knighthood." Queen Joan turned in her seat to look at Catherine. "I'm not sure what His Grace thinks of that."

"I am sure His Grace will do as he pleases."

"Your mother has already hinted … well, mentioned it to me." Queen Joan took a breath. "He doesn't really have the status that he should have, the status that you should have. This was not the match that your parents had hoped for you. But it's the best they can do under the circumstances."

"A knighthood for selling silk?" Catherine rolled her eyes.

The queen hesitated for a moment, as if thinking "A knighthood would help the situation. It would make things look better."

"Yes," Catherine said. "She'll have dangled it in front of his nose like a carrot. He gets a knighthood; she gets silk dresses imported from Venice. Everyone's happy."

"Good. I'm glad." Queen Joan smiled.

Catherine looked at her. Was she being serious?

"You're not disappointed?"

"I only seek to serve, Your Grace," Catherine said carefully.

"A very good answer." Queen Joan smiled. "Now tell me the truth."

"I thought"—Catherine hesitated for a moment—"I thought Sean would be here."

"Sean?"

"Sean Campbell."

"The sewer rat?" Queen Joan grimaced. "Yes, I know." She shot Catherine a sideways glance. "That's the trouble with these kinds of men. They go off to fight, and you never know when you're going to see them again or if you're going to see them again."

"My mother's plan is to have me married off before he comes back."

"What you don't understand is ..." Joan hesitated slightly. "All your mother wants is for you to be happy."

Catherine let out a snort. She picked up the comb again.

"Your mother does not want you to be undone by the folly of youth again."

"I've had my youth."

"Whatever it seems like, your mother is acting out of love."

"Love for whom?"

"When you get to your mother's age, you'll understand better."

"Then why did you bring me here?"

Again, the queen hesitated. "Sean Campbell is a good servant to the king. But that's not the same thing as being a good husband." She paused for a moment. "I was hoping ... I was thinking that ... Maybe, if you had some time together, maybe you'd realise he's not the right man for you."

"Your Grace married for love."

"That wasn't so easy."

"You're fond of telling us you married a beggar."

"He was homeless and a fugitive; he wasn't a beggar."

"He came back here to reclaim his kingdom; you came with him."

"Do you know what my mother said to me?" Queen Joan stood up in her seat. "Oh, stop doing that!"

"She told you to stop?"

"No, I mean put the comb down."

Catherine put the comb down on the dressing table.

"No. What my mother said was … You've made me forget, now. Oh, yes, she said she would never see me again. So far, she's been right."

For half a second, Catherine pictured the queen being scolded by a large woman with knitted brows and wagging forefinger. Then she pictured herself jumping onto the back of Sean Campbell's horse and riding off to the ends of the earth, her arms held tightly around his chest and her head lying against his shoulder—far, far away from all this.

"I could have married for money," Queen Joan said, "and I often look back and think how easy that would have been. I could have lived on a large estate with my parents only a few miles away. I could be going to sleep every night without having to make sure the doors were locked. I could be getting up every morning to have breakfast with my family, not travelling around the country to hold council meetings while leaving my children locked up in a castle because they're safer there than they would be on the road."

A big house with a large garden and servants to cook and clean. Or a knight on horseback with nothing to his name but a sword? All Catherine knew was that one man left her feeling dead inside, and the other sent a thrill down her spine.

———— † ————

Catriona MacNaughton, her white kirtle stained with blood at the shoulders and hanging loosely across her emaciated body, picked her way across the courtyard. Her skirt was bunched up around her thighs, exposing her shins, as she stepped over one body and then another. Then she let go of her skirt and let it drop, looking up at Janet MacRory on the battlements but saying nothing.

Janet's eyes were on a crow circling overhead. Its wings spread out, it was watching the goings-on in the courtyard. Then it glided over to the wall on the far side of the courtyard and perched on one of the battlements.

The smell of dead meat would attract the scavengers. But that was not what had caught her attention. Why was it peaceful enough for a crow to land on the battlements?

Where were the arrow shafts?

"What's happening?" she said.

"What did you say?" Baldred MacDuff asked.

She had spoken aloud involuntarily. She pushed open the wooden door of the tower and went down the winding stairs like the walking dead. She had no energy, no feeling, no passion. She no longer knew if she wanted to win this fight, no longer knew what she wanted. She wanted to survive only for the baby that was growing inside her.

How simpler things might have been if she had not become pregnant. Then she could have lain down in the courtyard and gone to sleep, not caring if she ever woke up.

Round and round and down and down she went till she reached the bottom of the tower. She came out into the castle courtyard, where crows were beginning to settle on the corpses. One crow perched on the nose of a corpse, surveying all around it.

With a bow in one hand and a handful of arrows in the other, Baldred MacDuff stood above them on the battlements. Somehow or other, he was still alive. Stronger men than him were dead. Better swordsmen, like James Duncan, were dead. Men of higher status, like Nichol Wallace, were dead. Innocent women who'd never wanted to be part of this, like Alison Gow, were dead. And here he was, Baldred MacDuff, still alive at the end of the attack.

But he was alive only in the sense that he was not dead. Every bone in his body ached. Exhaustion swept through him till he felt like the walking dead.

Beneath him, Catriona MacNaughton took a few steps across the courtyard, and the crows quickly spread their wings, taking to the air and circling above her head. An arrow shaft lay at her feet. She bent down, feeling as she did so that she might faint with exhaustion. She picked the arrow up, taking a knife tucked into the sleeve of her kirtle and quickly sharpening the tip.

She stepped over to another corpse that lay face down on the cobbled courtyard and pulled the arrows from its back. The crows watched her from above, perhaps wondering why she was taking the least edible bits.

A woman was lying face down on the cobbles. Sean Campbell went over to her, bending down and carefully turning the body over as if he thought he might hurt it.

"You broke their will," Janet said, looking at him. "They saw we had provisions and gave up."

Campbell felt uneasy. Something about it did not seem right. "They gave up very easily."

"If Cowal had stayed any longer, he would have been caught between Loch Awe's army and our stone walls. His time was up, and he knew it."

They made a strange couple as they stood together in the courtyard, both of them liking each other and both of them desiring each other. They looked more like father and daughter than friends or lovers, the man being tall and broad while the woman was small and slight.

Sean Campbell slowly shook his head. "Either Cowal's coming back after dark or …" he hesitated.

"Or?"

"Or this was just a diversion. A distraction."

"A diversion for what?"

"If I knew that—" He let out a sigh. "You bring Loch Awe's galleys down here because they're nowhere near—"

"Nowhere near what?"

"If I knew that." He shrugged. "Whatever else you want to attack."

"Cowal's not that clever," Janet MacRory said.

"Then he's coming back tonight."

Her shoulders sagged.

"Maybe you're right," Campbell said, trying to cheer her up. "Maybe it's over."

"Come," she said, leading him into the keep and up the stairs and out onto the battlements.

Squinting as he looked into the setting sun, a hand shielding his eyes, Sean Campbell scanned the birch trees. "Where are they?"

"Your reputation has preceded you." Janet rested her folded arms on the battlements. She shot him a sideways glance. "When you left, I used to walk through the birch trees on my own. I used to think that's where we would meet again—under the shade of the birch trees."[28]

"I always intended to come back alive."

"You were away a long time."

"I didn't want to come back until I was famous."

"Until the balladeers were singing songs about you?"

"You're going to tell me I was a daft wee laddie?"

"You weren't so wee."

"I don't hear you saying I wasn't daft."

"We were all daft when we were young." She left the battlements, going down the winding stairway and across the courtyard, with Sean Campbell following her. They went into the keep and back up the stairs and along the long the corridor. "You can take your pick of the rooms," Janet said.

She seemed to have decided he was staying for a while.

"I'll stay tonight," he found himself saying, "just in case Cowal comes back."

"This is the best room we have to offer you."

They had stopped outside an open door.

"This was Nichol's bedchamber."

"He took the best room?"

"He took the biggest room," Janet said. "My room gets more sunlight."

The room was almost bare, with only a small pile of straw on the floor. "You chopped up all the wood for fuel?"

"And arrow shafts."

"He should have let you have this room. If he had been a gentleman—"

"Oh, he tried to be one, most of the time."

"It will be cold in here," Campbell said, thinking about stone walls and no fire burning. "But it's cold everywhere."

"And uncomfortable," Janet added. "There's not much straw."

"I'm so tired I could sleep anywhere."

---

[28] It was a Celtic belief that birch trees grew in the Other World. In the old Scots poem "The Wife of Usher's Well," a woman's three sons die at sea, but they come back to visit her, one last time, with birch leaves in their hair.

"You could sleep in my bedchamber." The words popped out before Janet really knew what she had said. She blushed slightly. "What I mean is, well, what I meant to say is …" *It was such a relief to see you. I didn't know how tired I was, or how frightened. Fear keeps you awake at night, fear keeps you going without food, without sleep. Then a man takes the fear away, and you find yourself collapsing into his arms.*

"How much straw do you have in your room?" he asked.

"More than you."

"Is there enough for two?"

Janet stepped over to the pile of straw that was the remains of Nichol's bed and gathered up as much as she could in her arms. "There is now," she said playfully.

He hesitated. "I should return to Blackfriars," he said stiffly. "There is work to finish."

It was the wrong thing to say, and he knew it.

"Stay a few days; there is work to do here."

Stay a few days. Then days become weeks. Winter turns to spring and spring to summer; we could go swimming in the Firth of Clyde when the water is warm and the seals' heads break the surface to watch us like mermaids. Or we could swim under the night sky with the reflection of the distant stars on the black water. There was a beauty about the deep silence of the night, a silence as deep as the river itself.

And you, with your wet hair clinging to your naked shoulders.

"Stay for a week," she said.

To stay and sleep with you in your bedchamber like I never did before—like I should have done when I was nineteen years old. I wanted to back then—oh, how I wanted to—but I didn't have the courage.

To sleep with you now on a pile of straw because you've torn up the mattress and used it to make bandages, to sleep with your head on my shoulder and your fair hair across my chest, to sleep with your fingers working their way through the hairs on my chest.

To do it now because we didn't do it when the moment was ripe. To sleep with you now and your belly expanding day after day. To sleep with you, now, and Patrick O'Donnell's child in the same room.

Then I'm patrolling the battlements every day with a dagger in my belt, watching for O'Donnell's silhouette on the horizon.

"I should go to Blackfriars."

"Oh."

"I'll come back," he said.

"Yes."

But where's the purpose in making false promises? When will I come back? When Catherine Douglas has married Alexander Lovell? When King James has no more use for me? When I've picked up a mace and broken every bone in Patrick O'Donnell's body and left him lying on the slopes of Beinn Ruadh for the crows to pick over?

Maybe then I'll come back.

"I understand," she said quietly.

Yes, I think you do understand. We were a time and a place, but the time and place is not here—not here, not now. I made a mess of it back then because that's what I always do, and now we're in a different time and place. "I'll go in the morning," he said. "Once I'm sure Cowal's not coming back."

"You must eat before you go. We'll cook some bannocks and some barley bread and wash it down with whisky."

She smiled to him, but it was a weak smile that masked a lot of pain.

It was a weak smile with lips that were cracked and dry from standing outside in the cold winds.

Once upon a time, those lips had been red and moist and swollen with claret. They'd been open and inviting him to plunge down onto them—to plunge down like an eagle spotting its prey on the hillside and knowing this is its moment, swooping downwards in the blink of an eye.

But you dithered, you fool. And then the moment had gone like the hunter taking aim at a stag only to wait a moment too long for that perfect shot and then let the arrow go after the stag had bolted.

CHAPTER 36

"How was the council?"

"Taxes, taxes, taxes! The king wants more taxes," Atholl complained. Then his tone changed. "Everything is set," he said quietly.

A blast of sleet blew up the High Street. Robert Graham shivered. "The bolts are still in place."

"They will be removed at the last moment, so there is no time to replace them."

Graham was stamping his feet to keep warm. Two men approached from halfway down the street. Between them, they were leading three horses by the reins.

"You wait for the signal from Robert Stewart," Atholl said. His voice was quiet. Then he turned away, striding towards the approaching men.

"Lord Atholl?" a voice said. A man was holding out the reins to his horse.

Atholl mounted. Then the other two men mounted their horses.

"I envy you," Atholl said. "By the time we're on the bridge, you will be enjoying a hot bowl of broth in the Thrissil Inn."

The three men rode off, riding towards the river and then clattering across the wooden bridge.

"Whisky's what I need." Graham watched them, shifting his weight from one foot to another. Then he turned and walked briskly up the street towards the Thrissil Inn.

The bannock came hot off the griddle. Mary MacLean cut it into segments and held out the silver plate.

A DAGGER FOR CATHERINE DOUGLAS

Catriona MacNaughton took a small piece, leaving the bigger pieces for him. He took one from the plate even though he had a quaich of whisky in his other hand. The bannock was soft and warm. He took a bite. They were grateful to him; they wanted to share the moment. He understood that.

But all the time, the feeling was gnawing at him that he needed to be somewhere else. Cowal was away, most likely to hatch another plot, and here he was breakfasting on whisky.

He could be across the river, roasting fish over an open fire with his horse resting and ready to ride.

Ready to ride to Stirling or Blackfriars or wherever Catherine was.

What do I want with this life of breaking into castles and breaking out again? Doing a job and then travelling to the next one? Selling a horse to buy a boat and then selling the boat to buy another horse? Sleeping under the stars, never comfortable, never warm? Never settling down, never enjoying the simple things like a walk along a riverbank in the evening sunshine?

He was never enjoying his food—eating handfuls of porridge cooked by the heat of the horse's belly as it hung from the saddle in a leather pouch.

There was Gilchrist Muir, living in a small smoke-filled house, sleeping with the same woman every night. The two were getting comfortable with each other, understanding each other, relying on each other. He knew that she was thinking about him as she weeded the vegetable patch when he was away hunting.

Whenever he rode off to hunt, she stood at the door of their cottage watching him go and waving to him. Could that be Catherine? Giving me a kiss before I leave, my arms around her, her body pressed hard against mine?

Am I really going to let her marry that sycophantic, double-dealing, money-grabbing, saffron-wearing marrowless lickspittle that her parents have picked out for her only because he's never likely to ride off and get himself killed in a battle or a joust one day?

What if I asked the king for an appointment? I can read and write in Latin. I have travelled through France and through Germany. I could sit at a writing desk with a quill in my hand scribing charters on leather scrolls. And spending the winter making the ink we'll use all summer—peeling the bark off a hawthorn tree and grinding it down to a fine powder. Then dropping it into a cauldron of water and boiling it and boiling it till there's nothing left but a black paste.

Then, every night, I'd sleep with Catherine—her long brown hair spread across the feather pillow like a spider's web, a mattress of hair and feathers and her soft body underneath mine.

"I should leave now."

Mary MacLean looked at him. "Not yet, surely?"

Had he spoken aloud? He had been thinking to himself. He'd been thinking about Catherine—thinking about how he wanted to feel the touch of her against his skin, to walk with her hand-in-hand through the streets of St John's Town and then out of the town into the meadows where the cattle grazed and lie with her in the soft clover enjoying the endless summer heat and listening to the buzz of the bees and the song of the birds in the trees.

"We'll cut some wood and get a hot fire burning," Mary MacLean said, putting a comforting hand on his shoulder.

"You brought a barrel of whisky," Catriona MacNaughton said. "You must let us share it with you."

Or I could be across the Firth of Clyde tonight. And tomorrow, I could be riding for Blackfriars.

"My work here is done," Campbell said.

"Let your hair down. Enjoy yourself for a day," Catriona MacNaughton said.

Baldred MacDuff came into the kitchen.

"You will help me push off?" Campbell asked him.

"As you wish."

Sean Campbell put the quaich to his lips and titled his head back, emptying it. Then he put the quaich down on the table.

He knew, if Janet came into the room, she would try to persuade him to stay. He did not look at Mary MacLean, could not look at those blue eyes and long black hair. "Come," he said to Baldred MacDuff.

The two men walked out of the kitchen without looking back.

Mary picked at the warm bannock with her fingers. Soon, they would be making butter again, and she would be cutting chunks of butter with a knife and spreading it on the bannock.

After a while, Janet MacRory came into the kitchen. She looked at the table; there was a silver plate with a half-eaten slice of bannock where she expected Sean Campbell to be.

"Are the men in the banquet hall?" she asked.

"No," Catriona MacNaughton asked.

"I didn't think so," Janet said. "The fire's not lit."

Baldred MacDuff came back into the kitchen.

"Where's Sean?" Janet MacRory asked.

"Gone," Baldred MacDuff said.

"What?"

"He's rowing across the Clyde."

"You didn't try to make him stay?"

"Mary chased him away," Catriona MacNaughton said.

"What do you mean?"

"She put a hand on his shoulder; he jumped and left the kitchen."

"I barely touched him!" Mary protested.

Janet shook her head. "You've no idea how to talk to men. How many times have I told you that?"

———— † ————

He crossed a calm sea with the winter sun rising and the castle casting its shadow over the waters.

The empty boat was light and harder to row, being blown back towards Dunoon by the wind whilst also being sucked out to sea by the current. He rowed, pulling hard on the oars, while his breath condensed in clouds in front of his face.

Why did the journey back seem harder—and longer—than the journey to Dunoon? Was it only the different weight of the boat? Or had he been so tense with fear on the way across that he had not had time to notice the strain on his arms?

Eventually, he was stepping out of the boat and dragging it onto the beach at Gourock. Then, with soaking wet legs and boots, he was walking among the small houses and looking for Gilchrist Muir's door.

Which house was his? Could he remember? They all looked the same—stone-built houses with thatched roofs and wooden doors but never any windows.

There was the scrape of a bolt being drawn back. A door opened halfway; a cloud of smoke belched out.

Then the door fully opened, and Gilchrist Muir came out, stopping to stand in the street in front of Campbell, his arms folded. "Sean Campbell, it's yourself!"

"I need my horse," Campbell said.

"We were not expecting you back so soon."

"I was only dropping off the supplies."

"We thought …" Muir hesitated.

You thought I'd be dead by now? "Where's my horse?"

"You've just rowed across the Firth. I can't let you travel today."

"But I have work to finish in St John's Town," Campbell said.

"St John's Town will still be there in the morning."

"I know, but—"

"Eat with us and then rest awhile first."

"I should—" Campbell was about to protest, but he was tired from a bad sleep on a cold stone floor and a hard row across the river. He knew Gilchrist Muir was right.

"Loch Awe and Cowal can carry on their feud without you. And the king can order Cowal's execution if he wishes to. None of these things are our concern." Muir gestured towards his house. "Come inside, have a quaich of whisky, and tell us all about your adventure."

"I did not come for your hospitality. I came for my horse."

"You're going to ride one hundred miles? Let yourself rest awhile first." He took hold of Campbell's arm. "Come inside."

Campbell found himself ducking under the lintel and stepping into the house.

"Blow up the fire," Gilchrist Muir said. "We'll roast a fish for our guest."

Seonaid Muir, long red hair against green tartan, got down onto her knees with bellows in her hands. She pressed the handles together quickly; there was a puff of dust and then a red spark.

"You must be relieved to be back," Seonaid said.

Relieved? Yes, partly. Could he explain this mixture of emotions? He was pleased with a job done well. But he was also exhausted. And he was excited to know he would be riding back to St John's Town and Catherine.

And angry. He was angry with Janet MacRory. Pregnant with Patrick O'Donnell's child! What were you thinking about, Janet? Where's your self-respect? You were a better woman than that.

"You must tell us all about it," Gilchrist Muir said.

What is there to tell? Campbell wondered. You go back home. When you get there, either it has changed, or you have changed. It's not your home, any more.

"Something about it doesn't feel right."

"What do you mean?"

"Cowal. Why did he attack?"

"He's always had his eyes on Dunoon. You know that." Gilchrist Muir picked up a handful of sticks and put them on the fire. Seonaid blew on the fire with the bellows as her husband picked up a log and put it on top of the sticks.

"Then why did he retreat so quickly?"

"You men. You're always making things complicated." Seonaid stood up, walking across the stone floor in her bare feet. "He realised he was beaten, and he left."

"Good commanders never know when they're beaten. Zizka was never beaten, no matter what we did to him."

"We're eating salmon tonight," Seonaid apologised. "That's all we have."

"Something's not right," Campbell said.

"You don't like salmon?"

"What?" Campbell looked up. "No. Eh, what I mean is, salmon will be lovely."

"He's our guest!" Seonaid scolded Gilchrist Muir. "We always give our guests mutton." She picked up a stoneware bottle, put a quaich on the table, and then poured out some whisky.

Gilchrist Muir unhooked the iron pot that hung over the fire on a long chain. He looked at Seonaid. "Where's the griddle?"

Soon Campbell was sitting cross-legged on the floor with a quaich of whisky in his hands and the smell of salmon cooking in the air. He was enjoying the whisky, letting it warm his insides.

"The siege is broken?"

Campbell nodded his head.

"You must tell us about it."

Campbell opened his mouth to speak just as there was an excited banging on the door.

Gilchrist Muir went to the door and opened it. Young Tam Beaton rushed in. "You broke the siege!" he shouted.

"Yes," Campbell smiled.

"How many men did you kill?"

"I don't know."

"Ten? Twenty? My dad says you must have killed two or three, but I think it's more."

"I don't know if I killed anyone."

Young Tam looked confused. "How many did you fight?"

"You shoot an arrow. Then your attention is on loading the next arrow. You don't know what the first arrow hit."

"Anybody can shoot an arrow. Tell us about the sword fights."

"I wasn't in a sword fight."

"How did you get over the wall? Tell us about that."

"I didn't."

"What?"

"They let me in the sluice gate."

"What?"

"I stood under the garderobe and shouted through the grille."

"He thinks you should have climbed the wall with a sword in your hand, all the time fighting off Cowal's men." Gilchrist Muir laughed.

"When Robert the Bruce captured Lochmaben Castle, he swam across the moat and then climbed over the wall," Young Tam said.

"That's not fair," Seonaid scolded him. "You cannot compare Mr Campbell with Robert the Bruce."

"Dunoon Castle doesn't have a moat," Campbell said. "I couldn't swim the moat."

"They climbed the rock and scaled the wall to get into Edinburgh Castle."

"They were very brave men."

"Mr Campbell is a brave man," Seonaid said.

But young Tam seemed unsure.

"You should go home," Gilchrist Muir intervened. "It is getting late." He took young Tam by the arm and led him to the door.

"Loch Awe will reward you," Seonaid said to Campbell.

Maybe. "I didn't do it to be rewarded." Campbell took another sip of his whisky.

The door banged shut. Gilchrist Muir poured himself a generous whisky. "Give our guest some more whisky," he said to Seonaid.

He had been proud of himself, rowing back over the Clyde. Now he was not so sure. He'd stood under the garderobe and gone in by the sluice gate. Wouldn't Lady Douglas love that? He could hear her loud voice echoing along the corridors of Stirling Castle—"the man who crawls along sewers; that's all he's good for."

Why did he feel like a failure every time he broke into a castle? He had not cut the boy's throat, but everybody blamed him for it. He saw it in their eyes every time he looked at them. And he knew what they were thinking: Sigismund had sent him away because he would rather lose a war to Zizka than win it with cut-throats.

King James had given him a second chance and what had he done? He had left the king to come back to Dunoon. Then he'd stood underneath the garderobe at Dunoon Castle and waited for the defenders to let him in if they didn't urinate on him first. He'd politely asked to be let in by starving, exhausted defenders while he sat outside like a servant waiting at the king's table.

Robert the Bruce had swam through moats and climbed walls to capture castles, fighting his way across the battlements. What had Sean Campbell done?

Why do you think Janet MacRory didn't wait for you? She saw you for the loser you were and tried her best to forget about you.

"You must be very tired," Janet MacRory said.

No, that wasn't Janet MacRory's voice. That was Gilchrist Muir's wife. What was her name? Seonaid. Yes, that was it. Seonaid.

Yes, I'm tired. I'm tired of trying, and failing, to be a knight. I couldn't break into Dunoon Castle. I couldn't rescue anyone. Janet had to let me in. Was that not the ultimate embarrassment?

"Have some more whisky," Seonaid Muir said.

He looked down at the empty quaich in his hands.

Seonaid was bending over him, pouring more whisky from the stoneware bottle she was holding in two hands.

What do you want with a man like me, Catherine? Why should I wreck your life the way I've wrecked my own? You will be better off with Alexander Lovell. He'll provide you with a nice house and buy your mother dresses of silk. The best thing I can do is ride off to the Highlands.

"The salmon's nearly ready," Seonaid said.

And if there are no earls wishing to employ a cut-throat like me, there are deer in the hills and salmon in the rivers; there's plenty to eat in the Highlands.

"I'll make some porridge and let it harden overnight; you can take it with you on your journey tomorrow," Seonaid said.

"Yes," Campbell said.

"If you leave at dawn, you might get to St John's Town before nightfall."

Just to be told that I didn't do the job the way it should have been done? The ladder was too short; the sewer was too high. Were these things my fault? I could not walk around to the drawbridge because Cowal's men would have seen me and killed me. So I stood underneath the garderobe, and they took pity on me and let me into the castle before I froze to death. "I never do anything right," Campbell said.

"You broke the siege."

"A pregnant woman broke the siege. She held out against Cowal. Then she let me into the castle."

"You did your part."

"A small part."

"Let the balladeers decide that."

"Cut-throat Campbell, the disaster of Dunoon. A woman let him into the castle when he couldn't get in."

"The king will be expecting you in Blackfriars," Gilchrist Muir said gently.

Campbell took another sip of whisky.

"You shouldn't drink so much on an empty stomach," Seonaid said. "Have some salmon."

The king is expecting me, yes. But does he want me? I'll take him back his horse and go to Linlithgow to block up sewers and put bolts on doors because that's what I do. I crawl around sewers. The king can go to Stirling where he doesn't have to put up with people asking him why he entertains a cut-throat in his court.

And Catherine—you'll forget about me. The spring will break, the flowers will blossom, and you can marry with your mother's approval.

If I really loved you, I would get out of your life. Maybe you'll miss me in these cold winter nights. But by the summer, when the heather is in bloom and the blaeberries are ripe, by then, when Lovell brings you a wedding dress in beautiful silk, by then you'll have forgotten me.

CHAPTER 37

Sitting on a cold stone bench in the cloisters, she felt the cold stone through the flimsy kirtle.

She fingered the silver crucifix in her hand as if it held the answers. In the dining hall, the king's presence chamber, the courtyard, the nursery—wherever she was—Robert Stewart always seemed to be there, undressing her with his eyes. Meanwhile, her mother was about to march her up the aisle to a man who left her feeling dead inside. She was looking up at the cold, grey skies as if she thought Sean Campbell might descend on a winged horse.

A voice behind her said "You should put it on."

Catherine turned around. "Your Grace! I wasn't expecting—"

"Oh!" the queen snorted. "How many times can I watch my husband win games of royal tennis? I came here to be on my own." She smiled. "Like you, I suspect."

Catherine clutched the silver crucifix in her hand.

"You came here to pray?"

Catherine stood up. "It's cold. We should go inside."

"The weather doesn't stop the monks praying," the queen said. "They make me feel inadequate." Then she changed the subject. "Put on your cross. It will look nice against your blue kirtle."

"It's just a simple silver cross. I bought it from the silversmith in the High Street."

"What did you pay for it? No, I shouldn't ask." The queen smiled. "You should put it on."

Catherine hesitated.

"Let me see you wearing it."

Catherine did not move.

"Don't be shy. You must wear it. Put it on now!"

"I didn't buy it for myself."

"For your father?"

"No."

"No, I didn't think so." There was a pregnant silence. Then Queen Joan said, with a growing sense of dread, "Who did you buy it for?"

Catherine did not answer.

"I know you didn't buy it for Ballumbie. He already has a large crucifix of gold, which he wears to the church on Sundays. He would not have much use for a small one made of silver."

"Then he will not be disappointed if I do not give it to him."

Queen Joan grimaced. "Who did you buy the crucifix for?"

Again, Catherine did not answer. She was looking at the stone angel, its hands clasped in silent prayer.

"He gives you a dagger, and you give him a silver crucifix?"

"I want to give him something that will keep him safe. I want to know the Lord is with him."

"When he leaves you to ride off to fight in a foreign war, you mean?"

"Something like that."

"You're worrying about him?"

"The king sent him to Dunoon."

"His Grace did not send him."

"The king allowed him to go."

"It was a request from Campbell of Loch Awe."

"And if Sean seeks an appointment at court, he must do as the king wishes."

"They have their duties to the king, and their duties always come first." The queen let out a sigh. "This is what the men do, Catherine. They ride off to war."

"Then it will be comforting for me to know he has this." Catherine gripped the cross tightly, winding the chain around her fingers.

"Men like Sean Campbell, they do not make good husbands."

"He will give everything up for me."

"Is that what he says?" The queen shifted uncomfortably. "After a few years, he will grow bored. The house will become a prison. Look what happened to Margaret FitzRoland."

"Sean is different."

"That's what we all think about the men we love. Then it turns out that they're all the same." She eyed the crucifix. "Put it on."

"I wanted to give him something."

"Then I hope he does not give you heartache in return."

"I suppose the man you love will give you heartache?"

"Especially the man you love."

"I just wanted to give him something silver. And to put it around his neck myself." To see the silver shining against his naked skin.

"I used to watch James walk through the garden at Windsor Castle in the summer evenings when the shadows from the rose bushes lay across the grass." Queen Joan smiled to herself. "I used to like to look at him with his shirt off."

"Especially from the back," Catherine said unconsciously.

"What?"

His bare shoulders, the shoulder blades. His body tapering into tight-fitting hose that emphasised the muscles in his thighs. The hose clinging to the crack between his buttocks as he walked.

Oh, how she wanted to grab the hose by her fingernails and rip it off.

The hills were sparkling white under the rising sun, the horse trotting along the earthen track that passed for a road.

What kind of a man stands underneath the women's toilet and looks up? That was how Dunoon Castle was relieved—or that's the way Lady Douglas would tell the story.

Who do I admire? I admire one-eyed Zizka, with no money, no titles, and no land. A man with no tenants to drumbeat into an army with threats of eviction if they don't come. A man who lost an eye but kept on fighting, a man who'll give his life for his people and his country.

Then there was Elisabeth—a young twenty-five-year-old woman who saw Sigismund's army coming and shut the castle gates in its face. Boulders were launched at her walls, and stinking corpses were flung over them. Sigismund would break down the walls if he didn't starve her out first, and there was nothing she could do except wait for Zizka.

A young woman constantly cajoling her servants and keeping their spirits up, whatever she thought or felt herself. She didn't know where Zizka was or even if he was coming. She could only hope that he was on his way. But she had two things Sigismund did not have—courage and determination.

Yes, I admired Elisabeth and Zizka—not that they admired me. A man who does as Sigismund commands without asking questions, a man who breaks into the castle to raise the portcullis not thinking about the slaughter that will take place. I made so little impression on you, Elisabeth, you did not even learn my name. But what would you think of me if you did? What did you say to Zizka about the stinking, sewer-climbing, throat-cutting depraved diabolists you fought off?

The horse was trotting along quite happily. On either side of the road the trunks of the trees were dressed in frost and twinkling white under the winter sun. We couldn't raise the portcullis at Melnik Castle and keep it up. We didn't deserve to. I was fighting for fame and gold in my sporran. Then I was sent to Dunoon Castle—a second chance; and maybe I can say I'm fighting on the right side this time. But, this time, I can't get in through the sewer or any other way, so I wait under the garderobe for someone to piss on top of my head. They must have seen me and taken pity on me; they let me inside before I froze to death.

Why did I ever think I wanted to be a knight? You're the second son of a second son; nothing to inherit, you must make your way by the sword.

Sitting in a castle on a Savonarolan chair with a quaich of whisky in one hand and my feet resting on a stool while I issue orders like the Earl of Atholl or Campbell of Loch Awe—these things were never for me.

The compacted snow made an uneven dirty grey line with soft virgin-white snow on either side. He knew he should give the horse a rest; he pulled on the reins to reduce the trot to a walk. He jumped down, but his numb feet would not move; he stamped them on the ground. His fingertips were red and stinging with cold.

The distant howling of a wolf could be heard through the white trees. How he envied the wolves at these times, lying with their bellies flat on the ground and waiting and watching. The weather was never too cold for them or too hot—or the deer, pushing the snow aside with their noses and nibbling at the grass underneath. When the weather was cold, they knew what to do and how to get food.

He was too cold to walk himself warm. The fireplace in the great hall at Stirling Castle—get your attention on that, he told himself, on a cup of wine and a crackling log fire.

It's not so far away.

Stirling Castle stood imperiously on the hill above the town with a crust of snow on its battlements. Through the bars of the portcullis, the guard watched a man lead his horse up the hill, with rows of cottages on either side.

"Sean Campbell," the man said as he approached.

"Leave your weapons here." The guard made a signal; the portcullis began to rise.

Campbell ducked underneath it. "The horse needs a rest."

"I will take it to the stables." The guard reached out a hand and took the reins.

Sean Campbell patted the horse and walked towards the royal apartments. He felt the heat as soon as he entered. It was a subtle heat at first, getting warmer as he came through the king's presence chamber. This was where he'd first seen Catherine. And where he'd first met the king, down on his knees looking at the king's pointed shoes.

The king had given him a chance to redeem his reputation. Had he done enough with it?

Maybe they thought I could jump ten feet, grab the iron bars of the garderobe with my bare fists, and prize them apart. Maybe they thought I could fight Cowal's men two at a time, breathing fire as I did so.

He was through the king's presence chamber, now, and in the great hall. A man dressed in black with a frill collar was sitting on his own at the long table. He was drinking from a silver cup with his left hand and carefully writing on a scroll with his right hand, occasionally dipping the quill in the inkwell that sat next to him.

The smouldering embers of the log fire glowed red. A stack of logs lay on the fireplace, set there for tomorrow. Sean Campbell picked up a log and placed it on the bed of embers, watching a thin trail of grey smoke curl around the log and embrace it.

"Sean!" Sheona ejaculated.

He turned around.

"You gave me a fright. I heard footsteps—didn't know who it was!"

"Sorry."

"Don't apologise." Sheona turned to the clerk. "You wouldn't be doing that if the king was here."

"It's warmer here."

"Go back to the scriptorium," Sheona said.

"It's all right for you. You're always in here, sitting by the fire and drinking the wine."

"Leave him alone." Jean Lockhart had entered the room.

"Quiet!" Sheona barked. "You'll wake up the children."

"I'm going." The clerk carefully rolled up his parchment. Then he stood up and walked out.

Sean Campbell sat down on the long bench and rested his elbows on the table.

"You must be very tired," Sheona said to him. "We weren't expecting to see you tonight." She apologised. "We haven't made your bed."

"I'll sleep on the floor."

"Not until you've had a cup of wine!" Sheona turned to Jean. "Go and get some."

"Why should I go for it? You're the one who drinks it all."

"Not when you're around. I don't get the chance." Sheona disappeared from the room.

"You must tell us all about your journey," Jean Lockhart said.

What is there to tell? Campbell wondered.

When Sheona came back into the room a few moments later, she had taken off the white smock that she had been wearing under her green kirtle. Now her shoulders were bare, apart for the straps of the kirtle, and a generous amount of cleavage was exposed. She carried a silver jug and three silver cups on a silver tray. She set the tray down in front of Campbell and then picked up the jug and poured out two full cups.

"What about me?" Jean asked.

"You can pour your own." Sheona raised her cup. "Slainte."

"Slainte." Campbell took a gulp of wine, but his hands were still shivering and unsteady. Some wine dribbled down his chin. Here he was, making a fool of himself at court again.

The two women were looking at him expectantly.

Campbell shrugged. "There's nothing much to tell."

"That's not what we were hearing," Sheona said.

"News travels fast."

"News about you does."

Campbell frowned. He could picture all the courtiers laughing about him. "People don't understand how difficult Dunoon Castle is to attack."

"But you broke the siege," Sheona said.

"Lamont of Cowal backed off as soon as he saw you were coming," Jean said.

"I think Cowal just realised he'd taken on too much and left."

"You're being too modest," Jean said. "He left because you were there."

"I doubt it."

"Another successful mission!" Sheona raised her cup. "Here's to the illustrious Sean Campbell."

Was this a joke? What was she talking about?

Jean Lockhart seemed to read his thoughts. "You're very highly thought of."

Me?

"Your reputation travels faster than a horse at full gallop." Sheona was talking excitedly, spitting the words out. "King James always talks about you with respect in his voice. And I should know; I hear him talk about all the others. The way he talks about his chamberlain, for example; there's no comparison."

"Or Atholl," Jean said. "He hates Atholl."

"Oh, yes!" Sheona agreed. "How he hates Atholl."

Campbell's cup of wine was empty; Sheona leaned over and refilled it, letting Campbell's eyes travel across her bosom.

"And we see the fear in other men's eyes when they look at you."

"Like Alexander Lovell," Jean Lockhart added as if she wanted to get in on the act. "He's an overbearing boastful braggart when he attends court, but he turns quiet when you're in the room."

"Puffed-up peacock," Sheona said.

Campbell had one eye on the log that was sparking into life. There was no heat coming from it. He wanted to put another one on the fire.

"You're a man who breaks into castles, a man who stops at nothing," Sheona continued. "A man who will ride one hundred miles in one day till his horse is exhausted and then sail a boat across the Clyde to break through the ranks of Cowal's men. You fought in Germany. You fought in Bohemia. Even Zizka could not kill you."

"I cut a little boy's throat," Campbell blurted out ungraciously.

"Nobody really believes that."

"Nobody?"

"The people who matter—they don't believe it."

"Alexander Lovell believes it," Jean said.

"My point exactly," Sheona said.

"Can we put another log on the fire, please?"

"Yes, of course. You'll be frozen after your long journey." Sheona went over to the fire, putting two logs on it and then looking at it for a while and putting on a third log. She came back to the table. "King James was furious when he got the request from Loch Awe to let you go to Dunoon on your own. That was a job for two dozen men, not for one, he said. Anyone else would have made excuses but you just went off on your own and did it."

"One dozen men," Jean said.

"He said two dozen."

"I was sitting right here, and I heard him say one dozen."

Campbell had one woman on either side of him. Sheona was sitting close to him at the table, her whole body turned towards him and her right breast caressing the tabletop. "You've made a big impression at court," she said. She moved closer to him by about an inch. She was looking up into his eyes.

"He likes Catherine." Jean's loud voice shattered the silence.

"I'm not doing anything."

"Keep it that way."

"Just because he never looks at you?"

"You've had too much to drink."

"He could have any one of the ladies in waiting if he wanted to. It's not my fault if he never looks at you."

"I don't remember seeing him looking at you either."

"You don't want to remember."

"Catherine's his woman. She's always been his woman. The way she looks at him, the way she talks about him." Jean turned to Campbell. "Alexander Lovell is travelling from Berwick to Blackfriars. Go now and get there first."

Campbell was unsure what to say. "I—"

"You're the only man she wants. Don't disappoint her."

There was a sudden tingle of sensation in his loins. His heart was beating a little faster. "I'll go to Blackfriars tomorrow." It took him a couple of moments to realise what he had said. Inverness, the Highlands, standing over a river with a burning torch in one hand and a leister[29] in the other. These things were forgotten now.

"The king stays up late after a council," Jean said. "He has guests to entertain. There's minstrels, harpists, pipers; they'll be awake for hours yet."

Sheona gave Jean a sharp look. "He's exhausted; he needs to rest."

"Somebody's got to stop you making a fool of yourself."

"What do you mean?"

"You've already started taking your clothes off."

"I'm not playing with the children; I don't need to wear a smock."

"The king will be sleeping late in the morning," Campbell said. "I'll have plenty time to travel tomorrow.

"Once the children are awake in the morning," Jean said, "they'll expect you to play with them—especially Isabella. But you can leave now and be in Blackfriars while the minstrels are still entertaining the king."

"My horse is exhausted."

---

[29] A three-pronged spear

"Take another one."

"I've only just got here," Campbell said.

"Take a rest," Sheona said. "You can travel in the morning."

"You want to be in St John's Town before Ballumbie, don't you?" Jean said. "Lady Douglas is there, and she'll be pushing Catherine onto Ballumbie."

"The Formidable Lady Douglas," Sheona muttered.

Jean Lockhart turned to Sean Campbell. "Go now," she said. She stood up to let him pass.

Campbell stood up.

"You know where to find a fresh horse," Jean said.

"Yes," Campbell said.

"Off you go then!"

He looked from one to the other. "But it will be midnight before I reach Blackfriars!"

"And you couldn't arrive at a better time," Jean said. "The pipers will be playing; the courtiers will be singing. Jugs of wine will be laid out on the table. The king will be reciting his poetry."

Campbell seemed to hesitate.

"Go!" Jean urged him.

He did not move. Then, suddenly, he turned and walked out of the room.

Sheona watched him leave, her eyes on his broad back narrowing at the waist and the movement of his legs in the tight-fitting woollen hose. The bottom of the doublet obscured his buttocks, but she had had a glimpse of them before, when his back was turned. She turned to Jean. "You can't have him, so you're going to make sure that I can't have him, either?"

"You need to start growing up."

"Jealous cow."

CHAPTER 38

"Where's Callum?" Robert Graham complained, his breath condensing in the frosty air.

"The stables," Thomas MacMillan said.

"What does he want a horse for? Is he going to run away?"

"He left his dirk in his saddlebag."

"There's always someone who'll let you down." Graham was stamping his feet in the freezing night air to stop them going numb and rubbing his hands together to keep them warm.

Five men were standing, fidgeting, on the south bank of the River Tay. Swords dangled from their belts; the carved bone handles of daggers protruded from the uppers of their boots.

"What was that?"

"What?" Graham looked towards the monastery.

"There's someone there."

"It's a man waving."

"That's the signal."

Suddenly Graham was nervous; his legs would not move. Then he was running through the wet snow towards the monastery with the others following.

———————†———————

The night was as black as the Earl of Hell's waistcoat. Grey dirt coming out of blackness showed the way like the hand coming out of the priest's black robes and the fingers opening to spread the grey ash on your forehead.

The road was a dirty furrow amid fields of unbroken virgin white. Ice crystals glistened under the starlight. White merged into blackness and a dirty trail of compacted ice trodden down by horses' hooves.

The town of Stirling was behind him now. Where had his tiredness gone? All he could think about was walking up the High Street in St John's Town with Catherine Douglas on his arm. And then sharing a hot bath with her afterwards, her nipples floating on the surface of the water.

Who cares about castles and knights and foreign wars? Who cares about minstrels singing ballads about your exploits? Whatever kind of man your parents want for you, Catherine, that's the man I will be. I will sit all day in the king's scriptorium writing out letters for the king to seal or charters and grants. If your father needs a tacksman, Catherine, I can do that; I can ride around his estates counting the men who are fit for military service and checking that the oats and barley are growing in the fields. The king needs a constable; he needs a man he can trust. I could be that man.

Whatever you want me to be, Catherine, that's what I will be. I will dress in saffron and learn to play royal tennis. I will go to Venice to buy silk, let your mother take the best, and sell the rest in Edinburgh and Glasgow. I will hide my sword in the roof of our house and never tell our children I owned one. I will never breathe a word about Zizka or Sigismund; nor will I speak about Bohemia or the Holy Roman Empire. Our children can think their father is a boring old man who knows Latin. I don't care what they think, but they will respect their mother.

All they will know about their father is that he loves their mother. They will see that he loves your long brown hair, your blue eyes. He loves your skin, your perfect skin like the cream at the top of the milk. He loves your thighs and your shins; he loves your feet.

I can't wait to get to Blackfriars and kiss every one of your toes. I will kiss the top of the foot and then the bottom. I will kiss the heel and then the ankle. I will kiss the big toe and then that long second toe.

My hands, my fingers, my mouth will be all over your soft body—all over your cheeks, your neck, your plump breasts. My wet tongue will inside your ears, my leaking penis on the smooth skin of your stomach as you lie underneath me like a soft mattress, moist and warm, waiting for me.

"You're not wearing your new crucifix," Queen Joan said.

Catherine shot the queen a horrified look that said, *Not in front of my mother!*

Lady Douglas was sitting a little farther down the table, her attention on the harpist.

"You should wear it while you have the chance," the queen persisted.

"I did not buy it for myself," Catherine hissed under her breath.

Queen Joan rolled her eyes. "Remember how nice you said it looked against your blue kirtle?"

"No," Catherine frowned. "I didn't say that."

Queen Joan grimaced. "Do I have to spell it out?"

"Spell what out?"

"Where is it?"

"In my bedchamber."

"You think it's safe there?"

"We're in a monastery."

"How many monks do you see?"

Catherine looked around the room. The harpist was playing; the piper was taking a rest, standing by the fireside with a cup of wine in his hand. The king had his head turned away, discussing something with his chancellor. Servants were coming in and out of the room with jugs of wine.

"Who made your bed tonight?" Queen Joan asked.

Catherine suddenly realised she did not know.

"Who has been in your bedroom?"

Catherine stood up, suddenly worried. "I'll go and get it now."

"A good idea."

Catherine left the dining hall and made her way through the rooms to her bedchamber. She pushed open the heavy door, her heart racing. Three strides took her across the room to her bed. She put a hand under the pillow, and her fingers closed around a metal chain.

She relaxed immediately, pulling out both the crucifix and the dagger that Sean Campbell had given her. She turned back to leave the room. The door was half-open. She could not see the bolt, which should have been lying against the wall.

So this was Robert Stewart's plan? He would wait till everyone was asleep or drunk and come into her bedchamber? She left her bedchamber, her angry fingers gripping the dagger, striding back to the dining hall.

The harpist was still playing. The king was still talking to his chancellor. A servant was refilling the queen's cup.

Catherine walked over to Queen Joan. "Where is the chamberlain, Your Grace?" she asked.

Queen Joan looked up. "What?"

"Robert Stewart, the chamberlain, where is he?"

"He's here."

"Where?"

Queen Joan looked around the room. "I thought he was—" she frowned.

"He's taken the bolt from the door of my bedchamber."

"He's always fiddling with those bolts," Queen Joan said. "We must tell him to stop." Her eyes were still scanning the room, looking for Robert Stewart. "But if you're worried about your valuables, you can put them in a box and leave them in our bedchamber."

"I'm more worried about waking up in the middle of the night to find Robert Stewart in my bed."

People were shouting, their voices echoing through the rooms.

"What is that noise?" King James barked, annoyed.

There were running feet and armour clanking, sounds of commotion outside. Then someone shouted, "Treason!"

Thuds and thumps and metal clanking. A male voice, not shouting but screaming, "Tree-zon!"

"Treason!" Catherine gasped, looking to the door. The king, white-faced, was already on his feet.

"Come," Queen Joan said.

Men in armour, carrying swords and axes, came crashing into the dining hall. A servant threw a silver goblet at one, hitting him on the face. There was a splash of red as wine went over him and onto the wall.

The servant picked up a second goblet by its stem, holding it outwards like a sword. He stood between the men and the king.

But the king, with the queen following, was already out of the dining hall and running through the royal chambers. Catherine followed the trail of the queen's kirtle.

They went through Catherine's bedchamber. "Shut the door!" Queen Joan shouted over her shoulder. Catherine bent down to pick up the bolt from the floor.

But it was not there.

Her eyes scanned the room for the bolt. What had Robert Stewart done with it?

"Give me your dagger!" Queen Joan shouted.

Catherine realised there was a dagger in her hand. She threw it to the queen.

The king and queen were out of Catherine's bedchamber now and through the door to the next bedchamber. The clatter of armour was getting louder and louder as the men approached. Catherine picked up a wooden chair and put it against the door. Then she turned and ran.

Then through the next bedchamber with the Queen shouting, "bolt the door!"

There was a glimpse of the queen's kirtle vanishing into the nursery. Catherine looking around frantically. She scanned the room with her eyes. Where was the bolt? She grabbed the bed, but it was heavy and would not move. Again, she picked up a chair and pushed it against the door.

She could hear the scrape of the other door opening and the chair being pushed aside.

Into the nursery now, shutting the door behind her. She could hear Queen Joan screaming, "Bolt the door! Bolt the door!"

The bolt should have been left by the door, propped up against the wall. But where was it?

Again, a chair was pushed against the door, and Catherine turned and ran out of the nursery.

They were in the king and queen's bedchamber now. There were no more rooms to run into, no more doors. The queen was rolling back the carpet; the king was kneeling on the floor with a poker in one hand and Catherine's dagger in the other. He was working the knife into the cracks between the floorboards.

"Bolt the door!" the queen shouted at Catherine.

Catherine looked around. Someone had taken away the bolt. Was there anything else she could use? A broom handle, perhaps?

Through the door, she could hear the clatter of armed men bursting into the nursery.

The king had put the knife down; he had a floorboard in both hands.

"You'll get out through the sewer," the queen said. But even as the words left her mouth came the realisation that Sean Campbell had blocked the sewer up.

"Bolt the door!" the king shouted.

Queen Joan turned to Catherine. "Bolt the door!" she shrieked in desperation.

Without a bolt? Catherine had her back pressed hard against the door. She turned around, put her shoulder to the door, and bent her knees to push as hard as she could.

Then there was the thud of men hitting the door, and the door was being pushed back into her face, and she could not hold it—knew she could not hold it.

"Bolt the door! Bolt the door!" the queen was screaming.

Catherine pushed her left arm through the brackets. There was a jolt as the men battered into the door which shook on its hinges. Catherine felt the nip of the iron bracket cutting into her skin. But her arm had kept the door shut.

She looked back to the king. He was down on the floor. One leg went into the hole and then the other. Only his chest was visible and then only his head.

The door was pushing forwards, forcing her arm back against the bracket. She was pushing with her shoulder, pushing as hard as she could to take the pressure off her white and bloodless arm before it snapped.

"Hold the door!" the queen shouted.

King James had disappeared under the floor. The queen quickly put the missing floorboards over the hole and then stamped them into place.

The door was rattling and shaking and vibrating as the men banged on it from the other side with their axes. She couldn't pull her arm out, and the bone was ready to snap.

CHAPTER 39

"You told me you'd removed the bolts!" Robert Graham shouted.

"I did. I removed all of them!" Robert Stewart protested.

Robert Stewart had left open the outside door to the monastery, allowing five men to come rushing in with swords drawn. They came running along the passageway to the dining hall. A servant, carrying wine, stood in their way, and a stoneware bottle of wine went up in the air as they hacked at him with their swords.

But he'd had time to shout, "Treason," and alert the king. Now there was no time to lose. They ran into the dining hall, only to see the king and queen and a chambermaid disappear behind a door. They followed them, one abreast into one bedchamber and then another, only to see the door to the next chamber being shut every time they entered one.

Now they had come to door of the royal bedchamber. But it was bolted shut.

How had the door been bolted shut?

But it was too late to stop, now. The king knew who they were. If they went away and let him live, he would come after them breathing fire down his nostrils.

Graham took the heavy axe from his belt and, holding it in both hands, swung it hard at the door. The whole door shook, and a female vo ice gasped on the other side. He swung it again, aiming for the same spot. Again, the whole door shook. He swung it again. And this time, a panel caved in. He hit it again, knocking splinters into the room. He could see a woman through the hole in the panel; he pulled out his sword and stabbed the tip through the hole in the door, expecting the woman to step back.

She did not move; the tip pierced the kirtle and the soft flesh underneath. Then the five men were battering at the door with axes and kicking it with their feet while the whole of the door seemed to shake and reverberate on its hinges.

Catherine's arm was caught in the iron bracket. She was pushing hard on the door with her shoulder, her knees bent and her feet on the floor. Let them break her arm. It would heal again. And if it didn't, she could live the rest of her life with one arm. One-armed Catherine, that's what they would call her. Oh please, God, please help me keep this door shut.

Her soft leather shoes with their smooth leather soles were not gripping the floor. Her feet kept slipping back; she could not push hard against the door, which was open a crack, just enough to get a sword blade through and cut her arm.

Catherine shot a glance at the queen; she was on her knees replacing the carpet over the hole and smoothing it out with the flats of her hands—trying to get the carpet smooth and hide the hole underneath.

There was blood on the floor and on her kirtle and running down the door. Catherine pushed hard against the door with her shoulder, holding her arm with her free hand to stem the blood. Above her head, there was loud and violent banging as the whole door shook.

She looked up as a panel of wood caved in under an explosion of splinters. Her left eye just went black. Queen Joan was beside her, now, pushing at the door but that blade was poking through the hole and stabbing at her shoulder and tiny splinters of wood were dropping onto her hair because the hinge above her head was about to give away.

Then Queen Joan jumped back as the door broke apart and collapsed inwards, part of it coming down on top of Catherine whose arm was still caught in the bracket. Her whole body twisted under the weight of the men tumbling in, all in armour, clambering over the broken door on all fours. She tried to get up; a man swung an axe into her ribs.

Above her head, people were shouting. "Where is he?" Robert Graham demanded. He had fallen forwards onto his face as the door gave way. He stood up, putting a foot on Catherine's twisted legs and pointing his sword at Queen Joan's chest.

Queen Joan stepped back and then back again as Graham came forwards. She stepped back and stepped back until she was pressed against the wall. She was looking past the broken door and through it into the nursery, but no one was coming to her assistance.

"Where is he?"

"His Grace is not here."

Robert Graham looked around the room, suddenly experiencing a moment's doubt. "Check the other rooms," he said.

"We would've seen him."

They all knew that was true; they had followed the fleeing party through the bedchambers. King James seemed to have vanished like a magician.

One of the men climbed back over the broken door, stepping on Catherine as he did so. She let out a groan.

"No, no, no!" Robert Stewart was shouting. "He came in here. We saw him."

"Then tell me where he is," Graham said. He got down on one knee to look under the bed.

"The king is not here," Queen Joan said.

"There's a wrinkle in the carpet," Robert Stewart said.

"What?" Graham stood up, looking at the carpet. The unicorn's horn rose over a bump in the carpet.

"This carpet's uneven," Robert Stewart said. He prodded at the carpet with the tip of his sword. Then he stepped on it carefully with one foot. "The floorboards are loose."

Queen Joan watched, her face a mask, as Robert Graham came forward to look at the carpet.

"The sewer's under there," Robert Stewart said. "They were doing some work in the sewer."

"Unroll the carpet," Graham said.

Two men bent down and unrolled the carpet to expose three loose floorboards hastily thrown back into place. They lifted them up to reveal the sewer and a dark passageway.

The men all looked at each other.

"You go first," Robert Graham said to Thomas MacMillan.
"You can't swing a sword down there," Thomas protested.
"Then use your dagger."
"We could take the queen hostage and force him to come out."
"Get on with it," Graham growled.

Thomas MacMillan reluctantly drew his dagger and clambered down in the hole.

James had run along the length of the sewer till he reached the end where Sean Campbell had put in the grille with iron bars like a prison.

He stopped and turned around. Slowly, his eyes grew accustomed to the darkness. He could hear the soft scuff of smooth leather soles on the stone floor of the sewer. He pressed his back against the wall to merge into the darkness.

The scuff, scuff came closer; it gradually grew louder.

James screwed up his eyes. The outline of a head and shoulders was barely visible.

All of a sudden, he jumped forwards, stabbing with the knife. The blade went in between the ribs, but the man slipped on something, and his whole body went into the water.

Back in the bedchamber, they heard the splash. Then they waited for MacMillan to shout to them and come running back.

But there was only silence.

Graham looked to the next man, whose face was drawn and grey. "Go down there and find out what happened."

The man took a deep breath, saying nothing, and then climbed down into the hole. Behind him, the queen took one step towards the door.

In the sewer, James waited. Again, he could hear the scuff, scuff of leather soles on the paving stones. His eyes were attuned to the darkness now, and his ears were picking up the sounds of the rats and the water dribbling through the sewer.

He pressed his back against the wall, keeping his outline to a minimum. He could hear the intruder approach. Then he could see him.

He waited. Then he stepped forwards, more confident this time, punching the blade hard into the stomach and twisting it and turning it upwards and then pushing hard on the man's chest to push him into the water.

In the bedchamber, they heard another scuffle, followed by a splash and then silence.

Again, Graham waited for the man to come back but nothing happened.

Eventually, Robert Stewart said, "He's got a weapon."

"We all go in together," Robert Graham said. A dagger in one hand, he jumped into the hole. Then he bent down, ducking his head under the floorboards and disappeared. This time, he waited as the other two came down behind him.

It was dark in the hole, and they had neither lanterns nor torches. Feeling the damp wall with his fingers, his dagger in his right hand, Graham inched his way along. The walkway could only take one abreast; he stepped down into the water. The trickle of water was in his ears; his feet were cold as he splashed along.

He kicked something, realised it was, a body and stepped over it. Then there was something else soft and bulky in the water—another body. He stepped over that. Then he stopped. Starlight coming through an iron grille made a human shadow visible.

Feet were sloshing in the water. King James could see the points of three daggers coming through the darkness.

Am I going to die here in this sewer?

This is not the place for a king to die.

King James lunged forwards with his knife, colliding with the man on the walkway and knocking him into the water. But he felt a *whack!* in his back as Graham swung around and stabbed him.

Two men were on him now, and the third was splashing about in the sewer. Someone grabbed his hand that was holding the knife; he threw out a punch. But there were blows coming into his ribs and into his back, and he stumbled and fell in the darkness and into the cold water, wet cold water in his face. He could not breath; the water was in his nose, and the blows kept coming down onto his back.

The first thing Sean Campbell noticed as he came up the High Street in St John's Town was the door of the monastery swinging open on its hinges.

Stepping inside, he could hear a woman wailing. Walking past the cloisters to the royal apartments, the wailing grew louder.

A monk was standing outside the royal apartments, holding a broom in both hands like a weapon.

"I am Sean Campbell."

But the monk seemed not her hear. He was shaking his head in disbelief. "On holy ground," he muttered, "on holy ground." He looked up at Sean Campbell.

Campbell was about to say, "Where is the king?" But he suddenly realised there was a body lying on the ground at the monk's feet. Stepping over it, he turned into the dining hall to find tables overturned and cups on the floor, which was stained with wine. The bodies of two servants Campbell vaguely recognised were lying across the floor.

"The king is dead."

What? Campbell turned around. The monk was standing behind him.

"We were asleep; we were woken by the commotion."

"What?" Campbell began to walk towards the royal apartments.

"Don't go in there," the monk said.

Campbell walked out of the dining hall and along the passageway to the bedchambers. As he walked, the sobbing became louder and louder till it was hysterical.

The first bedchamber was empty. The nursery was empty. Then he passed into the next bedchamber.

A DAGGER FOR CATHERINE DOUGLAS

Lady Douglas was sitting on her own on a Savonarola chair. She stood up when she saw Campbell coming. "Sean!" she shouted. Then she rushed towards him, arms open.

Suddenly she was holding him tightly, her head on his shoulder. She was sobbing loudly; her whole body was heaving. Tears were rolling down her cheeks. Already, his shoulder felt wet.

"If … if only … you'd been here." She was sobbing, struggling to get the words out.

What?

"I-I knew it … was a mistake."

"What was a mistake?" Campbell was confused.

"Let-letting you go to Dunoon. I had a-a bad feeling about it."

What?

"I didn't-didn't say anything at the time. I should have … should have said something."

"I'm here now."

"Sean!" That was another female voice.

Campbell turned around. Queen Joan was standing in the doorway. Her hair was dishevelled, and her kirtle had been torn, exposing more of her bosom that was customary. She rushed over to him, holding him. But Lady Douglas would not let go, and now he was holding both women, both of them sobbing on his shoulders.

Queen Joan lifted her head, her eyes wet. "We must go to Stirling tonight," she said between gasps.

"I've just come from there."

"The children are safe?"

"Yes."

"Young Jamie is safe?"

"Yes."

A wave of relief swept through the room. "We leave for Stirling tonight."

"What?"

"You will accompany me."

Another journey? I was already exhausted when I left Stirling at nightfall. "Yes, of course," Campbell found himself saying.

"We don't have a carriage," Lady Douglas said.

315

"We'll go on horseback," the queen said.

"Yes," Lady Douglas said.

"If only you'd been here," Queen Joan said to Campbell.

"They wouldn't have dared attack if he'd been here," Lady Douglas said. "I knew it was a mistake to let him go to Dunoon. I said that to you at the time."

"I know you did," the queen said.

Now Lady Douglas looked up at Campbell. "You will always be welcome in my house," she said. "You must come and visit us in Tantallon."

What? "After you've made Catherine marry Ballumbie?" Sean Campbell snorted. "I don't think so."

There was a moment's silence. Lady Douglas glanced at Queen Joan. "You haven't told him?"

Queen Joan could not speak. She shook her head.

"Told me what?" Suddenly, Campbell's heart was racing.

Lady Douglas opened her mouth as if she was about to speak. But she was unable to say anything.

"Where is Catherine?"

"She ... she ... she ..." Queen Joan's voice was faltering.

"Where is Catherine?" Campbell looked at the open door that led to the bedchambers.

"Don't go in there," Lady Douglas said.

"Remember her the way she was," Queen Joan said, "not the way she looks now."

Campbell ran out of the room and into the next one. Ahead lay the royal bedchamber, but already he could see that its door was in pieces. Underneath the broken pieces of wood was a mass of long hair.

There was a monk in the room. "Requiesce in pace," he said.

Campbell took one step towards the door. Suddenly his stomach was in spasm. His eyes were full of water, but it was not a sob that came out but a howling, tortured scream.

Through the broken pieces of wood, the back of Catherine's hand lay on the floor, its white fingers reaching out for help that never came.

He bent down, carefully lifting up the broken pieces of door and leaning them against the wall. He got down on one knee and then both knees, putting an arm under her shoulders and under her thighs.

"Let me help you," the monk said.

Sean Campbell got back onto one knee and then pushed himself up, holding Catherine tightly. Her broken arm swung as it dangled; her head lolled backwards.

"Come," the monk said, and Campbell followed him through the bedchambers and out into the cloisters where he laid her on a stone bench under the gaze of the stone angel. He held her cold hand between his; he kissed her cheek that was cold like the stone bench. Her hair was hanging down; he picked it up and laid it across her shoulder. "I should tie it with a ribbon," he said.

CHAPTER 40

Isabella came running through the rooms. "No, I don't want to play with Jean. I want to play with Lady Cat," she shouted with heart-wrenching sobs.

Sheona Crockett ran into the room after Isabella; Isabella turned and ran out again.

"This is where I met Catherine," Campbell said. *She walked into my life, turned it upside down, and then walked out of it again.*

"It's also where you met me," Lady Douglas said. "You were sitting next to me."

They were in the dining hall at Stirling Castle.

"You found my company so interesting that you fell asleep," Lady Douglas said gently.

"I need someone to go back to Blackfriars," Queen Joan said.

"Let him drink his whisky," Lady Douglas said. Her voice was weak and tearful.

Campbell was sitting at the long table with a quaich of whisky in front of him.

"We left everything in the monastery," Queen Joan said.

"The monks will look after it for you," Lady Douglas said. "Or you could give it to them."

"All of James's possessions."

"Most of his belongings are here," Lady Douglas said.

"There was a poem he wrote to me and gave me in Windsor Castle. It was the first thing he ever gave me. I used to carry it around with me in my brown leather purse."

"Oh, yes," Lady Douglas said. "That brown purse with the drawstring?"

"I cannot see it anywhere. I think I must have left it in Blackfriars."

"There's plenty time to go back for it," Lady Douglas said.

"I'm never going back there."

"I really wish—" Lady Douglas was sitting beside Sean Campbell at the long table. She turned to him; their heads were very close. "If you'd been in Blackfriars"—she clasped his hand in hers—"Catherine would still be alive."

And if I want to meet her, now, and be with her, it will have to be in the Other World. "I'm going to Blair Castle," Campbell said. He was thinking aloud, not realising what he was saying. I don't want to be here; I want to die. But first, Lord Atholl, you're going to learn what it feels like to be afraid. I'm coming after you. I'm going to knock down the walls of that castle if I have to.

"Don't," Queen Joan said.

Atholl has destroyed my life. I will destroy his.

The queen seemed to be reading his mind. "Wait a month," she said. "I need time to raise an army."

Campbell avoided her eyes.

"Did you hear what I said?" the queen repeated. "I need time to raise an army."

Lady Douglas's fingers tightened their grip on Campbell's hand. She was looking at the queen. "He'll stay here with you. Don't worry." She turned back to Campbell. "You're not going to do anything stupid, Sean, are you?"

Campbell did not speak.

"I've spent a lifetime being stupid," Lady Douglas said. "It's time we all stopped."

"You have not answered my question," Queen Joan said. She was looking at Sean Campbell.

"I've answered for him," Lady Douglas said.

"Very well." Queen Joan turned and walked out of the room.

Sean Campbell watched her go. "I was going to give up everything for Catherine. I was ready to give up everything."

"I know," Lady Douglas said. "I wish I'd let Catherine ..." Her voice was wavering. "I wish I'd told her to marry you. Her father would have come around eventually. We could have persuaded him."

Campbell stared hard into his whisky. "What am I going to do now?"

"The queen needs a man."

Campbell shot her a surprised glance. He picked up the quaich of whisky. "What do you mean?"

"She needs a man she can trust."

"To do what?"

"To be with."

"What?" Campbell frowned.

"It will be good for you." Lady Douglas smiled weakly. "The children all like you."

"The queen. She's not going to—"

"Until she gets over the shock, you fool. She needs someone here she feels safe with." She squeezed his hand. "The children are demanding. They don't give you time to think. They don't let you grieve; they force you to get on with your life." Again, she smiled a weak smile. "My children were very young when my father died. I couldn't take time to feel sorry for myself. I had the children to think about."

"I just want to go away," Campbell said, "somewhere far away."

"Stay here with us," Lady Douglas said. Her voice was weak; her eyes were moist.

He shook his head.

"I'm serious," she said.

"Ballumbie will visit you."

"Huh!" She snorted. "That puffed-up peacock is in for a shock. He'll be thinking he's going to marry my other daughter now. It was always my younger daughter he was interested in. I had to work very hard to get him interested in Catherine."

"That last night in Dunoon. I stayed a night too long. They wanted me to stay. We couldn't be sure Cowal had gone. If I'd left earlier, I could have been travelling all night." Sean Campbell picked up the quaich to have another drink of whisky but noticed that it was empty. Had he drunk it all so quickly?

"You've had too much already," Lady Douglas said.

"I haven't had enough; that's the problem."

Lady Douglas stood up. "I should go and look for Her Grace. Maybe she just needs to be alone with her grief. Maybe she needs company. It's so hard to tell." She took a few steps out of the room.

"Lady Douglas."

She stopped and turned around. "Call me Marjorie."

"I could have got here quicker. I didn't have to stay that last night in Dunoon."

"Don't blame yourself."

"If I'd been here—"

"We could all have done things differently."

"I let Catherine down. I let myself down."

Lady Douglas blinked a couple of times. She seemed to be holding back the tears. "I let her down, not you," she said and quickly walked out of the room.

The smell of cooking was wafting through the castle, but no one wanted to eat.

Someone else was speaking, maybe Lady Douglas. But Campbell couldn't listen any more, didn't want to listen. He walked out of the dining hall and through the royal Apartments till he found himself out in the courtyard.

A woman walks into my life—a perfect, beautiful woman. Suddenly, here's a glimpse of what life can be like—coming home from a day's hunting with the smell of roasted pheasant in the air and this woman standing over the griddle with bare feet peeking out from under the folds of her kirtle.

Her hand on my chest, her fingers in my hair. Her gentle touch, her soft smell.

I was going to spend the rest of my life with this woman.

Then she is taken away.

Sean Campbell found himself looking at the tall figure of a man walking across the courtyard.

The man was walking hurriedly. Then he stopped, noticing the tears rolling down Campbell's cheeks.

"Where were you?" Campbell challenged him.

"I was in the Thrissil Inn," Walter FitzRoland said. "I didn't know anything about it."

"You were getting drunk?"

"I was sleeping."

"You could have stopped it."

FitzRoland flinched slightly. "What were you doing?"

Sean Campbell looked away. Then he said, "Getting it all wrong, as usual."

FitzRoland stepped forwards, putting a gentle hand on Campbell's shoulder. "Never fall in love with a lady-in-waiting. They have their duty to the queen, and their duty always comes first."

"I stayed one night too long in Dunoon. If I'd come back earlier—"

"If I'd stayed in the monastery that night." FitzRoland tried to give Campbell a sympathetic smile, but his face muscles were not working.

They walked back into the royal apartments, sitting down in the dining hall. A stoneware bottle sat on the table. Campbell eased the stopper from the bottle with both thumbs and poured out a generous measure of whisky. He passed the quaich to FitzRoland, who took a drink and passed it back.

The men sat in silence for a while. Eventually, Campbell said, "I'm going after him."

"Atholl?"

"Yes."

"We have to wait here. The queen will raise an army."

"I'm going now."

"Don't be stupid."

"The queen has to send out couriers first. Then all the clan chiefs will say they have to wait till the glens are clear of snow before they can march. That means Atholl has one month, maybe two, to prepare his defences." He shot FitzRoland a glance. "But I could catch him by surprise if I go now."

"You'll get yourself killed."

"Not before I've cut Atholl's throat."

"How will you get in? If he has any sense, he'll have blocked up the sewer."

"Then I'll disguise myself as a merchant delivering silk," Campbell said. "If I'd thought about that earlier, Lady Douglas would have let me marry Catherine, and she'd still be alive."

"I'll come with you," FitzRoland said.

"Now you're being stupid."

"So that makes two of us."

"I'll go on my own."

"This isn't a job for one man."

"All I have to do is walk into Atholl's bedchamber with a dagger in my hand."

"He'll have the door bolted, if he has any sense."

"Then I'll get him when he's on his way to bed. Whenever his back is turned. I'll give him as much of a fair chance as he gave Catherine."

FitzRoland was looking at him with critical eyes. When the question came, it was practical. "How do you get out of there?"

"What do you care?"

"Maybe you want to get killed, but I don't."

"Stay out of this."

"I told you; I'm coming with you."

"Why?"

"I owe it to you."

"No, you don't." Campbell picked up the quaich and put it to his lips.

"You followed my brother into Melnik Castle. And you took the blame when he cut the boy's throat."

Campbell paused with the quaich suspended in mid-air. "How do you know that?"

"I know my brother," FitzRoland said. "And I think I know you."

Campbell slowly put the quaich down.

The sound of running footsteps broke into the room as Jamie came running in. He stopped and pointed at Sean Campbell. "I will make you my field marshal, Mr Sean!"

"I am honoured, Your Grace," Campbell said.

Jamie climbed up onto the bench. "What are you drinking?"

"Whisky."

"The king drinks claret," Jamie said. "I should have claret." He looked around for a servant.

"Mairi!" Campbell shouted.

A young woman's head poked into the room.

"His Grace would like claret," Campbell said and winked. "Remember to serve it the way his father liked it—with honey and some water in it."

"My father didn't put water in his wine," Jamie said.

"Yes, he did," Campbell said. "He always put water in it. You taste the wine better if there's some water in it."

Jamie looked confused. "I don't remember Father saying that."

Mairi curtseyed. "Claret, as Your Grace wishes," she said and left.

"I need to attack Blair Castle," Jamie said.

"That's what we were discussing," Campbell said. He turned to FitzRoland. "If we can get inside the castle, we could seize Atholl in his bedchamber."

"It's dangerous," FitzRoland said.

"I'm not asking you to come."

"You want to go up there alone and get yourself killed?"

"What have I got to live for, now?"

"Don't talk like that."

"I told you; I'll go on my own."

"And I told you I'll come with you. Now what's the plan?"

"We catch him before he's ready. How did he kill King James? Because there were only a few servants in attendance. We can do the same to Atholl."

FitzRoland shook his head. "You can't kill him; the queen wants him alive."

"Kill him," Jamie said. "I give you my permission."

"Thank you, Your Grace," Campbell said.

Mairi came back into the hall with a silver cup. "Your claret, Your Grace," she said as she set it down in front of Jamie.

"Suppose we get into the castle. How do we get out?" FitzRoland asked.

Sean Campbell was silent.

"Going in and killing Atholl because you want to get yourself killed—that's not a good enough plan," FitzRoland said. "We need to get in and then get out." Then, almost as an afterthought, he added, "*Both* of us."

"We could take him hostage," Campbell suggested. "If you're holding a knife to this throat, the servants will let you walk out of there. They won't want to get involved."

"They'll despise him as much as he despises them. They'll be glad to get rid of him."

"Probably."

"If we can go in as silk merchants, that gives us a day to examine the castle's weaknesses and work out where Atholl's bedchamber is," FitzRoland said.

"I wasn't serious when I said I should go as a silk merchant." Campbell took a long drink of whisky. "I just meant—"

"It's a good idea," FitzRoland butted in. "They'll open the gates and let us walk in. It's a much better idea than taking a ladder with us and trying to get over the wall."

"I don't have any silk."

"What do you want silk for?" That was Lady Douglas's voice. She had come back into the room.

"We are holding a great council," Jamie said proudly.

"It's just an ordinary council, Your Grace," Campbell said.

Jamie pointed to Campbell and FitzRoland. "These are my field marshals!"

"Do you have a roll of silk, my Lady?" FitzRoland asked Lady Douglas.

"I can get you one. What do you want it for?"

"I want to look my best for the funeral," Campbell said.

"Catherine liked you just the way you are." Lady Douglas took a step forwards, holding out her right hand. "She wanted to give you this."

She was holding a silver crucifix. She pressed it into Campbell's outstretched hand.

He looked at it. "You should keep it, Lady Douglas."

"Marjorie. I told you to call me Marjorie," Lady Douglas said. Then she added, "Catherine bought it for you; she wanted to give it to you." Her voice was wavering.

Campbell looked at the crucifix for a moment and then put it over his head. The cross dangled from his neck and then came to a rest over his heart.

"May the Lord be with you," Lady Douglas said.

Campbell put the crucifix under his shirt, where he could feel the cold metal against his skin.

"You will come and visit us in Tantallon?" Lady Douglas said. She smiled weakly.

"Yes, of course." But first I'll saw off both Atholl's arms. I will peel all the skin from his body while he's still alive and puncture his eyeballs with the point of my dirk.

"My daughter ... my daughter." Lady Douglas turned away, walking quickly out of the room. "It's all my fault."

Campbell watched her go. A cottage on the hillside overlooking Loch Awe with goats munching on the grass and Catherine standing in the doorway, waiting for me to return home—that was all I wanted.

Now it's gone.

Because I was not there to protect you when you needed me.

We will meet again, Catherine, where the birch trees grow.

"You take people for granted. You don't realise how easily you can lose them." That was FitzRoland's voice.

"I know."

"If we have a roll of silk with us, we can tie it to the battlements and climb down."

"It's important to you to get out of there."

"Yes," FitzRoland said sharply. "After this business with Atholl is over, I'm going back to St John's Town to visit Margaret again."

Campbell shot him a glance. Was this guilt? "You don't have to do that."

"I know I don't have to. But maybe I want to."

"She'll have handed over your child by now. Some farmer down in Glen Esk will have it."

FitzRoland winced slightly. "She'll know where it is."

"Leave her alone; let her start anew."

"Why do you think we ended up in bed together? I always liked her. She'll never see my brother again; she needs a man in her life to look after her. I want to be that man." FitzRoland's eyes were moist. "And I want to see the child… Our child…I want to see our child."

Sean Campbell decided to change the subject. "You can't take your sword or your mace."

"What?"

"Silk merchants don't travel in full body armour. You can hide one knife in your armpit, another one in your boots."

They left at dawn, riding out of Stirling, following the River Forth and letting it guide them north-west. They passed a bare birch tree, its withered leaves brown like Catherine's hair. He had sat with her once under that tree, its bark sparkling with frost the way her eyes used to sparkle with love. They'd sat there once, hands clasped together, not noticing the cold weather, just being together.

Wait for me here, Catherine. Wait for me by the river with your long brown hair and your blue eyes. Wait for me under the shade of the birch tree with your kirtle matching its silver bark.

Wait for me here because I will be back to sit with you again under the shade of the tree in summer, like we never did, and maybe keep ourselves cool by wading in the river—you with your kirtle held up to your thighs.

Wait for me here. I'll know you're here even if I can't see you or hear you. But I'll sense your presence; I'll know you by your softness and your scent. I'll know you by your gentleness. I'll find you in that deep silence with the trees quietly rustling in the breeze and the river glinting in the sunshine. Leaves dropping on my shoulders in autumn will be your hair, and I'll lie on the ground with you all around me. Fifty years from now, when I'm dead, we'll walk hand in hand along this riverbank in the shade of the birch trees.

"How do we know Atholl will want silk?" That was FitzRoland speaking.

"He's clearing a path to the throne. He'll want to look like a king in waiting."

"We get into the castle and wait for him to go to bed?"

"Have you got a better plan?"

"Atholl might not be in a hurry to go to bed. He might stay up late in his banquet hall with a jug of whisky."

"Then imagine the look on his face when we walk in, daggers drawn."

Ahead of them, the old wooden bridge over the River Forth came into view overgrown with moss and its wood damp and dark. They clattered across it and rode on.

EPILOGUE

James I, King of Scots, was assassinated in Perth (St John's Town) on February 21, 1437. James II was crowned King of Scots on March 25, 1437. He was six years old.

Walter Stewart, Earl of Atholl, was executed for treason on March 26, 1437.

Catherine Douglas's bravery was remembered in folk tales and commemorated in the poem "The King's Tragedy" by Dante Gabriel Rossetti.

ABOUT THE AUTHOR

Euan Macpherson was born in Arbroath on the east coast of Scotland. He studied for an honours degree in English and Scottish Literature at the University of Stirling. He has made several appearances on television and radio, including BBC Birmingham, BBC Scotland, BBC Radio Scotland and Scottish Television. He has written for newspapers and magazines, in both the UK and USA. His first book, The Trial of Jack the Ripper, was published in 2004.

Lightning Source UK Ltd.
Milton Keynes UK
UKHW011457210222
399003UK00001B/52